OUT COLD

Book One
The Vampires of New Baltimore

by MISTY PROVENCHER

MISTY
PROVENCHER

ISBN: 978-0-9982110-9-1

For Shelley Custer
My dear friend and alpha reader
who read,
and re-read,
and re-read,
and re-read.
You deserve truck loads of Red Vines and Good & Plenty.

"Ahhh…Isaac Havrath has caught your eye!" A woman clucks beside me. "You school girls only see his pretty face, but you should know…that's the handsome mask of a murderer!"

The woman stretches out *murderer* with a dramatic whisper and a flourish of her fingers.

I turn my head and squint at her. It takes a minute to focus on the frizzy halo of her cocoa-colored hair and the wire rimmed glasses that dangle from a yellowed string of pearls around her neck. She reeks of rose perfume.

And I have no idea who she is.

Or what I'm doing here.

Unfortunately, neither of these things is new. Confusion has been my norm since the accident. I've learned it's best not to ask who people are, or where I am, but to figure it out on my own. Asking makes me sound crazy.

I turn my attention back to the white-washed sandwich board before me. The largest paper stapled to the board is a photocopied, sepia picture of a couple. The man, arms bent at the elbows, holds hands with the woman beside him, their fingers interlaced. She has small, sharp eyes and a severe center-part in her raven-black hair.

Beneath the photo, a headline reads: *Havrath Haunted Wedding Gown Exhibit—Open to the Public Wednesday, October 9th*.

More pictures crowd the article. One shows a tiny clapboard church; another, an old, burgundy-bricked mansion; and at the bottom is a glossy, modern photo of a sparkling wedding dress.

I notice the building beyond the sandwich board, and scan upward. The puzzle of where I am is finally solved. Wood letters spaced above the storefront spell it out: Grand Pacific House Museum. I'm on Washington Street in New Baltimore, which contains pretty much the whole shopping district of town, and spills into Walter and Mary Burke Park, which is cuffed at the very bottom with the sandy beach of Anchor Bay.

At least I know where I am — a precious luxury to me— but it still doesn't help with *why* I'm here. I should be used to the puzzles by now, but I don't know if that will ever happen. My brain has been a snowy TV screen ever since I showed up at my aunt and uncle's house about three months ago. My cousin, Meg, is a saving grace in making my bizarre reality seem normal. Try living without any memories of your parents, or your entire childhood, for a day, let alone months.

It's obnoxious.

Worse, every now and again, I blank out completely and end up in strange places with no idea of how I got there, or why I came. Like now—in front of the Grand Pacific House Museum.

A soft, clean breeze wafts up from the waterfront and rustles the edges of the stapled papers.

"I'm Dorcas Boyle, by the way," the strange woman says. She holds out her hand for me to shake. Her skin is Milligen and loose and she's got streaks of black, liquid eyeliner painted just below the rims of her eyes, like a football player. She slides her hand back when I reach for it and shakes with only her fingertips, as if she's the Queen of England. Her touch is so light, I barely feel anything.

"I'm the Curator of the Museum," she says. "You probably

heard about the Haunted Havrath Exhibit and I can answer any questions you have. *Literally.* I'm a savant." With a coy grin, she raises one shoulder and lashes the shreds of her crazy hair over it with an open hand. "I can answer, but if you're here to see the *century gown*, you're here too early! The garment is being...*readied.* The exhibit doesn't open until next month!" She waves her fingers in the air with a clucking laugh, but then her eyebrows sink and her thumb lands in her mouth. She nibbles the edge of her nail. "I was sure the fliers I sent to the high school had the correct date. You see, I have a profound recall when it comes to facts, but it doesn't equate with numbers. Such a misfortune! The Museum Board would be so angry with me! I've gone for so long with no mistakes! So, if I fudged that date...*oh!* Off with my head!" She crosses her eyes and slices a finger across her throat with another clucking laugh.

"I know the exhibit is a whole month away, but we're doing a fantastic build up to the opening! The restaurant on the corner is doing engagement dinner specials every week this month, and there is a paranormal tour company offering tours of local haunts and graveyards. The dance studio on Main is even offering ballroom dance lessons at a discount. They're also going to host a formal dance at the Community Center the weekend before the opening. Isn't that fun? It's geared up to be all the rage for you high school girls who are always looking for a new heartthrob!"

Who says *all the rage* anymore? And who would think anyone my age would consider a one-hundred-year-old, dead murderer a *heartthrob?*

I suppose the answer is a savant curator with an inconvenient case of dyscalculia.

What confuses me most is why my eyes keep returning to the photo of couple, but I'm really only looking at Isaac Havrath.

It's just a regular, two-dimensional, sepia photo, but his stare swallows me. I have a sudden craving to know if the true color of his eyes was a velvety, sweet cocoa or harsh, black coffee.

3

Knowing I'll never know is almost an itch that I'll never be able to rake my nails over.

I concentrate on breaking away from his eyes to view his ill-fitting suit. My gaze snags there too. Isaac Havrath was *stacked*. The jacket is tight across the shoulders, as if it was borrowed from a smaller man.

The curator drones on about how teenagers don't give the museum a chance because they never look up from their phones. I don't know what she's talking about. All of my attention is rooted on Isaac Havrath and his eyes, which keep calling me back.

Everything about him is captivating. His hair is slicked back and lightly oiled; his groomed mustache leads into the soft shadow of a beard. He has a soft, yet, direct gaze that reaches out of the photo, as if we're in a restaurant together, having our first date, staring across the table at one another.

As if he can't take his eyes off me.

I'm a little skeeved to admit it, but Dorcas Boyle was right—Isaac Havrath is a heartthrob.

I shake my head to release the connection to the photo. Seriously. I cannot be attracted to an ancient murderer displayed on a sandwich board in front of a museum.

That's just creepy.

"The official opening is October 8th at midnight, " the curator chirps. "I know, I know. Why not just officially open on October 9th, the original date of the Havrath wedding, you ask?"

I shrug even though I didn't ask.

Would never ask.

I don't even care…

except that I kind of do.

A wiry, little tinge of jealousy snakes through my heart at the thought of Isaac Havrath getting married, and I have no idea why. This is *crazy*. He was a *murderer*. Dead forever ago. I try to make it all sink in. I try to call up a shiver, and can't.

Instead, my eyes flick back to the photo of Isaac staring at me.

4

As if we're on a first name basis now.

Dorcas stabs an index finger through the air in front of my face. "The gown has a bit of a...shall we say...a *scent*. We want to air it out properly, and in time, so we don't want to miss the ghost that is said to appear in the gown, and the mysterious *toaster* who is rumored to visit her each year! We're having a special drawing for only a handful of people to attend the midnight opening on the eighth, so we don't scare either of them away!"

I squint at the curator again. My brain is stuck on a *one-hundred-year-old toaster*. I'm thinking ancient appliance, so it takes me a minute to realize she means a *person who toasts*.

"You know," she continues, "some say the toaster is Isaac Havrath himself, returning to conjure his beloved year after year, but if you ask me, I think it's a bit unlikely he'd still be able to make the trip at one-hundred-and-fifteen-years old."

I think Dorcas Boyle expects me to be dazzled, because she scoffs when I give no response. I can't. I'm silently freaking out over my sudden, intense, tingling desire to see ancient Isaac for myself. A thrill zips through me at the idea of Isaac stepping out of his sepia-framed jail where I can assess his eye color and touch the fabric stretched over his broad shoulders

"If you want to read all about it, the urban legend was published in The Voice and copies were sent to school last week."

"I've been out sick," I say.

The curator eyes me before taking a calculated step backward.

"Oh, it's not like that," I offer. "I'm not contagious. I don't go to school because I suffered a traumatic brain injury. From a car accident."

The look of pity on the curator's face is like draping a wet comforter over my soul. Cold, uncomfortable, heavy. She puts a hand over her heart. "Oh, you poor dear!"

I change the subject with an awkward smile. "Who did the groom murder?" I ask.

Dorcas Boyle gives me a groan. "I'll be right back," she says before turning away to climb the two crooked cement steps into the museum. She disappears, only to return moments later with a stapler and wrinkled newspaper, which she snaps open and folds back to reveal a full page story.

"You can read for yourself. It's going to be quite the event." She staples the newsprint to the edge of the sandwich board. The breeze picks it up and flaps the paper like the drooping sleeve of a preacher's robe.

The curator goes back into the museum. I stand on the sidewalk and read the entire article four times through—memorizing everything to tell Meg—before I start the walk back to Aunt Dena and Uncle Leonard's house.

Isaac Havrath's face drifts through my mental snow. The thought of him is an itch that moves before I can scratch it. It tingles in my brain and prickles in my heart. It irritates the soles of my feet and the centers of my palms. I can't shake the thought of Isaac's piercing gaze, and I don't know how I'm going to wait a whole month to find out more about him.

"I don't know why you stick around here, Nova. It's vile," Meg says to me across the dinner table. "Hell, I don't know why I do."

Her eyes roll up into her skull like slippery egg yolks, as if she's really trying to get a good look at her brain from the inside. I hate when she's like this, but I get it. I've been dying to tell her all about Isaac Havrath since I got home, but I don't want to do it here, over boiled hot dogs and cups of flat orange pop, as Uncle Leonard sneers at us from the other end of the table.

Uncle Leonard, Meg's dad—she's adopted—is drunk. That's typical. He's the reason I don't fault Meg so much.

"I want these dishes squeaky clean," he slurs, stuffing the last bite of a plain, hot dog in his mouth. He flips his paper plate in her direction.

"You can't wash paper plates," Meg tells him. "If you don't believe me, ask Nova."

Uncle Leonard's not having it, and Meg's just made his mood ten times worse by bringing me up. Uncle Leonard has resented my presence in his house from the first day I arrived. While he might verbally abuse Meg, he just pretends I'm not here at all. The side-eye glimpse he shoots me is more reflex than anything. He shakes his head as if berating himself for falling for Meg's trick. Having acknowledged me enrages him all the more.

"Don't give me that! You can clean them! I want those dishes spotless!" He pops to his feet, thumping against the table as he tries to keep his balance. This is how he is when he's stone drunk. He jumps up and Meg startles, but it's in slow motion because she's already messed up tonight. Uncle Leonard grabs hold of a good chunk of her long, glossy hair.

"I said you're gonna wash the dishes!" He seems just as surprised as she does that he got ahold of her. He uses her hair like a rein in his fist and jerks her off the chair and to the sink.

Meg is messed up enough that when she swings a fist at him, she misses by a mile. Uncle Leonard shakes his own fist, giving her a hard snap that wobbles her neck. Meg stumbles forward, missing the edge of the counter with her face by millimeters.

I scream. It's my one strength: Uncle Leonard fears the neighbors will hear the insanity.

He lets go with a snarling glance in my direction, but he looks away fast. Maybe it's the humiliation of making someone with a brain trauma shriek. Maybe it's because he's never liked that I'm here to begin with. He tries to ignore me most of the time, but I just made it so he can't. Either way, he lets go of Meg and with a huff, he stomps out of the room.

Uncle Leonard is half monster. The other half of him might be decent, but I wouldn't know. That part of him is usually passed out somewhere.

Meg just laughs as she plants a palm on the counter and pulls herself back onto her feet. She makes a big show of washing the plates, in case he comes back. They turn to mush in the water. She giggles as she scoops the papier-mâché out of the sink and into the trash.

I don't know how she even gets back on her feet after all of that.

All I know is that Meg is a warrior.

Once the dishes are done, I follow her to our room. We share her full size bed. She locks the door and opens the window before she strikes up a fattie. She calls it *the devil's lettuce* with a laugh that isn't.

It's no surprise why Meg likes getting messed up—and tonight, even more messed up on top of the messed up she already was—but it still breaks my heart.

She's one of those people with all this potential that never gets to surface. Meg's absolutely, gob-smacking gorgeous, with eyelashes as long as my middle fingers, skin like Cleopatra, and a mane of hair that shines so much it glitters. She's smart too, knowing exactly what to say, and when to say it, in order to ease a situation—like laughing about the dishes tonight. But she also has a great sense of strategy, so I'm positive that at some point, Uncle Leonard's going to get his for jerking her around by the hair.

She could have it all, but Meg forgets that. She lets her hair stay snarly, wears her tee shirts until they smell like armpits, and she weighs about twenty pounds less than she should. Meg only cares about pills, punctures, and weed, because those things don't bug her about living up to her potential.

I've waited all day to talk to her, but now I have to wait even longer. She inhales, the perfect points of her upper lip clamped around the rolling paper. I could look away, but what's the use. Half the time, I'm not sure my cousin even knows I'm still in the room. I'm busting to tell her all about Isaac Havrath, but I have to wait for the right moment, when she is relaxed, but still conscious, or Meg will just tell me to go away.

After missing her all day long, I can't bear to be shut out all night too.

She holds her inhale, the smoke leaking from the corners of her mouth. I look away.

"If I was you, Supernova?" she finally says, "with a couple of dead parents? I wouldn't hang out here. No way. Not with the *Breaking Bad* family." She coughs a cloud at her own joke and her head does one big wobble backward, as if her neck can't handle the weight.

"If you were me," I say, "with no place to go, you'd be happy to have a place to stay."

I don't tell her I also stay because I believe she needs me more than she'll ever admit.

She snorts. "*Happy* ain't something you're ever gonna find around here, Nova-caine." She fades backward, onto her pillow, her eyes just slits as she holds the joint out to me. I don't take it and her arm goes slack. "You can leave whenever you want. There's nothing keeping you here. You don't even got a bed of your own. It's vile."

It's my turn to laugh.

"Vile." I nod. If Meg didn't say it was vile, I would worry a lot more about her mental state. It's her word and she spouts it like she has Tourette's. As long as she's saying it, I know she's still in there and the drugs haven't completely fried her brain. I guess I consider it my safe word. "Is that why you stay? Because you have a bed?"

"I'm stuck here," she says. Her eyes roll involuntarily. "But I don't know why I stay."

Yeah, she's getting to that point where she stops making sense. Maybe she means because she's in her Senior year and has to finish. Maybe because she's always so strung out, she can't find any other way. I don't know.

She chucks the stump of her joint into the metal track of the window sill where it will burn out without setting the house on fire. It glows like an angry, orange eye, poking a hole in the darkness. Meg lays back on her pillow again. Her eyelids flutter.

"Meggy," I bark. She can't pass out. Not yet. Not before I've had a chance to tell her about *him*. "I read something cool today. An urban legend. You wanna hear it?"

"Yeah, sure," she drawls. "Tell me a story, Nova Spice."

"You have the newspaper in your backpack. Look at the article's pictures and I'll tell you a ghost story," I say. Anything to keep her interested and awake.

"I'm tired," she grumble-whines, but she fumbles an arm down along the edge of the bed for her backpack. She wrestles the paper out and the crinkling revives her a bit. It's already folded open to the right page. She squints at the photos and her brows furrow as she tries to focus.

I don't know why I'm so excited, but my stomach bounces like I'm about to tell her about a boy.

Which I guess is exactly what I'm going to do.

"It's about this couple that was going to get married, but it ends in murder," I tell her.

"Oh good," she murmurs.

"The actual, haunted wedding dress is going on exhibit at the museum on Washington Street. The bride was this girl...Silvia Pantazis. She was the daughter of a traveling carpenter who was commissioned to make pews for a church in a tiny town. The preacher's son, Isaac Havrath, fell in love with Silvia and proposed to her."

"The Havraths put this town on the map," Meg mumbles. "But they're all gone now. Super vile. I did a paper on them in sixth grade." She squints at the newsprint again, angling the paper as if it's the lighting that's faulty.

I can't stop the Isaac train, whether she wants to hear it or not. "Isaac's mom wanted her only son to have a huge wedding, but they were really poor. A preacher's family and all that. The mom claimed she had an inheritance, but, actually, she stole from the church treasury to pay for the huge wedding feast, fancy carriages, and a custom dress for the bride."

"I never heard any of this stuff," Meg raises her pinched nose like a blind mole. "Only about how the family was super rich from...doing stuff."

"The rich part came *waaay* later, after they moved here," I tell her. "Word spread about the wedding and people flooded in from all the surrounding towns for the ceremony. Turns out, it was a disgruntled carriage driver who spilled the beans about Isaac's mom swiping the money for church mortgage.

"Silvia's family called off the wedding and the Havraths were shamed. The humiliation was too much for Isaac's mom. She killed herself."

"How?" Meg asks. I'm delighted that she's interested. The newspaper crinkles in her grip.

"It didn't say *how*, but Isaac was so grief-stricken, he murdered the carriage driver, who he blamed for telling everyone. Isaac was thrown in jail. His dad was so ashamed, he left Byron and came to Michigan to start a whole new life. He built a new church. He even started a new family, and the creepiest part? He named his *new* son Isaac too."

Meg leans on her elbow, the paper draped over the edge of the mattress. Eyes still squeezed shut, she tilts her chin again. "What happened to the Samantha?"

"Silvia," I correct. "The bride hung herself."

"In the dress? That's sooo vile."

"It didn't say she was *wearing* the dress, but it was considered cursed after that."

"*Obviously*," Meg puffs, dropping the newspaper on the floor. "So, how'd the Havraths and the museum get the dress?"

"I don't know," I say. "Isaac's dad must have taken it with him when he came here. The dress was handmade by some fancy-shmancy European designer, so it was probably worth a lot of money. Maybe that's how he got the money for the new church. All the article said was that the dress was part of the Havrath estate, until it was donated to the museum this year."

Meg perks up again. "The Havrath Mansion has been abandoned forever and the building got torn down forever ago. It was on 24 Mile Road. All that's left is the Dorothy basement."

"A Dorothy *what*?"

"You know…" Her grin makes her look like a stroke victim. "A storm shelter, Supernova. Like, in the ground. With doors on it. Like the one in the Wizard of Oz?" Her grin smears into a sly smile. "We all used to go sit in there to get stoned, until the cops found out and kept busting us. Nobody goes there anymore."

"Huh," I say. I am bubbling inside to tell her the rest. "On October 8th, the night before the anniversary of the wedding—"

"The one that didn't happen," Meg says.

"Yes," I say, "The legend says that at midnight, a mysterious toaster—"

"A *toaster*?"

"Not the appliance. A person who toasts."

"Man or woman?"

"Some people say it's the groom, even though he'd be over a hundred years old."

"That's stupid. It's not him."

"Well, whoever it is, they show up because Silvia is supposed to appear in her wedding dress. The toaster leaves behind rose petals on the floor and two champagne glasses, one with a little booze still in it."

"Oh yeah, right." Meg snorts. I can tell she's losing all sense of herself by the way her words start running together. "They're trying to say somebody's been sneaking into that abandoned mansion for *years*? And with a bunch of roses and a bottle of bubbly, and nobody knows who it is? Yeah, right! Try locking a door for once! It's a bunch of crap! The museum just wants customers, or the mayor wants tourists…somebody wants some-thing. It's a scam, I can smell it. It's vile."

"I don't care," I say. "I still want to see it. It's better than sitting around here, doing nothing, isn't it? We should go down there tomorrow and see if we can see it early."

Meg nods and the nodding continues longer than it should. "Yeah, sure, Nova Lisa."

Her mouth flops open and a line of drool swizzles down her chin. I don't care if she meant it, but I'll remind her tomorrow that she said she'd go, and I'll tell her she promised.

I t took hours, but I finally convinced Meg that we should go down to the museum.

But she invited her boyfriend over and he's taken all day to get here. If there's anything worse than waiting all day to go see a picture of a dead murderer, it's waiting for Meg to get ready, but if there's anything worse than both of those, it's having to share oxygen with her boyfriend, Murray.

Mur. The walking, talking, Murphy's Law. Muriah Scary.

Meg looks like royalty, but Murray is a scrawny, ginger-haired idiot, so skinny his ribs look like his stomach is caving in. His spine shapes him into a giant letter C. Another delightful feature: his fingers look like he's growing a garden of hemlock beneath each nail. *And he chews them.*

The two of them met halfway through Junior year and Meg didn't dump him at the start of summer vacation like she should have. Meg's Mur-stake has no job, no ambition, and no plans for the future. When Aunt Dena once asked Murray about what he wanted to do with his life, he knocked the back of his palm against his forehead, wiggled the bull horns at her, and said, "We'll see."

Winner.

There is one good thing about Murray though: I always know when he's coming. The smell of him—sour laundry and rotted potatoes—sets the ambience, but it's the chain that connects his wallet to his belt loop that gives him away. Murray jingles like a belled hound.

It rattles as he drops onto the couch cushion beside me and kicks his nasty, greasy boots up on the coffee table. The stink of him wafts over me.

"Where's Meg?" He pulls out his switchblade and digs crud from beneath his ragged fingernails. He flicks the crust into the couch cushions.

Meg shuffles in, her hair piled up in a bun, lazy-princess style, with strands leaking out in every direction.

"It's about time you got here." She kicks Murray's boots off the edge of the coffee table. "We wanna go downtown."

"Who's we?" He asks, even though he knows. Hands in the air, the tip of his switchblade is pointed toward his ear. It would only take one *bonk* and that blade would slice through his ear hole and hit the wide open space in between.

I grin. Dreaming up Murray's demise is my guilty pleasure.

"Me, you, and Nova," Meg says.

"Come on. Can't we just leave her? We'd have more fun if it was just the two of us." Murray rolls his big dumb eyes, dragging his gaze right through me. He flicks the switchblade closed and dumps it in his pocket. He doesn't just hate me, he *loathes* me.

I adore that.

"Be nice," Meg says. "She's part of my life, so she's part of yours too."

I stick my tongue out at him.

He glowers. "I didn't sign up for that."

Meg glowers back at him until he gives in with a sigh.

"What's so special downtown?" he asks.

"There's a haunted dress at the museum on Washington and we wanna see it." Meg finishes with a pouty, little whine. She drops

16

down on the cushion beside him and curls up against him, kissing his stubbly, orange cheek and batting her eyes at him. He's chewing his thumbnail.

Total winner.

"I ain't draggin' ass downtown to see a *dress*." He spits a piece of the nail.

"It's *haunted* and it's from the Havrath House." Meg tugs playfully at one of his belt loops, jingling his wallet chain. She lowers her eyelids. "There's all kinds of old stuff at that museum that's probably worth a bunch of money, and museums probably don't notice stuff that goes missing like stores do."

Murray perks up. "I didn't think about that."

"Come with us and check it out, *Murlin*," Meg whispers in his ear.

"Wizards have skills and brains, not crusty, nail fungus," I murmur.

Meg plants a kiss on his cheek. "He's magical to me, and that's all that matters."

"You're my everything too, baby," Murray tells her.

When he leans in to kiss her, I mimic the sloppy hound dog kiss until Meg notices and shrieks a laugh.

Murray pulls away.

Mission accomplished.

"Come on, let's go." She nudges him with a smile. "Nova doesn't want to watch us kiss all day."

"She don't have to watch." He's as sour as his tee shirt, but he still gets off the couch.

I shrug him off like dust off my shoulder. She likes him.

That makes one of us.

By the time we hit Front Street, the decorative street lights are on. The soft gray flicker, coupled with the smell of fish wafting up from Anchor Bay, is a ton better than the dumpster-fire that is Murray's breath.

Meg and Murray slog along behind me. His chain jangles as he dives forward, trying to jam his hand up under her shirt. Meg squeals every time. It grates on my nerves.

"The museum closes at nine," I urge them from over my shoulder, but there's no hurrying them up. I doubted Dorcas Boyle would let us see the exhibit early to begin with, but now, showing up to beg a half hour before the museum closes, seems pointless.

Meg's shoes grit against the sidewalk as she squeals and ducks away from Murray again. "Stop it, *Murlin*! We got to hurry so we don't miss it!"

"You know you like it," he says.

I'd like to kick him in the throat and see how much he likes that. I don't know why Meg hangs onto him as if he's a kite string, dangling from the moon.

Meg dodges him, but then she lifts the hem of her shirt and

flashes her neon orange bra. He dives at her again, and when she squeals *again*, I groan and look away.

The two restaurants near the water are closing up. One offers specialty wines and dinners à la carte with waiters in bow ties; the other sells stuff you can eat while walking along the beach, served in biodegradable paper baskets by teenagers in jeans. Both places are lit, but empty. The bow-tied waiters refill salt shakers and the teenagers lean on the counter eating food they didn't pay for. None of them seem to notice us as we round the corner from Front Street and work our way up Washington.

"We're not going to make it if you guys don't hurry up," I complain over my shoulder.

It's hopeless. Meg acts like she can't hear me as Murray slings an arm over her shoulders and whispers who-knows-what in her ear. She laughs. Murray drags his loser-boots even more slowly over the concrete and sticks a tongue in her ear, which makes her squeal again.

Yuck.

I trudge on.

"We're not staying long, right?" Murray says.

"Nova thinks it's already closed," Meg whispers.

He pauses to look into the window of a jewelry shop. He grunts at the reinforced bars inside the frame and moves on. "Nobody trusts nobody anymore."

I come to a jarring halt in front of the museum. All the lights are off and a slanted *closed* sign dangles on the door by a string.

Murray laughs as if he's won something.

"It's closed!" I roar at them.

Murray grins, but Meg's brows fall as if she suddenly understands how much this meant to me.

"Maybe we can see the dress through the window?" she offers, pulling away from Murray to join me at the glass. "Come on, at least we might be able to see it."

Meg cups her hands against the square front window to peer

inside. I follow suit, pressing the edges of my palms to the glass too. The moment I do, a sharp sting zips through my skin. I yank my hands away.

There is no bug, no cut I can see, but the pain is indisputable. The sting permeates my hands. Fiberglass needles explode in my arms, prickling through my muscles and veins, sticking like barbed wire. Scratching only spreads the itch through my torso and into my back.

Meg doesn't notice.

Murray doesn't care.

"The lights are off," Meg reports, still glued to the glass.

The itch spills into my belly and falls into my hips. I feel like I've been rolled in bed bugs. No matter how much I scratch, nothing is relieved.

"I only see a bunch of pictures, an old couch, and a piano," she continues, "but there's more stuff further back I can't really see."

I throw one hand over my shoulder and dance in a miserable circle, trying to scrape the unreachable center of my back. What I can reach, I can't scratch hard enough.

Murray pulls his switchblade from his pocket and flicks it open as he watches me twist, buckle, and dig at myself. "What's up with you?"

"I think something stung me!" The barbed wire itch drills into my bones. The core of me is one big itch I can't reach. I want to yank out my finger bones, jab them through my skin, and scratch the marrow of my femurs.

Meg pulls herself away from the window. With one look at me, concern breaks open like wounds across her face. "Show me your hands! If something stung you, there'd be a bump, or a cut, or something!"

There's not a mark on me, even though my body feels like it's about to catch fire, as if every nerve is packed with gunpowder and set to explode. No poke, no cut, no blistering bubble of venom. There's nothing, except the feeling that my body is packed in itches, each nerve full of gunpowder. I rake my nails across my skin, giving myself less than a heartbeat of relief. More fiberglass needles explode in the wake of each fingernail.

"Huh." Murray says, dismissing me altogether as he runs his switchblade beneath a nail. He turns back to Meg with a dull sigh. "Anything worth anything in there, Meggy?"

The itch plunges even deeper.

"Bees aren't out this late at night," Meg reasons aloud, ignoring him. She scans the front glass of the museum, the air around me, the contents of the street. Her initial splash of concern turns to a tidal wave of ferocity.

Meg doesn't get scared about things.

She gets pointed.

Determined.

Matter-of-fact in a way that could part fire.

"What *in the world* did you touch, Nova?" she growls.

"I don't know!" The prickling circulates through my veins like little fan blades, spraying stinging quills through my muscles. I rake my fingers over myself, too miserable to be worried about her tone.

"Tell me what it feels like!" she insists, her words clipped, clinical, stern.

"Itching…I'm itching all over!" I gasp out the words. "I want to run to get it out of me!"

"Then run!" Meg commands.

"I *can't!*" I shout at her. It's not that I don't want to; my brain won't heed the request.

My body echoes my desire, screaming up my spinal cord, *RUN*, but a stubborn, clinging sensation—one I can't even translate—anchors my feet. My soles itch so bad, I want to scrape them off on the sidewalk, but something in the far depths of my mind whispers commands in a language my body heeds.

I tremble, scared of this surfacing part of me that I don't understand. Commands are coming from inside me, although they are not mine and they don't have a voice. It's like this itch embeds orders in my muscles that override my own.

The first order isn't even translatable into words. It's only a feeling. An urge. One that is specific and indisputable.

Stay.

Like a dog.

The second order skips any semblance of words altogether and moves straight to raw urge. The feelings boil up, gathering together, forming an even fuller command.

Desire.

Need.

The urge pops open like a blood blister: *I must see Isaac Havrath.*

It's not a want. It's a *have to.*

My muscles ache to run away, but the urge holds them in place.

Peering past my own scratching image in the museum window, I stare at the ombre shadows of old furniture and antiques melting into the darkness. More urges bubble in the deep pot of my stomach. These urges, which are not mine, have a plan. A steaming tendril of a suggestion escapes and I gasp with the intention. I sway on the balls of my feet. The urge is to use my head as a battering ram to enter the museum if there is no other way.

"We've got to get inside!" I tell Meg, "before I hurl myself through this window!"

Meg whirls on Murray.

"Can you get us in or not?" she barks.

He jerks back at the venom in her tone, but then his gaze scales the wood storefront, over the museum sign to the bricked top level. Like he's going to spider his way up to a window. "Has there ever been a place I couldn't get into?"

"Then get us in," Meg commands. "Now!"

He releases a shot of breath from between his teeth and grabs Meg's hand. He tugs her past the front window, around the edge of the building. I follow them down the narrow, dirt passageway between the buildings until we end up in the alley.

Murray twists one way, then the other, checking for life. There's no sign of anything back here besides over-stuffed garbage bags, overflowing a dumpster two doors down like rancid soap bubbles.

"See? Back door," Murray murmurs, pointing to the museum's wooden back door. A blue gingham curtain covers the paned glass window inset at eye level.

The itch stops the moment I lay eyes on the door.

I drop my hands, relieved, but the urge takes over. The urge to see Isaac Havrath's photo fish-flutters in my chest, the soft hook of desire sunk into my sternum. The air around me is gelatin, the tug forward makes me feel awkward and light-headed.

I force a step backward, and achieve it, but when the severe itch returns, I can't convince my body to run. The urge to stay, coupled with the *pull* toward the museum's back door, is too strong.

Meg narrows her gaze at me. "What's going on? Did the itching stop?"

"Only if I go inside," I say. My voice trembles with my inner tug of war.

It must not show on the outside, because Murray cuts me a sly look and mumbles, "Faker," as he takes out his switchblade again and steps closer to the door. Hunching his shoulders, he jimmies the blade between the door and the frame. It only takes a shove of his shoulder to pop it open. "These idiots don't even have a deadbolt!"

A surge of stale museum air hits me—the scent of ages, the dust of an accumulated past.

Murray pushes the door open wide with the palm of his hand and steps back with a flourish to Meg.

"Open said me, *my queen*," he says.

He's such an idiot. Usually, I would relish the opportunity to rub Murray's nose in his stupidity, but a delicious, warm wash of tingles rush over me, washing away the horrible, stinging prickles in my veins. A fluttering tug appears too, pulling me forward as seductively as if I'm in the arms of a tender dance partner.

"Come on!" Murray growls to Meg. "You were the one who wanted to see the dress, so let's go see it!"

5

T he tug guides me softly past Meg and Murray, over the threshold, and into the museum.

The back room is piled with boxes, but there are nightlights plugged into the walls that create a glowing path like fairy lights. Murray kicks the boxes aside as he drags Meg inside, but I follow the glow into the front parlor.

To the right, there is a settee shoved against the wall. To the left, a wall display of old photographs and plaques. An upright piano beneath. Dorcas Boyle's sandwich board leans against the side of a glass case filled with accessories like discolored netted gloves, a beaded coin purse, and a frayed handbag. An ancient cash register that looks like it weighs as much as the moon, sits on top.

The pleasant *pull* draws me to the staircase landing, located directly behind the front door with its crooked *open* sign. I'm under the spell of this current that whisks me up the stairs as Meg and Murray stumble around the parlor. There is a thump and a crack before I'm even halfway up the steps. I force the pause and I'm a little surprised when the current allows it, rather than forcing me to the top floor.

"You could've just opened the case from the back," Meg says.

"It looked like it was going to break anyway," Murray grumbles. "What a bunch of junk! Maybe not the cash register—that's kind of cool, but I can't carry it all the way back to my house. We need a car if I can even carry it."

"Nova," Meg hisses to me, "Where are you?"

"Forget about her," Murray says as I continue up the stairs. "We've got better stuff to do."

Meg's giggle pauses my steps. I turn back to see Meg at the bottom of the staircase, and Murray, who is now cupping her face as he kisses her. He walks her backward, until her spine is flush with the wall at the bottom of the steps. They keep kissing and making noises that make me think of blubbery, white snot and gooey tentacles rammed in my ears. They pant in each other's faces and collapse on the stairs, Meg curling her legs around Murray's malnourished hips as he dry humps her.

It's like watching giraffes mate.

And it would turn my stomach completely inside out if the fascinating *pull* wasn't tugging my attention further up the staircase.

I turn away, continuing up the stairs. Moving forward feels good, like a healing massage in my bones that eradicates anything left of the itch, even if climbing the steps is completely involuntary. If I wanted to turn back and climb over Meg and Murray to leave the museum, I'm not sure I *could*. I think the current feels so good only because I've surrendered to it. My feet plant themselves, one step at a time, scaling each stair, until I'm at the top.

Urges aside, my brain isn't completely sold. I know I shouldn't feel this good, caught in a stream and letting the urge of this *hook* or *tug* or *pull* or whatever this is, guide me. I should go back down the stairs. Should follow my reasonable instincts and get out of this museum.

But the further up the stairs I go, the more excited I get. I'm going to see Isaac Havrath's photo. *A photo.* It's crazy and I know it, but I keep moving forward, following the stream, the tug of the fishing line, the invisible partner—whatever this is—to the top of the steps. A hallway leads to a pair of double doors at the very end.

Getting there, to what I assume will be the Havrath Exhibit closed away behind those doors, is the only thing running through my head.

Even as I hear the howl of the sirens approaching.

6

The '*idiots*' who didn't install a deadbolt on the museum's back door, had the sense to install an alarm system instead.

Two cop cars pull up to the museum. One car in the front, which parks quietly at the curb, and one in back that throws up dust clouds as it screeches to a halt. A seizure-strobe of red and blue lights blast through the front door and race over the tangle of Meg and Murray at the bottom of the stairs.

"Holy shit!" Murray jumps up, pressing his scrawny shoulders against the stairwell wall as if he can disappear through the plaster.

Meg crouches at his knees. "You said we wouldn't get caught!"

"Shit! Shit! Shit! There wasn't even a deadbolt!" Murray moans.

"Nova...Nova, hide!" Meg hisses, waving her hand at me.

I don't have the chance to answer her. The magnetism of the *pull* swells and with the surge, I'm sucked down the hall at a trot. Despite the cops crashing through the back room and bursting through the front door, reaching the double doors at the end of the hall soothes me.

I should be panicking. I should be terrified that Meg— Murray's on his own—is being busted downstairs. But, as I cup the knob in my tingling palm, I don't even try to turn back. I open the right door and slip inside the room.

I bite my bottom lip as the cops shout at Meg and Murray to stay where they are.

One of the officers orders them to put their hands in the air.

Murray says, *"It's cool, man, we were just looking for a place to...you know."*

The cop says *sure*, asks them if they have warrants. The jaws of the handcuffs close with a metallic growl. One of the cops asks if there's anyone else inside.

Meg says no. Not a hint of liar in her voice. Meg doesn't tell anybody what she doesn't want them to know, and she's good at it.

Murray just says *nope*, like the nose-picker he is.

A cop lumbers up the stairs despite what they've said. I hear the other doors in the hall open and close as he clears each room.

I press myself behind the edge of a curio cabinet, pushed almost into the corner, on the same wall as the double doors. The cop stalks toward the double doors. The knick-knacks rattle on the glass shelves. I squeeze deeper myself into the narrow space.

The footsteps pause outside the door. I hold my breath. The vintage ceramics still.

The cop's gun enters the room first. He sweeps one side, then the other.

Finally, the cop creeps all the way into the room, gun still drawn. I can see him with only one eye from behind the curio, but I am as motionless as death itself. He's a wiry old guy, bald on top, gray on the sides, glasses that glint when the streetlight catches them right. Somebody's Grandpa, I bet.

I keep my shoulders flat to the wall, my body breathless. There's no way I'm hidden enough, but it's dark. I've got that going for me.

Until Grandpa Cop pops on his flashlight.

He roves the sphere of light across the walls, right past me, over the cabinet, straight across the somber faces of Isaac's and

Silvia's families, hanging in dark frames. The cop scans the other side of the room too, dragging the light past a podium; a cake table; an arched arbor draped with fake ivy and a settee with a tiny rosebud print. Nothing is more interesting than the photos of Isaac, until the flashlight beam rolls over the dress at the far end of the room.

My breath dissolves in a soundless gasp.

A thousand crystals, on the background of creamy silk, all twinkle to life. They blaze and dance, casting colors like sugar sprinkled over a velvety custard cream. It's easily the most stunning thing I've ever seen.

My breath hitches as the cop takes a step backward. The knick-knacks in the curio shiver on their glass shelf.

The flashlight darts around, and I freeze, the beam splashing past me. He straightens up. Holsters his gun. Grandpa Cop locates the light switch near the door. He flicks it up and down, up and down, but no lights pop on.

My lungs sweat.

I squeeze my eyes shut.

I couldn't breathe if I wanted to.

The cop clicks the button of the speaker on his shoulder and reports '*all clear*' into the mic. He backs out of the room and closes the door.

Finally, his footsteps retreat down the hall and stairs.

The cops stand around blabbing down below. Grandpa Cop reports, "Upper level's clear. What's with the lights, Joe? There are no lights up top. Those kids couldn't have cut the electric, or the alarm wouldn't have sounded."

"I dunno," another cop answers. "Maybe they got some burnt out bulbs. You know these old buildings. They're all wired funny."

My shoulders plastered to the wall, I lock my knees, even though the *pull* that brought me upstairs now beckons me toward the dress. It drags up my chin, so all I do is stand and stare at the dress while the cops mill around downstairs, their radios shrieking with static and updates.

Not that I mind.

The gown hypnotizes me. The street light doesn't move, doesn't flicker, but the crystals on the dress glisten with a soft, pastel strobe effect. The colors drift around the room like a fairy's shadow. I could stand here and stare at it all week if I have to. The floor-length ball gown spills across the floor, the train wrapped around it in a billowing heap, as if it goes on for miles.

This is not the wedding dress I envisioned when Dorcas Boyle was babbling about the legend behind it. I assumed that the dress would be yellowed as the curator's pearls by now, crusted with homicidal blood, and as fragile as holy scrolls.

But this isn't a dress. It's a gown for a queen. It is made of a heavy, cream-colored satin with a bodice glazed in pearls and glimmering crystals, silk bows draped at the sleeves, and an empire waist. The gown dissolves at the bottom into Honiton lace, so satisfyingly thick and at the same time so intricate and delicate, it reminds me of the way a thick piece of chocolate melts in my mouth.

I stand still, admiring the gown until the cops finish their business. My fingers itch to rub the layers of the captivating gown. The cops call the museum curator, who never shows up, and finally board up the back door. The minute the cruiser tires grit away down the alley, I cross the floor to the gown.

My knees shake. My spine is damp.

I've just committed a felony. The cops could return. I could still get caught.

But the anxiety doesn't stem from the crime. It's rooted in the fact that at least three different photos of Isaac Havrath seem to be watching every step I make as I cross the room to touch his former-fiancé's gown.

Standing before it, I have a spooky sense that one touch will somehow change my entire life, or, at the very least, force Silvia

Pantazis from the shadows of death to shriek at me for messing with her gown. It's crazy, but the anxiety stops me from extending my fingers, even though my arm is outstretched, my fisted hand only inches from the gown.

Thoughts that think me, rather than me thinking them, return. The urges whispers in my limbs. *Just one touch. Just one.*

The urges whispers in my limbs. *Just one touch. Just one.*

I pant, fighting to keep my fingers curled and dug into my palms. It doesn't seem right to give in to the urge. I've already broken in and haven't considered leaving even once, but shreds of moral decency continue to flitter through my brain. I puff out a breath and suck in another, struggling against the urge to run my hands over the gown, when a strange scent tickles something in my head.

It is not the dusty aroma I would have expected.

The smell is good, and not good.

Sour as a lemon, biting as a pickle, it is a scent similar to rotting fish caught in a fresh gust off the lake. Whatever it is, it clears my head long enough for my obsession with the gown to dissolve. I step away, shaking my head, and breathe deep to clear my passages.

I really need to get out of here.

I avoid eye contact with any of Isaac Havrath's photos, but my gaze snags on the wedding certificate hanging on the wall. The document is so beautiful, I have to look closer. Written in flawless calligraphy, each line of the announcement is nestled within hand-painted ivy, roses, and tassels that surround the names, *Isaac Havrath* and *Silvia Pantazis*. It's weird to be holding such a masterfully artful wedding agreement for two people who never fulfilled the vows upon it.

I run my finger over the glass. Their names glide among the vines and flowers.

My finger stops dead on the date.

I read it twice.

And twice again.

Penned in that perfectly slanted calligraphy, the document reads: *In this, the ninth month and tenth day of the year, nineteen and twenty seven.*

The paper said that the haunted gown and its mysterious toaster appear at midnight on the anniversary of the foiled wedding. But the paper said the anniversary was October 9th, 1927.

I think of the museum curator drawing her finger across her throat. Dorcas Boyle and her dyscalculia reversed the date after all.

The wedding date was not October 9th. It was September 10th.

September tenth.

September...the tenth.

Today.

The framed wedding certificate slides off my lap and hits the floor with a *thump.*

One that is echoed by the door downstairs.

7

I wedge myself back into the corner, behind the curio, as footsteps tread up the stairs.

I knew it. The whole *toaster* thing reeked of an inside job from the start.

Dorcas Boyle is probably going to swish through the double doors in a cheesy Halloween cape, sprinkle some flower petals, and splash around some bubbly. But then, why would the toasting happen today, on the correct date of the wedding, when Dorcas Boyle printed the date in the paper as a month from now? The museum wouldn't benefit from the event happening without any ticket holders present.

Unless there truly is a mysterious toaster, who is coming on the correct date, to see the gown across the room…which is *actually* haunted.

I smash my shoulders against the wall and crumble up to make myself smaller. Less noticeable. My splintered nerves jab at the air trapped in my lungs.

The footsteps climb the staircase, solid and steady. They are heavy, measured steps, thoughtful as a wedding march…or sorrow-ful, as a funeral procession. I could be dead wrong, but recalling the way the curator flitted up the museum's cement steps the first day I met her, Dorcas Boyle's gait is nothing like the one closing in on the double doors.

It has to be a hoax.

Has to.

But the *pull* returns like a whisper of static racing over my skin. Goosebumps sweep up my arms. My muscles tug, as if they are made of metal shavings and a weak magnet is aimed at my hiding spot. I remain as close to the wall as I can be without sinking into it, although my bones tingle into the marrow.

The feel of everything changes with every footstep. The night grows darker than a deep bruise. The air congeals. The parchment-glow of the streetlights is too weak to make the crystals on the gown cast their shimmer. The shadows come from every corner of the room, stretching toward the gown as if one touch could bring them to life.

The door handle twists, the latch scrapes, and one of the double doors wafts open.

My breath turns to chewing gum in my lungs.

A man dressed in raven-black steps into the room like a hole in a shadow. With him comes a whiff of cold metal that sits on my tongue like a coin. Fresh static races over the threshold, my nerves swiftly prickling, my muscles twitching, summoning my body in the man's direction.

Who is this guy?

I lock my limbs in place and force my lips apart, so I don't grit my teeth.

His broad back faces me. Stepping further into the room, I can make out his black trench coat, draped across the breadth of his shoulders and cascading down his body like a smooth cape. He doesn't notice me. His gaze is riveted purely to the displayed gown as he elbows the door closed, the latch snicking softly behind him.

We're all alone now.

My tugging muscles, and my joints locked like rusted chains. I should concentrate on keeping myself still, but my entire being is fixated on every move this man makes.

He rolls his shoulders back. A cellophane cone of roses crinkles beneath his right arm. A bottle of champagne dangles from the same hand.

I squint at the man with my one eye, peeking around the edge of the cabinet. He runs his left hand, as square and broad as his shoulders, through his dark hair and lets out a deep, slow, sigh. It sounds like an admission of defeat.

I shouldn't be here, witnessing this event. I have no right to be part of this at all, to watch *whoever-he-is* pay his intimate homage to the gown. But, as I gaze at the hard cut of the man's jaw and the subtle shadow upon it, I am struck with how familiar his face appears.

And how impossible.

He looks just like Isaac Havrath. The Isaac from the photo— not what would be the gruesome current version, which has been dead for over a hundred years. This man must be a relative, and a doppelgänger at that.

The returned urge paralyzes the commands I give my body: to sneak away, to steal away unnoticed, or to just bolt from this room, destroying anything in my path of escape, like a cow caught in a pottery shed. My legs remain motionless.

"I've missed you," he rasps.

8

His soft, crumbling tone sends an entire quiver of itchy arrows shooting through me. The man is a mysterious stranger. I dig my fingers into my palms, desperately trying to override the itch—the one that commands me to respond to him—with pain. So far, that's working, but my resistance seems to weaken by the second.

The man sweeps across the wooden floor planks, halting before the gown and bowing deeply. As if he's going to ask the thing to dance.

The static in the air builds.

Desire sucks at my skin.

Dangerous doesn't even begin to describe this feeling. It's something far worse than that, because danger isn't so captivating.

He deposits the bottle on the cake table and lays the crinkling bouquet of flowers beside it. Tugging at the wrists, he removes his trench coat and tosses it on the couch. Beneath the trench, he's wearing a black suit coat with matte lapels. The jacket tapers from broad shoulders to his lean waist. Despite the lack of light in the room, I make out the way his muscles ripple beneath the fabric of his clothing as he plucks the bottle from the table and uses the corkscrew to open the champagne with a soft *pop*.

He fills one flute a quarter full. The soft hiss of the fizz is like another layer of the static surrounding me. I grind my teeth with it, but I can't take my eyes off this mysterious man.

Fake Isaac Havrath takes a seat on the rosebud couch. His eyes anchored on the dress, the vague details of him are visible in the dim light, the plate of his jaw barely shifting to down the bubbly in one swallow. He sets the glass down beside the gown's generous train, elbows on his thighs as he stares at the gown.

He goes still. So still, I can't even hear him breathe.

Then—

"Would you speak to me?" he whispers. The assured look of him is not the look of a man who begs, but his voice is tortured and wavering. He winces. "*Please.*"

I'm smothering in my last breath, unable to exhale. The itch crawls across my vocal cords. I'm about to answer—I can hardly stand to keep my position secret even one second longer—when he raises his head and sniffs the air, just once. I must be sweating off the spritz of Meg's perfume that rained over me while I stood behind her in the bathroom this afternoon.

"It's you," he says and I'm instantly confused. Is Meg's perfume familiar? Is he even talking about what he sniffed? My gaze darts around the room. Who is he talking to, when there's no one here but the two of us?

His eyes coast right over me in my hiding place. Maybe the haunted gown is going to cough up a bride after all. I stare hard at the dress, waiting for the murky fog of a ghost to appear, but nothing comes. The static races up and down my arms; my nerves crackle as if they're going to shatter.

The urge to run swells.

I should heed it, but all I do is look back at the duplicate Isaac Havrath.

A trembling grin twitches across the man's mouth and disappears. Tears glint like tiny diamonds in his eyes. "Please, let me see you. I promise, there's nothing to fear from me. I will explain everything."

Explain? To who? There's no one here but us, and he looked right past me. Who is this man that seems to feel so much?

If this guy missed the museum memo and showed up for publicity sake, then why do his pleading and his promises sound so sincere? The sorrow in his voice breaks my heart. He's so stunning in the dull haze of the street light, I almost *wish* I'm the one he's trying so hard to entice.

At the same time, something inside me keeps digging in its heels against the tow truck *pull* I feel toward him.

I grind my spine into the wall, standing my ground, and the beautiful man goes still again. Still as death. He sits for so long that I swear I will die and disintegrate before he ever moves again.

The first wisp of dawn sneaks through the spotless museum windows, illuminating the shadows. Fake Isaac Havrath finally speaks.

"I'm trying to be patient, but daybreak is coming, my love. I can't wait any longer. Please let me see you."

My eyes flick back to the gown. Nothing. Not even the rise of a dust bunny.

Hanging his head a moment, he sighs and gets to his feet. He lifts his trench and slides his arms into it. Picks up the crackling cellophane bouquet.

Every hair on my neck stands with him. My belly button gives a tug forward, but my spine presses backward, as if it's trying to feed me to the wall. The end result: I don't move a centimeter.

I ache from top to bottom. I have yet to breathe one normal breath this whole night.

Fake Isaac kneels in front of the dress, his trench coat pooling like a black puddle around him. The position he's in, he'd only have to turn his head a bit to the right and glance over his shoulder to see me. To my relief, he doesn't.

My stomach rolls over. I don't want to be seen. Or maybe I do. I'm not sure what I want anymore, as I study the back of his head. The way the layers of his hair lay so perfectly, they could be numbered.

He extracts three roses from the dozen. One at a time, he closes his fist over each flower, crushing it and scattering the bruised petals over the floor, in front of the coiled train of the dress. The scent of the ruined blooms clings in the air. A sorrowful sob shakes the man's back. He wipes his face on the shoulder of his jacket.

I don't know why…it's crazy, really…but tears bead in the corners of my eyes too.

This guy has problems. Whoever he is, and however he's connected to the dress—whether he's a great, great grandson with a warped ancestor fetish, or a random screwball with a history obsession, or even an actor hired by the museum—I still feel for him. His tears seem genuine. He stands and closes in on the gown, sliding his feet beneath the train until he's close enough to wrap his arms around the dress form. It kills me as he buries his nose to the shoulder of the gown and breathes so deeply, it's like there's nothing else inside him to take up space.

"If you are here and you can't speak to me, please don't stop trying. *Please.* Come to me instead. I'll be waiting for you at the Havrath House, the mansion, as I always have." He looks out the window at the growing streaks of the coming dawn. "You must find me, my love, since I can't find you."

He flicks up the collar of his trench and exits the room, his footsteps treading down the stairs. The sound of him disappears without a scrape, or latch of the front door, but I know the exact moment he is gone.

The urge prods me to follow the mystery man, but it's not so intense that I lose control. I press my feet into the floor to keep myself from rushing after him. The longer I stand, the more the *pull* weakens and I can get my head on straight again.

I slump against the paneling, gulping breaths. I've been here the whole night, witnessing the mysterious toaster. My aching limbs, my deprived lungs, my bones that feel like they're going to fall apart from standing still so long. The *pull* and the *push* that played tug-of-war with my whole being and continues even now.

The man's grief must have been a show.

The whole thing.

The toasting, the grieving groom, the roses, the pleading…it's all an act, somehow connected to the Museum Board. An inside job, just like I thought. All of it for the sake of being caught on a surveillance video, to validate the urban legend.

What hasn't made sense all night seems clearer now with the coming sun.

The museum will have recorded this on a scratchy loop of tape, I'm sure, to play on opening day, which will validate the legend as being true. Of course, no one will quite be able to make out much from the vague images. I can only hope my face won't be captured.

I nearly swallow my own tongue.

The man was probably some out-of-work actor. He must've known I was here the whole time, feeding me all the romance of that crazy urban legend and all that crap about the Havrath House when Meg said it was bulldozed last year.

The museum is stirring up the story of an urban legend to get people through the doors. *Money.*

That's what this was all about.

Meg got hauled away for nothing.

I can't believe I fell for it.

I steal down the stairs and let myself out the front door with my sleeves pulled down over my fingers. The *closed* sign *fwaps* against the glass as I slip out, but the minute I'm on the sidewalk, I run at a dead sprint toward home, listening for police sirens the entire way.

9

We don't have to sneak out of the house. Aunt Dena dragged Meg home from the police station after the museum incident and grounded her, but Aunt Dena has three jobs and Uncle Leonard sucks at being a warden. He's passed out on the couch, snoring over the yammering of infomercials, when we leave.

Meg plods along, hungover. Since Murray was retained, and his stash isn't available to numb her, Meg resorted to guzzling down one of Uncle Leonard's whiskey bottles from the garage. I'm sure the excitement of showing me where the Havrath Mansion once stood has dwindled with the miserable thunking in her head. I float along beside her like a sticky balloon until we reach Washington Street. The waves off the water sweep cool breezes up the sidewalk.

Meg stops suddenly, rocking onto the balls of her feet and gripping her right temple. "I don't think we should go."

"After everything I told you about the toaster, the only thing we *should* do is go!" I argue. "I want to know who he is!"

"Toaster." She laughs. She's thinking *appliance*, not *person*. Guaranteed. "Whoever the guy was, he's a fake. The whole thing is. I already told you, the Havrath Mansion is torn down. There's nothing left but the Dorothy basement. Whoever you saw, he's not going to be sitting out on a stump, in the middle of an empty lot, waiting for someone to show up like a leprechaun."

The tug, which hasn't left me since that night at the museum, flutters in my gut. The tug says he will be there, just like he promised. "I still want to see it."

"Well, I don't."

"Why not?" I can't believe she's not intrigued. Or that she's being so stubborn. "I told you about the feeling…the *pull*. Whatever this is, I want to get rid of it. I have to go."

"No, you don't. You can ignore it and you should." She slips her fingers down over her eyes, squeezing her temples between her fingertips and thumb. "None of this sounds right. I told you, tweakers used to hang out in that Dorothy basement. If you go, you're asking to get…I don't know…mugged…or something worse."

"Come with me then," I say.

"If I could tackle you and keep you here, I would." Meg winces from beneath her palm. "But I can't. So, go if you have to. It's that way. On the left." She shakes a hand at the scrolling street, the black top that leads straight out of town and into the underdeveloped parts of New Baltimore.

"How far?"

"I don't know. Three or four miles," she says. "There's a *For Sale* sign on the lot."

"Okay. Bye." Her back is already facing me as she walks away. She keeps going in that direction and I go in the other.

10

The *For Sale* sign, when I finally reach it, is crooked and stuck into the side of the road like a thumb tack on the rolling acres. Ditches lie between the lot and street, punctuated by the raw, dirt driveway snaking off from the road. The *tug* turns into a distinct *pull,* and an equally hard *push* springs up to combat it.

Caught between the two, it makes me a little dizzy.

Before me, the lot ripples with a vibe of emptiness.

The indentations where the mansion and other buildings must have stood are covered with crabgrass and bull thistle now, like hair plugs implanted on a bald man's head. The Dorothy basement lies to the left of the shallow bed. The peeling, white, wood doors are warped and closed with a padlock. Clusters of trees hover like peeping toms, their branches scraping phantom mansion windows, while others have been cut to stumps. A willow worries at the edges of the lot—hair thrown over a hidden face. My gaze traces the dirt driveway that branches off the mansion's footprint and leads off to the east. Far back on the acreage, the skeletal remains of an ancient barn splinter into the tall grass.

Another thing I notice: Meg was right. Isaac Havrath's mysterious doppelganger isn't perched on a tree stump, waiting.

I rock on my heels, stuck in neutral between the *pull* toward the empty lot and the *push* to sprint back down Washington and find Meg. But the longer I stand, the more the *pull* digs in with excuses for staying and exploring the lot. Like taking a closer look at the Dorothy basement, just to see where Meg spent her time before I came to live with her. The longer I consider it, the more brilliant the idea becomes.

I am overcome by the next *pull* and thrust my foot forward, stepping from the dirt shoulder of the road onto the pebbled drive of the lot.

I plant my foot on the Havrath estate and the moment I do, all color evaporates.

Everything turns a murky, milky gray. Silence sucks the breath from my lungs. Particles of dust blind me.

The *pull* drags me forward and I make a leap I don't intend or control. My second foot hits the Havrath soil and dark, rich colors swiftly blast up from my soles.

The sunny, fall afternoon is gone. In its place, a midnight blue canopy, dotted with silver stars that pulse like the adjustment of radio station sound. The air is thick with the smell of lilac; trees dangling the scented chandeliers like clusters of dark grapes.

A lightning bug flashes its lime green bulb before my eyes and I blink, taking my attention from the sky and trees.

I am at the bottom of a manicured lawn, its blue-black blades prickling beneath the moon. A towering mansion, similar to the one I saw in the museum photos, stands before me. On second look, the mansion is recognizable by the cascade of rounded steps that spill from a skirted front porch and the balcony directly above it, surrounded by a squat parapet. In fact, there's no mistaking it. This is the Havrath House.

I've hallucinated myself right into the past. I turn in a full circle. I'm in a world from one hundred years ago.

Candles sparkle from a dozen front windows. Real candles that could catch the house on fire. Not the plastic ones with flickering tea lights that Aunt Dena has in the bathroom.

I shake my head, trying to rattle my senses loose. I can't be crazy if I *know* it's a hallucination.

Can I?

This is a whole new flavor of traumatic brain injury, different from anything I've tasted before.

I circle around again at the clomping of horse hooves. Two horses lead a black, buggy, equipped with lanterns and large, wooden wheels over the dirt road. What was the black asphalt of Washington is now a raw road full of rain-washed potholes. The hooves and wheels throw up a cloud of dust that look like a dingy ghost in the moonlight.

I turn back to the mansion. It casts a dark, looming shadow across me. The enormous structure that wasn't there a moment ago. That can't really be there now.

I've *got* to be hallucinating. This must be bubbling up from my recent fascination with Isaac Havrath. It's got to be some kind of trauma-induced vision, but the mansion looks real. There is dust in my nostrils. I don't know how I could conjure the sound of a door banging in the distant carriage house.

I stumble backward.

Midnight sucks away from me.

I'm falling through a narrowing hole.

The colorless silence surrounds me again, but I fall and land with an *oomph* on my rear, onto the blazing hot black top of Washington Street.

The *For Sale* sign leans off the grass, but still stabbed into the empty lot.

Getting to my feet, I'm dizzy and lurch forward, falling face-first this time, straight onto the manicured lawn of the mansion hallucination.

There's no way I'm falling into a hallucination and feeling the spikes of grass beneath my palms, or hearing men's voices and laughter mix with the sound of a hammer striking iron.

I look up and squint.

Candles still burn in the windows of the hulking house before me. A horse whinnies from the far off shadow of a barn.

This cannot be real.

Scrambling backward, crab style, flinging myself through the gray chasm once again, I land flat on my back on the Washington Street blacktop. I squint this time against the full sun, slicing across the empty lot in front of me.

There is no mansion, no carriage house, no laughter. Nothing but an empty lot. The broken bones of a barn.

The *push* sprouts up beneath my soles, as if trying to turn me homeward again. I let it build in my bones until I am able to jump up and sprint down Washington Street, away from whatever that was.

11

I slam the door of our bedroom to wake Meg. She's stretched out on our bed, a streak of sunlight draped across her like a comforter, and the slamming works like a charm. She pops up as if woke by gunshot.

"Dang it, Nova!" she moans, clutching her head.

I don't waste any time. "Meggy, you've got to get up and come with me. You've got to see the Havrath lot—"

"I've already seen it. A billion times," she grumbles.

"No, you haven't. You haven't seen what I just saw. I might be going crackers, Meg. I don't know. I need you to come and take a look and tell me if you see it too."

"Staaahhhp, Nova-caine. You're making my headache worse." She rubs her fingers against her scalp. "What's the problem? What did you see?"

"I saw the Havrath Mansion!"

She lets go of her head, grimacing at me through the messy spill of her hair. "You are crackers."

"Don't say that!" I shriek and she goes back to clutching her head.

"Gah...shut up!" she hollers back. Then, in a tight whisper, "Why do you think you saw a mansion?"

"Not *a* mansion...*the* mansion," I say, getting down on my knees beside the bed. "I *know* I saw it. Meggy, I swear...I touched the grass and I could smell the road dust and there were horses and carriages there! There were candles in the windows—"

"You touched...wait...candles in the middle of the day?"

"It wasn't daytime. The stars were out."

She peers up at me, her hair sliding down her arms, although her grip is still intact. "Noves, this sounds—"

"Don't say anything," I whisper. "Not unless you're going to come with me and see it for yourself."

12

We are silent all the way down Washington, because I'm obviously crazy until proven otherwise. Meg's not saying anything, but it's not like she has to. I know how crazy it seems.

I slog along beside her, my stomach like a waterlogged hunk of driftwood wedged beneath my ribs. It weighs me down with the soggy thought that I might just be losing it for real. I don't know if Meg will be able to see the mansion, but I'm more worried that I won't be able to see it again either.

We arrive at the ditches, across from the crooked *For Sale* sign. I resist the tug inside me and it makes my limbs quiver. The hair on my arms stands up straight, as if I've been rubbed all over with a balloon. It's only about four o'clock. The sun flows over the patchy grass plots and the weathered Dorothy basement, spiking the willow's tresses with streaks of tan and gold.

We stand there a minute before Meg says, "I don't see anything." Her voice is swallowed up in the early dusk.

I take a deep breath. "I only saw the mansion after I stepped onto the driveway."

A streak of thick, sooty clouds drifts over head, sending

shadows racing over the lot. Meg walks to the edge of the driveway. "Is this where you went?"

I nod.

A fall gust blows out of nowhere and the leaves flutter on the trees all at once. A hundred tambourines of panic that startle my soul.

"Are you coming?" Meg asks.

I roll onto the balls of my feet and rock backward. The entire movement is involuntary. The *push* and *pull* suddenly rage up inside me.

My mind screeches, *leave*. My feet root themselves.

My ankles ache as if there are fingers wrapped around them, dragging me forward. My mind kicks into hyper-survival mode, struggling against the *pull* the same way a drowning swimmer panics to break the surface for air.

My brain and my body press in from every angle, battling for a verdict.

Push. Pull.

Struggle. Yank.

Resist. Drag.

Shove—

I can't take any more.

I lunge across the ditch, onto the Havrath lot. My feet hit the soil together and the mansion balloons into view, exploding like an airbag. It's all here—the mansion, the carriage house, the far off barn, and the darkness that I saw the other night, although it is a lighter shade of blue-black dusk.

Meg is nowhere to be seen.

The pounding of metal echoes from the direction of the carriage house and the conversation of disagreeing women, which comes from the west side of the house. I creep up to the mansion and edge to the side of the lot, looking for Meg. I spot the two arguing women instead.

One is old and one is young, and that appears to be their only difference. Two versions of the same woman, they are differentiated only by gray hair versus glossy brown, soft crow's feet versus flawless skin, the thickness of middle-age versus the willowy body of youth. Both, however, are dressed in stiff, black dresses with burgundy aprons covering them from chests to hems and each with a basket of wet laundry, I assume they are maids.

I cling to the edge of the brick, but the women's attention is fixated on hanging laundry on the dual lines strung between trees, as well as on one another.

"He is an affliction that you must overcome, Lucy." There is as much starch in the older woman's tone as the shirt she's attaching to the clothes line.

"You think anything that brings anyone the least little bit of joy is an affliction," Lucy snaps back. "I believe you're just bitter that you were not so afflicted."

The older woman yanks a sheet back to glare at the younger maid. "You were only chosen because—"

"Because I look like you?" Lucy smirks, but doesn't pause in hanging the linens. "We do look just the same, aside from our years, don't we, mother? So you could've been chosen just as easily as I, but you weren't."

The older woman's brows rise as she reaches down to drag a towel from one of the baskets. She tosses it over the line and pinches the fabric straight, blocking her daughter from view. But the mother's tone remains brittle. "Youth is often a preferable condition, since experience would likely hinder such whimsy."

"*No,* the truth is, bitter old biddies don't worry about hindrances at all." Lucy steps into a space between items to scowl at her mother. "And that's because whimsy has no interest in darkening the doorstep of the withered. This is none of your business, mother."

"And whose is it? Hoomstid's business, maybe?"

Lucy only snaps out a towel and hangs it on the line. They continue to hang the laundry in frosty silence.

I inch away from the building edge and take up my search for Meg again. The front door of the mansion is ajar.

She wouldn't...wait. This is Meg. Yes she would. Meg would totally walk into a stranger's house. And ever since she started using, she's not above stuffing valuables in her pockets that she thinks wouldn't be missed.

I steal up the stacked front steps of the mansion. My hand is on the front door knob before I even realize it and as I'm processing that, I slip inside. Reflected flames from the window candles dance upon the polished wood floor. To the left, a living room. Couches, chairs, and two low coffee tables, huddle around an empty fireplace. To the right of the entry way, a parlor with pristine upholstered chairs and a settee, almost identical to the dusty, old furniture I saw in the museum. Straight ahead, a lengthy hall with closed doors on the left, and a staircase full of dark steps rising upward on the right.

My toes are compass needles, tugging me forward, but I stand my ground and whisper, *"Meg!"*, like a sniper, aiming it into the parlor first. I fire the second round of her name into the living room.

No answer.

I tilt toward the stairs. "Meg!"

"Ohhh, I smell a beautiful perfume! Something lovely and *foreign*," an odd, voice whispers from somewhere down the hall. Odd because I can't make out if it belongs to a male or female. It's something perched right in between.

I am pinned at the dead center of the hall, like an imbecile in a horror movie.

The androgynous voice grows louder, moving toward me. "Sir, can you smell it?"

I expect the owner of the voice will burst through the door at the end of the hall, and I'm standing here like a thief. I want to hide, but my body has gone on hiatus from all commands again.

"Where is it coming from?" a second voice asks. This voice is unquestioningly male, with a deeply appealing undertone that turns my legs to rubber. It releases a flock of flutters in my stomach and then sets them on fire.

The warmth squirming through me is not wholly unpleasant. But it's not enjoyable either.

I am both drawn and repelled at once, unable to move and stuck solidly in this weird, immobile neutrality as my brain fires commands that my body ignores.

My curiosity fuses to my temper and sprouts razor blade teeth. I may not be able to move, but nothing is stopping me from tipping back my head and shouting, "Come and get me! I'm right here!"

A door further down on the right swings open and a strange man barrels through. He is spindly and pale in an ill-fitting, raven-colored suit that swallows him whole. He stops dead the moment he spots me, his tiny lips drifting apart, as if he's seen a ghost. I'm not even sure how well he sees, since one eye floats on a cheek, the other on his forehead. His two eyes blink at me in uniform disbelief.

I try to will my legs to carry me in the opposite direction. My brain only winces in response.

"Mr. Havrath, sir…" the man calls over his shoulder. His voice has that odd feminine lilt I heard earlier, a doily dropped on hardwood. Not male, not female. The sound hovers somewhere in between. "Mr. Havrath, the stench announces her! She has come, sir! I believe she has arrived!"

Stench? They can't be talking about me.

A different voice answers from behind the door.

Sensual, soft, unmistakably male. My spine melts and my leg muscles go fluid. I feel like my body is feinting, but I snap it upright with a severe surge of will.

"Please show her in, Hoomstid, and do not reply to her scent as a *stench*. It is offensive to refer to it as such, when it was necessary as a marker to identify her. It will wear off soon enough. Now, show her in, and then you are dismissed for the evening," the deeply male voice says.

Hoomstid's forehead eye gives an uneven twitch. "But she may be dangerous, sir."

"Even so…" the man's voice drifts away as if the threat has been properly answered, even thought it didn't sound like an answer at all.

I'm sure they're not talking about me. I don't stink. And I'm about as far from dangerous as anyone can be, yet, the servant's gaze is still rooted on me.

"Yes, sir. Of course." Hoomstid strides down the hallway toward me. He stops before one of the hall doors. His smile is forced as he hails to me with a gangly arm. "This way, Miss. Come this way."

I look behind me, even though I know he means me. *How can he mean me?* I just poofed here from…somewhere else. I'm still not entirely sure where *this* is. Back in time, I assume, from the looks of things. Hallucinations of a scrambled, traumatized brain, seems most likely.

As if I ate a pan of Meg's magic brownies.

My feet won't move. The *push* is now stronger than the *pull* and I think that if I can just unstick my soles, I'll barrel out of the mansion so fast, I might rip the carpet runner on my way out.

"Come, come!" Hoomstid scoops his hand through the air violently. "Sir will see you! You've come to see him, so come! Don't stand there like an imbecile!"

The invisible man's voice rolls out of the room and down the hallway. "Hoomstid, you are dismissed for the evening. Go *now*. I will speak with her alone."

A shiver aches to be loose in my spine. The servant frowns, but he turns and marches back to the door at the end of the hall. He disappears through the door and I'm alone. The house settles with a creak and the *push* pauses. In its absence, I take a minuscule step toward the door Hoomstid had indicated.

"Hello," the voice says. It's as if the voice is in my ear, instead of filling the hall.

The *push* returns fully, insisting I bolt for the front door, the street, home.

But the *pull* returns too, gripping me by the scruff of my neck, hauling my soul backward, holding me from my escape.

Caught between the two, the air is sucked from the room and the whole hallway spins. When it stops, I am face to face with the same, mysterious and horribly handsome man who left the roses and champagne at the museum.

Fake Isaac Havrath, who looks spot-on with the photo I memorized of the real man.

His eyes meet mine. There is no sign of surprise in them.

"I'm so glad to finally see you." He exhales with a grin, the skin around his eyes flawlessly smooth.

My thoughts gush out of my mouth. "You have the wrong person."

The air in my lungs disappears like punishment for the words. I'm paralyzed.

"No, never," Imposter Isaac whispers in the inches between our lips. He lifts his hand as if he is going to brush the back of his fingers down my jaw. I demand my body to shrink away, but my muscles won't obey. My feet won't come loose from their place on the floor. Something invisible separates me from my own will. "I am very experienced with the wrong people and I would never mistake you for one of them, Nova."

I feel the waiver, the crack in whatever binds me and my feet break free. The skin over my jaw feels raw, although he's never touched me.

I should bolt for the door, but I don't think I can outrun him, and I can't leave before I find Meg. Instead, I narrow my eyes on him to let him know I'm not intimidated. I hope he buys my bluff.

"How do you know my name?" I tip my head and peer at him through narrowed eyes.

Meg must be here. Maybe she was calling for me and he overheard it. Maybe he's caught her and is holding her somewhere.

Isaac the Imposter tips his head back with a hearty laugh, his midnight locks falling away from his forehead and cascading down his temples. "I've been searching for you all of my life. I think I know exactly who I'm looking for. It's you, Nova. It's always been you."

"How do you know my name?" I ask again.

He reaches for me instead of answering and I pull away. I catch a waft of him, a scent that sinks into my lungs. Fresh and cold, the scent is as clean as snow with a tang that is as sharp as a tongue stuck to icy metal. Despite the after-sting, I want to breath him in again as much as I want to get away from him. He reaches for me again and I am amazed that my feet obey when I decide to take a full step back.

His eyes widen as if I've slapped him across the face. Maybe it's because I won't let him touch me, but I get the feeling that he thinks I should know the answer to my own question.

"Please don't be frightened of me," he pleads, dropping his hand. As polished and collected as he appears to be in his tailored suit, the static between us mounts. My resolve is a flimsy barricade against his *pull*, but at least I can still resist him.

I think it surprises him too. I take another step backward. Shock drifts across his face as if he is wild inside; frantic about being out of control, and without any clue as to how to get himself straight again.

"You still haven't told me how you know my name," I say. Has he caught Meg? I'm not going to mention her if he doesn't.

"Stay." His voice is thin. Desperate. "There is so much to talk about."

My feet can move, but something in his voice compels me like any stupid girl in a horror flick.

The struggle inside me makes me anxious. My own will battles for dominance over this foreign will that coaxes and beguiles and drags me closer to Fake Isaac, into his world. My brain curls into a knuckle, battling against that other part, which speaks in the depths of my head and insists that I first find out who this man is, how he knows my name, and where we are. As if all the answers will tell me whether or not my brain has melted into a hallucinogenic gob of goo.

"Tell me who you are," I command. If he's not going to tell me where Meg is—since that's the only way he could know my name—then I'm going to have to keep my head on straight and find out whatever I can.

His eyes flick up at me as if he's convinced that I already know. "I am Isaac Havrath."

I snort a laugh. I hope he mistakes it for confidence or assurance, instead of the feral heartbeat of fear thundering through me. "The third, fourth, or fifth?"

"Whatever do you mean?"

"You're not *the* Isaac Havrath. You would be a great, great, grandson or a distant cousin or something?"

"I have no children," he says, spreading his hands wide.

"You aren't the first Isaac Havrath. He lived in the 1900's." Even hearing myself say it aloud is idiotic. This guy is either completely mental or screwing with me on an epic level. Or both. Time travel isn't a *thing*. I don't know why my brain whipped up the mirage of the mansion—maybe some of Meg's 'vitamins' got into something I ate, or maybe it's because my thinker's a little busted as of late—but people don't come back from being dead and the man in front of me is definitely nowhere near *dead*.

"I need to know," he says, breaking into my thoughts, "how did you get in here?"

"Traumatic brain injury," I snap.

You'd think we'd be fresh out of the short laughs at one another, but he pulls another from a chuckle behind his fist.

"You think you're in a dream? That none of this is real?" He adds a smirk.

A smirk like that, on a movie screen, might be charming. It might convince a girl in a twisted, imaginary story that she had it all wrong. But I'm not that girl and his stupid, condescending smirk turns my blood to lava.

The *pull* is battered down by my rage.

Shredded by pure wrath.

I turn my back on him, confident in my roiling fury that he wouldn't dare touch me or he'll pull back a bloody stump if he tries—

He grabs my arm and seems as shocked as I am when his fingers wrap around my skin. His touch roars into my veins. Flames of pain leap through me, dwarfing my fury and consuming it, bite by bite. My legs go weak. I haven't felt anything so painful, so shocking, or so vivid since…I don't know when. I clamp my lips to stifle the whimper.

I lunge away, battling to get loose, but his grip doesn't flinch. He's an anchor. His arm a chain, and I'm yanked backward without him even trying.

"Stay," he commands softly. The smirk is gone, but the brittle darkness of his eyes flashes silver, like petrified wood. Each of his fingers on my flesh is a row of fire.

"Then let go of me!" I spit from between my teeth.

He unclamps his vice-like grip so quick, it's like I'm the one burning him to the bone. I stumble backward, rubbing my skin, and staple my most rueful glare to him.

"I apologize," he says as I continue to rub at the drilling ache he's left in my bones. "I didn't mean to hurt you."

He's not forgiven. I'll repay it if I get the chance.

"Tell me how you found my estate," he says.

I shrug. "I walked here."

"No, you didn't." He flashes a sheepish grin.

Is he serious? I return a scowl and his expression flattens out as quickly as a hard snap to a bed sheet.

"No one knows the estate exists, aside from my servants and myself. Was there something in particular that drew you here?" His eyes are as unreadable as reflective sunglasses.

Does he mean the *pull*? That nagging draw that is sucking at me even now, as if it is waiting for one speck of weakness to sink its hooks back into me and drag me straight into this man's snare? Yes, that feeling of need, of want, of morbid curiosity drew me here, but I'll be blasted if I'm going to admit to it.

Chin down, I look up at him through my lashes. If he wants to play games, I can conceal my cards too. I'm not about to give him even one answer that he doesn't already have.

"If your property is so hard to find, I wouldn't be here, would I?" Oh. That was pretty bold. I should've eased back on it.

But his smile is easier than I think it should be. Innocent? Entertained? No, I don't think so.

"An honest answer would be very helpful, Nova, since I've been waiting an incredibly long time to see you."

"A little honesty would be great." Yeah, too bold yet again, but I can't back down now. I raise my chin, although it's far below his, and take a step forward to crowd his space. "How do you know my name?"

"We were friends once."

I force a short, flat laugh, but lose my nerve. "You're a liar."

"How else would I know who you are?"

I seal my lips before blurting Meg's name. I'll only give him questions for his questions. "Yeah, how would you? Because you're not who you say you are, and I don't remember you at all."

It's not a lie that I don't remember him—I don't remember anything before arriving at Meg's house—but it never occurred to me that this fake Havrath could be someone from that very same past that I can't recall. Meg says I lived far, far away, but the *pull* I feel, against every instinct I have otherwise, intrigues me. Maybe the *pull* isn't supposed to be as uncomfortable as it feels. Maybe he is someone I once knew. Someone I'm supposed to know now.

But that doesn't explain the *push,* or the pain that ripped through me from his touch.

"Let me ask you this," he says, dusting a finger over his top lip, "do you know how Isaac Havrath died? Because, from what I've heard, the urban legends are all different."

"Who cares? I asked who you are."

"I'm trying to tell you just that, Nova." He smiles as he says my name. A dangerous smile. Jagged. *Why am I still standing here?*

I glance the front door. Ten to fifteen paces, if I'm running. Maybe I can make it after all.

"Let's stop with the games. You need to know you can trust me, so let me tell you the truth," Fake Isaac says, yanking my gaze back to his. "You were correct. I'm not one hundred years old. I am *one-hundred-and-twenty* years old."

He gives that a moment to gel with me, ducking down a bit to hold my gaze hostage. His hands rise on either side of me, to offer aid if I pass out? Or to coral me? No idea, but neither is necessary. When I show no response, he continues.

"I do know you. If you stay, I will tell you everything. Would you, please?" His tone is soft and hypnotic. His gaze is loose and easy, as if he is already confident of my answer. "Will you stay?"

"No!" I make sure my feet are moving before I say it.

Imposter Isaac makes a swipe for me, but I pivot and he comes up empty. The *push* floods me with adrenaline. I race for the door.

The handle in my palm, I rip it open and shoot outside. I'm on the front lawn before I even take a breath. My feet hardly touch the ground as I sprint for the property line.

"NOVA!" Fake Isaac bellows from the threshold of his mansion.

The pounding in my ears mutes everything else. The dusk lights my way to the edge of the lawn. I launch myself over the ditch and see the horses too late. The swift thunder of the carriage rumbling down Washington pours into my skull all at once. I pitch forward, off balance.

Flailing.

My shoulder hits the dirt road hard, right in front of the oncoming horse hooves. Sharp stones bite my skin as I try to roll out of the way.

Hands over my head, I come to a stop. Dust in my nostrils. Silence.

I'm not trampled.

I lift my head, coughing up dust.

Washington Street isn't soft dusk now; it's darker than the skin of a black plum. I get to my feet, squinting in both directions to see if I can make out any familiar shadows in the distance, but there is no sign of Meg. Not one soul on the street, except me. I turn my gaze back to the empty plot where the old mansion once stood, before the bulldozers came for only a moment and then I'm sprinting down Washington to find my cousin.

15

"Go away," Uncle Leonard grumbles, turning over to bury his face in the couch after I shriek *'Where's Meg?'* enough times that he has to answer. "She ain't here."

The thing is, it's not exactly unusual that Meg goes missing, but usually, I can find her by tracking Murray down in his crusty, basement bedroom, or at his dealer, Beezo's, crappy apartment. But Murray's still on lock down. Under these circumstances—the ones that suggest Meg might be trapped somewhere on the grounds of an invisible estate, with a very enchanting imposter makes me frantic.

I check the Towne and Country party store, where Meg and Murray constantly fail to get adults to buy them 40 ouncers. Then, the tire shop where they beg the mechanics for smokes, and P&R Taxes, because Meg likes to stop and pet the owner's dogs. Finally, I check at the Hang Dragon, a Chinese restaurant where Murray's buddy does dishes and slips them boxes of sticky rice and fountain drinks sometimes, but no one has seen Meg or Murray in days.

I head back down Washington. The *open* sign dangles in the front window at the museum and as I get closer, an itchy aura draws me toward the door. Meg wouldn't have come to the museum to make amends or anything like that, but the museum curator might be able to provide me some clues as to why I can see an estate that no longer exists…or why, or how, Isaac Havrath exists.

I stand out on the sidewalk for an extra heartbeat, feeling like a criminal, and wondering if any of the shop owners on Washington Street will come running to identify me as the girl they saw sneaking out of the museum that night Meg and Murray were hauled away by the cops.

No one comes.

I step into the museum. The string of welcome bells tinkles over my head and I gasp at the sudden wave of pure itch that rushes through me. Unlike the first night I was here, the itch does not persist, but feeling it all startles me all the same.

And the museum curator.

"Good gracious!" Dorcas Boyle shrieks, jerking upright from the book on the counter, her hand planted over her heart. It takes a moment of licking her lips and staring at me before she regains her composure. She replaces her cat eye glasses on the perch of her nose and runs a hand over her head, a stray barrette rising out of the chaos of her tumbleweed hair. "I didn't see you there!"

"I'm sorry! I didn't mean to scare you," I say. It feels weird being back in the museum.

She smoothes her palms down the front of her olive cardigan with an uneasy laugh. "I was so engrossed in my book!"

"What are you reading?" I ask, hoping she'll refocus and calm down.

"Just some stories sent along with the dress."

"Oh?" I step closer to the counter, peering at the open book. It looks old and smells musty as I hover over it, beside Dorcas. There are hand-drawn pictures on each page. The left page has a drawing of a black cat with a white mask that covers its face. The cat's fur is covered with decorative patches that depict bones, eyeballs, the moon, the sun, and symbols I don't understand. It's adorable.

The right page isn't so interesting. A picture of a tube, with sparkles highlighting the wave of fluid inside.

"What is this?" I ask.

"A children's book of stories that came with the wedding articles from the Havrath Estate. I'm not sure they meant to send it along, but it is an interesting, old book. This one," she points to the patched cat, "is about a magical cat named Charkus. He's an omen of death, but the doomed can barter with him for one of his many lives."

"I thought they only have nine." I say. "He's probably pretty stingy if people are always asking him to give up one."

"Charkus's owner is Phane, a god of death. When Charkus comes home each year, Phane feeds him nine more lives, which he can trade in the coming year, and Phane takes the names of those who bartered with his cat, so he doesn't collect those souls by accident."

"Wild," I say.

"Isn't it?" Dorcas points to the vial on the opposite page. "And this one is *The Sunshine Vial*. That story is about a magical tube, which contains the powers of a superior deity."

"What's the rest of the story?" I ask.

"I don't know," Dorcas says. "The book is missing a lot of pages. Ripped right out." She turns the page and brushes the ripped fringe of the missing pages. "Such a shame that anyone would do that to such a lovely book." She jerks her head up with a grin, a bobby pin falling out of her crazy hair and onto the counter. She picks it up and drops it in her sweater pocket. "Oh well! That is that, so have you come in for more details on the Havrath exhibit?" She pushes up her glasses. "Ask me anything. I'm a savant, after all! Excellent recall, except for numerals. Those...not so much." She notices the slight tilt of a frame on the wall and walks over to adjust it.

"Did you hear about the big break in?" she asks, stepping back to assess the frame's alignment. I panic that she's going to say she recognizes me from some hidden camera security footage, but she only plants her fists on her waist and continues on. "A couple of kids broke into the museum! Thankfully, the police caught them and nothing was stolen…at least, not that we know of. Pranksters, I think. They left behind roses and bubbly in the Haunted Havrath Exhibit, just like the famous *toaster* does. I can't imagine why they did it, except to try to debunk the *toaster* and spoil the whole opening!"

I hadn't thought of the curator finding Isaac's bottle and flowers. I never would've guessed that the discovery wouldn't lead to her figuring out that her dyscalculia had jumbled the wedding date. Instead, Dorcas Boyle seems to think Meg and Murray are a couple of high-brow pranksters, rather than some kids looking for a sneak peak at a gown and to score some antiques they could trade for an afternoon worth of dope. I can't imagine what will happen when someone finally takes a good look at the actual wedding certificate, like I did, and figures out the mistake.

"I can't say the crime was a bad thing," the curator whispers to me, although I think we are the only two in the building. "After all that publicity, do you know that we had a crowd at the door this morning? At least two or three people were waiting when I arrived and they were so eager for me to unlock the doors! The board has decided to open the exhibit early. We're still going to have a candlelight vigil for our *toaster,* but we decided there'd be no harm in letting the public enjoy the rest of the exhibit early. I'm going up to dust the pieces, if you'd like to see it."

Guilt stumbles my tongue in a series of sounds that make Dorcas smile.

"Exciting, I know," she says, retrieving a fuchsia feather duster on a stick from a cabinet in the parlor. I follow her up the staircase, the tug from before still present but not at all as intense as it was when we broke in. The double doors at the end of the hallway are wide open, the gown in view.

I halt at the threshold. The gown is beautiful, it really is, but nothing like when I saw it the first time. There is no magic, no soft light of night painted over it, no aura of enchantment pouring over me. There is no itch, and therefore, no fantastic relief. The first time I saw the gown was just like having the first bite of a hot fudge sundae. And seeing it now is like eating the rest of the dessert with a numb tongue. It's nice, but seems like it should be so much better.

Dorcas Boyle waves the fuchsia duster at the gown. "Isn't it absolutely gorgeous?"

"Yes." I force a grin.

"You're welcome to take a look around," she chirps, going to the curio cabinet I hid behind the night of my crime. She opens the door with a twist of a tiny, silver key she leaves in the lock. "If you have any questions, I'm right here to answer them."

She lifts the duster and glides it over the shelves as I meander around the display. A frosted, cardboard wedding cake has been added to the table with the utensils, but otherwise, everything looks pretty much the same, except the wedding certificate on the wall.

Something is very different about it. The certificate I saw was hand-painted in brilliant color with crisp calligraphy lettering. Even in the dull spill of the evening streetlight, the certificate had been dazzling. The certificate I'm looking at now is nothing like that. The paper is too bright, the painted flowers bland, the black calligraphy appears flat, and it all looks like it's been smashed with a rolling pin. I'm not sure what I'm looking at, until I notice the slight shadow surrounding the document's date.

I draw a breath. This isn't the original document. This one's been doctored. The actual Havrath wedding date has been replaced with the mistaken date, the one that has been scheduled for the candlelight vigil for the *toaster.* I glance over my shoulder at the curator. Her feather duster hovers over the top of a ruffled, blood-red, glass bowl, cradled in a tarnished bride's basket.

"This certificate is altered," I say.

The feather duster drops to her side and the bridal basket crashes on the wood floor, shards of glass scattering across the planks.

16

"Would you *please* not breathe a word of this? The Historical Society was counting on me not to muck this up, and I was *certain* I read the date correctly this time. Besides, the lovely woman, the correspondent for the Havrath Estate, was the one who told me the original wedding date was in October! I'm positively certain she did; I made sure to write it down! I know better than to rely on information without documented proof, but the certificate only arrived the day of the robbery, and we really needed to book the events! Oh..." she moans, gripping her temples, "if the Society finds out that I made another whoopsie, after spending all that money to promote the exhibit...I'll get the axe! But you don't care about my neck on the line, do you? You probably don't have to worry about a roof over your head, but my job is all that's keeping me and Sir Furball off the curb! It's not like we're living in the penthouse as it is! Do you even *know* what cat food tastes like? It tastes like ten-year-old meatloaf, but that's what we'll be eating when we're living in a refrigerator box beneath the overpass!"

"I'm not going to say anything," I tell her. "I promise. I don't even care about the dates."

She fidgets with the knit of her sweater, smoothing it down, getting herself back under control.

I smile at her, as if it proves my promise. "I only came to ask you some things about the Havrath legend."

"Oh," she says with a soft sniffle. "What would you like to know?"

"I was wondering if there was any more to the legend? Something...*strange*?"

The curator crosses her arms, holding her forearms as if she's cold. "Since we're friends," she whispers, "I think you're referring to the *dark* part of the legend?"

I have no idea what I'm asking for, but dark part sound about right. I nod and Dorcas rewards me with a sly grin.

"You must have been digging deep in your research."

I nod again. She has no idea how deep this has gotten with me. Isaac's in my skin, and my thoughts revolve around him, whether I like it or not. That's why I am here and not out searching harder for Meg.

"Well," she licks her chapped lips and pushes a tuft of hair away from her temple. "There all sorts of variations of the urban legend, but the Havrath correspondent made it clear that the gift of the gown and the other antiques that came with it were conditional. She didn't want any of this to be presented in the exhibit, although it is fascinating lore, and I believe it would intrigue visitors. The dark part of the Havrath story flirts at the edge of things that some find less palpable. Things about the afterlife." Her eyes flick about, her whisper high and excited. "*Paranormal* things."

I swallow. Does she know the things I do? That Isaac Havrath and his mansion exist in some strange alternate dimension?

"This particular vein of the lore is very dark." Dorcas smiles as if this is just part of a good ghost story, rather than a real and frightening thing. "There are some stories that suggest that after Silvia died, Isaac disappeared. Some believed there was a sinister reason for the absence, which was eventually tied to his father.

"The pastor was reported to have gone...shall we say...*bonkers*. The death of his wife, the tarnish on his name, the disappearance of his son, and the loss of his church sent him over the edge. There was also a report that the pastor's brother died around this same time, although there are no other records of residency, or even a death certificate to substantiate that the pastor even *had* a brother. However, it would've been one more straw on the pastor's crumbling sanity if he lost his entire family and his congregation all at once.

"Anyhow, after the wedding tragedy, court records reported that Pastor Havrath turned up at various public functions to accuse the townspeople of gossiping him to ruin. There weren't any formal charges, but the good pastor had to be escorted home more than once after violent outbursts in town.

"When several local farmers reported finding their animals brutally slaughtered in their fields, it seemed only natural to point fingers at the one person who caused constant disruption: Pastor Havrath. Livestock was their livelihood and suddenly, their cows, mares, and sheep were found dead in record numbers."

My stomach churns.

"There was no firm proof that Isaac's father, the Pastor, was actually to blame, but when the Havrath homestead was found abandoned, it was considered as good as a confession of guilt.

"Strangely enough, Pastor Havrath was recorded to have come through Ellis Island when he came to America from Europe. We found records of residency in Illinois. He formed a small congregation there, but there are no records of Isaac. There are other Havraths who came through Ellis Island, but none with the name of Isaac.

"So, it's possible that everything the previous townspeople said was true: the pastor fled in guilt and Isaac was dead. Another interesting twist was that another small town, two towns over from the pastor's new residence, also began to report animals slaughtered and missing. Stranger still, all the butchered animals were pregnant," the curator goes on, "No males. The baby animals were birthed—the evidence of the birth was left behind—but the mother was drained of blood. Another development: huge chunks of the flesh, bone, and even hooves were removed, and the baby animal gone. But that wasn't all."

Dorcas pauses to peer at me and I give her the wince I think she's looking for. "Sick," I add.

"I would say so," she says. "Within a few months, male *and* female animals began to disappear into thin air. Large stock at first, then everything, right down to the cats. Dozens and dozens of cats, all went missing on the same night. Barn cats, known strays, domesticated cats. Poof. Scads of them.

"The first news articles suggested it could be someone stealing livestock to start their own farm, but it would've been next to impossible to steal a bull and hide it when it was branded. Even when the problem grew and authorities really put their noses to it, they didn't turn up any of the lost livestock, aside from the pregnant females they found slaughtered." Dorcas taps her temple. "And nothing explained the cats. Nothing explained the cats to the public back then, except witchcraft. They accepted that pretty easily it seems."

"But why was it connected to Isaac's father?" I ask.

"An investigator mapped the web of crime scenes and found Pastor Havrath's church at the center," Dorcas says. "The same investigator researched the pastor's roots and unearthed the stories of Isaac's tragic wedding, the theft committed to pay for it, Isaac's disappearance, and the previous, similar crimes of animal slaughter. Word spread faster than torched gasoline.

"Once the pastor's parishioners heard of the thievery, they turned on him. They accused him of animal sacrifice, pagan rituals, and practicing witchcraft, in order to erase the memories of his current congregation."

"Witchcraft," I whisper with a shiver. I am riveted, drinking in the details as fast as I can, even though I still don't know what to make of it all. If Isaac Havrath died in a foreign town, who have I been talking to? Is it all some perverse magic?

"The pastor relinquished the church and fled again, eventually coming to New Baltimore. He built a new, even smaller church on the lot down on Washington Street, with money from an undisclosed benefactor. The basement that was part of the church still exists on the lot. Unfortunately for the pastor, gossip spreads faster than fact. There were never any parishioners in the pastor's new church. The good people of New Baltimore solemnly believed the pastor would try to establish a church of witchcraft.

"From what we can gather, via brief mentions in donated private letters, court records, and news articles, the church rotted into weeds and the pastor was a recluse. He wed a foreign woman and since no more animals were reported missing in neighboring towns, the rumors faded for a time.

"The Havrath name was absent from further public record until the pastor and his wife had a child. It wasn't the birth that stirred suspicions, but that the couple named the child Isaac. It seems the pastor and his wife were seen rarely, if ever, in town, and the child wasn't seen at all. Besides those mentions, however, the Havraths seemed to be *out of sight and out of mind,* for nearly the next two decades.

"The second Isaac Havrath grew into a man and he seemed to have taken care of the pastor and his wife until they both died. Isaac the Second took over the homestead. He built up an impressive lumber business and a freight company and, with his wealth, constructed the Havrath Mansion. There are several newspaper accounts of his charitable works, including establishing orphanages and providing financial support to the poor. It took decades, but Isaac the Second was able to redeem his family name. Money is magical like that."

Isaac the Second. It still can't be who I'm speaking to. The Isaac I met can't be over twenty-five years. He's probably the crazy grandson of Isaac the Second, just like I originally thought.

Now I just have to figure out how he makes a whole estate appear and disappear. Unless the stories of witchcraft are true.

I look at Isaac's pre-wedding photo on the wall and, just like before, his lovely fiancé at his side disappears. As I stare at the photo, I notice the urge creep over me again. The more I look at his image, the more I crave seeing Isaac again—his midnight hair, his dark eyes streaked with shadows. I even want to hear his lie about how we were friends once. My craving for the handsome liar is a deeply annoying sensation I can't shake.

I feel like I'm free-falling, against my own will, for an imposter who lives in an unexplainable, impossible...invisible mansion.

Like that could ever work.

"Did Isaac marry and have kids?" I turn his name over on my tongue, bittersweet, like a square of too-dark chocolate.

"Not that I know of. He remained a hermit all of his days, operating through various correspondents. Such a shame," Dorcas says as she bends to pick up the pieces of the bridal basket. I don't know if she means his lack of marriage, kids, or the shattered antique.

"When did he die?"

"Rats. I'm going to need a dustpan for this," she grumbles, straightening up with a handful of the glass shards. "I don't know when Isaac the Second died, but it must've been recently, since the estate was dissolved and the gown donated to us. The correspondent was supposed to send along a death certificate, with the gown and the other items, but it never arrived and I've had a bugger of a time getting ahold of her. Lovely woman, but she's about as dependable as Michigan weather. She had the most interesting name."

I look away from Isaac's photo altogether, leaning in the curator's direction. "What is it?"

"Machara Milligen," Dorcas Boyle says. "A bewitching name, isn't it?"

M achara Milligen's name is on repeat in my head as I make the loop, looking for Meg again. RJ's, the tire shop, the party store, dealer Beezo's apartment, Murray's house, home.

Meg is nowhere and no one's seen her.

The worst part is, even as I slog all over New Baltimore searching for my cousin, all I can think of is Isaac Havrath. My cousin is missing and I'm ashamed to be hoping, and working so hard to convince myself, that she's somewhere on Isaac's estate.

Yes, I want to find Meg, but the honest-to-gods truth, I'm no hero. I've got this insane craving I can't shake to see Isaac again and I'm using my cousin's disappearance as an excuse to go back there.

To see him.

The other honest-to-god truth is that I'm not this girl. There might be a whole lot of things I don't remember about myself, but the one thing I do know is that I'm not a girl who needs a guy to make me feel like I'm whole, or worthy, or powerful. I know I'm a solid equal to anyone I meet, but being whole, worthy, and powerful doesn't change the impact of the butterflies racing around my stomach. Or the excitement they promise with each ripple of their wings.

I have no doubt that Isaac Havrath is a dark shadow. Whatever he is isn't good for me—probably not good for anyone—but at least I know the risks. I'm not a dumb girl running blindly into the clutches of a murderer. I snort. I'd rather think I'm a clever girl, fascinated by a mysterious stranger and curious to find out why.

I also need to make sure Meg hasn't fallen in a ditch on Isaac's estate, or gotten trapped in a well or something.

This is everything I tell myself as I walk down Washington toward the Havrath land.

I reach the lot with its lopsided sign and curse low, far beneath my breath, just in case there's a god listening.

I have to go back. I do. It's not just the craving that drives me. It's intrigue. Curiosity. Fascination.

And it's for Meg.

It's not as hard as it should be to put my foot over the mansion's lot line.

A scream nails me in place.

I'm in the yard again, but the doorway of the mansion is dark, as if I've zapped back into a different point on the clock altogether. Fake Isaac isn't waiting for me. No one is. But the scream is female, and after I hear it, I can't get it out of my head that it might be Meg.

That it's probably Meg.

That it *is* Meg.

The tips of my ears tingle. I turn, and there is Liar Isaac, at least a yard away, staring at me as if he's looking at a ghost. I let the *pull* close the distance between us, until I am toe to toe with him, shouting in his face.

"Where is my cousin? I know you have her here somewhere! I heard her scream!"

"Your cousin?" He rocks backward with a wince, as if it's the most ridiculous thing he's ever heard. "The scream came from one of the maids. In the house. A girl...full of nightmares." He reaches for me and although I try to avoid it, my hand betrays me, drifting up to meet his like static cling. I cringe upon contact, expecting the pain from before, but instead, there is only the softness of his skin.

The warmth pulsing in his palm. The feeling of him, spreading out over me, weaving wires between us that seem to bind together and become thicker by the moment.

"It doesn't hurt if the contact is not forced," he says, glancing down at my hand cradled in his. "I am so sorry to have caused you any pain before."

It's stupid how I am flooded with forgiveness. That I don't question why it doesn't hurt, or why I want to move closer to him. It is undeniable how quickly the wires bind between us, becoming far less flimsy and far more dangerous, as they fuse together. Whatever we are to each other is being welded, like the links of a chain.

How is he doing this to me? And what is he doing exactly?

I am not a victim.

But I am willing to forgive what I wouldn't before. Willing to stand here patiently, as whatever is between us builds and bonds together. Willing, even though I'm not sure I should be willing.

My thoughts vanish as his beautiful, dark gaze rolls over me. Every thought of Meg drops right out of my head. All that sticks with me is a vague sense of something I forgot about her, but nothing so important that I want to work at remembering it. Isaac's pure attention is suffocating, but feeling myself grow weaker beneath his gaze seems like the most pleasurable way to die.

The *push* I felt before straggles now. It has become only a silly and annoying compulsion, like waking from a delicious dream in a warm bed with a relentless urge to pee. I surrender to the *pull* and let it drag me into Isaac's dark gaze.

"I've missed you," he says.

"I was gone an hour or less." I try to scoff, but the muscles in my face don't comply. It's like nothing in my body will oppose him, no matter how trivial.

"It was nearly a whole day, and it felt like forever."

I peer around us. "It couldn't have been that long," I laugh. "It's still dark."

"The sun never shines on my estate." The smirk that made my fury boil before only seems charming now. "I've chosen this location for just that purpose."

"You're afraid of sunburn?" I wonder aloud.

"I love the night," Isaac replies, breathing his allure all over me.

I inhale.

His enchantment buries me. From the muffled depths of my soul, my ego still manages to sputter about what a fool I am, but I don't care. It's easy to think of the tingling butterflies in my belly. Easier to ignore everything when the reflection in Isaac's eyes is so fascinating. Easiest to believe I want the cage and the chains when they make me feel so good.

"Come with me," he says.

I let this fraudulent man lead me into his house, ignoring the somber understanding that I will go anywhere he asks.

Isaac kicks open the front door with his boot. I follow him into the bronzed darkness of the candlelit foyer. Shadows streak the floor and slide over the walls. Besides the noise of the door thrown open, the mansion is silent as a mortuary. Until a paralyzing shriek plunges through the hall.

The sound cuts the silence, as much as it cuts through the threads that keep me at Fake Isaac's side.

A vision of Meg streaks through my head. "I want to see her!"

Isaac doesn't answer me. Instead, he bellows, "Hoomstid!"

I startle, pulling back my hands, although Isaac keeps his palms open and steady. Confident my touch will return. My nerves are still reluctant, but little good they do besides spill adrenaline through my veins.

The flicker of a floating candle at the end of the hall raises the hair on my neck and it doesn't lay back down when the servant's disfigured face appears over the flame.

"Sir? You called for me?" Hoomstid's effeminate voice is no less startling than it was the first time I heard it. He stands with a stick-straight back and the eye at his cheek blinks. The other, in the low center of his forehead, remains steady and open.

Isaac's voice is a sharp contrast. "Light the house!"

"Yes, sir." Hoomstid jerks a bow. The highest eye never loses sight of me.

"And bring Ms.—" Another icy shriek cuts him off.

This time, I can track it. Not in the house. Out back. It doesn't sound like Meg after all, but the scream sounds as though it has good reason. Knowing it's not Meg doesn't put me at ease.

"I apologize for that, sir," Hoomstid says with another lumpy bow. "I was looking after Miss Milligen, but she's having quite a night. There is nothing I can do to make her comfortable. I have run out of the nectar that settles her, sir, so she only asks for you to grant her more. Forgive me..." Another gratuitous bow. "I don't believe the lady is otherwise suited to appear in such heavenly company as you find yourself at the moment."

Milligen...the name rings a dull bell somewhere deep in my head. I try to follow the sound of it, but am distracted as Isaac gives his servant a long look, as if the butler can read Isaac's mind. But the servant doesn't move a muscle or blink an eye and Isaac looks away with a grimace. "I think we've all done what we can for the lady, Hoomstid."

The servant offers a half nod, the lower eye blinking consensually, while the upper remains on me, rooted and unblinking.

Isaac's attention is elsewhere, his stare cast into the shadows of the dark hall. "She requires different amenities, or at the very least, an establishment with a nurse who can look after her as she requires."

Another wobbly bow, but the eye is steadfast. Gaze or glare, I cannot tell.

"Agreed, sir." Hoomstid backs away and retreats down the hall, wall sconces lighting as he goes. I smell the wax, but candles do not light themselves.

I turn to Isaac. "I thought you said it was a maid with nightmares? It sounds like she's an addict."

I've known enough of Meg and Murray and their acquaintances to know the signs.

"Come with me," Isaac says as his arm slips around my waist.

It brings us uncomfortably close, the length of him heating my ribs, but his body lights a wildfire across my skin. Logic mumbles, *get out of here, get away from him,* but as Isaac presses to me, I care less about reason than the movement of his body guiding mine. I'm both disgusted and enamored with him. *How can those two feelings occur together?*

I should be running out of here like my pants are on fire, but with Isaac's hand laid against the small of my back, the heat of his fingers seeps through me. I can't concentrate on anything else. He is breathing fast and I like the idea that I am responsible for his quickened heartbeat. My concerns scatter faster than I can gather them.

We go down the hall, through the door at the end into the kitchen, until we stand at the back door. Isaac places his wide, flat palm against the wood and pushes it open ahead of me, but before I can step out onto the short stairs, Isaac pulls me back.

"Nova...before you meet Machara..."

I inhale his cursory groan. "Machara? I know her—"

"Doubtful. Machara Milligen is a correspondent of mine." His eyes rove away from me. What is that? Embarrassment? Frustration? I can't read what I can't see. Isaac's gaze stretches beyond the door and across the back lawn, far away from me. His throat bobs with a swallow. "Before you meet this woman, there's something I want to tell you first."

"She was a maid, then a correspondent, and now she's a woman? What exactly is she to you?" The growl in me is pitiful, but whoever this Machara Milligen is to Isaac is coming back to me. The correspondent Dorcas Boyle told me about...it seems like years ago, the memory is so dull. But it sounds as though this woman has meant a great deal to him. Enough that he doesn't know what to call her, doesn't know how to explain her to me. The tug-of-war inside me is dizzying. I'm jealous. I'm furious. I'm hurt —but over what, I don't know, since Isaac and I have no relationship. A surge of forgiveness spills over me. "I don't care what you have to tell me, Isaac, or who this woman has been to you."

His gaze swivels back to me, harder than expected.

"But you will," he says, silver streaks flashing across his pupils. "I'm going to tell you everything, Nova, starting right now."

He drops back from me, the heat pulling out of skin like carpenter tacks. This emotional whiplash is wearing thin and I want it to end.

"Look at me," he says as I take his hand again. He lifts his upper lip and I'm terrified that he is going to tell me some cruel truth.

Instead, he bears his teeth at me. Curved, white incisors slide down from his gums, engulfing his regular teeth. The new teeth are almost the same size as the normal ones, except they taper into razor tips, sharper than any needle Murray's poked into Meg's arms. From the very points, the fangs dribble a liquid, clear as water.

Saliva.

I've had it all wrong. What's fake about this man is that he isn't a man.

Isaac Havrath is a vampire.

M y scream doesn't come. There's not even one stuck in my throat.

I stare at Isaac's fangs. His saliva drip, drip, drips on the back of my hand and rolls off my thumb like tears. Every drip seems a little more usual. As if it's perfectly normal to be standing in front of a vampire, in a different time, in a mansion that no longer exists.

"You're a vampire." I'm half awed, a quarter intrigued, a quarter weirded-out.

"And you," he says, lids lowering as if his words alone are able to kiss me, "you are—"

Another high-pitched scream rifles from the back yard, and the spell is broken again. I tear my eyes from Isaac Havrath's mouth. The mythological mouth of a murderer. The sound of the scream knocks me into my right mind. With another glance at Isaac, I see shadows I didn't notice before. They frame him, smoking at his edges, as if he is on fire inside and his body can't quite contain it. The innocence in his expression doesn't seem to fit.

I bolt past him, out the back door and down the steps. I race across the grass, dimly lit by the moon, but am brought up short by a carriage. It pulls around the loop of the worn dirt drive behind the mansion, dust clouds instantly caking in my nose. I jump away at the whiny of a horse who rears slightly in its harness to avoid me.

"Whoa! Whoa now!" The dark-coated driver clicks his tongue at the gleaming horses. The animals settle and continue past me, stopping before the cottage, short of the loop's turn.

A footman jumps off the back of the carriage and opens the door. A candlelit lantern hangs outside, casting a somber glow on the padded seat within. The gleaming horses whiny again. One stamps a nervous foot.

I whirl around, wide eyed for an escape. I'm caught between the mansion's back door, the carriage before me, darkness to my left, and on my right, a red wood cottage that stands at the edge of the wide driveway loop.

It would be a charming place if the windows weren't covered over with iron grates and the door didn't have such an intricate locking system, visible from the outside. Which means that the cottage is a place of detainment, rather than a place for guests.

The door of the cottage is suddenly thrown open and Hoomstid stumbles out beneath a bundle of a woman. Definitely not Meg. The woman's hair is long and ropey, dirty gold. Her gown flows all the way to the servant's feet, tripping him up as her head lolls back over the awkward crook of his arm. Her mouth hangs open. Hoomstid, only just a wick of a man as it is, stumbles on the fabric of her and fumbles not to drop her altogether.

Isaac materializes behind me. I feel him like the waft of a summer wind bringing in a storm. He was telling the truth - it wasn't Meg screaming. I'm pretty sure Meg was never here at all. She's wandered off somewhere, but she didn't come here. My shoulders loosen only slightly.

Hoomstid grunts the woman into the carriage, stuffing her in like loose, slippery pasta. He gets most of her dress in and one of her shoes tumbles out onto the dirt. He tosses that in, and her hand flops out.

I turn on Isaac. "Is she messed up on drugs, or is she dead?"

"Neither," he says and Machara Milligen's blood-curdling scream, so near from inside the carriage, makes me jump. I glance back to see her fingers, knuckles straining against the skin, clamped to the opening of the carriage door.

"Isaac! My moon!" she shrieks, hefting herself up in the seat. Her eyelids move like they're sticky, as if someone's poured glue in them. Hoomstid blocks her way out of the carriage, but she oozes into the open spaces and pokes out, reaching in our direction. In Isaac's direction. "Please...I need you, my lovely moon! Please!"

"Hoomstid!" Isaac commands, "Have her trunks loaded quickly!"

The servant casts a look of despair over one shoulder. The conundrum, at keeping the screaming Miss Milligen in the carriage, and following his master's command to load the woman's luggage, is expressed equally in each of Hoomstid's skewed eyes.

"Let me out, you rotted melon!" Machara Milligen shouts, clawing at the servant. "Isaac! Isaac! What are you doing? I am in *pain*!"

"Hoomstid! Trunks!" Isaac snaps and the servant, still trying to guard the door from escape, swivels his head to command the useless footman, who has been standing by and giggling at Hoomstid's efforts, to fetch the lady's belongs. The footman slinks to the cottage and goes inside.

"What does she want?" I ask.

"Her needs will be sufficiently met, but there is no use in her upsetting everyone on the grounds. Hoomstid will quiet her."

I doubt it. It seems like the only way it could happen is if Isaac gives her whatever it is she wants, and he isn't making a move.

She continues to plead, arms threaded through Hoomstid's elbows, hands clawing at the air as if she can dig a tunnel to Isaac. The servant struggles to retain her, but manages.

The footman returns, one small trunk beneath his arm and dragging a much larger one across the gritty drive. Both are black cases; both covered in an inconsistent, white pattern. As if drawn on with chalk. The metal edges shriek and rub against the dirt, but the footman passes Hoomstid and manages to heave the luggage and secure it on the back of the carriage.

"Isaac! Why won't you help me, my moon? I have nowhere else to go! I've done everything for you! Help me!" Miss Milligen continues to beg from every unoccupied opening, poking out windows and whatever isn't blocked of the door. Finally, Hoomstid wrangles the carriage door and gives the woman a shove backward to slam it shut. Her shifted weight rocks the carriage and Hoomstid, out of breath, pounds his fist against the closed door.

At the sound, the driver whistles. The horses shoot forward, going from stand-still to a runaway speed. I stumble back, into Isaac.

The carriage lurches with a thump from within. I assume Machara Milligen is being tossed around inside like a bingo ball. The horses thunder around the loop, throwing up a swirl of dark dust. The harnesses clatter and squeal, the carriage swaying and thumping. The whole business roars toward the straight part of the driveway that leads to Washington. The driver hollers a great, *hyah!* at the turn, and the horses take the bend, the carriage pitching onto two wheels before it disappears around the edge of the mansion.

Isaac and I stand at the center of the settling remains of a dust-hurricane.

"Who is she to you?" I ask with a cough.

"She is a revenant and a witch. That's what she was to me and nothing more."

Another scream fades quickly along with the rattling of the carriage. It seems like she thought she was more. Much, much more.

"What do you mean, *a revenant and a witch*?" I cough out the question as the dust clears. Was this the *witchcraft* the museum curator mentioned?

Isaac looks at me long and hard, as if he's considering what to tell me, what to leave out. I start walking and he stays in step right beside me without questioning me. I have to do something to keep my body busy so my brain can process whatever he's going to tell me, or piece enough together from whatever he's not. We head around the edge of the mansion, following the dirt driveway toward the street, the same path the carriage travelled.

"Tell me everything," I say, so there is no confusion about what I want to hear. "The whole truth."

"Revenants are souls," he begins softly. "Those who have passed and returned, without being traditionally reborn. The soul takes a body that was not theirs, to continue living in the same period of life they just exited. A witch is a—"

"I know what witches are," I return flatly, even though I'm not sure I do. Machara Milligen isn't of the Halloween variety that wears pointed hats or drag around broomsticks. "Revenant...like taking over a body? Like a poltergeist? Or a vampire?"

"Revenants are neither," he says, lightning bugs blinking around his head. He steers me, with soft fingertips on my elbow, off the driveway and across the front of the yard. "But they particularly don't enjoy being called *poltergeists*. It is an offensive term to them, as if they are only borrowing a body and suppressing the soul. Revenants rid the body of the soul, and slide in before the body dies." Isaac's fangs aren't visible now, but his arrogance is. "And revenants are far inferior to vampires. They are weaker beings, since they don't drink the blood of life, but when they take a body, the skin thickens, the organs rejuvenate, and the bones strengthen. They don't get sick and it takes great, concentrated effort to wound them. The revenants can live eternally, as vampires do, but if a revenant's body manages to be physically damaged, they do not heal. Vampires are indestructible. Revenant bodies, however, can not be repaired."

"How can you tell a revenant from a human?"

"It's tricky. The body has its original organs, and they take on the traits of the ghost who inhabits the body. Humans create diseases through their thoughts and beliefs about mortality. Ghosts are eternal beings, so the organs of the body align to function eternally, unless exterior events damage them."

"So you're saying they're human, besides the birth part."

"Oh no," he laughs. "Not at all. Humans are weak. Flimsy. Revenants are far more durable. It's the reason vampires choose to drink from them, rather than humans. Humans can be sucked dry too easily, and it's far easier to either crush or break them."

Sure. That's not insulting. He should be slapped. There's nothing easy about me. I've been tested and proven, having lost my parents and all memory of them. Crushing and breaking me is impossible.

But instead of outrage, acknowledging my lack of thick skin embeds a glinting sliver of jealousy in my heart. Isaac chose to drink from a so-called revenant, Machara Milligen.

Maybe it's just a more proper way of saying *addict*, which

seems more accurate from what I saw, but whatever she is, I saw Isaac's fangs and I know she was his juice box of choice.

I've also seen a couple of vampire movies with Meg and I know what else vampires usually do when they drink. They're usually thirsty in more ways than one.

I stop beside the long ditch that separates the yard from the graveled street and stare into the muddy trench.

My humanness repulses Isaac. I should be strapping on a party hat, but the multitude of live, pulsing wires between us, which continue to weld us together, overrides my sanity. Weirdly, I feel as though I should be sobbing for all the ways in which I am lacking. All the reasons why Isaac Havrath will never desire me.

He lifts my chin with the side of a curled finger. "What's the matter? Your countenance has changed considerably."

I don't want to tell him, but I can't gulp the words back down, even with my hardest swallow. All that squeaks out of me is misery. A weak confession that proves him right. "I'm human."

The gleam disappears from the cold metal in Isaac's eyes. The irises soften and his pupils melt toward the edges, encapsulating my reflection.

"Oh, no, no, no," he whispers with a grin, laying his palm to my cheek. Half a day ago I would've laid him out flat for saying that, doing that...if I hadn't already run away. Now, I'm digging deep into his gaze, wanting to find myself in it at every turn. "You have no idea, do you? No idea who or what you are! I told you that we were once friends. I let you call me a liar, because I didn't want to overwhelm you with the truth. But we *were* friends, Nova. More than that, actually."

I swallow. That strange new part of my thoughts whispers that it doesn't matter that he is a stranger. There's no sense in it, I know, but this foreign beacon planted inside me throbs, wanting this stranger to want me, to find the core of me, to take my place as my primary guidance.

His eyes search mine. I'm not sure what he expects to find as panic pushes my heartbeat through my ears.

"What were we to each other?" I ask.

"You were to be my bride," Isaac says.

Nothing feels right about this.

Tears gather in the corners of my eyes and a brick lodges itself in my throat, but these responses don't match my real emotions. The responses don't even feel like they are mine. Just like the itch, the tug in my bones, and the static that pulled at my skin—all these things are being drawn from me, pulled to my surface, and called to Isaac as if my emotional responses are his belongings.

What he doesn't seem to understand is that my instinct toward self-preservation, though buried, remain intact. I am still hesitant, apprehensive, and wary of a century-old vampire who doesn't look a day over twenty-five. My defense mechanisms battle the tugs and itches and static, but they're there.

Panic rises up and I can't dissolve the tears it brings. Fear spills into my hands and over my lips, making both tremble. My deepest instincts say this is a lie; there is no way I could've known Isaac over a hundred years ago. I am only seventeen. My parents died in a horrific car accident only months ago. My whole body quakes. It's all lies to manipulate me. It must be lies. I do not want to be a vampire's bride.

"What is happening to me?" My voice quivers.

A smile splits Isaac's lips and relief flows over his face. He lifts my hand and kisses my knuckles. "You were spelled, my darling, that is all this is, and now that we are together, it is wearing off. The final act of the spell is to show me your true feelings and I am so pleased to see you are filled with such relief and excitement as I am!" He scoops me into his arms as if we are victors, crossing a difficult finish line together.

I let him pull me against his chest, but I am limp. He is interpreting my tears and quivers as relief, instead of stemming from the panic over what he said and continues to say. I don't know what more is to come, if there are truer emotions inside me that will come bursting from me, but my muscles and bones are slowly coming back under my control. The battle against his magnetism lessening. Once body is able to obey me fully again, I think I'd like give a whirl at strangling him.

"I had Machara—" he begins and I stop him flat.

"She had something to do with this? Your *kept woman…*" I shrill, letting the sound of frenzied jealousy burst through my tone. Anything to buy myself time and let my body come back fully under my control.

"It wasn't like that," Isaac explains. "You are all that has ever mattered to me, Nova. Machara was only a revenant that I could drink from, and a witch that could conjure spells for me. Hers were not even that potent! I only had her place the additional spell because—"

"Additional? How many spells are on me?" I try to sound amorous, as if I am in awe of what's he done, instead of flipped out. I flex my fingers into a fist at my side, just to see if I can, and I succeed. The *pull* is slowly drizzling off me like sand washed off at the beach, but I keep my eyes steady on Isaac, leaning into him, lips open as if I am hanging on his every word. Anything I can think of, to keep him believing his spells are still working, while I quietly test my body and reflexes to find out for myself.

His smile couldn't be more dazzling as he spills the rest of his trickery. "I am only sorry it took me so long to bring you here! I apologize for keeping you waiting, but powerful spells are expensive! I had to pay a great warlock first, for the spell that drew you to me."

A light bulb in my brain ignited.

The day I appeared at the museum and didn't know why.

The obsession I felt after looking at Isaac's photo.

The insane itch that burst through me when I touched the museum's window.

The pull that dragged me up the stairs to the exhibit, and then to the empty lot, and then onto Isaac's invisible estate.

I've been a mouse in an easy maze. Every avenue led to bigger and bigger hunks of cheese.

I knit my brow, as if saddened. "What did you have to pay the warlock?"

"Oh," Isaac chuffs like a humble human being. "He demanded several things. He needed a great number of animals for his village, so I supplied those. I slaughtered pregnant females and took the newborns for the warlock's village, other ingredients from the animal that the warlock needed for his spells, and I also supplied myself with a meal. Those days were lean for me. Killing the livestock saved me from slaughtering the entire town of New Baltimore."

I hold my jaw tight so I don't gape. Those were the animals Dorcas Boyle told me about, the ones that disappeared and were thought to be killed by Isaac's father.

"And I took the members of the warlock's coven who were exiled from his village—"

"Machara?"

Isaac nods. "Yes, she was one of the exiled. I needed a revenant and she agreed to become one so I wouldn't starve. I also needed her to distribute the spells, as I can only travel in the dimensions allowed to the vampire colony. She did a marvelous job and she was of great help in the spells that have helped you to see me as I am."

I tip my head innocently to the side. "How else would I see you, Isaac?"

"I wanted you to see me as the man who loves you," he says. "Not as a repulsive vampire."

"You are the furthest from repulsive I've ever seen," I say. It's the truth. He's got an incredible body, and his raven hair and silver-streaked eyes make him the most attractive man I know.

Isaac's shoulders roll back slightly with my praise.

"But trying to control how I feel about you through spells," I draw back slightly, "That makes you a little ugly."

His expression takes the hit, visible by the twitch in his jaw and the silver wall that swiftly slams down over the softness of his gaze.

"I apologize for that," he says tightly. "I didn't want you to be afraid of me."

I can't lose my edge with him just yet—not before I know if he has Meg—but it turns my stomach to even pretend that I feel anything for him. The bizarre affection I felt before has finally disappeared, leaving an aftertaste of words that make me want to spit in his face. But not until I know Meg is safe. The best I can do is to tell him the truth, in the way he wants to hear it.

I drizzle sweetness into my tone as I smile up at him. "I'm not afraid of you, Isaac. "

He's still beaming, so pleased with himself and the outcome of his spells.

I wipe away whatever moisture is left from the corners of my eyes and make a three-quarter turn, looking in all directions. "Are you sure my cousin isn't here somewhere? I was almost positive she followed me when I first came."

"No one can come to my estate unless I've invited them personally, but if you tell me what she looks like and her name, I will be sure she will be welcome on the estate if she comes looking for you."

If. He obviously doesn't know Meg at all. Meg is definitely not an *if*. She's a *when*.

He's still smiling as if this makes everything okay between us. Relief and helpfulness are layered on his face like warm blankets. He must believe that whatever lies he's told, and whatever spells he's put on me, wewe'rere fine. Worth it.

I return my most sincere smile, to encourage him to buy that crap he's working so hard to sell me.

Whatever relief might be showing on my face is the last bit of truth I have for him. He doesn't know Meg's name or what she looks like. She is safe.

Just like I will be.

I lunge across the ditch for the road, to escape this despicable vampire and his creepy estate for good.

I don't jump far enough and land in the middle of the opposite side of the ditch. I counted on the ground being hard and easy to scale, but instead, there is only mud beneath the grass. My feet sink in. I claw at the gunk, scrambling up the edge for the road.

Isaac's splashes into the muck below, growling my name. He grabs for my ankle and I snap my leg back, kicking him in the face. His grip isn't solid and the hit jerks him momentarily off balance.

I take my advantage, yanking my left foot out of the muck. It sucks off my shoe. I dig my toes into the rising edge of the ditch and launch myself to the top of the ditch. I throw myself forward, into the street. Isaac's fingers wrap around my ankle as I break into the dirty gray fog between my world and Isaac's.

"Let go of me!" I shriek.

My scream echoes in the void.

With wide eyes I search for something to grab, but there is nothing here. Literally, nothing. Only bleak, shifting billows of gray fog. Clouds stir above, below, and beside me. Particles dance in it like unsettled attic dust. I breathe in the filthy air and it clogs me with panic. I can't tell anymore if I am standing up or lying down; if I am on my stomach or my back, if I am standing on my feet or my head.

All I know is that the cold fog makes me feel dizzy and disoriented.

I can't see the vampire's grip, but I feel it digging into the skin of my ankle. He hauls me backward through the dusty brume. Or maybe it's downward. I glance over my shoulder, at the length of my body. Obscured in patches of fog, I can't see my feet at all. The vampire pulls again and I scream as my joints stretch. My knees disappear completely, eaten by the billowing dust.

I claw at the ground, terrified to be captured and equally terrified to remain in this void. I scream and claw, but there's nothing to grasp, nowhere to sink my nails. I rake through the smooth fog, hands searching for a tree root to hang onto, stones to throw at the vampire—anything—but I only shred the dusty brume. The murky smog fills in the furrows as quickly as I make them.

I close my eyes as Isaac hauls me out of the thick, cold fog and back into his world.

My feet land on something solid. I stumble on the sprawling
lawn of the Havrath House. Unable to get my balance in
my single shoe, I fall backward on the dewy grass, the shoots damp
and prickly in my palms. I'm in the middle of the yard, closer to
the house than the street. The same hands that pulled me out of the
gray-blue emptiness yank me to my feet.

I am abruptly toe-to-toe with the seething vampire.

He grasps my right wrist like an iron cuff, indifferent and unre-
lenting. Darkness drapes itself over any answers I might find in his
eyes.

If he thinks I will fold to his fury, I am not the girl he assumes I
am. I will not cower, no matter what happens. That in-between
pocket of nothingness scared me more than the metal grip of my
liberator.

We glare at each other.

"Why did you do that? I could've lost you!" he finally roars.

I wrench my hand from his grasp and, this time, he doesn't
resist.

Even more shocked when his shoulders crumble and he drops
his forehead into his palm.

"Please don't ever do that again, Nova," he whispers. He doesn't sound angry anymore. He sounds frightened. Desperate. "You could have been lost forever in the *vias*."

"The fog?" I try to scoff, even though just his name for it shreds my spine with fear.

"Yes." He lifts his head, eyes guarded but soft again. "That fog is called the *vias,* and it's deadly. It is a barrier that protects my estate from the outside world and it is treacherous to cross."

"It never was before."

"Luck and only that," he says somberly. His brows furrow over his hooded gaze. "Why did you run from me?"

"You don't know?" I rub my wrist where he'd held it tight. "You lured me here with spells, to tell me you're a vampire, and that I was going to marry you a million years ago...and you can't figure out why I ran?"

"You think I *lured* you here to harm you? Or to tell you lies?" He captures my hand and lays it against his chest. "I've only ever loved you, Nova."

I yank my hand away. "That's hard to swallow, since I didn't exist a hundred years ago."

His smirk doesn't help things. "I like to think you've loved me longer than that."

"I haven't, I don't, and I didn't." I glance over his shoulder at the road. We're half way up the lawn and although my body is solely under my command now, it is too far to sprint in one remaining shoe without believing I'd be caught. Not surprisingly, Isaac the Vampire is pretty supersonic for his age and he notices me measuring the distance of my escape route.

"You don't want to do that," he says. Although his stance appears relaxed and peaceful, something changes. He plants his feet and narrows his eyes. Raw strength pours off him in waves. Heat slices through the air between us like the furnace blast of a coming storm. As sure as I am of myself, I shrink away, but I can't avoid it. The surge of his power crashes over me and I gasp. What hits me is more than emotion. It has a tangible grasp that steals my breath and throws a dark blanket over my soul.

For a moment, it feels like the whole world has gone dark and I am utterly alone in it.

I have nothing and no one.

I am nothing.

"Nova," he says, and the despair is swiftly yanked away. The colors of the Havrath Estate rise up and I gulp a breath spiced with the scent of mud, grass, air, and the metallic tang of Isaac. I lock my knees so as not to shrink away when he leans in close to whisper in my ear. "If you insist on leaving, I will call you back to me again, and again, and again. As long as it takes. I will be patient with you because I know you wouldn't want me to give up. You may not have your memories of us, but we will create new ones. Even better than before. I can help you remember what you've forgotten."

"How? With another spell?" I raise my chin, along with my sharp tone. I can almost reach out and wrap my fingers around the temptation he's offering. As frightening as it may be, I want my memory back. I ache to know who I was, so I can start being who I am, without feeling like I'm playing the lead in a movie without a script.

"First you need to know what you are." His eyes flash and the sudden streak of silver telegraphs something into my soul. A warning. An ominous signal of danger ahead.

He's a vampire, after all. And I'm wherever this estate is— somewhere Meg won't be able to find, and someplace I'm no longer sure I can escape. That should be the danger I recognize from that flash in his eyes, but it's not.

It's a more sinister feeling than any of that. He said I need to know *what* I am and something about that swirls anxiety all through me.

"I don't want your help," I snarl. "I just want to go home."

Isaac's hand closes on my wrist again, though he casually

slides his other hand into his pocket. He leans in, his breath drifting across my neck as he croons in my ear, "Oh, you need my help, Nova. You'll stay on as my guest so I can do that. You need to know what you are, and who you are, and how we can light up this world together. But, for now, since Machara's weak spells haven't held as they should have, we'll have to rely on what she left behind."

He retracts the hand from his pocket and unfurls his fist. I only have a blink to notice the powder in his palm, before he blows it over his fingers, into my face.

I don't cough.

I don't choke.

I pull myself up through mental sludge, thicker than the mud in the ditch. Moving my limbs is pure disaster. I wobble and jerk. Something presses into my stomach so hard, I want to barf. I open my eyes to shifting fabric and further down…someone's butt under the fabric.

I'm over Isaac's shoulder.

"Do not fight, miss," Hoomstid's unisex voice pleads behind me.

"You drugged me," I slur. My lips are loose, my tongue is tight, and the words are all smeared.

"It's not a drug," Isaac says. "I only subdued you."

"What do you think drugs do?" I say, but it only comes out as a messy heap of sounds. I try to raise an arm and elbow Isaac in the temple, but nothing works the way I want it to.

"Stay still," Hoomstid pleads. "It's for the better, miss."

Sure. I'll just give up because I'm told. I pour all my energy into jerking and wobbling as hard as I can. Unfortunately, despite my efforts, the vampire manages to keep his grip. No getting him off balance this time. But I keep trying until my head slams on the edge of a doorframe.

Then, I stop moving to groan.

"Are you alright?" Isaac asks. He deposits me on an unfamiliar bed and runs gentle fingers over my temple.

I do my best to jerk away and glare at him, but none of my muscles are responding as they should. Instead, I knock against his hand and try to curse at him instead. Those words don't work either. I only blow bubbles that pop on my lips.

He straightens up. "We'll talk when you are recovered."

"No, we won't." The words skid out on slobber. It doesn't even matter, since the tone of my mumble communicates my sentiments perfectly.

"I'll take care of her, sir," Hoomstid says with a low bow to Isaac.

I flick my gaze back to Hoomstid, but when I look back for Isaac, he's gone. But gone where, I don't know. The door that we entered through is gone. Or, at least hidden by the series of long tapestries draped over the walls.

Hoomstid, recovered from his bow, looks where Isaac last stood before turning to me. He retrieves a blanket from the end of the bed, shakes it out over the top of me, and bends to tuck it in around me, like I'm a mummy. The flowery smell of a woman's perfume wafts around me and breathing leaves my lower lip dry.

"Miss, you need to remember who you are," he whispers as he tucks. The eye on his forehead stares at me, unblinking, while the one on his cheek tracks his tucking. "You are much more than you know. Much more than what Mr. Havrath says, or what any of the faithful servants here might tell you. But there are those of us who know you, Miss Nova, and we'll do what we can for you, but we are limited. It is most important that you remember who you are."

"How?" The question spills out of me in a blur, but Hoomstid 's gulp is audible. He understands.

"This could get me killed," he mumbles in my ear. "Revealing anything to you puts my life in danger; please be mindful of that. I am frightened of your wrath, but terrified of what will happen to my master if his heart is broken. Be kind, my lady, please, be kind."

His fear peaks my interest and his tender sentiment takes me by surprise. He's concerned about Isaac's black heart? Why in the world would he be afraid of me? I'm hardly the harbinger of death with my mouth that won't work and my arms tucked in hard at my sides.

"You will be safe in the cottage, but look to the night for your answers, miss," Hoomstid whispers against my ear. "Magic is the only thing that might save you."

26

After Hoomstid's confession of fear and his weird advice, the last thing I expect is the brutal shove. He pushes me onto my side, and by the time I roll back and get loose from my blanket restraints, a door slams somewhere and the servant is gone.

It takes hours before whatever Isaac blew in my face wears off. Once I'm back to normal, I scout the bizarre room where he and Hoomstid abandoned me. The walls are draped with heavy tapestries and I can find no windows or doors behind them. Only scribbles on the walls. No windows. No doors.

There's got to be a way out, since there was a way in. The only thing similar to a door is a small room with a toilet inside. The tapestry is its only 'door'. I note the design on the fabric as it wafts back against the wall.

All the furniture in the room is claw-footed, which seems appropriate. It's all upholstered with gold and cream brocade, which also seems appropriately old, like Isaac. Also, the styles fit —a camelback sofa and two armchairs that each look like they could swallow me in a gulp, a claw-footed bathtub in the corner. I'm surprised the toilet in the closet isn't claw-footed too.

A hardwood bureau sits beside the four poster bed, all four

posts draped with chiffon. Candles from the middle ages, flickering, fat, and dusty, are stuck to the top of the dresser, adhered by the bubbles of wax that have melted around their bases. The dust on them crackles and dark smoke twists upward from the wicks. All five drawers of the bureau are empty, except for a sachet in the top drawer that smells of Machara's flowery, talcum perfume, a hatpin with a long, red tip that I realize is not coated with paint, but blood, and a group of tiny, knotted loops of various colored hairs. A stack of decorative bed pillows sit piled on the floor.

For Machara living here, she sure cleaned out fast.

I lift the skirt around the bed when my toes stub on something beneath. Silver-striped buckles and strips of leather. I reach under the bed to fish out what I think might be a belt, but it's attached to the bed. I let go the moment I get a good look.

Restraints clatter on the wood floor.

The buckles aren't striped.

They're spattered with blood.

That pervert was tying Machara Milligen to the bed to drink from her. She must've gone insane in this cottage. From what I can remember of her screams as she was carried out, I have to think she fell in love with her captor. Maybe pretending to love him was better than the torture that left splatters of her blood on the heavy, leather restraints.

A tall china pitcher nestles in a wide bowl on the dresser, both china pieces are hand-painted with delicate, pink rosebuds. I lift the pitcher carefully from the bowl.

And lob it at the cement floor.

The beautiful pitcher shatters in a million pieces, some of them lodging in the skin of my legs.

No one comes.

Huh.

I kick the restraints back under the bed and go to the two-top kitchen table with straight backed, claw-footed chairs. More thick candles flicker and melt behind hurricane glass.

The table is oddly set for dinner for two, with rose-painted china dishes, salt-and-pepper shakers, an empty sugar bowl, a full cream pitcher, a covered bowl of butter with a fitted lid. Inside, there is a glob of soft-peaked, white butter beneath the lid.

From the contents of the room, a few things become obvious.

First, Hoomstid is a terrible housekeeper.

Second, the cottage is actually locked down better than a jail cell.

Third, Isaac is every bit as wealthy, and psychotic, as I can imagine. Probably even more so.

I work my way around the room, slipping a finger, one at a time, beneath the wall tapestries again, to look at the dark drawings that caught my eye. I draw back the fabric to reveal weird bits of graffiti and lines of poetry scrawled all over the paneling beneath. Some of it is gouged into the wood, some smeared like it was drawn with eyeliner. Other symbols are chalky gray and faded, as if written in ash.

Most aren't legible, but I find a verse that I can make out:

CURSES *upon the sweeter blood that tempts him*
May the moon strike down the thunder
let our chains be bound together
beneath our own stars and the damnable sun.
Release us, deep night, from the torture that pulls us under
Let us escape into and beyond.

I ASSUME Machara wrote this about Isaac, but what does it mean? The first line sounds like she wanted to keep him from cheating. But the part about the moon and thunder? She called Isaac her *moon*, but then, what's the thunder he'd be striking down? Her? The line about their chains being bound together...that woman needed some serious self care and rehabilitation. And the whole thing about being released from the torture makes too much sense, but escaping into their beyond?

She loved him. At least, she seemed to think it was love. It's sick.

Machara Milligen wasn't a maid, and she wasn't some impartial, business correspondent. Isaac meant a lot to her, but he used her for her blood and her spells. I wonder what the symbols on the walls did, or do, and if they, or the tapestries, are connected to the reason that the windows and doors have disappeared. Considering that I've seen Isaac's fangs and I've seen his mansion that disappears in a snap, magic isn't a far stretch at all anymore.

I pull a tapestry away from the wall and get under it. My face is so close to the drawings, my nose almost rubs the wall. That black smeary ink isn't ink. I think the symbols and words are written in *blood*.

I quickly drop the tapestry and scramble away from the wall to lean against the bureau.

27

One moment, I'm alone in the room, and the next, Isaac is lounging against a tapestry, one of his square shoulders making a dimple in the fabric. I do a double-take and nearly jump out of my skin when I realize he's standing there for real.

"I'm sorry for trapping you," he says, his gaze flicking to the broken pitcher pieces. "Believe me, if there was any other way—"

I don't mention the restraints I found. The trapping before me. The trapping he might think he'll do again. Instead, I grab the rose-painted porcelain bowl and, twirling on my heel, fire the delicate bowl at his forehead.

Vampire Fact: *they have probably been attacked enough that it's easy to see what's coming.*

Isaac reaches out a hand and plucks the pitcher out of the air. He sets it down on the coffee table without so much as a *tink* of the china.

"You've got an anger management problem," he says, sweeping aside the previously shattered pitcher pieces with the toe of his polished shoe. "Do you feel better now?"

"I haven't even started," I snarl, despite the slightest hint of a *tug* that beckons me to him. Who knows what was in the stuff he blew in my face. I lock my knees and hold my own easily, but I keep the distance between us. "I saw what you did to Machara Milligen. The restraints under the bed. You're sick."

"It's not what you think," he says, stepping toward me.

I step back to the side of the dinner table, lifting one of the dinner plates. It may not do much good against a vampire, but I have a whole table full of things to fire at him if need be.

"Let me out of here," I say in the calmest, angriest tone I can muster, "or I will destroy this cottage."

"This is for your own—"

"Good?" I roar at him. "Are you going to say this is for my *good*? Don't you dare! Is that what you told Machara? Restraints were *good for her?*"

Isaac tightens his lips and crosses his arms, rocking forward and back on the balls of his feet as if he's the one who is stuck.

"This isn't how it was supposed to be," he says. "If you'll just let me explain everything, I don't believe you'll hate me at all."

I knot my arms over my chest. He's had the chance to explain 'everything' a few times now and fat lot of good it's done. "Explain the restraints first."

"They weren't for her," he says. "They were for me. I didn't take any pleasure in drinking from Machara. She wasn't happy about it. She wanted an emotional relationship, rather than just one of…*satisfaction.*"

A blush creeps across my face. I already knew what Meg told me of vampire's appetites, and I assumed it was true with Machara, but the way Isaac hushes the word—whispers it—presses a heat through my veins that should not exist. It embarrasses me that anything he could say could have any warming effect on me.

"She was unhappy, so she spelled me," he says in that deep, guttural tone that continues to spread through me. "She made it so I couldn't drink from any of my other willing servants. Only her."

"There are others?" I rub my temple.

"Most of my servants are revenants, Nova. I saved them all

from exile to the nothingness of the *vias*. Any of them would be willing to serve me in any way necessary, and most would do it with pleasure. You've never had a vampire's teeth breaking your skin, but if you did, you'd know that the cost of the drink is exquisite pleasure to the cup."

The surge of desire comes like a white-hot snap through me, but I still manage a sneer. "You call the *people* you drink from, *cups?* That's what they are to you?"

"They're called *Bottles. Cups. Vessels,*" he says, the fringe of his eyelashes dust his cheek. "You don't understand. Whoever I drink from desires to become my possession, Nova, so sometimes it is easier to look at them as objects. You think I'm being callous, but I'm protecting myself too."

"Because a vampire is so helpless—"

He throws his fists to his sides, anger slicing the air between us. "I was the son of a pastor! You don't think I don't know what I am? I know it every time I feel my damned hunger! It wasn't my choice to be this way! The thirst burns me up inside until I drink! Guilt and morality don't change the fact that I am alive and I have to eat, Nova."

He takes a breath and settles back toward the wall. He wipes a hand across his forehead, presses splayed fingers over his mouth. His calm demeanor returns in pieces, his face like a puzzle being put together in a different way.

He inhales and begins again in a calmer voice, "What you don't know is that vampire venom is addictive. Whoever I drink from, they will be chemically addicted to me. They will desire me. And what you don't understand is that not one of them satisfies me. Only my true mate can do that.

"Every meal I take only shaves the faint edge off my hunger. That's all I ever get. I've learned to control myself, but it still makes me anxious, never being able to be completely satiated. I resist feeding, but imagine a fire inside you, burning up your organs, blazing in your throat and the only thing to quench that painful fire is to drink!

"At the same time, every meal I have ensures that I have *created* an insatiable stalker for myself. Every one of my *cups* craves my fangs in their neck every moment of the day and night, in varying degrees, depending on how much and how often I drink from them. They all crave the focused attention a vampire showers on their true mate, and they are furious when they don't get it from me. Do you see how we all lose in this arrangement? I am obsessed with finding my true mate and having complete satisfaction, while the *cups* strive to keep me tethered, because they are addicted to my venom and adamantly believe they are enough to be my true mate. I resist drinking because I know I will not be satisfied and I also know the *cup* will only become more addicted to me the more I drink from them and the more often I do it! But the pain increases until I cannot take it anymore. The restraints are there to control *me* from turning my frenzy on the *cup* and draining them to death!" His eyes are glossy, his pupils beads of mercury. "Don't you understand how exhausting this is for me? If I start looking at my *cups* as people, the guilt is overwhelming. Every meal for me means more and more ruin for them. The torture only ends when I can drink solely from my true mate and the addiction is reciprocated."

"If you think I might be the true mate you're looking for, I believe you're wrong, Isaac," I tell him.

He shakes his head, not as if he's telling me I'm wrong, but as if he is sad that I don't believe it. Lacing his hands before him, he tucks his chin.

"Would you like me to tell you about your mother and father instead?" he asks, looking up at me from his downturned face.

Despite myself, my spine melts at the mention of my parents. "You knew them?"

"You couldn't find a couple more respected," he begins. The silver in his eyes turns to soft, fluid beads of mercury. "People looked up to them. Your mother was supremely peaceful. She exuded worthiness, and she was as beautiful as midnight itself. Your father...there isn't enough words to describe his regality! Powerful, good natured, and generous would probably describe him best."

Regality. I didn't come from money. If I did, I doubt I would've ended up as I have: penniless and left on the doorstep of my equally penniless relatives, having to share their daughter's bed.

Still, everything Isaac says rings bells in my soul. It doesn't wake memories, but it wakes the feeling of them. My parents were good. They were regal, powerful, and worthy. My intuition recognizes them in the essence of Isaac's words. As if *regal, powerful, peaceful,* and *worthy* are physical pieces of them; as real and meaningful as their faces and arms and legs.

Isaac might be flattering the memory of my parents because he thought I was going to marry him, but his eyes aren't on me. The warmth in his tone and the affectionate smile that plays around his lips makes me wonder if he genuinely admired them.

"They loved you with all their hearts. They would move worlds for you, if they could." Isaac says.

My shoulders drop a millimeter. "You're telling the truth. You did know them."

"Of course. Who didn't?" he says with a soft, sad laugh. I'm not sure he knows how he's just poked a gaping hole in my armor.

"Me," I say, a lump in my throat stifling any other words for a moment. I clear my throat. "I don't remember anything about them, except that they died in a horrific car accident. They died and I didn't."

The guilt weighs down my heart.

Isaac's brow wrinkles. "Who told you that?"

"What do you mean? What difference does it make? They're gone."

"They are gone, but, Nova...your parents did not die in a car accident."

I open my mouth and realize there aren't words. I'm not sure who told me. I never thought of it before, but I can't remember anyone actually telling me how my parents died. I never questioned it, since I didn't remember anything before the moment I found myself standing on the Nichols' front steps, feeling like I was supposed to be there. I only rapped on the peeling door with the tarnished knocker and waited for the door to open. The sick feeling of loss glued my feet to the porch and I was sure I couldn't have left if I wanted to. Meg opened the door and my eyes stung at the sight of her. I couldn't remember anything, much less having met Meg before, but I was hollow and lost, when she opened the door, it was like a break in the dark clouds. Like meeting a stranger that feels like an old friend. Her wide smile and the way she stepped right out on the porch with me…she instantly made me a survivor. *"Hey, are you okay?"* Meg asked. *"Come in, cuz! Come in! It'll be alright!"*

I replay that moment, just as I've done dozens of times before, and I don't know how I never noticed it.

"No one told me my parents died. I just knew," I say. "It's called *closed head brain injury.* Post traumatic stress disorder."

"A hospital released you, set you loose to find your own way home?" Isaac asks carefully. He probably doesn't want to lose anymore china, but there is a gentle prod in his tone, like the way Meg feels for a vein before inserting a needle. "Were you wrapped in bandages? Did you have discharge instructions?"

No.

"Don't you think it a bit strange, Nova? No newspaper articles? No follow up visits to a doctor? How did you find your way to your relative's home?"

"I…I don't know. I was in shock. Someone must've dropped me off." I wish I could hide the tremors in my voice. I never knew how I arrived at the Nichols' house, only that I was suddenly on the porch, knocking at the door.

"And who told you that you had a brain injury?"

Now that I think of it, no one ever mentioned my brain injury. *I* explained it to *them.* It never felt like a lie. It came so easily across my tongue and it explained everything I couldn't, so I'd accepted it as the truth.

I want Isaac to stop asking questions. It's uncomfortable, as if he's lifting the edge of a rug and pointing out a mountain of dirt that's been hidden underneath.

"Sweetheart…" His soft voice is filled with pity and that old, lost and hollow feeling returns. "Did anyone ever deliver any of your belongings?"

Again…no.

I dig my fingertips into my arms and look down at myself. I'm wearing the same stuff Meg always wears: long tee, black yoga pants. I don't remember putting them on, much less owning them.

When I think of the room Meg and I share, I can't think of one thing in that room that is completely mine. Or even partially mine. Not a hairbrush, a pillow, nothing. It never occurred to me how strange it was until now.

"There's something else you need to know," Isaac says, but I stop him by raising a hand.

"No," I tell him, my stomach churning. "I never want to know. I don't want the gruesome details."

"It's not about them." The mercury in his eyes gathers. "It's about you."

"Okay...what do you think you know about me?" I ask. I don't know what I know about myself, so it's getting harder for me to figure out if Isaac's been lying or telling me the truth all along.

"This might be hard to hear, and I apologize, but your parents didn't die together. Your mother passed first. You stepped into her shoes after her passing. You tried to shoulder her responsibilities."

The claws of one of the kitchen table chairs scrapes across the planks of the wood floor as I pull it away from the table. I sink down on the cushion.

"When she left, you weren't destroyed. You couldn't be. You had to take care of everything she left behind, including your father."

My heart knows the story Isaac is telling. His seemingly insignificant details overwhelm me. A lie couldn't clang inside me like this. Sorrow stings my nose and the salt of it sits on my tongue. *I had to take care of everything, including my father.* Something in that is more than just true. It's absolute. I can feel it. My throat itches; my lungs are spongy and waterlogged as if I've been crying hard for days. I hide my face in my hands and try to stifle a sob that surfaces from that veiled part of me that keeps my memories hidden.

I wish I could make sense of it. Wish I could verify what he's saying with just one memory, but all I have to corroborate his story are the emotions of loss, guilt, and responsibility.

"Is this a spell? Tell me the truth," I plead.

"No spells. No lies. I am telling you the truth." Kneeling before me, he surprises me by touching my face. I'm destroyed by my flood of feelings and not at all prepared to defend myself against the soothing heat in his palm. It radiates through my skin and without really thinking of what I'm doing, I rest my cheek against his open hand. "I'm so sorry," he whispers, "but there is more."

I don't know that I can handle more. I'm already swallowed by my emotions and struggling for air. I can't imagine anything could feel worse...only *more*. I take a deep breath. I'm going to have to hear it all, get it all out, if I'm going to make it through this.

"Tell me," I say.

His fingers spread out on my cheek, his other hand grasps the one in my lap. The mercury in his eyes is pure liquid. He takes a deep breath.

"You are a ghost," he says softly.

30

His thumb strokes my cheek. A slight frown drags down the corners of his mouth.

I throw my head back and let out a crazy laugh.

"*Ghost!*" I shriek. The grief vanishes, the laughter trouncing it like the crisp snap of a sheet. It's the deepest, loudest laughter I've ever laughed.

Funnier yet, Isaac's face is dead sober. He leans back on his heels and the sight of his furrowing brow and stunned gaze makes me laugh all the harder. I laugh so much, he swims in my vision, distorted as if he's trapped in a funhouse mirror. The muscles around my middle lock up and ache.

Yes, I'm *sure* ghosts have a tough time with their *muscles* aching like this!

He wants me to believe I'm a ghost!

I have to stand and stretch my seizing muscles. Hysterical tears run down my cheeks and into my mouth. Leaning against a wall tapestry, I clasp my stomach so the laughter doesn't shake my guts loose.

"If I'm a ghost," I try to catch my breath, "I'll just pass through this wall—"

I lift the tapestry and rap my knuckles against the smooth plaster.

"Oh, that's right!" I stop laughing long enough to shoot him a smirk. I let the tapestry fall back into place. "I can't move through walls because I've got a body!"

Isaac hasn't moved from the floor. The mercury gathers and turns to metal again. His eyes follow me around the room as I laugh at him and pound the walls.

"Where did you hide the windows and doors, Isaac?" I taunt. "Amazing, isn't it? I still need doors! I can't seem to get the hang of evaporating! Did you make Machara Milligen a ghost too?"

"I didn't 'make' her anything," he says, getting to his feet. "But if you don't believe what I'm telling you—"

"No, I don't think I believe anything that comes out of your mouth!" I snap at him. "It's ridiculous! But you really had me with all that crap about my parents...you really had me! Was that another spell? Because, I actually believed you for a minute. But if you think—"

"I don't think anything, Nova. Nothing. " He says it so softly, my laughter disappears.

The pure craziness over being trapped in this cottage, and about the whiplash emotions he's given me is really sinking in.

"I'll let you consider everything I've said and when you're ready to hear more, I'll be back."

And like that, he's gone.

If I wasn't hysterical before, I am now. Especially since being left in an empty room makes me feel like a toddler in a time out.

After I overturn the furniture and smash the dinner plates, I whip the full cream pitcher against one of the tapestries, followed by the sugar bowl, and finally, the salt and pepper shakers. I send the lid of the butter bowl crashing against the ruined tapestry too, but the bowl itself, and the hand-churned ball of soft butter inside...*that* I keep in my palm.

I swipe my fingertip across the ball of oil and put my finger in my mouth.

I smile.

That butter is salty.

Just like me.

31

T ime is as valuable as gasoline. Or butter.

I pick my way through the ruined room a few dozen times, searching for an exit again—as if one will turn up as magically as it disappeared. When I don't find anything, I gather everything I need to hatch my plan. It's so simple, it's brilliant—although my scheme has great potential for getting me killed.

If I'm not a ghost, like Isaac claimed.

Which I'm pretty positive I'm not.

I drag a pillow from beside the bed and rub butter all over the fabric case as if it is a huge puff pastry. I wipe the last of the oil from between my fingers and dump the pillow in the middle of the bed. All the other pillows that were piled beside the bed are now arranged around the butter-smeared pillow like the rays of the sun.

The table candle flickers as I remove the hurricane glass. The flame is solid as I touch it down on the greasy pillow.

It only takes a second to catch.

The flame jumps up and spreads faster than gossip, chewing up the pillows and leaping on the gauzy fabric draped over the four posts. Shreds of the delicate fabric float, the embers landing on the wall tapestries. The fire eats the cream and gold threads, a flaming mouth that grows larger and larger, gobbling up the next tapestry, and the next.

And no one's coming.

I might've gone a bit too far. The smoke chokes me down to the floor. I lay down, trying to get under the fumes. I might've really screwed the pooch. I thought Isaac would get me out of here.

I pull my shirt collar over my nose and try to breathe through it.

The fire crackles, the orange flames fan out across the walls. The heat doubles. The whole room has been thrown into a furnace.

I should've thought this through a little more.

A door throws open somewhere and the fire responds with a roar, leaping to escape.

Heat rolls over me, presses me to the floor. I can't get up and run because I'm not sure which way is the exit and which way leads deeper into the flames.

"Nova!" Isaac bellows.

I choke on his name.

Isaac's hands hook around my arms. He yanks me to my feet. He throws a cloak over my shoulders I glimpse an open door where there wasn't one a half hour ago. The blaze licks at the threshold. Smog escapes through the opening in roiling, black clouds that stain the darkness outside. Isaac tugs the cloak over my head and pulls me into his arms. Scooping me up, he rushes straight through the fire. The staggering heat smothers any air left in my lungs.

Once we are safely outside, Isaac throws off the cloak. The garment lands on the dirt driveway, a circular heap of flames clinging to the fabric.

Isaac deposits me on the sharp grass.

"Nova?" His fingers brush the hair away from my face. "Are you alright?"

The fresh air is like swallowing ice cubes. My lungs spasm. I cough out the smoke and inhale the sweet smell of the ground, the living grass, and the humidity from the surrounding trees. Gazing up at the sky, the sight of the stars settles me and the coughing fades.

Maybe that's what Hoomstid meant by looking to the night. It eases me.

"Are you alright?" Isaac leans over me, raking his terrified gaze across my body.

"I told you," I say between breaths, "I'm not a ghost."

He doesn't laugh. "How did the fire start? What happened?"

I cough again. And grin.

I got out of his damned cottage, that's what happened.

Servants pour from the house with buckets and bowls, cook pots, and anything else that will carry water, but it's already too late. The cottage blazes like an angry fist shaking at the sky. The scorching heat keeps the servants and their buckets of well water, assembly-lined from the stables, too far back to be effective. They may as well be spitting on the fire as it gobbles the cottage. The smoke twists into the sky, painting the estate a smelly shade of sooty black.

Panic and chaos streams around us as the servants turn their efforts to safeguarding the backside of the mansion. They douse the wood porch and house brick with their buckets of water, but there is no wind to brush the blaze toward the main house. The flames shoot straight up and the embers rain straight down.

Isaac doesn't even glance back at the destruction I caused, until I am sitting up. He sits beside me, an arm stretched out behind me, supporting my back and shoulders. We stare together at the servants rushing around the burning cottage as if we're watching fireworks on the fourth of July, instead of a house fire that is entirely my fault.

"How did it start?" he asks. I roll my tongue in my cheek.

"It started when you locked me up," I say. Someone else might feel regret for ruining his cottage, but any guilt I may have felt burned away the moment Isaac hid the windows and door from me.

He turns to look at me, but I don't give him my gaze. "You did this?"

"Sure did," I say. "I buttered a pillow case and threw a candle right on top."

I ignore his hard stare.

"Do you realize how dangerous that was?" he says from between his teeth.

"Oh yeah," I nod. "But you can't kill a ghost."

I cough for impact.

His scoff rolls off my cheek.

I peer up, through the stringy clouds of smoke, at the stars. I imagine each twinkle as silent applause.

We stay seated on the lawn until the flames eventually die, along with the rest of Isaac's cottage. The charred beams that remain upright, stand like eerie bodies burnt at the stake. The air thickens with the sour scent of ruin. Servants file past us, dumping buckets of water on the foundation. The remaining piles of strobo-scope embers die, extinguished in an angry hiss of steam.

Hoomstid lugs a full bucket past us and on his return trip, he stops beside Isaac. "Sir, would you like me to prepare a room inside for our guest?"

"Where else would you put her? I won't have her sleep in the barn!" Isaac snaps as one of the last upright beams surrenders and collapses in the ash. A plume of soot shoots into the air. Isaac rubs his jaw. "Have the things I acquired for her placed in my room. She will sleep with me."

"Over my dead body," I say. Ironic and punny, but also bluntly accurate. "I will not sleep beside you or *with* you. If you think burning down your cottage is harsh, try locking me in your bedroom."

"It's a very large room, miss," Hoomstid worries the bucket

handle nervously in his palms. His forehead eye blinks, the eye on his cheek stares. I'm not sure which I should be looking at. "The footage of the bed chamber is larger than the cottage."

"Do as I tell you and don't forget who you serve," Isaac snarls at the servant. "Her wishes are none of your concern."

"Yes sir." An awkward grin freezes beneath Hoomstid's skewed eyes as he thrusts a leg behind himself. He drops into a jerky curtsey, drags himself out of it, and scurries off to disappear through the back door of the mansion.

I pull away from Isaac and get to my feet. If I could run for the lot line, I would, but I'd have to dodge two dozen servants to make it. Fat chance. Instead, I plant my feet and stare down my nose at him. "If you think—"

He startles me by jumping to his feet and meeting me toe-to-toe.

"You've burnt down my cottage and the sigils on the walls that protected you." The strain of his patience tightens every word.

"The graffiti? You're sure about that?" I scoff, but maybe I was wrong about the marks. Wouldn't that be a blast of bad luck. "Those marks weren't there to hide the windows and doors?"

"They were absolutely there to hide the windows and doors! Machara used the sigils to spell the cottage at my request. The exits were hidden so no one could get into the cottage unless they knew the correct sequence of sigils."

Uh huh. I narrow my eyes. "And so no one could get out."

"There was an emergency egress in the water closet, if you had looked. All you needed to do was pull down the ladder behind the commode," he says. "I didn't mention it because I wanted you to settle down and hear what I have to tell you. There's a lot you need to know, but you battle me at every turn and refuse to listen."

Well…rats.

Despite how many times Isaac proves me wrong, it never occurs to me that maybe I ought to give him a chance. That maybe being a vampire doesn't automatically mean he's a liar.

Except that thing about me being a ghost.

A trusted vampire. Ha. Two things that don't seem to go together.

I remember what Hoomstid said about me being something more than what Isaac tells me I am. Isaac said I am a ghost. Maybe Hoomstid meant I shouldn't let Isaac play mind games; that I should not doubt my humanness.

Or maybe Isaac is trying to protect me from Hoomstid?

"You don't trust your servants to stay out of the cottage?" I ask.

Isaac scoffs. "Of course not. My servants are mostly steadfast."

"Mostly, but not completely."

"Well," his grin is sheepish, "most are loyal to me because I've had to drink from them. That tends to create some jealousies that are beyond my control. Not one of them would harm me, but there have been incidences between them at times.

"So only most of your servants are trustworthy because you've drank their blood."

"All of them are trustworthy, or they wouldn't be here. Some servants are faithful to me because I saved them from exile, others because I've proven myself worthy of their devotion."

"Then who are you trying to keep out of the cottage?"

"The most dangerously competitive creatures that exist," he growls. "The Brethren."

3 3

"You have brothers?"

"No." He lowers his voice as a maid, the younger woman who had been hanging clothes with her mother the first night I appeared at the estate, passes by us. She scowls at me, her emptied bucket banging against her leg. Isaac flicks his chin for her to keep moving and she scowls at him before moving along. I guess I've lost any hope of a fan club among the servants. Isaac doesn't continue until she's out of earshot. "The Brethren are nothing like *brothers*. The Brethren began as a hoard of male vampires, but in time, females joined the colony too."

"So there is some sibling rivalry?" I lift my hands in the air. "Why are you so worried about them getting into your cottage?"

"Oh no...I *worry* about them discovering my estate, despite all the spells and precautions I have taken to hide my home." He takes my hand, encasing my one between his two. "But I am *paralyzed* by the thought of the Brethren getting into the cottage, because that was my safe house, for myself and my true mate.

"I told you, vampires are the most competitive creatures in existence. My estate is not unique; every vampire's estate is charmed, spelled, illusional and anything else we can think of to hide our dwellings from one another. If one of them located this estate, they wouldn't hesitate to kill me, simply to take control of what is mine. Luckily, I am the newest vampire to the Brethren, so rising up in the hierarchy isn't one of their motives. But there are plenty more. The worst is if they knew I had found my true mate. It would instill fervor."

"Good thing you haven't," I say and he smirks.

"If you were," he says, "they would all want you, because it would destroy me. They would desire you, simply because they would want you to desire *them*. For a true mate to choose another, other than their true match, is the ultimate victory for a vampire. The Brethren would rather add you to their addicted collection of *cups,* than an existence of satisfaction, which they cannot obtain for themselves."

"But I'm not your true mate," I say.

He flashes me a pained grin. "I apologize, but what I believe is the only thing that matters to them and I do believe it, Nova."

"Even if it's going to get you killed? I'm telling you, I'm not the one. I would know it if I was. I'm sure I would feel something, and I'm sorry, but I don't."

"Be that as it may, situations often change," he says. I only let his stubbornness go because he's not smug with it, but at some point he's going to have to accept that I'm not 'in it to win it'. Right now isn't that moment, though. Isaac's tone grows darker and more anxious as he continues. "I know they will do everything in their power to steal you from me, once they know I've found you. Upon meeting you, they will each try to charm you away, and when it doesn't work, they will search for our estate."

I don't bother to tell him that they can't steal what isn't his, or that he shouldn't be worried at all, because I don't want *any* vampire. Hard stop on that.

"The hunt will become a priority," he adds darkly.

"I need to cross that ditch out front and go back to where I came from, and you need to leave me out of this," I tell him. "Quit saying I'm *the one*, because I'm not, Isaac. Even if I was, then you should have brains enough to shut up about it, if saying it could get me killed."

"I'm sorry, but I don't have any control over this," he says and from the brutal sorrow on his face, I almost believe him. "Males have to claim their true mate. We must announce it, so that other males in their colony don't kill a true mated female accidentally."

"But they can steal her?" My voice climbs in my throat. This whole thing is insanity. "How is that any better?"

"True mated females are symbols of status among males. Stealing her away bests another male, but whenever males are fighting over a female, it will turn violent. That is why the law was created. A male cannot rob another male by killing what he cannot have. When that has happened, all the vampires turn on the murderer and kill him. It is a risk I've never been willing to take.

"That's why I employed Machara and her skills with magic. She made the cottage into the fortress I required. In the event of an attack, those cottage walls could not have been destroyed or breached." He looks back at me with a grin so dry, he should be spitting dust. "Unfortunately, I overlooked the possibility of a fire intentionally set from the inside, that was my fault. Machara did a brilliant job otherwise."

"You addicted that woman, so she'd do anything you asked," I say. A male servant walking by stares at me, his bucket sloshing water down his leg. His stare is strange and intense. Angry, almost. He doesn't seem to notice his pants, soaked all the way down and into his shoes.

"I paid her," Isaac corrects in a sharp whisper, pulling my gaze away from the servant. "My attention and my venom were the payments she demanded, in exchange for the spells and blood I required. Magic does not come cheap, and luckily I had something to barter."

"Come on, Isaac! She was in love with you!"

His eyes scan the back yard and he keeps his voice low, our

conversation as private as it can be. "She may have been, but I was honest with her from the start. I told her she was not my true mate. She may have believed I would change my mind once I witnessed all of her talents, but I never once encouraged that belief."

"You're a saint!" I laugh. "You said yourself that your venom is addictive, and your attention is what the addicted crave, so why wouldn't she fall in love with you and do whatever you asked?"

"She was a lonely woman," he insists, "and she begged for the illusion of a true mate, so I gave it to her. She knew my venom was addictive and she was aware that she would be sent to a rehabilitative facility when our agreement ended! Our agreement was fair. I never asked Machara for one thing more than what we originally agreed upon. Not for extra spells or added charms, and I never once asked her to fall in love with me."

"You are either incredibly stupid, or ridiculously arrogant."

"It was an agreement!" he snarls, throwing his hands in the air.

"Stupid it is, then," I snap.

The servants swiftly halt all around us. I glance up, and then circulate my gaze through the staggered lot of Isaac's employ. Every eye is tacked to me. A woman pours her water out on the ground and throws her bucket down in the puddle. It splashes over the hem of her dress, but she never stops glaring at me. I guess I insulted their master, lord, sir—or whatever they call Isaac—a little too loudly. I stand at the prickly, center pit of them and panic wriggles down my back, but I will not let them see me cower.

There is just something about backing down that doesn't work for me at all.

I turn back to Isaac and narrow my eyes. "I guess all that time and effort addicting Machara was for nothing, since I wrecked the cottage."

"You certainly did." He agrees with a tranquil nod, crushing his top lip with the bottom. He leans in close, his breath stirring my hair as he murmurs in my ear, "Remain close to me, so that I can keep you safe."

I turn my face to his. "You said the Brethren don't know about me yet."

His hooded gaze takes in the servants, standing like statues all around us. He wraps his fingers around my upper arm and his grip is firm as he tugs me in the direction of the mansion's back door.

I jerk my arm loose, but keep walking, because the servants are still all silent and creepily rooted in place. Each one of them watches me go, and I am not given one nod, or smile, or even a vague, overt glance of sympathy. Their expressions are unanimously blank and teeter on a mysterious ferocity I don't understand.

"The Brethren don't know about you," Isaac murmurs as he falls into step beside me, "but the servants do, and as I've told you, they can be a jealous lot."

We go through the back door, into the safety of the mansion kitchen. I'm relieved when the servants' bustling begins again and no one follows us inside.

A matronly maid—when I can focus, I realize she's the older of the two maids who had been at the clothesline—kneads bread dough on a broad, chopping block island in the center of the kitchen. Pots bubble on the stovetop behind her, the steamy scent of boiling ham permeating the room. Graying strands of hair have escaped her baker's hat near her temples, and are plastered across her forehead as if they've been marinated in sweat and swiped sideways with her forearm.

The woman pauses the moment I come through the back door. Her eyes narrow as if I'm an intruder, but then, Isaac walks in behind me and his presence instantly douses her fiery disapproval. The wrinkles around her eyes smooth out at the sight of him and her eyes glimmer.

"Good day, sir." Her smile is sweet and welcoming. And completely aimed at him. I'm not sure she remembers I'm standing beside him, the same way I felt when I saw Isaac's pre-wedding photograph.

"Good day, Esther." His chuckle is short and wooden, as if the last thing in the world he wants to do is to be stuck yacking with the maid.

Esther, on the other hand, continues to bloom in his presence. She scrubs her doughy hands down the front of her apron and runs floured fingers over her sweaty forehead, grimacing as she skims the wayward strands. Her frown really brings out her jowls. She scrambles to brush the hair back into place, but only manages to smear flour everywhere she touches. In mere seconds of frantic grooming, she's coated herself like a gummy chicken leg.

"Excuse my appearance, sir," she trills. "I'm making bread for sandwiches, since everyone will be wanting a hearty lunch after extinguishing the cottage fire."

"Very thoughtful," Isaac says with another wooden chuckle.

Esther glows with the mild praise.

"Lunch?" I ask, glancing out the back door. "The stars are still out."

Turning back toward Esther, I can see my awareness is not appreciated.

"The stars are always out," she says. Her scowl enhances the jowls too. "That's the way Mister Havrath prefers it, and I agree with him. Darkness makes the heart grow fonder."

I have no idea what that means. From the look on Isaac's face, he does, and he's becomes all the more intent on getting away from the maid.

"Keep up the good work, Esther," he says and this time, he clasps my elbow and steers me toward the door leading out of the kitchen.

"You'll be entertaining in the parlor, sir?" Esther asks, skittering along parallel to us, on the opposite side of the island.

"No," is all Isaac says.

"The sitting room, then?" she chirps.

"Not today," he says.

"Maybe some tea on the front porch?"

Isaac reaches past me, sliding the swinging door open with his palm. "No," he says as I walk through.

"I could bring something to the dining room for you?" Esther's high, hopeful question is met with a final, *no,* as Isaac lets the door swing closed behind us.

His fingers remain on my elbow and the mansion's front door is straight ahead of us. I can see it is also locked up tight. Bolting through a window seems extreme, and just as impossible as getting the front door unlocked with enough time left to escape.

"That maid is one of your *cups*, isn't she?" I ask, stalling as I scour the hall for another exit. There are doors that lead who-knows-where and not worth the risk.

"She was," Isaac answers as he leads me to the base of the staircase, "a very long time ago."

"And she's still that attentive?" I pull my elbow from his palm, pausing at the bottom of the stairs. "How long does the addiction last?"

He grimaces. "Esther is not addicted. She's obsessed. She hasn't been my *cup* in over seventy years."

"Seventy?" I look back at the swinging door to the kitchen. The maid was older, but not that old. Maybe mid-fifties, tops.

"She's a revenant," Isaac explains, flicking his chin at the staircase to coax me forward. I don't move. "Remember, I told you that revenants don't age? Not like humans, at least. Revenants reach about twenty-five years of age and stop aging, unless the body they chose was older when they took it. Then they stay that age."

"She's middle aged forever? No wonder she's so cranky!" It's all so weird, I laugh louder than I should and throw a hand over my mouth to stifle it.

Isaac's fingertips return to my elbow and urge me up the steps. This time, I go, but plodding upward as slowly as I can. Everything about going to a vampire's bedroom suite is a bad idea, but I don't have a lot of choices. At least, not right now. I also think that if I'm nice to Isaac, and can get him to relax around me and trust me a little, more opportunities for an easier escape will come my way.

We reach the second floor and Isaac steers me to the right, down a long, wide hallway with white walls, black doors, flower vases on narrow, white tables, and black and white pictures displayed in charcoal frames. A burgundy runner leads to a huge, leaded glass window at the very end. The window is a clear glass with black threads of intricate designs that cast moonlit shadows of filigree roses on the floor.

Isaac stops at the door in the center of the hall; the last door on the left from what I can see. His hand on the knob, I reach for his arm. He pauses, turning to me with a questioning brow.

"You make deals…" I say. "Compromises."

His brow rises a bit more as he turns to me. He clasps his hands in front of himself. "Sometimes I do."

I let my fingers slide off his arm and back to my side. "I want you to promise…I don't want you to enchant me."

"How do you mean?" His smirk stands at the crossroads of curious and smug. At least, that's how I interpret it.

"You know…I don't want you to put me under any vampire spells. I've seen the movies. Probably all of them. I know what vampires do." It's the truth. That's all I did while Meg was away at school—I waited for her to come home, and I watched movies.

"Vampire spells?" he scoffs. "Who told you that? There is no such thing! Vampires have skills, but we are not magical."

His amusement annoys me. "Vampires hypnotize people and seduce them. If I'm going to like you at all, Isaac, it has to be real. I have to be able to trust you. No tricks or spells."

"If I could hypnotize anyone, I'd have hypnotized every single *cup* I've ever had, so they would forget I've drunk from them! That could've saved me a lot of bother! Let's go in and talk about this." He turns back to the door, twists the knob and walks into his softly lit bed chamber. I inch in slowly, staying close to the door, even as he closes and locks it.

I stand against the side wall and peer into the sprawling room. It is lit from end to end with dozens of candles, though the air smells fresh and crisp, as if a window is open and a steady breeze is sifting through it.

A dining table and serving area occupies the far left of the suite; a sitting room spread across the center of the suite, followed with a bathing area—a claw-foot tub resting beneath a giant, circular, stained-glass window, and, on the far right of the room contains an enormous bed stands on a high platform. The bed itself is thick; I would guess there are at least two mattresses on the frame. The four posts surrounding the bed are carved mahogany, each one as shapely as a belly dancer, but also as tall and solid as bodyguards.

I stand there, gaping like a yokel, as Isaac melts into the room with the ease of a man who is used to wealth and luxury. He takes a seat on one of the settees in the sitting area, and continues our conversation, as if walking into his palatial bed chamber wouldn't temporarily stun me.

"Now, the seduction that you were talking about…that's different," he says, settling back against the upholstery with a sigh. He crosses his legs as if we're in a business meeting. His gaze could puncture a manhole cover. "Vampires are masters of attraction, but to think of seduction as a spell is an insult. It would be far more accurate to say we are naturally skilled.

"Consider this: beauty is the mark of a vampire, and who isn't attracted to beauty?" He picks lint from the knee of his pants and releases it into the air. "Beautiful people are always favored, that's no secret, and vampires were given the gift of eternal beauty. Can you imagine being thousands of years old *and looking it*? What a dismal existence that would be!

"Along with beauty, another 'secret of seduction' is something that's accessible to everyone: confidence." He lays two fingers on his temple, his thumb on his jaw. The candlelight enhances the shadows that settle beneath his cheekbones. "It's not magic. Confidence is an unavoidable condition, especially when you're nearly indestructible and have been alive for hundreds or thousands of years. Confidence is what happens in the absence of fear. There's nothing that can harm us and when you have lived a hundred years, you realize that there's not an opportunity that won't come twice, let alone a thousand times. There is always more money to be had. There are billions of gorgeous *cups,* and more born every day. And that sort of knowledge leads not only to confidence but to the last facet of a vampire's unparalleled ability to attract who and what we want.

"Patterns," he says simply, lifting the two fingers from his temple. His pupils are wide and dark in the soft light and his sharp angles muted. The vision of his innocence could easily be mistaken as that of an angel.

"People live by patterns," he goes on, "and after hundreds of years of observing those patterns, identifying them is simple. In fact, ignoring them becomes impossible.

"Sometimes I wish I could. It makes life dull, you know, being able to anticipate every single thing that is to come. There is no excitement, no suspense anymore. No thrill of the chase left.

"I know every single pattern of a woman's interest. When they will giggle, when they will laugh, when they will twirl their hair, when they want me to kiss them. I know the patterns of men too. The patterns may vary, but there are no surprises anymore. It is maddening sometimes, how easy it is to seduce a *cup.* There is no challenge to it at all.

"I have more understanding for the older vamps. They often turn to perversions not because they are perverse, but because they crave the surprise and the shock and the revelation again. But the perversions aren't unique. They have obvious patterns too and it doesn't take long before they become as dull and predictable as everything else."

He tips his head to the side and the light spills into the hollows of his neck, shadows lost in the muscle. "Can you understand why vampires are considered odd? We are categorized as manipulators, but how do we ignore the patterns when that's all we can see? And how do you deny humans or revenants what they beg for?"

I'm watching his lips form the words and suddenly, I don't know any of the answers either. Isaac smiles and my tongue sticks to the roof of my mouth. I realize my lips have been hanging open and it breaks the spell.

He smiles again as if he knows exactly what he's doing.

"That," I say. "Don't do that to me anymore."

He gets to his feet and crosses the room to the serving area. He takes out a bottle from a low cupboard and pours honey-colored alcohol in two stout glasses, dropping in ice from the bucket with a clink and splash. He carries the glasses back to the settee and places them on the coffee table.

"Come sit with me." He invites me with a flourish of his hand toward the alcohol. "What else would you like to know?"

"I want to know why it never gets brighter than twilight on your estate."

"When you build a house, don't you want to feel at home in it? It would've done me little good to live in a place where I couldn't go out of doors whenever I please."

"So you *are* afraid of the sunlight?" I ask, taking a seat on the opposite settee and sitting back on the cushions.

"I'm not *afraid* of anything," he corrects me with an amused grin. "But the sun is highly uncomfortable, so I prefer the darkness."

I'm about to ask if the sun can damage him, when I think of a better question.

"I want to know what the Sunshine Vial is," I say.

He pauses, staring at me as he lightly rolls his jaw. From his deadened expression, maybe I shouldn't have asked after all. I bite the inside of my cheek.

"How did you hear about that, I wonder?" he asks sweetly and the sparkle in his eyes makes me want to gush everything I know.

"There was a book at the museum with a colored drawing of it. It's a tube, with sparkling, yellow liquid in it, right? The Curator said the book was included in the donation pieces that came with the wedding gown."

Isaac tucks his chin. "Ah, yes."

I am able to breathe only when his shoulders relax and he smoothes one hand down the top of his thigh. Isaac latches an ankle over his knee, reclining across from me.

"I did own a book of children's fairy tales once," he squints at the far wall, past my shoulder. "Now that I think of it, I do believe one of the stories in that book was titled, *The Myth of the Sunshine Vial*. Surely, that old rag isn't the one this curator is studying? It was just a collection of nonsensical children's stories, given to me by my mother to lull me off to dreams at night!"

"What was the story about?"

"The myth was something about a deity whose essence was captured in a vial, or something like that. As if a deity would ever be so foolish!" Isaac chuckles.

A myth. *Huh.*

As mythical as the vampire sitting across from me?

Isaac surprises me by continuing on. "I shouldn't be surprised that the book wasn't tossed in the rubbish. Many Revenants believe that the fables are true. Some even say the vampires have possessed the Sunshine Vial for decades, and are holding it for valuable trade."

I don't miss the way his gaze scans me like a lie detector. I try not to move a muscle, try to keep my expression smooth, as if I'm guilty of knowing something I shouldn't.

"Others," he continues, "myself included, say the vial never existed, except within pages of fairy tale books. Some say it's real, but it's been lost forever."

"Wouldn't you know if the vampires have it?"

"I would never know unless *I* was the one who had it. Vampires aren't family. They're not friends. They don't share secrets without one of two things: advantage or bloodshed." Isaac leans forward and lifts a glass, the ice tinkling as he takes a swallow. "I've answered your question. Now let's talk about what you don't want to discuss."

"I don't have anything to hide," I insist, "but we need to make a deal first."

The only thing I won't talk about is Meg, but he doesn't need to know that. Stroke of luck to have the low table between us. If he thinks about sinking his teeth into me, I'll overturn the table and stake him with one of the legs.

"Another compromise?" His soft laugh is as welcoming as the scent of bread through an open window. He replaces the glass on the table between us.

"I don't want to stay here. I'll tell you what you want to know, on the condition I can go home when we're done."

He considers it a moment, the shadows of his eyelashes fanned out upon his cheek like dark, exotic feathers.

"Alright, I agree," he says, chin down, his eyes shifting upward to meet mine. "I agree, as long as you are completely honest with your answers."

"Deal," I say. The ice cubes shift with a soft *tink* in the drinks.

"Let's drink on it." He leans forward, pushing one of the glasses across the coffee table toward me. Condensation leaves a wet streak behind.

I don't reach for the glass. "No thanks. I don't drink."

"No?" He grins, chin angling to the side. "Why's that?"

I shrug. "I just don't. I'm not old enough."

"I see." He picks up his own glass, swirling the liquid, his gaze intense. "Exactly how old are you?"

My mouth opens, closes. "Seventeen or eighteen."

"You're sure about that?"

"No." I lift my chin. "I don't remember. I told you—"

"Yes, you said it was a brain injury," he finishes.

And now I know what he really wants to talk about. Big surprise when he says, "Do you want to talk about why you can't remember?"

I roll my eyes. Hard. "This again? The ghost thing?"

"When was the last time you had something to eat?" Isaac asks.

"This morning," I say, but when I trace my short memory, I can't remember eating anything.

I think about the last time I've eaten anything. Ever. Meg used to make eggs…I don't know that I ever had any. The night we had boiled hot dogs and Uncle Leonard made Meg wash the paper plates…I sat at the table, but I don't remember putting anything in my mouth. There were only two plates that turned to mush in the water.

Not that it means much. My memory is Swiss cheese at best, with blackout blocks that rarely stack together in a solid sequence of events.

There must have been dozens of breakfast, lunches, and dinners, but I can't remember one. Aunt Dena gobbling casserole before heading off to her third shift. Uncle Leonard eating tuna from the can with his fingers. Meg sharing bags of chips with Murray. I don't remember putting one morsel in my mouth.

My spine turns into a long, tight nerve of panic and Isaac's question strums it with one solid *twang*.

When have I felt hungry?

I grab the glass of booze off the table in front of me and hold it up beside my lips with my own smug smirk.

Isaac quirks a brow. Waits.

I put the drink back down on the table. "I can move things. Ghosts can't do that."

"It's easy enough to prove if you're not," he says. "Take a drink."

"How do I know you didn't put something in it?"

"I didn't," he says simply. He reaches out, lifts the glass, and tosses back the contents. He sets the empty glass back on the table with a grimace.

"Your turn."

"I thought vampires only drink blood," I say.

"One of many myths," Isaac says. "I enjoy whiskey from time to time. Maybe because many of the *cups* had the taste of it in their veins and the taste is familiar, I don't know. I am able to eat as humans do, but I prefer not to. The taste is uniformly either bland, sour, or rotted, or a mixture of all three. Blood varies from *cup* to *cup,* but even a terrible *cup* tastes like ambrosia compared to *food.* Blood nourishes me and I crave it above any other food."

"Animal blood too?"

A short nod. "If I must. Choosing between animal blood and human blood would be like choosing between eating a handful of meal worms or a feast of my mother's home cooking. But I digress," he says, waving his index finger to indicate the drink in front of me. "I drank mine."

I shake my head. "I told you—"

"Yes, Nova, you told me and told me. I don't mean to offend you, but you're being a bit of a coward." He smiles devilishly.

I pick up the glass and toss the whiskey across the table, at his face.

What a stupid thing to do...especially to a vampire.

He jumps to his feet, grabbing my wrist before I have a chance to withdraw it. The glass tumbles from my grip and hits the table with a *crack*. Isaac yanks my hand down, throwing me off balance. I plant my knee on the coffee table to steady myself, but it only helps the vampire to draw me closer.

His wet face is an inch from mine. I breathe him in, alcohol drizzled on metal.

"Would you let me kiss you?" he whispers, but doesn't wait for my answer. He tugs my hand down again and we collide, his mouth on mine. The whiskey flavor is on his lips. I should try harder to pull away, but don't. His fingertips glide up the back of my arm. He grips my shoulder softly, coaxing me toward him.

I hate to admit it, but this kiss isn't the worst thing that's ever happened to me. Far from it.

I shouldn't be pleased with the small, pleading groan that escapes his throat either, but I am.

I don't fight it when he drags me across the table and into his lap. My legs fit on either side of his hips.

He was lying about hypnotization. His kiss pulls feelings from me that I'm not sure he's earned, but I still respond to them. I slide my arms around his neck. I open my mouth to him. The only thought I can keep in my head is the sensual movement of his lips against mine.

His arms, wrapped around my waist, haul me even closer. My stomach quivers, adrenaline replacing blood. He holds me as if he is incapable of letting go.

My heart races. It has no clue that it's being pan-fried and shoveled straight into Satan's jaws. Heavens help me. I suck his bottom lip between my teeth and run my tongue along the velvet skin.

He groans as I release it.

And then he bites me.

One fang pierces the edge of my bottom lip. I shriek and he releases. My skin is pulled up slightly as the fang slips out and I scramble off his lap, holding my mouth, already tasting the blood on my tongue. I can feel it oozing in a warm stream down my chin.

"What did you do that for?" I keep my fingers over the wound, but I can't tell if his fang went all the way through my lip or not.

Concern etches lines across his forehead.

"Look at your hand," he says. He reaches for me and I back away.

I pull my fingers from the escaping ooze at the corner of my mouth and peer down at my fingers. There is no blood on them. I wipe my chin, feel the wetness on my fingertips, but when I look again, there is no blood.

"Notice anything?" he says.

"You bit me!"

"And there is no blood."

"Drop the ghost fetish already! All the blood is in my mouth! I can taste it!" I shout at him, the salty taste welling on my tongue at the mention.

"The main difference between a ghost and a revenant or human is that they have no blood," he says evenly.

"Ghosts don't have feet or feelings either, but I have both!

They don't breathe, and look, Isaac!" I inhale so hard my nostrils are sucked in with my breath. "I'm breathing! A ghost couldn't kiss you, or feel pain, or talk to people, or—"

"Why not?" he says. "Why would you think that?"

"Because they're *ghosts,* Isaac!"

He taps his temple. "This is the problem. Humans make up all sorts of fantastic myths, and then, they believe them. They spread the myths around and everyone believes it too. Of course ghosts have feet, and feelings, and breathe. Ghosts are living beings! They passed out of one existence and into another, but they are alive all the same. You are fully living, just in your own bit of time and space."

"The point of a ghost is that it doesn't have a body. Because it just died and left its body. I have a body." My forearms are clammy talking about death.

"I am still Isaac, whether or not I am living outside the conventions of a certain existence. You will always be you, and you will always recognize and interpret yourself, as a whole being. You have the *senses* of life force, even if you don't have all the components of it—like blood. The thing you're missing is that you are co-existing within the human world, behind a thick veil. You can see everyone, but not everyone can see you."

"Everyone sees me!"

"You haven't noticed how they interact with you? Or, more specifically, how they don't?"

I shrug. "I haven't noticed."

"A gorgeous girl, with no memory, who no one notices—"

"People notice me," I say. "My cousin talks to me all the time. Her boyfriend can't stand me. My uncle..." The last two might prefer not talking to me, but they do when they have to.

I don't dwell on it, but I am extremely aware of how people often ignore me in obvious and strange ways. They walk around me, look right through me, ignore me when I talk. I figured it was this town, these people, the strangeness of someone with brain trauma, the tragedy of my parents, something to do with being a teenager. There are a dozen reasons more reasonable than being a ghost. I've just learned to ignore it.

The one who bothers me most is Aunt Dena. She never speaks to me, never looks at me, never acknowledges me. But she's always tired from work and seems to save her conversations for yelling at Uncle Leonard and lecturing Meg. I've always assumed she resented having another mouth to feed, since she can barely keep up with the ones she has.

Isaac rubs his upper lip. "Do any of these people who converse with you happen to suffer from alcohol or drug addictions, by chance?"

I open my mouth and close it.

All of them.

When I don't snipe him with an answer, Isaac lowers his chin as if he's proven his point.

"How about conversations with normal, everyday people? People without addictions? Has that ever happened?" He looks up at me without lifting his jaw.

Staring at him, I work to ignore the soft shadows that paint him into a god, and decide that the kiss we shared wasn't that good after all. And then I remember.

"I talk all the time with the museum's curator. She was the one who told me all about the exhibit and the legend of the gown and you—"

"She's an expert?" His long fingers cup his chin.

"Yes, she is! She's a savant!" I jab a finger in the air triumphantly.

"She has altered brain function, then," he drawls. "People whose minds are altered due to substances, mental illness, or unusual brain chemistry, are much more likely to see you."

I knot my arms over my chest. "You see me just fine. All your servants talk to me."

"Death tends to alter the brain chemistry," he says. "Vampires, revenants, and the magical are all aware of ghosts."

"I have skin."

"You feel an essence of skin, but what you are is pure energy, Nova. Would you like proof?"

"Sure," I whisper, but I don't need it.

Vampire Isaac is insane.

I saac lunges forward, capturing my arm. He lifts it to his mouth, holding tight so I can't jerk away and his fangs extend, sliding down from his gums.

"What are you doing?" I yank back in panic, but I'm not quick enough. Isaac rakes his fangs across my skin, splitting open my forearm.

Pain spears through me and I squeeze my eyes shut. I feel the muscle, and fat bulging from the split skin, the blood stinging as it pours out of me and drizzles down my fingers.

"Look!" He gives my arm a shake and I envision blood spattering on the floor, the settee. "Open your eyes!"

"I don't want to see it!" I cry. I'm not going to watch myself bleed out.

"You're imagining what isn't even there." His scolding is soft, calm. "You need to see this! The wound is going to close in a few minutes, and we'll have to do it again if you don't see it."

I force my eyes open, expecting to be tricked into a sick game.

There is no blood. With my lip, I couldn't see it, but I could taste it. I peer down into the bloodless slit Isaac's made in my arm. There is no fat, muscle, or bone inside the open wound.

Beneath my skin, there is a thick, opal fog that looks like soft, pearlescent meringue. I run my finger alongside the wound and wince.

"If you don't expect pain, it won't be painful," he says softly.

Staring into the bizarre wound, it's not hard to let my curiosity overtake my expectation of discomfort. The moment I do, the sensation of pain dissolves. The skin begins to knit together slowly at both ends of the wound, the skin reaching over the open split, coming together and healing, closing up the laces of a football. Before the center closes, I stick a finger into the wound and wiggle it. I feel the strange sensation of squirming inside the space, but there is no pain. Until I think there should be. Then, I yank my finger out and grip my arm as the wound seals itself shut. The angry tingle makes me grimace.

Isaac fingertips glide down my opposite arm. They feel like feathers and raise goose bumps on my skin. The pain of the wound is instantly replaced.

"You see? When you focus your attention, your senses rise to your expectations," he says. "You're alive, just not in the way that you thought."

One of his fangs drips. I hold my healed arm close to my chest, my gaze bolting from his sharp incisors to his dark eyes.

"You're not going to drain my soul," I say. I'm not about to volunteer to be his groceries.

"Of course not!" He laughs. "I don't drink *souls*. I drink blood."

"And you've proven I don't have any, so why are your fangs still out?"

"I can't help it," he says, closing his eyes. His brow furrows and with a pained grunt, the fangs begin to retract, sliding up centimeter by centimeter. So, he can help it. Once the fangs are completely withdrawn, his eyes flutter open. "Your spirit emits a scent that still sparks every avenue of my desire. I look forward to the moment I ignite your desire in the same way."

"Nah," I say dropping one of his trademark smirks on him, "I'm not weak like that."

He strokes his jaw between his fingertip and thumb. "You are right, Nova," he says. "I am the weak one. You are my weakness and vulnerability is dangerous. Truthfully, I crave you a hundred times more than Miss Milligen ever craved my venom. You considered me a monster for making the agreement I did with Miss Milligen, but I was particularly empathetic and did not take advantage where I could have, because I understand unsatisfied desire. I felt it every second that I waited, throughout these decades past, for you to come to me."

"What about Silvia?" I ask. "Did your bride-to-be know you were waiting for me?"

"Silvia was your best friend, so she was heartbroken when she learned that we'd fallen in love."

"My best friend? And I did that to her?" I sink down on the edge of the settee. My soul weighs more than the world. I don't want to believe it, but truth tingles inside me.

"This is not an easy tale to tell." Isaac rakes his fingers through his hair. "Who...no, *what* we are now...began with my wedding."

A quiver laces up my spine. This is the truth. *The scary truth,* is what that quiver says.

"I want to know everything," I say as evenly as I can, which isn't the slightest bit even. "Tell me all of it."

"Alright." Isaac tugs up his pant legs over his knees and lowers himself down beside me, pressing his spine against the high back of the settee. "When I came of age to marry, my parents urged me to find a wife and start a family. There weren't any young women in my community that interested me, so there wasn't much hope of me marrying, unless I settled for one of them. But one day, a traveling carpenter came to town and offered my father his services. My father commissioned the man to build a proper pulpit, alter, and pews that would replace the split log benches we'd been using.

"Alexandru Pantazis was a skilled carpenter with no mind for sums, but his daughter did, so he brought her along. Silvia was smart and pretty and didn't shrink from hard work, assisting her father in every way she could. I was young enough to think those qualities were all I needed to be happy with making Silvia my wife.

"Within a few weeks, my parents saw how well Silvia and I were getting along and encouraged me to consider marriage. Silvia's parents were god-fearing people, so they were quite pleased with the perspective match to a pastor's son. Both sets of parents pressed for an engagement. I liked Silvia and did not want to disappoint anyone.

He exhales, long and slow, staring up at the ceiling. "Everything was running on schedule until about two months before the wedding, when Silvia insisted I meet you. It was important to her that I get along with her best friend and I agreed.

"I expected a farmer's daughter, or a girl who giggled behind a blush, but Silvia did not prepare me for your beauty and grace. I will never forget my first glimpse of you. It was at twilight, and the two of you walked through the field, the pollen still thick in the air, flowers tucked in your hair. You were a vision, laughing together, and the sound of it came on the wind to me, like the music of birds. I never intended it, Nova, but it happened all the same. I was instantly enchanted with you. You talk about hypnotization—you are the one who was guilty of taking me under your spell. No man could've resisted you. You were a…" He shakes his head, looking away shamefully as the words drift. "A beauty. Like no other."

I feel the bloodless blush creep into my cheeks. Not at the flattery, but because that moment led to me betraying my best friend.

He sucks his bottom lip between his straight, white teeth and releases it, licking his full, perfect lip. "I hated it, but Silvia just couldn't compare. I never faulted her for it, but I couldn't help that I wanted you so much more. I knew the problems my weakness would cause for everyone and I was embarrassed by it, but I still couldn't help myself."

He sits beside me, pressing back against the settee. "If a strand of your hair fell from your braid…there was only so long I could admire the color of it, how the sun played on it, before I craved the right to be the man who would tuck it behind your ear." He smiles, his gaze, distant and blissful. "You tortured me with your presence. I suddenly knew what it was like to want a woman, to truly want her, and the timing couldn't have been worse. I was committed to wedding someone else; your best friend, no less. The more I saw you, the less I could think of anyone but you.

"I counted the days when you would be coming with Silvia to see me—well, not me, but that's the way I preferred to think of it. And when you couldn't come, for whatever reason, Silvia probably wondered why I was less tolerable. I convinced myself that Silvia was suspicious of the way I looked at you, and how you could make me smile when she couldn't, or how I would do anything I could think of to make you laugh. Your laughter has always been music."

I am queasy, but what am I going to do? Barf ghost guts? I need to know the rest. How I played my part in this deception. I turn to Isaac. "Silvia knew what was going on?"

"No. I learned later, she never suspected a thing." His eyes travel toward his chest, long lashes dusting his flawless skin. "I convinced myself that she knew, because I wanted so much to finish things between us. I decided to confess to her, so she would call off the wedding and I would finally be free to pursue my interest in you. There wasn't an opportunity until a week before the wedding. I confessed my true feelings for you to Silvia. "

I reach for clues inside myself, but my memory is hollow and no feelings drift to the surface. If I felt so much for him back then, I can't tell now. All I feel is regret and grief, moving like fan blades, blowing through my confusion. I rub my fingers on the upholstery but I'm so numb, I can't feel a thing.

"I told Silvia how I felt about you, and she broke down. I was sorry, but I felt such relief. I was sure she saw that we were not meant to be together, that you and I were, but I was wrong again.

Silvia dried her tears and told me she understood. She loved you deeply too. She said she understood how I could fall in love with you. But she said she loved me too, enough for both of us. She believed my love for you would be fleeting. Like a common cold. She insisted this was just a stumble and that it would strengthen the bond between us, since I would value how compassionate and dedicated she was to me, in the end."

"That's heartbreaking." My voice is stringy. His lips curl into a sad grin.

"It was the happiest I'd ever been," Isaac says. "And the most devastated, when Silvia reminded me that the expenses were already paid for the wedding and canceling everything would financially devastate both our families. Not to mention the humiliation she and her family would endure. She would likely never have the opportunity to marry again. People would talk and they would assume.

"I tried to tell her she was wrong, but I knew better. Continuing on with the wedding wasn't right, but Silvia refused to cancel it and I was trapped. I couldn't be the one to ruin her. From that moment on, my world turned dark.

"I went to my father and told him what was happening. He was a well loved pastor, and I often saw him guide people to follow their own paths, rather than trying to reroute them to what he thought they ought to do. I thought he would understand when I told him I fell in love with you. But he didn't understand.

"My mother was furious. She and my father were poor and married without celebration, so she wanted the best for me. She had used everything we had to pay for the wedding, including funds set aside to pay the church mortgage. My mother assumed the wedding gifts would, at the very least, repay the money spent, so there had to be a wedding." His eyes flash. "The custom gown my mother ordered for Silvia never fit her properly. She thought she'd gained weight. The truth is that when my mother asked for yours and Silvia's measurements, to order your gown from the town tailor and send Silvia's via post to an impressive European designer, I was so certain that you were meant to be my true bride, I gave her your measurements instead.

"I suppose I inherited my mother's romanticism. I was steadfast in my belief that things would sort themselves out. I had faith that you would be standing at the altar with me, instead of Silvia."

I catch myself leaning forward, hinged on his every word. It all sounds so eerily familiar, as if I know this story, even though I don't. I am miserable with the details of my wrongdoing. I force myself to relax my fingers that dig into the edge of the settee. I swallow. "Did I know about all of this?"

His frown creases his cheeks and breaks his words. He scoots forward, takes the hand I'm not clawing into his cushion. "You were as deeply in love with me as I was with you." He presses soft kisses to my knuckles. "You told me to marry Silvia, and you said you would be happy to be my mistress. You wanted everyone to be happy, everything to be smooth. You wanted to keep everything a secret."

It feels like boulders are rolling inside me. Landing on my heart. I am a liar? A betrayer?

"But I only wanted you, Nova." He squeezes my fingers in his. "On the day of the wedding, I went to Silvia again, right before she was dressed in her gown, and this time, I gave her no choice. I told her I could not marry her, that you and I were meant to be together instead. Silvia threw me out of the bridal room and screamed for her father and brothers. In front of all of our relatives and friends and parishioners who were present, celebrating the ceremony, she announced that I'd been unfaithful. With you.

"The place went dead silent. I could hear every breath I took, until all the voices exploded around me. You were in shock. You were willing to be nothing more than my mistress, and you thought I would actually allow that to happen. What devastated me was the vision of you standing there with your bride's maid bouquet dangling at your side.

"Silvia's mother turned on you and accused you of seducing me. I tried to get to you, but Silvia's family created a barrier between us. The women formed a circle around you. The shouting was ear splitting. They were spitting on you! One of Silvia's cousins got hold of your hair. Another pushed you down. I thought you were stunned. You weren't fighting back.

"I lost my head. It wasn't supposed to happen like that. We were supposed to have our chance to be together." His voice fades as he meets my gaze. He pauses and something shifts in his demeanor, but he continues on. "I thought…I *believed* our love was indestructible. I fought my way across the church to you, but when I got there, you were lying at those women's feet…and you were dead."

Dead. The finality and the guilt and the truth tumble together. I died there, ashamed, and the love of my life tried to stop it. It's all true. I feel the truth of it in my phantom bones.

I slide my hand over Isaac's collarbone, into the silky thread of his coal-black hair, and draw him to me. I kiss this vampire who loves me more than I realized…until now.

39

The kiss is so deep and so long, we end up on the settee again, my legs bent on either side of his hips, me hovering over him, sliding a hand along his jaw and behind his ear, in case he pulls away. He doesn't.

The more I kiss him, the more I want to. He lays his head back on the firm upper edge of the settee. Lifting slightly on my knees, our chests crush together. His kiss sends sparks racing through me, sharp and exciting. I run my hand along the back of the settee, noticing the narrow edge beneath his neck. The idea of his discomfort wears on me. I try to ignore it, but can't. It spreads an uneasiness through me that tugs at my brain like the *push* did before.

It's creepy.

I sit back on his lap and he lifts his head.

"Something wrong?" His voice is as husky as the baritone chords of an acoustic guitar.

"You spelled me again, didn't you?"

"No."

I stare at his lips, wanting to kiss him, to be kissed by him again. Oh yes, he definitely did something. His lazy hand rests on my waist and I am enjoying the heaviness of it there. The warmth. I'm not this needy.

"The truth, Isaac," I say sharply.

"It's not a spell, I swear it," he says. "You must be getting some effect from my venom."

"You're addicting me? How can you if I'm a ghost?" Just saying the words makes me feel the dizzying, disorienting truth all through me.

"I'm not doing it intentionally," he insists. "Vampires have heightened levels of desire. Ghosts translate emotion. I can't addict you without sharing my venom. But you must be translating my attraction to you and feeling the effect of how strong it is. I'm not going to apologize for that. I plan to do everything in my power to prove my feelings for you and help you remember what kind of man I was to you."

I plant one foot on the floor and ease off his lap. He reaches for my hand, but I slide it out of his grasp.

"It can't happen this way," I tell him. I'm suddenly aware of how quiet the room is, how it is just the two of us within this large space, how his eyes glisten in the candlelight. I'm standing between his knees, and whether or not it is real or just some translation, I feel the heat radiating from his body in a steady pulse.

"Then tell me how you want it to happen," he says.

His gaze is mesmerizing. I tear my eyes away and step over his leg, returning to the opposite side of the coffee table, where I hope to be able to breathe normally again. I lower and perch on the edge of the cushion.

"I want to know who you are and who I am," I tell him. "I want to know the rest of the story."

"Alright," he says, spreading his arms across the back of the settee. It makes the furniture look small and delicate.

"The legend said Silvia hung herself and you disappeared."

His eyes steel a bit. "That's inaccurate. My wedding day was also the day of my death, although not many knew that. When my mother's squandering of the church funds became known, the parishioners turned against her. They attacked her, but at the front of the mob was my very own Uncle Silas. Do you recall mention of him in any versions of the urban legend you heard?"

"No."

"Not surprising," Isaac lets out a long sigh. "Silas was my father's reclusive brother. He was as dedicated to God as they come, having trained to be a pastor himself, but never made it that far.

"Silas lived, or you could say *hid*, in the cellar of my father's church and acted as the caretaker of the structure and the grounds. Cleanliness is next to Godliness, so Silas was meticulous in his maintenance of the church. He believed his atonement was: rising at dusk each and every night to scrub every inch of the church, clean the chalices, make and bottle the wine. He made the original split-log pews in my father's church and laid the first floor. No one ever laid eyes on my uncle; my father didn't trust his brother's thirst. I'm not sure Silas trusted himself. My father kept his brother alive on raw meat and animal blood. Silas kept himself alive by dedicating every waking moment in service to the church. My father insisted the wedding be held at dusk and Silas did something he'd never done before. He came up from the cellar to attend my wedding, but when he saw the grandeur, he was suspicious. My father told Silas what my mother had done and Silas was livid, but when he realized that I was calling off the wedding and that the church would be lost because of it, he went after my mother, and I was the one who stood in his way."

The realization hits me, steals my breath. "Your uncle was a vampire."

Isaac responds with one slow nod. "It began long, long ago. My Uncle Silas was a grown man, already a bit of a family disgrace because he was an alcoholic who drank away every dime he made, never married, and still lived at home. My grandmother would not turn him out.

"The night the disease came to my family was the night my grandfather sent Uncle Silas out to collect the firewood Silas had procrastinated collecting during the day. A vagabond bit Silas--obviously a vampire with no idea of what he was doing, as Silas was left to die. But, instead of dying, Silas dragged himself home before his second death overtook him. Once my grandfather, also a pastor, realized what happened, he cast Silas out of the house. He knew he'd become a demon. My grandmother was distraught. My father also tried to convince my grandfather to help Silas, but my grandfather wouldn't hear of it. My father dragged Silas to the root cellar of a burnt-out house, a mile from the family home, and there, Silas became a murderer—"

"You mean, he *fed himself*," I correct.

"Silas tried to do what he'd been told was right—he denied himself feeding. He tried drinking himself into a stupor, but vampire blood neutralizes alcohol. He tried eating only human food countless times. Each time, he nearly starved to death. Then, he would go on binges, killing townspeople in our their own town and neighboring towns.

"My grandmother passed within three months of the bite, from grief over losing Silas. I was told my grandfather died as he came home through the woods one night," Isaac's eyebrows twitch upward, "supposedly attacked by a bear."

"Silas killed him?" I swallow, my compassion for Isaac's brother waning.

"No. My father did." Isaac's lips drop into a grim line. "He blamed my grandfather for exiling Silas and destroying my grandmother by denying help to my uncle. Upon my grandfather's death, my father inherited his first congregation. He was eighteen. He moved my uncle into the basement of the church and began supplying him with animals. The solution evades death, but animal blood is a miserable substitute for human blood. Silas dedicated himself to my father's ministry in absolution for his own soul."

"Is there a way to overcome the urge to feed?"

Isaac shakes his head. "Silas constantly tried to exist on animals, but he knew he was damned each time he came to the point of starvation and could not keep himself from killing another human to stay alive. The cycle drove him insane.

"The townspeople were terrified by the rash of murders. The congregation gave alms, hoping to appease the monster they didn't realize was living in the basement of their own church."

40

"Silas was hidden, right under their noses," Isaac scoffs. "My uncle slept in the empty coffins that my father stored in the basement of the church. No one was going to go searching in there. Whenever the killings began to appear less than random, we moved to a new town and established a new church. Starting over again and again was difficult, but my father was committed to doing anything he could think of, to help his brother from committing murder. Including nailing him inside the coffins, in hopes that the urge would pass, or that Uncle Silas would die before succumbing to yet another sin."

I gulp at the idea of being nailed inside the tight confines of a casket. "That worked?"

"Not at all. A vampire can subsist on animals for only so long, and when we reach our base hunger, we turn wild. My uncle smashed caskets and escaped every time, killing in town, or in the surrounding towns, and after he had fed, he would return to my father again, humiliated and penitent. The cycle would start all over again. Silas grew unstable over time. My mother wouldn't go into the church without my father and she wouldn't let me go in without both of them.

"On the day of my wedding, Uncle Silas was already suffering from hunger. Hearing that he was going to lose his home made him wild. He risked the pain of the setting sun and attacked my mother."

I'm reeling. "He bit you to get to your mother?"

"Yes." Isaac says, his gorgeous, olive skin flushing a sickly pale. His smile flickers and dies. "He bit me and drained my mother. My father's screams interrupted Silas's rage long enough for him to see what he'd done. He fled back to the church cellar, and Silvia's family set fire to the church. The death of a vampire is like no other, especially one who dies in flames. His screaming was heard for miles. It still rings in my ears when I think of it."

He leans forward, his elbows on his knees and turns his head to the side as if the sound will pour out of his ear. His muscles are tense. I wait for him to finish, rather than disturb him.

"With an initial bite, the venom paralyzes the bitten momentarily," Isaac begins again, staring at the floor, his head hanging between his shoulders. "The parishioners presumed I was in shock when my father dragged me away from the chaos. Silvia was killed when the fire collapsed the church."

I hide my mouth behind a hand. "That's awful. I can't believe it. It's completely different from what I heard."

He raises his head, his crow-black hair falling away from his cheek. "I'm sure it is. Stories change over time."

"I read that you murdered a carriage driver for spreading gossip."

"I am a murderer," he says with a sad grin, "but it was my father who killed the carriage driver. Pulled the man off the high seat, right onto his head, when the driver wouldn't give my father the carriage. My father knew what the mob would do to me if they knew I was bitten. It would confirm the suspicions that followed us. My father loaded me into the back of the carriage, along with the corpse of the driver, which was to be my first fetid meal. We left town forever and I began my life as a vampire."

"And I was there?" I say. "Was my father there? Was he still alive?"

"He was. Your father had to attend to work duties and he didn't want you to come to the wedding."

"Why?"

Our gaze pauses, as if he doesn't want to break my heart with answers. "It was such a long way to travel and he considered it dangerous."

I gasp. "He died *after* me." Sorrow washes over me for a father I can't remember.

Isaac gets up, comes around the coffee table and sits beside me. "You were his only daughter. His heart broke and he wasted away after losing you. I'm so sorry, Nova."

He draws me into his arms and I let him. I even tip my chin up for his kiss and it does just what I expect it to. The velvet of his lips and the warmth of his mouth draw away my grief. It's dangerous how a simple kiss can dull out every emotion I have, except those connected to Isaac. When I break the kiss, he rests his forehead against mine.

"If you'd like to remember your past, there is a way," he whispers.

I pull my head back, gaping. "You know how I can get my memory back?"

He gives one solemn nod. I don't like the look of that.

"You mean magic." A shudder works through my legs at all the things that could go wrong about that.

"Of sorts," he says. "The only way to get your memories back is to replace them with the memories of someone close to you."

I melt a little, reaching for his hand. "You'd do that for me?"

"I would if I could," he says with a pitying tilt to his head, "but since I was reborn as a vampire, my memories are tainted by venom. It could turn another being into a homicidal maniac, quite literally."

A silver streaks dart across his pupils and I follow the movement, wishing on them like shooting stars. But what I'm wishing for, I can't really define.

A sharp rap on the bedroom door startles me from the confusion.

"Mr. Havrath, sir, there's been a sighting on the grounds!" Hoomstid shouts through the door.

41

Isaac jumps to his feet and I grab his sleeve. "What's going on?"

"My Brethren," he growls.

After what Isaac's told me about his Brethren, my vertebras shiver.

"How many?" Isaac growls. He takes my hand and hurries me across the room to the door, throwing it open. The shocked face of his disfigured butler greets us.

"At least one, sir, but Esther thought she spotted more."

"Where?"

"In the pasture and fields beyond, sir." Hoomstid sidesteps the doorway to avoid getting trampled as Isaac drags me along with him into the hall and toward the stairs. "Do you think it best to take the lady with you? I could keep her in the barn for safekeeping, if you wish."

We're down the steps and out the back door by the time Isaac answers. The humidity of summer is claustrophobic. The way my feet sink into the grass, which is still soaked from extinguishing the cottage fire, makes me feel trapped and vulnerable as I peer into the outlying darkness and try to detect movement.

"Yes, yes, the barn is the best option." Isaac's answer is distracted as he drops my hand. Shadows of trees and tall grass are all I can make out, but Isaac's eyes seem more adapted as scans the distant darkness. "Go with Hoomstid, Nova. There is a spelled stall that may keep you safe."

I stick on *may*. What happened to sticking by my side? Never leaving me again? Doing his all to keep me safe?

Isaac turns back to Hoomstid. "If any of my Brethren show their faces, you know what to do."

"Yes, sir." Hoomstid bows his chin to his chest, while the eye in the center of his forehead anchors on me like the traveling eyes of a painting. The servant grabs my upper arm, as if he's going to jog me off like a five-year-old. The only reason I don't resist is because he yanks me out of the way of two approaching horses.

The beefy coach driver who took away Machara Milligen sits atop one and ignores the fact that he nearly tramples us. He ignores us altogether, shrouded in a fresh dust cloud, as he leans down from his saddle to offer the reins of a jet-black stallion to Isaac.

"Your horse, Mr. Havrath," the driver says from beneath his handle-bar mustache. "The other servants are saddling up. They will be right behind us."

"Excellent, Eustace." Isaac plants a foot in a stirrup and swings himself onto the back of the glistening, raven horse. His movement is fluid, more graceful than birds, and I drink in every detail. He winds the rein around his fist, sitting tall and regal in the saddle. Small quivers radiate through me.

Isaac pulls on the reins, aiming the horse's head toward the fields. "Take her now, Hoomstid!" he shouts. "It will likely take us till dawn to locate them. Defend her with your life if you must!"

"Yes, sir!" Hoomstid's fingers renew their grip on my arm.

Isaac digs his heels into the horse's flanks and the stallion races off into the darkness. Eustace follows. Moments later, dark horses and their riders merge from beyond the carriage house, creating a cloudy cluster behind Isaac and Eustace, racing into the outlying shadows of the pasture and field.

The coach that took Machara Milligen away ambles from the carriage house toward us. Drawn by two deep brown horses, Esther, the cranky older maid who nearly beheaded me with her scathing glare after the cottage fire, is perched on the driver's seat. She pulls up hard on the reins, bringing the horses to a neighing halt in front of us. Hoomstid opens the carriage door and, his grip still tight on my upper arm, pulls me toward the opening.

I yank my arm away. I'm not sure getting into anything Esther's driving is a brilliant plan for me.

"Miss," Hoomstid says, a strangely weary pleading in his voice. "We must hurry."

It's not like I can argue. The aftershock of quivers continues to pulse through me too, urging me to follow Isaac's instructions. It's either Esther or Isaac's Brethren, and I think it's better to take the maid's seething hatred than whatever a few vampires might do to me.

I climb into the coach, the car wobbling beneath my feet as I step up, not so different from the way my emotions are sliding around inside me, on tilt. Hoomstid scrambles up behind me and drops on the opposite cushioned seat as Esther shouts, *hyah!*, and the coach jerks forward with such aggression, my head knocks against the back wall.

Esther probably did that on purpose.

"There is someone in the barn, miss," Hoomstid says, wrings his hands between his knees, both skewed eyes anchored on me.

"Who?" Veins of sweat swiftly streak down my back. It's a setup. My voice is solemn as I ask, "Is it the Brethren?"

Hoomstid's forehead smoothes as he releases a tense laugh. "Oh no! You are in no danger, miss. This visitor would only like a word."

"A visitor? Isaac said there's no one but servants on the estate—"

"Quite rarely do we have visitors, but they do come from time to time, when it is important." Trickles of sweat stream from the servant's temples now and it's not because the interior of the coach is stagnant or hot. "This visitor has only requested a word with you."

"About what?" I sit back.

"About who you are, miss." Hoomstid wrings his hands so thoroughly, his knuckles crack. "If you want your answers, you must go now!"

"How would this person have *my* answers?" I ask as the coach bounces over a pothole in the ruts leading toward the barn. Hoomstid is thrown forward, landing on his knees in front of me, his head sunk in my lap. He skitters off the floor and back onto his seat, straightening himself feverishly. I have no time for his blush, which punches a darker shadow into the lightless coach.

"Who is this person, Hoomstid?" I press again, craning toward him so I can hear over the pounding of the horse's hooves.

"If I may ask your trust and discretion, miss…" His color drains as he fidgets. "This visitor is a fellow revenant. Have you looked to the night for clues, as I've told you?"

"What does that even mean?" I shout as the carriage strikes another pothole and tosses us both from our cushioned benches. Our heads slap together like chicken cutlets, but Hoomstid seems unfazed. I moan and grasp my temple as we regain our seating.

"Regretfully, I'm unable to explain any more than that," Hoomstid says.

"Of course not." I lean off the bench, narrowing my gaze that flicks between the servant's misplaced. "Did Isaac spell you with magic so you can't tell me anything?"

"Yes, miss. I am also a revenant, a servant, and have been a cup to Mr. Havrath. There are things I am not at liberty to say." He winces, wiggling on the bench as if he is wrestling with another ghost. His breathing turns short and fast as he writhes, but from locked teeth, he grunts, "However, there are things I can *do,* things I can help you to see clearly. Understand, I would never betray Mr. Havrath...except that he betrayed me first."

What? A hard bounce over another pothole sends me to Hoomstid's side of the coach, closer than expected. He leans away, as if repulsed. I lean in, fascinated.

"How did Isaac betray you?" I ask.

Up close, I can see just how sweaty our conversation has made him. Each answer squeezes another rivulet from his brow. He closes his eyes and his neck bobs with a swallow.

"Mr. Havrath," he begins. Another gulp. More sweat. The muscles in his jaw jump as if he's drinking down lemon pulp. "Mr. Havrath used my intended...for a cup."

The servant emits a hard exhale, as if he's just moved a cinderblock house from his chest. The coach jolts me backward on the seat, but I hang onto the seat and regain myself quickly.

"Your girlfriend? Who is she?" I ask.

"Lucy VanBjorn is my fiancé. Esther's daughter," he says, both eyes blinking in unison as he pokes his index finger at the ceiling of the coach, toward the driver's bench over our heads.

Lucy was the younger maid, the one who was hanging laundry that first night I came to the estate. She was with her mother, Esther. I remember their discussion—the two of them were arguing over a man who Lucy had, but Esther wanted.

It wasn't Hoomstid they were talking about.

They were arguing about Isaac.

It's all so clear now, even in the dark, dusty air of the coach. Isaac addicted Lucy and now she only wants Isaac, instead of Hoomstid.

I knew Esther was infatuated with Isaac too, but now I can

understand why she hated me too, while wanting to help me at the same time. Isaac took Esther's daughter from her, and then ditched them both to be with me.

The knowledge presses buttons that send off explosions in me that feel dangerous, exciting, jealous, beautiful, and loathsome. I want to pack Lucy and Esther in a carriage, the same way Machara Milligen was removed. I want Hoomstid to do his job. I don't hate Isaac, even though whispers of feelings keep bubbling up in my head, suggesting I should. I keep my mouth shut.

The coach hops again. They are probably driving me to my doom and I'm taking the ride willingly. Maybe they are getting even with their master. Maybe I am the sacrificial lamb who's supposed to do the leveling up for Isaac.

The coach rumbles to a halt, a dust cloud fogging the view out the window.

"Who is waiting in the barn, Hoomstid?" I ask, but Esther leaps down from the driver's seat and throws open the carriage door.

"Hurry!" she barks. The urgency in her voice sounds artificially concerned to me, as if she is shrieking stage lines to an invisible audience. "She's not safe out here!"

I don't know what's waiting in the barn for me.

I could run. I could scream. I could panic.

But, I don't and I don't and I don't.

Instead, a bizarre curiosity overtakes me. Whoever Hoomstid wants me to meet, I'm pretty sure Isaac doesn't know about it, and probably wouldn't approve, which intrigues me a hundred times more. It could be an executioner. It could be something else.

I climb down from the carriage and walk, sandwiched hostage-style, between Esther and Hoomstid. The combined animal sounds swell as we approach the door. Slipping inside, the permeating smell of the barn coats my nostrils.

A single lantern burns from a hook in the center of the aisle, casting shadows on pigs, goats, horses, and bundles of chickens lying on shelves and nests of hay. Esther takes down the lantern and we follow her to the back of the barn where the last two stalls are empty, swept clean. The servants and I enter the second to the last stall, the wood panels painted with sigils, which look more like a child's chalk drawings than protective insignias to me.

"This is the visitor I mentioned," Hoomstid says, but he peers back over his shoulder, checking the now-closed front door, where we entered. There's no one else in the stall besides Esther and me, nothing in the surrounding stalls but animals.

I think they're nuts, until I hear the rustle of hay.

A surge of adrenaline bolts through me as a man appears on the opposite side of the wood panel, which separates our stall from the last.

Stranger yet, my mind blanks as I stare at the man. My tongue doesn't work. He is nothing special, and at the same time, breathtakingly handsome; like comparing the gaudy paper tube of a cheap kaleidoscope to the brilliant designs inside it. He is a layering of browns: carob hair, mahogany eyes, skin the golden color of the whiskey Murray used to lift from the corner liquor store. Nothing outstanding, but the longer I stare at him, the more I'm left with a hazy softness, as disconnected a feeling as stars drifting between clouds.

My god, I'm falling in lust with every man I see. And from the way his mouth has drifted open as he stares back at me, I would say he feels the same blast of static shock that I do. The sharp tug of guilt that comes with the thought of Isaac doesn't even distract me.

"Say something!" Esther hisses. "We don't have all the time in the world to stand around! Do you have it or don't you?"

The man closes his mouth. Swallows. "I do."

He hands me a tiny chip of glass. Puts it in my palm as if it's something important, and as if I know what to do with it.

As if I can concentrate when his touch tingles against my skin.

He motions for me to put it away. I reach down to my side. I let it slide off my hand and into my pocket. I'm incapable of keeping my eyes off him.

It's the first time I've had such an intense desire to see every aspect of a person—I haven't even felt this much for Isaac, and it worries me. I stare at the man before me as if he's the most interesting piece of art ever created and I must devour every detail. Twice.

"I think I know you," I whisper, "although I don't know how."

The mysterious man's mouth opens slightly and closes. His neck bobs with a small nod and swallow.

"Yes, yes…that's the way it is, being a revenant," Esther snaps. "Let's not dawdle! Is there anything else? Otherwise, she's got the chip, so you need to get out of here before Isaac returns! Let the others know, the vial isn't here."

"What others? And what vial?" I ask. I remember something about a vial…something Dorcas told me. "Do you mean the Sunshine Vial?"

All three of them look at me wide-eyed. The moment is broken when Hoomstid shoots Esther a look and she clamps her lips. So, the Sunshine Vial *is* what they're talking about.

Why, I don't know, and from the grim, closed mouths around me, I can see no one's about to tell me.

When I look back to the stranger, is eyes are on mine and air freezes in my lungs.

"What is this chip for?" I ask him, tapping my dress pocket where the chip is hidden.

"It's a warlock's monocle," Hoomstid answers instead. "It will help you see Isaac for what he is, so you may remember who you are."

The stranger doesn't even blink.

I look from the stranger to Hoomstid. "What do you mean—"

"Alright, you delivered it, now go!" Esther reaches over the stall wall and gives the man's shoulder a shove, but he may as well be made of rock. Her momentum doesn't so much as sway him, which seems to fluster her all the more. She turns on Hoomstid. "I am here betraying Isaac, for what? It's not like you have any proof of what she is!"

I wonder if they think I'm a revenant, instead of a ghost—full of stolen guts, instead of clouds and dreams.

"Mr. Havrath believes it," Hoomstid says. "That's proof enough for me."

"What do you think I am?" I ask the butler, but since my eyes are still on the handsome stranger, I may as well be asking him. He still doesn't blink.

"Isaac doesn't know!" Esther scoffs. "He's always seduced by a pretty new face! He's also been leaning on Machara's magic and making assumptions! Lest we not forget, what a jealous woman Machara was? She could've drawn in a dog to appease him!"

I think she's calling me a *female dog*, in the worst possible terms, but I have bigger concerns.

I'm torn in two, gazing at the stranger in the stall beside me—half amazed by him and half furious with myself for looking at him at all. Isaac is the one who melted my emotions hardly a whole hour ago. If anyone is betraying Isaac, it's me.

"What do you say, Athen? Do you know her?" Hoomstid asks.

Athen. The stranger's name doesn't strike any familiar chords. Neither does his face, but there is something about this man, his...*his-ness*...which makes me feel as weightless and out of control as a feather in the wind.

Athen hasn't blinked once. "I don't know," he says, but the softness in his gaze intensifies while somehow slipping deeper inside me, as if he's unlocking doors in me that I can't even unlock myself.

"She could be no one in particular," Esther flicks her chin toward Athen, "just like him. Just like the rest of us!"

"Machara thought he was someone!" Hoomstid counters sharply. "And we all remember *something* of our past lives, but they don't! It must mean something—" Hoomstid turns back to

Athen and me, looking between us with a peaked brow, like the crook of a branch, disconnected and floating in the center of his face. "We hope you will accept our help, and in exchange, keep us in your good favor."

"What he's saying is we'll help, if you will grant what we wish." Esther bristles, crossing her arms over her chest.

I break Athen's gaze. "What do you two think we are? Genies? How would we grant you wishes?"

They must mean telling Isaac. They don't want us to tell Isaac that they're traitors.

The doors of the barn burst open before she can answer. Athen drops like he's been shot, plummeting below the panel of the stall between us.

"Nova?" Isaac strides down the aisle toward us, his black boots smacking the floor. He stands beside me in seconds, shoving the servants aside. "Are you alright? I'm glad you made it to the charmed stalls! Who is here with you?"

I open my mouth, but the words disappear like a wisp of smoke in the air.

Isaac lunges for the stall wall, grasping the wood and peering over the edge with fangs extended, ready for battle.

Hoomstid and Esther exchange a horrified glance.

Isaac retreats from the wall slowly, turning back to me, fangs invisible.

He must've seen Athen. Must have. There's nowhere for the stranger to hide on the other side of the wall, but Isaac shows no sign of it.

"Who was here?" Isaac barks, his dark eyes swallowing me.

Everything I felt for him before rushes back, but I bite down on the edges of my tongue to keep Athen's name, and the general admission of his presence, silent.

"No...no one was here." The guilt makes me stutter. My fingers find the mysterious chip in my pocket and trace it.

Esther and Hoomstid gather themselves and the butler steps forward. "It was only us, sir."

Isaac moves closer and my thoughts melt away like sugar in the rain. I close my eyes. It only helps me to concentrate on the specifics of the handsome stranger a little, and then, not at all, when Isaac touches my cheek.

"You don't need to be out here any longer," he says.

"You've found the intruder?" Hoomstid asks.

"There was no intruder. Only Wayne, the boy from the carriage house, breaking the new mare in the pasture." Isaac's eyes flick to the stall wall again. Suspicious. "I want a full inspection of the grounds to be certain there is nothing else."

I can't explain why, but I place my hand on Isaac's cheek to draw his attention back to me. Maybe it's not to betray him by lying about the stranger. I can convince myself that it is simply because Isaac's attention feels as strong and good and relaxing as the sun, radiating on me.

"I'll come with you," I say.

His shoulders relax, but he shakes his head. "The hunt is work for my men. Not for you."

Wow, that's chivalrous. Or misogynistic. I'm not sure which.

He turns to the servants. "The two of you will saddle up and join the rest. I want the entire estate scoured, every inch. Go, get out of here. Nova is safe with me now."

The dismissal is so harsh, I cringe. Esther's displeasure is audible, but I'm not sure if it is because Isaac's lumped her with 'his men' or if it is because of the way he rubs his thumb gently over my cheek and I curl my face into his touch, closing my eyes on the maid.

All I know is that I will do anything in my power to please Isaac.

As I stand with my cheek resting in his palm, listening to the servants guide horses from the stalls and out of the barn, I understand her jealousy—the yearning that follows Isaac like a trailing cape. He's the kind of man that is loved or hated, and nothing in between. Isaac is patchouli in a close room, and me...all I can think of is how lucky I am to fill my lungs with him.

I'm busy memorizing the smooth softness of Isaac, basking in the glow of his gaze. My enchantment with Isaac feels methodic and pleasantly numbing. Steadily, it erases the fascination I had with the mysterious stranger who gave me the glass chip in my pocket.

"Tell me truly," he murmurs, running his hands over my shoulders and down my arms, "were you frightened?"

I sigh. "Not at all."

The truth spreads my eyes wide open, which is my undoing. His gaze locks on mine, instantly dissolving my boldness. Isaac's thick lashes remind me of a Venus fly trap, but their beauty turns me into a brainless fly.

I don't need to peer into any itty bitty piece of glass that will show me who Isaac is. I already know.

He is everything.

He is weakness.

He is mine.

And beyond all reason, I want to encourage it.

My back against Isaac, I sit cradled between his arms, behind the neck of his ebony stallion, as we ride back to the mansion. His icy metal scent is refreshing and it clears my head of every other thought besides him. Isaac brings the horse to a swift stop at the back porch and helps me down before hurrying me inside.

"What's the rush? You said the estate is safe, isn't it?" Our fingers are latched like loose links in a chain, but there is no slowing his pace as he leads me up the stairs and down the hall to his suite. He's moving so quickly, his finger slips from mine.

"Safe enough that I can't wait another minute to be alone with you," he says, reaching for me again. A static spark snaps in the space between our fingertips. The sharpness stings so much, that for a moment, I don't remember why I am standing in this hallway.

Isaac reaches for me and the panic disappears as quick as it came with his touch.

Inside his suite, Isaac closes the door, drawing me back with his opposite hand. He presses my back to the wood door, his fore-arms on either side of me, caging me in. There's nowhere else I want to be. He kisses me so deeply, sparks run into my toes. When he breaks away, I try to recapture his lips, but he turns his head and lays his cheek against mine, his breath stirring my hair.

"I want you to come with me, to meet the Brethren. I want them to know you are mine."

"I'll come." *What?* Why did I just agree to meet a murderous band of vampires that treat him so badly? I have no clue, except that whatever Isaac wants, I want to give him.

"I want to present you as mine to them." He leans closer. "I want to claim you, so you are protected."

"Claimed? Like luggage?" I laugh, but I am intoxicated. I am willing to be his backpack, clinging to him forever.

Isaac's expression is somber. "Claimed, as in, you will never be theirs."

I can't keep the offense of being *claimed* sharp enough in my head. Not when my body is busy having an entirely different reaction to him. A fever of illusions works its way through my thoughts, all versions of Isaac and me, happy, together, doing things only humans could: feeding him, lying with him, having his children.

I curl my fingers into my palms and dig the fingernails into my flesh.

It distracts me enough to focus on this *claiming* thing.

But only barely.

"How does being your luggage protect me?" I ask. I hope I sound bratty and disgusted, but I don't think I do. I'm lousy at being anything but what he wants right now, and the most I can do about that is to be angry about it out loud.

He pulls back from me and his gaze turns distant, but not from my weak attempt at rage. I think he considers my fury with the same concern that he might regard kitten claws snagging his sweater. He murmurs about the Brethren, his gaze narrowing as if he is considering them through some portal that is invisible to me. I study the darkness in his eyes and the determination in them.

"I've kept you a secret as long as I've been able, but secrets always find a way to the surface and often before it is convenient. This time, we need to be prepared for what is to come. Claiming always spark a great competition amongst the Brethren," he says. "They will come to steal you away if they can find the mansion, but as of now, the safeguards that keep the estate hidden are still working."

"Like the *vias*."

"Yes." The fringe of his lashes drops against his cheek. I visually trace the planes of his face as he continues. "The *vias* keeps all the Brethren's estates hidden and separate, but it can still be traversed. It is not without great risk, but it has been done. The claiming and the obscurity spells Machara put in place still do not guarantee the Brethren won't try to draw you away from me. It will only make it a bit harder for them."

"What can I do?"

"You could become a Revenant," he says. "Meet the Brethren as a ghost, so they cannot bite you and lay claim to you in that way, and once you've been introduced, you take a revenant form. That is when I can truly claim you and you will become mine. Then, you will never be tempted to leave me, no matter how they try to seduce you from afar."

"I would never be tempted anyway," I say. The craziness of it settles into my head like a practical plan.

"When can I meet them?" I draw him to me, our lips only inches apart.

"The sooner, the better," he says, lowering his mouth to mine. "But first, I want you to know how to escape them."

45

W ant. There is nothing in me but want.

I want to kiss him again. I want him to kiss me until I'm numb. I want to feel every inch of him. I want more in every possible meaning of the word, but Isaac draws away. A cruel taunt. I reach for him, but he traps my hands in his.

He's been tempting me all this time, and now that I'm giving in, he wants to talk.

I let out a long, frustrated exhale.

"It's time I showed you how to move through solids," Isaac says. He leads me across the room to the dining area, with its marble counter.

"Why didn't you tell me before?" I ask.

He shrugs. "You weren't ready to hear it."

Well, that's a lazy answer, if I've ever heard one. It would've come in handy in the cottage, to walk through the walls to escape, rather than crisping the place.

"And I didn't want you to be frightened," he continues. "I knew if I told you this part, I'd have to tell you the rest. It is dangerous to remain a ghost. Whether or not you know it, you become less able to enter a revenant's body every day. There is only so long you can remain a ghost before that is all you are and can ever be."

"Why? What happens?" I ask mildly. I'm hardly listening.

I've become a girl who can't think of anything but a boy.

It's obnoxious.

"You'll disintegrate so quickly in the presence of a revenant body that you won't be able to get inside it in time."

His worries bounce off me like rubber. All I want is to get this all over with, so I can kiss him again. Stick to him like glue.

I lift my hand and bring it down on the counter top beside us. Nothing. My hand thunks down on the marble hard enough to vibrate my bones like a tuning fork.

"Don't *try*," he says softly.

Don't try. That's as helpful as adults telling teenagers to just *be yourself*. How can you be something you don't know you are? I am extremely aware of how difficult it is to *try* to be me without any reference.

"Just expect it," Isaac coaches.

I drop my hand on the counter again. It crashes once more.

"We could try again later," I say, moving closer to him. There are other things I'd rather be doing right now.

He steps back with a patient grin. "Don't try so hard. Don't *think* about what you're trying to do. Just *know* that you are doing it."

I want to know how to be a ghost, but when I press my hand against the marble counter, I realize it's the fear of it going through that is what is stopping me. It's freaky to consider passing through something so whole, to accept that I am what Isaac's been saying all along. And all of what that means.

But I'm also a little obsessed with doing it. Like the first time Meg spoke to me and I wanted to get her to keep talking all the time because it made me feel less hollow. And like kissing Isaac... I can't start thinking of that or I'll never find out how to control my ghostliness, which I might need if he tries to lock me in a room ever again.

"Just know that you're…" he begins and I shush him. He's not going to stop until I accomplish this.

"Let me do it," I say. I place my hand on the cool marble and splay my fingers wide. Close my eyes. Picture my hand sinking through the marble, floating inside the wood beneath it, touching whatever utensils might be in the drawers.

I pop my eyes open with a gasp.

I yank my hand out of the marble, banging a whisk inside the drawer as I do.

"Yes!" Isaac laughs in triumph.

I shove him away, stunned. I like the feeling of his hands wrapped around my waist, our torsos touching, and our hips so close, but when I shove, he moves.

I plunge my hand back down into the marble. My hand slides right through this time, as I know it will, since it already has. Second times are always easier.

My finger connects with sharp metal and I panic. I'm gripping a knife. I open my eyes to see my arm lodged in the counter, through it. I can feel the blood dribbling out of my cut palm and I shriek. Isaac leaps forward and tries to yank my arm out, but I am not completely free. Instead, I'm stuck, my fingers caught in the marble as if they'd developed there.

I scream.

"No, no, relax, relax," Isaac chants, although his tone is alarmed. "Close your eyes and do what you did before."

The marble goes from cool to icy. The rock squeezes the bones in my hand.

I scream again.

"Breathe, Nova. This kitchen smells like home, doesn't it?" Isaac asks, his voice soft and calm.

My hand trapped in rock, and he wants to talk about kitchens? I take a deep breath and I'm flooded with the taste of warm bread, rich cocoa, whipped cream. Even so, all I can do is pant, *"Yes."*

Isaac's lips splay over mine.

The pain swiftly subsides.

I draw another breath.

My hand numbs within the marble.

Isaac's lips knead mine in a slow, passionate rhythm. It sends a wild shiver down my spine and all I want is to cup his face in my hands...and I do. He halts the kiss and I open my eyes, both my palms planted on his cheeks, instead of one hand lodged in the marble.

He smiles.

I drop my hands, turning over the one that was stuck moments ago, inspecting it. Not a broken bone. Not a scratch or a bruise. Nothing.

"I can't believe it," I say.

"That might happen more and more, now that you've done it a few times," he says. "You could get stuck in walls and spaces, so you'll have to be careful."

The thought of it—getting stuck within plaster, or dropping into the wood floor, or disappearing into a sewer pipe, or a grave—my mind rushes to the worst possibilities.

If I ate food, it would certainly be splattered all over Isaac's polished shoes right now.

"It's going to be alright," he says, roping his arms around my waist. His touch is magical. It convinces me that everything he says is right and true. I just nod, entranced, wanting his enchantment to never end.

"How can it be?" I ask. "I can't stay this way."

"No, you cannot. So, after you meet the Brethren, we will procure a suitable body for your revenency," he says.

I nod, even if it feels as though everything is progressing faster than I am. "When can I meet them?"

"Soon," he says. "I promise you."

46

Isaac keeps his promises. But I didn't expect *soon,* to mean *immediately.*

Before dinner, Esther brings up a burgundy dress, swinging with long ropes of pearls at the open back, and a pair of skyscraper sandals with glass heels.

"You must be dressed as a desire when you meet the Brethren," the maid says. "Or else they will kill you both, on the spot."

She scans me, the scowl on her face suggesting that my current attire, ripped warrior leggings and a sliced tee, is the absolute opposite of desired. It's Meg's style, but I have to agree, it looks like I've been in a sword fight with a pirate. Knowing how much Esther despises it, I go to great lengths to fold each of my items as if they are relics, before hanging them over the back of a chair. Esther waits with several sighs, groans, and continual shuffling of her feet.

She finally puts the dress over my head and tugs it down so hard that, if I had skin, she might've yanked it clear off. Next, she drags over a chair and shoves me down by the shoulders to sit, facing a dark wood vanity with an oval mirror. Esther hands me some bobby pins and rakes my scalp with a bristle brush.

"Why do you hate me so much?" I wince as she tugs her way through a snarl.

"You are a ghost."

"So?"

She rips at another snarl, my head jerking back with each brush. "So, you are nothingness. Mr. Havrath has better options available to him. Revenants who are more suitable to his…taste… and we are capable of loyalty that you would never even consider."

"You don't know a thing about me!" I throw down the bobby pins and they skitter across the top of the vanity. "I am more loyal than you could ever be!"

"Oh?" The hairbrush pauses as Esther's eyebrows spike into the wrinkles on her forehead. "To whom?"

"Okay, that's enough," I say. "You're in love with Isaac, that's it, isn't it? That's the problem you have with me?"

She cracks my skull with the back of the brush. I jump out of the chair, hands on my head, and swivel around to glare at her. She glares right back.

"*Everyone* is in love with Mr. Havrath!" she sneers. Maybe, but after seeing how she turns to goo whenever Isaac walks into the room, I think she's drastically minimizing her own feelings. "That you would ask me such a thing only reconfirms my worst fear! Of course I am in love with him! As is my daughter! As is every servant on this estate who is worth their keep! Aren't you?"

I don't know what to say to that, but she doesn't give me the chance to answer. Esther shoves me back down on the seat and drags the brush through my hair again.

"Don't tell me that you aren't," she snarls. "I'll thrash you to death right here if you do."

Love? I'm not sure I can call the connection between Isaac and me *love*. Beguiled, magnetized, captivated…those are words that better fit us. I meet her gaze in the mirror, as steely and indisputably as I can muster.

"I am enchanted with him," I say, but the words are hollow

194

bullets, aimed to shoot down Esther's disbelief. Unfortunately, the intention blows apart as they leave my mouth. I've been apart from Isaac for the last couple of hours while getting ready, but now, *enchanted* seems like a huge stretch. In fact, I'm barely interested. It's confusing. When I try to pin down what I've ever seen in Isaac at all, I can't explain it to myself.

I look in the mirror and see disbelief twisting Esther's lips and disappointment painted all over my face. I wonder what I'm even doing here, as I catch Esther staring at me in the mirror. She drops her gaze and slides the brush through my hair.

I can't will myself to leave, even though I don't want to stay.

I let Esther fix my hair.

Two hours later, my hair is styled in complicated plaits and I'm encased in a gown that Meg would call, *sick.*

"You should be delighted," Esther tells me through thin lips. "Mr. Havrath chose the garment himself."

I turn in front of the full length mirror beside the bed. This dress is beautiful in a way that makes me wonder what Isaac really thinks of me. The front is burgundy lace over a sheer shift. It hugs my best parts. In the back, long strings of pearls hang in graduated lengths to mid-thigh. With every movement, the pearls sway and sing Isaac's name in a soft, gritty whisper. I listen carefully.

On second thought, they don't sing his name at all. They chant, *mine.*

Esther steps away with a sigh. Her eyes scan me up and down, and up and down again, as if she's caught between silence and words. I wait for the verdict and finally, she motions to my bodice and then taps her own. "If you get into trouble," she whispers. "This will help you see what you need to."

"Like what?" I ask, tapping my bodice. There is absolutely something buried between the lace and the shift. A small, stiff area, but before I can inspect it, the maid snatches my hand away and tugs me toward the door.

"Don't dawdle." Esther makes *dawdling* sound as heinous as

murder. "Mr. Havrath is waiting for you downstairs. You best be gone."

Honestly, I'm glad to get away from the maid. The mixture of mysterious talk, grim glares, and mixed feelings confuses me.

I forget Esther as I concentrate on picking my way down the stairs in the monstrously high heels. I slide my palm down the polished handrail and the pearls sing with every step.

Isaac is waiting at the bottom of the stairs and his reaction is unexpected, because there isn't one. He is distracted, staring off at nothing in particular He looks to me only when I'm beside him, but his gaze remains distant.

"Quite beautiful," he murmurs.

He could be talking about a chandelier. I feel like one, the way the pearls sway against my backbone, but as I near him and smell his cologne, it clicks what is *enchanting* about Isaac. It's the scent of him, which is both fresh and hard at once—a captivating mix of ice and metal.

We make it only a few steps before I refuse to follow behind him anymore. Not when I'm going to all this trouble to endure beatings with hairbrushes just so I can look like a trophy girlfriend to his fellow vamps. I stop dead on the porch, although Isaac proceeds to the carriage. He doesn't notice I'm not there until he opens the door and stands for several moments, waiting for me to climb into the buggy.

He blinks out of his funk and traces the route back to where I'm standing.

"Come, Nova." His tone is pinched flat. "We do not want to be the last to arrive."

"Esther said I am not your best option, and maybe I'm not…" I let the rest of the sentence evaporate. Best option for a girlfriend? Just a lover? A wife? Now that I'm here with him, dressed in a dress that sings about me as a possession, rather than *of* me, I think of everything Esther said. That if I am not desirable the Brethren will kill me—how, I don't know, because being a *ghost* makes me pretty dead already—I only feel a sliver of guilt about tossing her under the bus. "It's obvious you're worried about what's going to happen tonight. If you don't believe in this, maybe you need another option."

He curses beneath his breath, scraping the sole of his boot on the dirt drive. "You are my only option. Esther sometimes speaks when she shouldn't." He jiggles the door handle. "Please come along now. It's very important that we are not late."

47

I climb into the carriage with the help of his hand.

It hardly seemed worth all of Esther's annoying fuss for me to look so pristine, until I really get a good look at Isaac in his own formal attire.

He sits back on the carriage bench in his fitted, black suit, crisp white shirt, and black satin vest. There is not a hair out of place, not a speck of dirt on his shoes. Isaac is as clear as a photograph—retouched, perfected, static.

And still disturbingly distant.

The same leathery driver who drove Machara Milligen away—the thick man Isaac called *Eustace*—urges the horses down the driveway.

Isaac isn't even moved by the jolt of the carriage.

His silence is bristly and annoying, but I understand. As much as I can. He's worried about seeing his Brethren. I was confident that Isaac could handle everything, but his gaze remains glued to the window as he strokes his knuckles. I hope I can handle everything.

It stops me from questioning why there is a small chest and a stack of blankets piled on the bench across from us, especially when the carriage windows are shut tight and the air inside the cab grows humid and stifling. I'm grateful that the bundles of heavy fabric, roman window shades—probably meant to block out any light—are rolled up and tied securely above the windows. I fold my arms across my chest and sit back, staring out the window too, worrying over what lies ahead for us.

The carriage takes a left at the end of the drive and continues down Washington Street, moving away from town. The wheels churn over the dirt road, the estate parallel to the carriage window. We leave behind the shadows of the carriage house, the barn, and a far-off candle-lit windows of what I think are the servant quarters set far back from the road. Isaac's endless property runs into tall weeds and finally rises into trees.

We ride along for maybe two miles and then there is a flash— only a flash—of gray sky, filled with lint. The horses jolt forward through the *vias* and then everything outside goes dark again. The Havrath estate has vanished. A bustling, snow-covered city street appears in its place. People in thick coats rush by on the sidewalks and cars honk behind the carriage, upsetting the horses. The carriage continues on, but an icy chill clings to my skin and makes it tingle.

A second wintry gust blasts through the carriage. Isaac shivers out of his stupor and scoots forward on the seat, retrieving a blanket from the opposite bench. He shakes it out, encasing us both. One arm around my shoulders, he draws me close to his ribs.

I inhale, disturbing the pearls, but their chant is muted beneath the blanket.

"You've enchanted me, haven't you?" I say. "Even though I told you not to do it."

"Of course." He flashes me a wicked smile and any annoyance I have about his admission drifts away as I take another deep breath. Isaac's gaze travels away from me to the passing landscape outside the window.

"You're really scared of them, aren't you?" I whisper.

"Scared? No. Nothing scares me." But his laugh is a bitter stutter. It doesn't convince me even a little bit.

"Tell me their names," I say. "They'll think you've told me all their secrets, and I'll yawn and show them how bored I am with them."

He peers down at me with a devilish grin. His joy washes over me. My heart, tethered to even his tiniest joy, floats.

"Sarkazian is the oldest and leads the Brethren," he squints as he says it. "Murial is second oldest and might be the smartest."

"That sounds like a girl's name," I giggle. The joke works. It does me good to watch his shoulders relax, the muscle below his ear soothed from its previous twitching.

"There are fourteen of us in the clutch right now. You don't need to know all their names, but you should know I am the youngest, so they respect me least." He wipes his lips with his index finger and thumb and lets out a surrendering sigh. "Grehnold is the next youngest and always trying to justify himself. He will be the most aggressive in courting you, I think."

I sit back from him. "You're worrying about being able to protect me?"

His expression is grim. "Desperately."

"Isaac," I brush my fingers down his arm, "It's not like I need saving. I'm a ghost. What are they going to do? Kill me again? Stop worrying. There's not much that can happen to me now."

"You're wrong," he says, still grim. "You don't understand how they could charm you. They will do everything they can to steal you away from me."

"That would be a *choice,* and it's one I wouldn't make."

"They would take everything I had if they could. They've tried before, but they didn't count on me being clever. That's why I hid the estate from them. Now they all do the same, although I'm better at it. They hate me all the more because they not only envy what I have, but how I'm able to keep it from them." He places his hand over mine. The delicious, comforting Fahrenheit of his touch rises up through my veins, spreading out in my mind, where it melts every thought that isn't about Isaac.

A car honks and the carriage jerks. One of the horses neighs.

"Ridiculous," Isaac grumbles. Eustace calms the animal with a guttural, *whoa girl!* and the carriage continues on. Isaac drops the curtain on the right side window. It cuts the chill, but doesn't eliminate it. "The Brethren chose this location with every intention of annoying me."

"How?"

"By upsetting my horses," he growls. "We agreed to a meeting place that was secluded and private and they purposefully chose a bustling metropolis! This is exactly the opposite of everything we agreed to."

I let him complain, paying less attention to anything more than the melodic sound of his voice. I am not worried about choosing anyone else and besides, he's got the most musical voice, it's easy to be calm as I listen to him. It's as if each syllable he utters is a serenade, even when he's not saying anything remotely comforting.

"Tell me some more about the Brethren," I say. "Which is the least threatening?"

"None of them," he says. "Every single one is competitive. You might not suspect Laumer or Cinq, because of their dispositions, or Venice, since she is a small female, but—"

"One of the vampires is a girl?"

"Cinq and Venice are both female," he corrects with a slow nod, "but no matter the sex, no vampire can be trusted. Cinq appears frail and frightened by everything, but don't let her trick you. She'll sneak up on you as much as any of them. And Venice, she's...well, she's small, like I said, but again, don't let it fool you. In her human life, she was married to Verlac, but since she changed him, they've despised one another. Worse for him, Urbis fell between them in ranking, so Verlac has to answer to Venice. It obviously grates him."

It's a little surprising to hear that there is a whole symphony of drums beating out of tune beneath the surface of the Brethren's ominous existence. That could be to our advantage, even if I'm not sure how yet.

"You said you're the youngest?"

"Yes. I am the newest vampire and I have no *stirp*—no established creator," he says. "My uncle was a hermit, not just from the human race, but from the Brethren too. A vagrant, who was driven out of his own clutch, bit him. That sort of lineage makes me less trust worthy."

"What's a clutch? Like a family?"

"Family shares love and respect for one another. Clutches are nothing like that. It is only a term for the groups of vampires we have descended from or were created from. The Brethren is made up of those of us who represent our clutches, or you could say, the lineage we were created from. My lineage is the lowest of all, because my clutch evolved from derelicts who often rejected the rules governing our existence."

"How many are in your clutch?"

"Only me," Isaac says, looking away. "There would have been my Uncle and me, but he was killed in the fire on my wedding day. That's the way most clutches are, though. As I told you, vampires are competitive by nature, so having anyone else in their clutch that could take their position in the Brethren, doesn't suit them much."

"You live a life of worrying who's sneaking up on you," I say and Isaac scoffs.

"Not when I'm the most clever vampire in the Brethren, and not when I have the most incredible mate at my side." He lifts my knuckles and kisses them. The velvet touch of his lips scatters my thoughts like pick-up sticks. "Once we are mated, the Brethren will no longer be of concern to us. We will be more powerful than all of them combined. That's why they will each seek to pull us apart."

I shake my head. "Is it because I'm a ghost?"

"Yes," Isaac says, this time with a stiff brush of a kiss against my knuckles as if he wants the conversation to end. He raises the shades from the window and a fresh shock of wintry air takes my breath.

Eustace guides the carriage off the main road and through a group of snow-coated pines that obscure looming iron gates from public view. Peeking out the window, high, black spires of a structure pierce the sky beyond the veil of trees.

The gates open automatically, although there are no attendants or cameras. Eustace only whips the horses into a trot and the metal clangs shut behind us. The only sounds are the horses' clopping hooves and the grinding tremble of the carriage wheels as they move along the winding drive.

A blur of small shadows breaks from the tree line. Dogs. They come running toward the carriage. Isaac sees them too and curses under his breath. He reaches for the chest on the seat across from us. I expect him to pull out a gun, but instead, he extracts a large bundle of bones wrapped in cloth. The fabric has absorbed the blood of the joints and hunks of intact meat, leaving it smeared with deep, red stains.

Isaac takes down the window and heaves the whole bundle out onto the snowy ground. The dogs, who were running full speed at the horses, detour and leap at the bones instead. They snarl and attack one another as they try to claim the bones.

Isaac certainly seems to have visited his enemies a lot.

I sit back on the carriage bench beside him, wondering if this is a foreshadowing of what is to come when I meet Isaac's brethren.

"At least it's secluded, like you wanted," I say to break the tension. It hardly helps.

"It's a safety precaution," Isaac says stiffly as the sound of the guard dogs fades away. "Not just for me, but for all of us. We meet in a neutral place because none of us will grant access to our estates."

"Why?"

"We are vampires, Nova. We hunt for each other. We want one another dead. It is what and who we are, do you understand? We fight for what is ours. But each of my Brethren believe everything in the world rightfully belongs to them."

"Do you believe that?" I ask. I feel his pride with a skitter of disgust. "That everything belongs to you?"

"I only desire to be the master of my destiny."

That sounds like a *yes*. At the same time, it sounds like what anyone would want and I'm no longer sure what his answer means or if I am opposed to it.

"Vampires are territorial. We will kill for what we believe is ours. In a group, if one of us attacks, the others will choose sides and fight also. When the battle is won, the victors fight one another to claim the prize." He clutches my hand and my disdain falls away like sand between my fingers. "This meeting may become us against them. My brethren will stop at nothing to seduce you and draw you from me, but as mates, we have the advantage. We battle together and we will claim the prize of remaining together. Remember: trust no one but each other."

The pearls of my dress shrill as I ask, "Can't we do this some other way?"

The carriage cuts through the underbrush, the sturdy leaves raking the bottom of the carriage. I rest my quivering fingers at my throat.

"It is a requirement of our law," he says. "I must present you, so that my Brethren can verify my claim is real. Once you are claimed, they are bound by law to respect our relationship. This night will be treacherous, but I have plans in place, should things get out of hand."

The carriage halts in front of mansion doors. I trail my fingers down, over the bodice of my dress where the stiff little piece of fabric lies. Esther didn't tell me what it was for, only that it was there in case of trouble. "How do I know if things are going badly and what should I do?"

"There is nothing for you to do," Isaac says with a less than reassuring grin, "except stay near to me."

48

The carriage wobbles as Eustace climbs down and opens the door. Isaac steps out first, and before he can offer me a hand, a male voice breaks through the night.

"Havrath! You've finally arrived! We've been waiting…and I see you still have your enormous body guard! How are you, Eustace? Considering more beneficial employ yet?"

"No, sir," Eustace says to the mystery male. "But I thank you for the consideration."

The masculine voice drips with what I believe would appear to be a baiting smile. "What does he give you? It must be nightly doses of venom to garner such loyalty!"

"I'm not at liberty to discuss our arrangement, sir," Eustace answers.

"The relationship must be quite profitable for you to be so faithful," the male muses. "Or, possibly, amorous?"

Eustace is silent. In the darkness of the open carriage, a sour wave rolls through my stomach. I cringe, thinking of Isaac sinking his fangs into Eustace's beefy neck and the carriage driver's eyes rolling into his skull in ecstasy. The thought of Isaac holding anyone else in his arms, besides me, curls my fingernails into my palms.

"Your envy is flattering, Grehnold." Isaac's tone is lazy, flat, bored. "But no less rude. My servants are not looking for alternate employ."

"As if they could..." Grehnold's answer whispers across my skin and raises goose bumps. The stranger suddenly samples the air with a sharp sniff and releases it with a theatrical gasp. "It can't be!" Grehnold laughs. "Not riding in this bumble trap carriage of yours! But I would swear to it..." He takes another fierce sniff and I shrink from the door as if he's smelling my neck. "Do I scent the presence of a *goddess* amidst your stench, Havrath?"

Isaac wasn't kidding—they really are shameless with the compliments. And completely minimizing of me as a human being.

Isaac's hand reaches into the carriage, palm up. Despite understanding that I am little more than a trophy to Isaac's Brethren, it is still a relief to place my hand in his. My palm is beaded with sweat, but Isaac's grip is firm and steadying. I step into the opening wishing I didn't have to duck down and get my first glimpse of Grehnold.

"This is the woman I shall marry," Isaac hisses as I descend the carriage steps. "Treat her thus."

"Ahhh, so you *have* come to claim her!" Grehnold laughs. The moment I lay eyes on the new vampire and my breath dissolves, as if caught and pulled away by the wind. The vision of him could do no less. The vampire before me is stately and bald, despite a heavy, bearded jaw. His small, green eyes appear sharp and clever as he assesses me with them.

"Of course," Isaac says with an ease that floats like oil over the tension showing on his brow.

"Well hello," Grehnold says with a small bow. "May I ask how this simple cad was able to persuade *divinity* and capture even a glance in his direction?"

"I chose him." My tone is more wooden than I'd like, but I shift my hips so the strings of pearls sing my meaning for me.

Grehnold's gaze lingers as if it is seeping into the cracks of me. The lifted edge of his grin leaves a grimy shadow of his imagination all over his face. His eyes slide over my body, visually groping my shape while trivializing my soul. Despite this, I've fallen into the deep standing water of Grehnold's eyes. Both charmed and paralyzed, I sink into the depth of his minimizations.

The other vampire takes my hand and shivers shoot up my arm as he kisses my knuckles. It's the same sensation Isaac's touch gives me, which rattles me. I didn't expect another vampire—anyone else, really—to elicit the same response from me that Isaac does.

Grehnold's eyes slide up to meet mine. "And what shall I call you, other than *goddess?*"

He's laying it on thick and I know it, but he appears so sincere —as if nothing in the world matters to him except me.

"That introduction will wait until we are before all the Brethren," Isaac says, taking my hand from Grehnold's.

Isaac's grip tightens around my fingers. I wrench my attention from Grehnold and the moment I meet Isaac's gaze, he smiles. There is a reminder in that adoring smile. I give my head a shake, emptying myself of all the things Isaac had warned me about: the vamps' territorial natures, their desire to charm, the urge to kill for what they believe is theirs.

Being caught up in the other vampire's gaze was a small betrayal to Isaac, but I am back where I should be now. Isaac's smile also says I belong to him. He will fight for that. For me. He will die before he allows any of these vampires to take me from him.

There is something horribly weak and something gloriously powerful battling it out within that knowledge.

Grehnold offers me his arm, but I straighten my back so the pearls sing *mine, mine, mine,* as they sway across my chest and hips. I take Isaac's arm, along with the pleasure of Grehnold's defeated smirk.

"Apologies, brother." Grehnold drops his arm and bows his head. "I was just expressing my admiration of this supreme creature that you've somehow managed to acquire."

"Somehow," Isaac repeats darkly. We stride away, toward the front steps, with me still attached to his arm.

The darkness of the estate closes in around us. Moonlight swiftly breaks overhead, glazing the sizable house and the line of odd vehicles parked on the crescent drive. The cars are odd because, despite their four wheels, I've never seen anything like them. Sleek pods, glinting eggs, geometric wings and flames with seating compartments. On second look, everything is a bit strange, from the old fashioned house with mirrored glass in every window, the futuristic cars lined up out front, and even the spiky grass, which looks like it's made of splinters of glass. All together, my surroundings make me feel that Isaac is the safest thing in this whole place.

"If you should require a more suitable escort..." Grehnold calls after us. Isaac continues forward, but I jerk him to a halt and turn back.

"Just so you know what it is that I consider suitable," I tell Grehnold, "I was the one who sought Isaac out. Not the other way around. I tracked him down, followed him home, and insisted on staying with him."

That's a dead lie, and both Isaac and I know it, but as I stand beside him, reeling from the sensuous feeling of his body so close to mine, I begin to wish that I could rewrite our history. That maybe I'd met him first, before Silvia. That I could've worn the dress he had made for me. That it hadn't taken amnesia and a hundred years to find him again.

I certainly won't have any of his *Brethren* treating him as if he is substandard. I turn away from Grehnold and decide right then not to cast even another glance in that idiot's direction, no matter what he says, and no matter how hard he tries to steal my attention from Isaac.

Grehnold doesn't give up easily.

"Times change," the bald vampire purrs. "Maybe you'll follow me home one day too."

"Doubtful." I dismiss him without even a glance over my shoulder. Instead, I squeeze Isaac's bicep. "Do you have more interesting friends here, Isaac? I think I'd like to meet *them*."

Grehnold's eyes warm my back as we walk away.

We go through a tall, burgundy door into a round entry hall, big enough to use as a skating rink. Twisted branches interlace above our heads with tapers tucked into the snarls that cast a sepia glow on the marble floor as we stride across it. Isaac's soles barely whisper, but my heels clink like ice in a glass. The moment we enter, a band of ten men, standing in front of a broad-stoned fireplace, turn in unison to look at us.

Every single one of them is as stunning as stars, although they all appear a little too perfect to be human. Grehnold got it mixed up. These men are the gods.

All eyes on me, all of them so similar to Isaac, so breathtakingly beautiful, and all scanning my body as if this is an auction, rather than an introductory meeting. I raise my chin and the pearls trill, *mine, mine, mine*. I'm sure they were designed to sing for Isaac, but in my head, they are singing for me. I am my own and nobody's shrinking violet.

The cluster of vampires turn toward us, their chins ticking upward as if catching the scent of the perfume Esther poured all over me. My arm still looped through Isaac's, I exaggerate the swish of my hips as we cross the room. The pearls don't whisper. Instead, they shrill their message like an enthusiastic opera singer. Their smiles drop from their glorious faces—all of them, except Isaac's, whose haughty smirk spreads across his lips and seeps into every other feature on his face.

"Good evening, my brethren," Isaac says.

"I'd like to introduce you to my claimed, Nova Ford."

"*Sure*," the vamp furthest from us sneers. "Don't know how you did it, but it's a very convincing scent with which you've imbued her. Good stunt, Havrath."

"It's not a trick," Isaac insists. Even I cringe at the whine in his tone.

"He didn't coat me with any scent," I snap. It's like they're saying Isaac is a dog and I'm a fire hydrant. But the vampires only glance at me before turning back to their conversation and collectively ignoring that I said anything.

A vampire with a low brow drawls. "You never dare to leave your little hidey-hole. How would you have come across her? Even if you ventured out and got so supremely lucky, how would you have fooled this beauty into being with you?" His chin flicks up slightly again, taking another whiff of me.

I hope it's sweaty.

"He didn't have to fool me into anything," I insist and stop myself from continuing. Their snobbish, minimizing behavior makes me defensive and if I've learned anything from Meg, it's that defensiveness is weakness.

Still, the vamps look amongst each other, one pressing his tongue into his beautiful cheek as if he knows better.

I tug Isaac's arm and he obliges me, dipping his ear down so I can whisper in a dull tone, loud enough for all of them to hear, "I thought you said these Brethren were competitive? They only seem petty to me, and very jealous of you."

A young vamp steps forward and a low growl breaks loose from Isaac's throat.

"Hello to you too, Isaac," the vampire flicks him a casual nod, though the vamp's eyes are on me. Ancient in their depths, his eyes are mahogany brown, as if drinking blood has permanently tinted them. Every inch of this vampire is slicked back, straightened and suave, but his shoulders are relaxed and his smile is easy. His nostrils flare slightly as he offers me his hand. "It is a pleasure to meet you, Nova Ford. Please know that you will be safe the entire time you are here. I personally guarantee it." He scans the other vampires with a wilting glare. "You will all behave yourselves, gentlemen."

I would scoff at him for calling them *gentlemen* instead of what they are—bloody murderers, nearly cannibals, and mostly condescending brethren who aren't brothers at all—but the vampire's stately demeanor is so soothing, I relax my forearm which is still looped around Isaac's.

But Isaac doesn't have the same reaction. As I relax, he clamps his elbow to his ribs, as if he needs to prevent my arm from slipping away.

"Don't tell me you're going to allow Havrath's claiming, Sarkazian," the vamp with the brooding brow says. "It's like allowing a child to keep a diamond ring to play dress up!"

A diamond...*really*. I've had about enough of this, ridiculous heels or not. The vampire's compliments are so over the top that it's not difficult at all to see them for what they are: shameless attempts at manipulation. They're so unsophisticated in their attempts, it's offensive.

I scramble inwardly, trying to recall what Isaac told me about the vampire called Sarkazian. I believe he said this vampire was the oldest, and from what I can tell, it makes sense, because he's also the most polished.

"I do believe it," Sarkazian answered in a measured tone. "The scent is real, though I can see she's fading at her edges. You're a fool to delay her revenancy."

I thought it was just my eyes, but even in the dim candle light, I can see it too. My fingertips are blurry, as if I'm looking at them through greasy glass. I can't make out whether or not I have fingernails.

"It is her decision," Isaac says and my heart swells with his respect for me.

"Her decision might be to fade into oblivion? Lost forever?"

Sarkazian chuckles, but his gaze is harder than stone. "Or is it your decision to postpone acquiring a vessel so that none of your Brethren can take what should belong to the highest ranking vampire who can look after her properly?"

"Take that to the bank, Murial," another vampire chuckles, his sapphire eyes rooted on me. Ah yes, Murial is the second, highest ranking vampire, and Isaac claimed Murial is the smartest.

Sarkazian adds, "Do not taunt him, Faverus. Having been a vampire from the very beginning—"

"Yes, yes, everyone knows you were the very first and Murial second." Faverus rolls his gorgeous, sapphire eyes. There's very little humor in Faverus's tone and I'm a little surprised when Sarkazian does little more than shrug off the insult.

"He's right," Murial warns, flicking his chin in Faverus's direction. "You ought to think before flaunting that position, Sarkazian. I doubt that any of us savor the position you've put us in, and lest any of us forget, the hierarchy can change at any given moment."

"Though it has not for nearly a millennia." Sarkazian's fierce expression becomes an apologetic smile as he turns to me. "Forgive their outburst, Miss Ford. Children don't always honor their elders, or the gifts they've been given."

"Gifts?" yet another vamp sneers as he slips a pocket watch into his vest.

"Gentlemen!" Sarkazian bellows. To my surprise, all the vampires silence, A willowy female and equally reedy male skulk into the room, joining the group of vampires. Although they are gorgeous as the rest of the Brethren, this must be Cinq and Laumer, with their anxious glances and looking as though they're about to be kicked or ridiculed at any moment. These two are the ones Isaac said appeared weak and scared, but actually aren't. Flinching at each movement of the vamps around them, they put on a good act if it isn't true. "This is no way to introduce a goddess into our company!"

"*My* goddess," Isaac corrects, even if he does it in a bleak whisper and chased by a hard swallow. It's shocking to see him, usually so powerful and commanding, cowed by his Brethren.

I can kind of understand why the vamps find weakness unappealing.

Sarkazian drops his chin slightly.

"For now," he answers Isaac, stepping back from us with another smile that erases my distaste at Isaac's intimidation. Sarkazian is not only a bully, but a statement like that diminishes me too. Whether or not Isaac can defend me doesn't matter. I'll do it myself.

"Forever," I say, delivering Sarkazian a gritty, *back-off* smile.

The eldest vampire only returns a *we'll see* tip of his head, announcing, "We'll have dinner first, and then we will convene to the billiard room to discuss matters."

D*inner.*

My legs go weak and I sway on the lousy stilettos. There's only one way to interpret *dinner,* when I'm the only one here who isn't a vampire. I'm not sure what these vampires want from me, but from the quaking in my stomach, my intuition tells me it might be an arm or leg.

I walk into the dining hall, palms sweating, at the nucleus of these beautiful men. They surround Isaac and me and leave no way to escape. Isaac's arm beneath mine feels less assuring and more like a leash, leading me to my last supper.

We enter a dining hall which is unusual in many ways. White walls, ceiling, and floor, there are no tables. Instead, a low, white platform stretches down the center of the room—like a cat walk for a fashion show. Fourteen, formal sitting chairs line the right wall; only two chairs are against the left. The chairs are uniformly black, upholstered with shining leather, the backs of which each appear to be embroidered with various patterns in black thread. I'm not sure what the designs mean.

Isaac takes a seat in the first chair on the right, still holding my fingers as the Brethren file past us, each casting me long, sultry looks, before taking their seats in the other chairs against the wall. It is a mixture of flattery and insult to me; each gorgeous creature eyeing me as if they are choosing a cut of meat at a buffet.

Isaac tugs my fingers, guiding me to the front of him, and then gently pulling me down onto his lap. I perch on his legs, uncomfortable with the intimate seat I'm given, aware of the hard muscle of his legs. While I fidget and shift, Isaac runs a steady hand down my back, making the strings shrill.

A female saunters in through the open doors and the rest of the vampires' conversations drop into silence. With one look at her, I lean back, suffocating the sound of the pearls too.

The female is obviously vampire, breathtaking in the way that turns 'ugly'...exotic. A drastic shorty, she's boosted up on 60's patent leather, knee-high, white boots. Her eyes and mouth are both too large, her nose a tiny, drifting snorkel in the center of her face, her body shape straight as a stick. Her hot pink jumper doesn't even attempt to imitate feminine curves.

Not that any of it matters.

Confidence pours out of every one of her pores. Hair hidden away beneath a sparkly white scarf, a few long twirls of glossy-black locks spiral from her temples to her shoulders.

She's incredible.

"You're late, Venice," Sarkazian drawls, inspecting his nails.

"Nothing's started yet," she counters without breaking stride. She casts a graceful nod and somewhat wily smile at me as she continues on to the only empty seat. Isaac's grip at my waist tightens. Once Venice reaches her seat, she coats the chair with her body, rather than just sitting down. In fact, she's so relaxed, she's almost lying flat, her rear teetering on the edge of the cushion, shoulders flush with the low back. Her legs latch lazily at the knee.

A servant, in tails, bow tie, and with a completely neutral expression, closes the great doors of the hall with a grind and squeak that echo. The sound sets me on edge and Isaac doesn't relax his grip.

Another door at the opposite end of the dining hall wafts open and the sharp clap of polished shoes announce the two more servants who enter the room together. This time, it is a young man and woman who saunter in. Despite the plain black and white serving uniforms, they are attractive, each carrying a covered, silver platter in front of them.

The male has delicate elf-ish features and sandy hair brushed in a thick wave across his forehead. He is sprinkled with freckles and his pale skin has pink undertones, like a baby pig.

The female is brutally tall, narrow shouldered, and has storm-cloud colored hair tied into a heavy braid that reaches her waist. Her face is moon-shaped and she's painted thick, goth-black wings from the edges of her smoky eyes. She walks across the room with a model's stomp, but every inch of her vibrates with a perpetual quiver.

There is no table.

No place to put the platters.

Unlike me, the servants don't seem confused by that.

They come to the base of the low cat walk, the man's chin held high. The woman's silver lid rattles against the platter.

"Dinner is served," the male servant says, eyes straight ahead instead of gazing at the vampires, and me, lined up in our chairs against the wall.

Sarkazian stands. "Dinner manners apply," he announces simply.

I bend down toward Isaac and he cranes upward, so I can whisper in his ear. "What does that mean?"

"The servants are revenants. They walk, one at a time and the highest ranking vampires have first choice. If Sarkazian wants the servant, he takes them."

"You mean, he drinks from them?"

Isaac's beautiful brow wrinkles. "Yes, he can drink, but it is a show of personal control and power for each higher ranking vampire to pass the meals on. Manners dictate that no vampire should eat, until all their subordinates have had their fill."

I gulp, my eyes drifting back to the male and female servants at the end of the runway. It's stupid that it shocks me, but it does. I really hoped the silver platters contained salads or steaks. Now, I have no idea what they contain and I don't even care. Ghost vomit scales the back of my throat, strong as vinegar.

Leaning on the arm of the chair, an ache shoots up my wrist the arm and I sit up straight on Isaac's lap, peering down at him as I rub my hand. "I'm going to have to watch you drink from one of them?"

"They don't usually get this far," Isaac murmurs. It doesn't really help. "Part of the game is that the lowest vamp in the hierarchy also gets to choose the servants that will be offered for meals. I know Verlac has a penchant for waifs with braids, and both Murial and Urbis enjoy freckles. I picked all fourteen of the servants to correspond with my Brethren's particular tastes."

"You could've chosen your own type, but you are tempting them instead," I whisper. It's kind of sweet, in a really sick and disturbing way, that he chose for them, instead of himself.

"I already have the one who satisfies me." Isaac's eyes flash silver and he flicks his thumb at my back, making the pearls croon. "I have fourteen chances to entice them to succumb before I do."

"What happens if they do?" I ask, leaning my arm across Isaac's shoulders.

"Whoever eats before their subordinates are fed is humiliated and must clean up after the meal."

The vamp beside us, blond and square-faced leans from his chair toward ours. "Dream on, Havrath."

"We'll see, Carmen," Isaac returns with a sharp smirk. "I believe those were the same words you used at our last dinner, weren't they? Did you bring an apron for this evening?"

The vampire's hazel eyes flick to me and despite myself, I melt a little. "When he is proven wrong," Carmen says with a dry smile, "you are welcome to sit on my lap, dear lady, while he tidies up."

Isaac is interrupted from his come back as Sarkazian points to the male servant and commands with a flick of his wrist, "Walk."

The male servant answers with a brief nod and steps onto the catwalk, holding his platter in front of his chest. He walks with an agonizingly slow pace, traipsing past Sarkazian with a glimpse to the alpha of the Brethren. Sarkazian watches the male pass, giving no indication of hunger or even interest, aside from a bland, complimentary nod.

The male can't conceal his frown. The confidence in the man's eyes disintegrates as he moves on to Murial, who sits stroking his chin as if he is bored, despite the fact that Isaac chose the male because of Murial's love of freckles. The servant's visible disappointment in being unable to entice Sarkazian is swiftly replaced by stony determination. The male brazenly locks eyes with Murial, even pausing to blow the vampire a kiss.

Murial only yawns. Faverus's sapphire eyes scan the freckled man, but Faverus too allows the male to pass by with the now-rattling platter. The vamp even leans slightly off his chair, smirking, as he watches the servant stride past the fourth, fifth, and sixth vampires.

"Not for you, Drake? You either, Venice?" Faverus taunts. "Oh! And not your taste either, Urbis?"

The sixth vampire, Urbis, pinches his heart shaped lips. He's as beautiful as a china doll. "He looks lovely, but I'm feeling generous. Verlac or Okuda should have a taste first."

The male servant slows his gait, feet caressing the floor. The man's biceps strain within the arms of his white shirt, as if he is perpetually flexing. More nervous than he was at the start, the male lingers in front of the vampire, Verlac. The servant balances the platter and draws his fingers slowly through his hair. At the same time, he casts a longing gaze on the next vampires in the line of chairs.

Isaac said vampires are extremely competitive and I'm not sure that the male knows exactly what he's doing, but the longing gaze he's casting at the next vamps in line, while still standing between Verlac and Okuda, the latter vampire gripping the intricately carved arms of the chair, fangs so far extended, they slash into his lower lip.

"Verlac?" Murial chides from the second chair, "are you going to deny your inferiors and eat in front of all of us?"

Verlac's fingernails dig into the chair arms. "No," he pants. "My lesser Brethren are weak and must eat first."

Even if I wanted to ask Isaac what's happening, it would do no good. He's panting even harder than Verlac.

Okuda's fangs have skewered through his lower lip and the venom drizzles from the tips, making dark stains on the chest of his suit coat.

Isaac lets out a low growl that vibrates through my rear. I can feel the intensity of his hunger permeate my body.

Faverus leans off his chair with a sly smile at me. "You see, my love, the strongest vampires offer the first crumbs of the meal to the weakest."

I would tell him Isaac's already told me, but I'm focused on bracing myself on the chair as a barrier between Isaac's tense body and the servant on the runway. The pearls sing. Despite the male being seven vampires away from us, Isaac's brow is furrowed as if he is being branded and Carmen begins to hiss beside us. Faverus chuckles. "We shall see who the weakest is tonight. Okuda? Would it be you?"

The vampire beside Verlac looks sick. Like Verlac, Okuda grips the chair arms so tightly, the wood lets out a crack like ice in his palms. The servant strolls in front of Okuda and the vamp's almond eyes crush shut. His mouth contorts as he grits his teeth and the fang in his lip grinds downward, spearing a larger hole in the skin.

"Cinq, it looks like you will not get the first taste tonight!" Murial laughs.

The servant pauses as Okuda's first finger pries free of the chair arm and rises, as if summoning the male to stay.

"Would you take me, master?" the servant asks. The sound of his voice shatters Okuda's desperate resolve.

"Yes!" Okuda howls, clapping his mouth shut and grinding his teeth. Then, "No! Pass on!"

"What is it, Okuda?" Drake, the fourth vampire in the hierarchy and who the servant has already passed by, removes his pocket watch, leisurely swinging it around his finger. "Yes or no?"

"Yes!" Okuda howls and this time, he doesn't recant his desire. The servant steps down from the cat walk and strolls over to stand before the summoning vampire. Okuda writhes in his seat as the man lays the silver platter at the vampire's feet and removes the silver dome. What lies on the platter is strangely normal and completely unexpected: a white, linen napkin, folded like a swan. The servant lifts the napkin and shakes it out.

Isaac shifts beneath me, but he doesn't try to get up. I glance at him, both his eyes are squeezed shut.

I look back at Okuda, his fangs dribbling venom down his chin as he tries to open his mouth wider and release the skewered fang from his lower lip. The other vampires laugh as Okuda abandons all hope of releasing the fang and lunges for the servant. The vampire clutches the servant's shoulders and whether or not the male seemed to want to entice one of the vamps, now that it has happened, the male lets out a shriek. Okuda thrusts his head back and dives forward, sinking the tips of his fangs, one free and one still caught in his own lip, through the servant's skin. The male's expression flattens out in shock from the brutal attack.

"Like a *shrieking*, drinking through your lip!" Faverus hoots, slapping his leg. Sarkazian turns his head away in disgust, but the other vampires shriek and shout insults, as the servant's legs go limp and he slumps in Okuda's arms.

"Don't drain him, you *child*!" Murial sneers. "He'll have to find himself another skin, and this one is quite lovely."

"A shame to waste," Cinq agrees, dabbing at the venom that drips from his own fangs.

"You're going to waste the bottle!" Urbis snaps with his baby-doll lips, but Okuda continues to suck, straining at the servant's neck even as the male's eyes roll upward and disappear, leaving only the zombie-whites.

"Stop!" Verlac jumps up and curls his fist into Okuda's hair, yanking his brethren backward. "It's a waste of a cup!"

Okuda's fangs rip from the servant's neck and blood spurts into the air from the gaping wound. The man falls in a heap, flipping the platter. It flips over with a clatter and as if it is a dinner bell, Verlac dives from his chair, lunging for the servant's neck.

I think he means to drink the male dry, but instead, Verlac, panting, slides his tongue along the man's skin. Instead of circular puncture wounds, a dark, purple scar forms where Okuda's violent removal had ripped the flesh wide.

The six lesser vampires, including the one skittling around on the chair beneath me, are hissing and growling. Cinq bites the vampire, Laumer, who strikes Cinq with a sharp back hand.

"Control!" Sarkazian bellows from the front of the room. In an instant, the chaos stops and the vampires freeze. Sarkazian rises from his seat and the only sounds in the room are the panting, the turbulent rattling of the female servant's platter at the end of the catwalk as she stares in horror at the male servant, lying on the ground before Okuda and Verlac.

"Okuda," Sarkazian continues in his oddly, measured voice, "you *know* you do not drain a bottle if a skin is not required for another revenant!"

Okuda drags his forearm across his bloody mouth, the wild look seeping out of his eyes. He turns from one side to another, surveying the servant slumped at his feet, the elder vampires to his right, and then the inferiors—us—to his left. His fangs fully retract, the one fang yanking up and out of his lip, as Okuda puts his hand over his mouth in shock.

"I didn't mean to—" he stammers.

"No, you weren't thinking at all! Just look at your shirt," Grehnold scoffs. I don't know why he is so haughty when his own fangs were hanging out and drizzling like open fire hoses.

A clatter at the end of the dining hall pulls all of our eyes in that direction. The female servant has dropped the platter and darts toward the door where she and the male had entered. She grasps the handle, but it's shut tight, and no matter how she yanks at the handle or pounds against the wood door, it doesn't open.

Sarkazian watches her calmly, clasping his hands in front of himself. "My sweet lady…" he says, his tone deep and soothing, as the female continues to scream.

I try to rise off Isaac's lap, but now he is the one holding me back. When I glimpse him, he shakes his head, a signal for me to mind my own business.

Sarkazian pinches the bridge of his nose between his eyes. "Murial," he says, "would you please explain to this servant again what is expected of her?"

Murial crosses the room to the female, who screams and claws and tries to bite him as he nears her. With one quick movement, like a steel trap, the vampire moves in, pressing his body to the back of hers as he grips each of her wrists. She whimpers, but stills, against the door.

Murial tilts his head and, at first, I think he's going to bite her, but his lips only dip to her ear. He tips his head like a lover and his mouth moves, stirring her hair, but his words are too quiet to hear. The female's body relaxes in waves, and if I didn't know any better, I would think I was witnessing an intimate moment between lovers, rather than a hysterical woman being gently subdued by a vampire.

"What did he say to her?" I ask Isaac, but he only shakes his head, as if he doesn't know.

Murial releases the female and rather than fighting him, her arms drop to her sides. He turns away from her and walks back to his seat and she follows all on her own. Eyes wide as an owl, she gathers up the platter, napkin, and dome, reassembling them as they were before. Her hands still quiver, but she uses her thumbs to hold the dome to the platter, staring straight ahead until Sarkazian, still standing, gives her a flourish of his arm, inviting her to walk.

Her foot shakes, but she steps onto the catwalk. She staggers, the platter rattling, but she continues forward. As she crosses in front of Sarkazian's seat, he stands and she jerks to a halt, her face crumbling into a silent sob.

"Come here, darling," Sarkazian purrs, holding out his hand to her. She clutches the silver handles to her chest and stumbles off the catwalk to Sarkazian. He waits patiently, neither moving nor helping, until she stands before him. She rattles the silver with a soft, *oh,* and ducks down to set the platter on the floor before the vampire. She lifts the dome and removes the disheveled napkin.

"Leave it," he tells her softly. "Will you sit on my lap and watch the show with me?"

His voice is buttery and innocent. Her wide eyes stare at him a moment before she nods.

Her gaze darts to Murial. The second strongest vampire gives her a brief, encouraging nod. The female shuffles forward and takes Sarkazian's extended hand. He sits and guides her onto his lap, the way Isaac did to me. The woman perches stiffly there, just as I did on Isaac's too.

Sarkazian lifts the female's hand, examining her rigid fingers. Without a glance in our direction, he says, "Isaac, take care of Okuda's mistake, please."

Isaac shovels me off his lap and onto his emptied seat before I can object. I don't want to be left in this room full of vampires, alone, but Isaac does as he's told, hefting the male servant's body up and over his shoulder. Although it doesn't seem like a strain, his gaze is dark and brooding as he crosses over the catwalk and goes out another door, across from the servant's entrance. He goes out without a glance back in my direction and the stares of all thirteen hungry vampires fall on me in his absence.

I saac disappears and a thread of terror stitches itself to my spine. Sitting in a room full of vampires who are geared up to feast is unsettling, no matter how ghostie I am.

Sarkazian claps his hands. The moon-faced female on his lap startles, but Sarkazian casually rests one arm across her legs as the servant door opens.

Two more female servants, each holding a platter, step into the room. One has curly, bleached-blond hair with an inch of pure black roots spread down the center part of her hair; the second female, makes a weird statement wearing black tights, a pink tutu, an artfully shredded tank top, and rainbow eye shadow that extends from eyelashes to eyebrows.

Both seem as steady and confident as the male servant had been, although the blond with the roots spots the female on Sarkazian's lap and the contented lift in her lips goes flat. The girl with the tutu scans right past Sarkazian and the girl on his lap, to the seated line of beautiful vamps. Tutu gives a small squeal and wiggles her hips, rattling her platter as she bounds toward the edge of the catwalk.

"Please," Sarkazian gives the welcoming wave of his arm again and the females look at one another.

Tutu squeals and dances in place again, but Roots plants her foot on the catwalk first. Roots moves down the catwalk with a distinctive sway to her hips, stomping one booted heel in front of the other. She struts past Sarkazian and pauses for each subsequent vamp to twirl, lick her lips, and shoot them a risqué smile.

She even beckons Cinq and Laumer with a teasing finger, but both vamps wave her on. She passes Carmen's gritting leer and comes to Holifeld with a stiff smile, as if it hurts her cheeks. Her eyes are glossy, as if she's going to burst into tears, but the moment Holifeld raises his hand, eagerly summoning her, she breaks into a broad smile and struts off the catwalk. She deposits the platter at his feet and shakes out the napkin as if it's a prom dress. She snuggles onto Holifeld's lap and he wastes no time pushing her hair back and sinking his teeth into the flesh below her ear.

Holifeld slurps and the female lets out a groan. I notice Carmen and Grehnold grip the arms of their chairs, knuckles white as they watch. Roots finally slumps in Holifeld's arms, his head following the movement of her body. The outline of his fangs ridges the skin of her neck like weird bones. I look away.

I need Isaac to come back.

Sarkazian motions to the female with the tut and it all starts over again. Once Carmen claims her, Sarkazian summons the next two servants. The ritual of servants and claiming continues, the slurping and moaning nauseating; the occasional scream or, plead to stop altogether, disturbing. It goes on until all the vampires, except Sarkazian, have fed.

The last two servants to enter are males. Sarkazian lets out a disappointed sigh and the female on his lap, who had relaxed slightly, stiffens again.

"Isaac considered these two the cream of the crop? None of these revenants are a worthy skin!" The alpha vampire's words carry the tone of a curse.

"Maybe she is interested in slipping into a male skin..." Grehnold turns his smile in my direction.

"Nova," Sarkazian leans off his chair, the girl adjusting awkwardly around him, "are any of these bottles pleasing to you? However, I'd prefer you have a fresh bottle, rather than one of these cast-offs."

To me?

I press my back to the chair. "I...I didn't know it was something that might happen tonight," I stammer. I didn't expect to be offered a man's body either.

Where is Isaac? Did he know this was going to happen? He talked about finding a skin for me, but he never mentioned that it might happen tonight.

"I don't know what you mean." Sarkazian turns his glittering gaze on me and I am pierced with a thousand slivers of metal. "You're a ghost only for this moment, my goddess," he croons as if I am his, rather than Isaac's. Or, maybe more like I am a pricey adornment he has acquired for his finger. "You deserve a form more useful to you."

Isaac appears in the doorway and relief spills through my veins. I want to shout to him what his Brethren have proposed, but the way his shoulders curl, eyes glaring up from beneath the low tilt of his forehead, it's obvious he already knows.

"She is *mine*," Isaac snarls.

Considering the fire around me, I'm fine with sizzling away in Isaac's frying pan. He stalks back to me. I move to stand, but he stays me with gentle pressure on my forearm. He positions himself at a passive angle, but he is still standing between me and his Brethren.

"Yet, you have not drunk from her." Sarkazian chuckles. "She has no skin. Your claim is weak."

The dining hall is so stiffly silent, I'm afraid to crease it with a breath.

"The law is that I present her, which I've done." Isaac reaches back, extending his hand to me. I take it, even though his touch triggers an urge to run. "We'll be going."

"Now, now…there's no need to be offended. Stay." The strength behind Sarkazian's command rolls through the air and crashes against me. It's like an airborne sting that momentarily paralyzes. "We can retire for a friendly game of billiards instead."

The female on Sarkazian's lap remains frozen. The other vampires use the napkins to wipe their faces. The servants are alive, but once deposited on the chairs they sat in with the vampire who fed from them, the servants slump with satiated smiles that I don't understand.

Sarkazian remains seated as the vampires file from the dining hall. Isaac follows them, my hand in his. Sarkazian smiles at me as we pass. The girl on his lap seems more relaxed now that dinner is over.

"I'll join you, once I've finished," Sarkazian says from behind us.

The female with the moon-shaped face screams as we enter the billiard room down the hall.

Other than my dress, the house is a tomb. Not a stretch, considering I'm in the presence of fourteen vampires. The billiard room is so dark, I feel my pupils widening. The walls are polished red wood. The short green carpet swallows our arrival in one gulp.

Three pool tables are spaced across the room, racks of sticks on the wall, billiards waiting in triangular wood frames on the sharp, green felt. I'm surprised the table felt isn't vampire-themed: red.

Murial, picks up a cue ball and spins it in his fingers as if the ball is weightless. "Play for stakes, Havrath?"

"Wouldn't you like that," Isaac sneers, sliding his arm beneath the pearls. They shrill, *mine,* as exciting as the feeling that Isaac's touch sends racing through my stomach. "I'm not playing for her."

I draw a slow breath of relief. Isaac's scent rolls from him, icy-sharp and clarifying. None of the other vampires can come close to measuring up to him. The thrill zips through my stomach again.

Who is this person I'm becoming? I've never been so beguiled, so willing to be considered property. The idea of that nags at my brain. I should be disgusted, but instead, I'm breathing in Isaac's scent and daydreaming of more.

The longer we stand together, pressed close, the less I can tolerate the thought of him taking even one step away. It's not intimidation from the thirteen other pairs of admiring, hungry eyes on me. Every moment Isaac's touch remains on my skin, it is clearer and clearer to me that I am his and he is mine. Considering any other situation sends a frantic vein of panic whipping through me.

"You're right not to play, since you'd lose." Grehnold turns his smoldering gaze on me. "Nothing would be so sweet as to hear those pearls singing *my* name."

I curl my toes so hard inside my stilettos that if I wasn't leaning on Isaac, I'd fall over. His body responds to the pressure of mine, muscles tightening to support me as well as root us both in place.

Is this what love feels like?

Isaac flashes a brilliant, biting smile at his brethren. "As if you would be so eager or willing to gamble the same prize."

Murial throws a devilish smile my way. It is every bit as handsome as Isaac's, but the heat of Isaac's body running down the edge of mine makes the other vamp's charms less than inspiring. "Or is it that Grehnold is no coward?"

"Are you saying I am?" Isaac growls.

He tears away from me to stand toe to toe with Murial. I teeter on my heels, as if his momentum will drag me along behind him.

The guttural, piercing growls sound like scraping metal. The noise erupts all around me. It takes a moment to connect the bared teeth of the vampires with their foreboding snarls.

"You've come to present your prize to us, Havrath, but it seems rather weak to parade your spoils without any proof that you deserve them." Sarkazian's says from the doorway. His voice is like oil floating on a puddle.

Isaac and Murial move away from one another as if their bodies have no other choice.

Sarkazian casts a flawless smile in my direction. I return it on impulse, rather than instinct.

"Ms. Ford deserves a victor. That should be a vamp who is fully capable of protecting her." Sarkazian says.

"Like you," Isaac sneers.

"Satisfaction is of highest priority to all of us." Sarkazian says. "You should honor that."

Whose? Mine or theirs?

Isaac's shoulders bow beneath the weight of Sarkazian's scrutiny. "I am her victor," he mumbles.

I cringe inwardly at the bend in his voice. It's more like he's trying to convince himself, rather than making a statement to the alpha vampire and the rest of his Brethren who all watch us with sharp eyes.

"Come now, Isaac," Sarkazian drawls as the razor sharp points of his fangs extend, "I have no doubt you would give it your best, but you hardly inspire my confidence that you are the most suited for such a mate."

Isaac's snarl pulls my nerves to the surface. Even I know it's stupid to disrespect the alpha in such a way.

Sarkazian lunges, snapping his fangs and barely missing Isaac's neck.

Isaac spins out of the way, dropping into a squatting attack position at the Alpha's knees.

Poised to leap, Isaac's stare is so hollow and black, I churn backward, pearls screaming as I ram against Faverus's chest. Faverus grabs my upper arms. I shriek as his fingers dig into my skin. The pearls' shriek cuts through the snarls and tears Isaac's attention from the danger in front of him.

The alpha lunges again. Isaac darts out of Sarkazian's path.

I feign a faint and slide right out of Faverus's unsuspecting grasp. I scuttle away, as the rest of the vamps close in on Isaac.

The vamps press forward, trapping Isaac between a semi-circle of bodies and Sarkazian.

Faverus makes a grab for me and I tumble to the side, avoiding him once again. The smile on his face tells me he's been toying with me, cat-and-mousing me to keep me distracted as the Brethren close in on Isaac. Skittering backward against the wall, I break through the edge of the vamps and end up within the bubble they've created to corral Isaac. I'm parallel to him.

Fangs extended and snapping, Isaac lashes out at his Brethren, barely keeping them at bay. He said vampires will fight to the death for what they believe is theirs. He also said vamps believe everything rightfully belongs to them.

They're going to kill him.

His scent pours from him, the terror of coming death. I breathe him in and the thought of a future without him turns my own blood to ice. Yanking off my shoes, I stumble toward Isaac and hold up the heels like wooden stakes, ready to plunge them into whoever gets close enough.

I may only last a moment, but I'll die before I see Isaac hurt.

Verlac knocks one of the heels from my hand and Esther's words shout through my head. *In case of trouble...*

I grope my bodice with my free hand. My finger slips over a circular object. I tug it from the fabric pocket. The warlock's monocle slides from the fabric, into my hand.

What am I supposed to do with this?

A pale rainbow appears in the clear chip. I squeeze it in my fist. The sharp edges dig into the flesh and blood trickles down my fingers.

The Brethren raise their noses all at once like a pack of hounds scenting my blood. They turn their attention from Isaac to me in one wave, emitting a collective, frenzied hiss.

This isn't how I planned to help Isaac—by becoming a meal for his Brethren—but Isaac takes advantage of the distraction. He lunges at Sarkazian, sinking his teeth into the alpha's neck.

Sarkazian lets out a shout that shakes the walls.

My head feels like it will explode from the sound.

The vampires fall away as if the shout was a command to retreat.

I stumble backward, my bloody hand to my temple. The chip falls from my palm, hits my cheek and sticks before sliding sideways over my skin. I shriek as the cold glass slips between my eyelids and fuses to my eye. I shake my head and claw at my face, but I can't remove it.

I lift my hand in front of my face and can't see it.

Glancing up, I'm frozen by what I see. A filmy gauze slides over the top of the ballroom, creating a completely different version of the room and the people in it.

The room is a foreboding cavern with dark stains on the floors and pool table felt; the Brethren are no longer the beautiful men I first saw. Their glamour fails as I focus on them through the warlock's monocle.

They are skeletons with grim, gray bones, draped in shreds of decayed flesh held to their frames by their fine clothes. Strips of gore peek from shirt sleeves and hang from collar bones like grimy, mummy wrappings. Sarkazian, the most skeletal of all, claws at Isaac. Isaac, the least ruined of all of them, stumbles backward. His sickly gray face is riddled with so many cuts and gashes, he is barely recognizable.

I gape, paralyzed by the sight of the vampires.

"Kill him!" Sarkazian points a sharp finger bone at Isaac and the Brethren attack at once. They sink their calcified teeth into the rotting remains of Isaac's arms and legs.

Isaac doesn't scream in agony.

He screams a name.

"EUSTACE!"

The carriage driver bursts into the room, brandishing an ancient, black rifle with a muzzle like a bugle.

"Get over here!" Eustace jerks his head for me to come to him, but then he trains the business end of the rifle right at me. I stop short. Eustace squeezes the trigger anyway. A spray of wooden bullets blast past me, through me, and slice into a thigh-hunk of Okuda's already dead flesh. The bullets that hit Okuda don't kill him, but blast him backward. The other vamps use their arms to shield themselves from the bullets, the wood bouncing off their ulnas and radiuses. Okuda claws the wooden shrapnel out of his remaining skin.

"Get over here!" Eustace barks at me again and I run to him, as he aims the barrel of his gun at the swarm of Brethren surrounding Isaac. "The bullets only slow them down, unless I can skewer their hearts!"

Skewering seems like an impossible dream, considering the vampires' hearts are locked away behind their ribs. The vamps deflect the bullets with their bones the way superheroes use their shields.

There's no way I can mistake the dangerous zombies I see through my eyepiece for heroes.

My feet move through mud until a wisp of Isaac's cologne reaches me. It's not the rot and stench I'm expecting, but the smell of fresh ice and metal. It rushes through my lungs and awakens my brain.

The scent of *my* Isaac.

Everything clicks together in my head. He is still Isaac. The horrific vision of him that appears through the magical chip attached to my eye must be false. This is Isaac and he is *mine*.

"You're going to hit Isaac!" I scream, grabbing the muzzle and jerking it toward the ground. Eustace fires, a blast of wood bullets exploding against the floor and spraying splinters across the room.

At least it clears a path for Isaac to break free. He sprints to us, the corpse of him grabbing my hand and hauling me along with him, behind Eustace, out the door of the billiard room and down the hall. We race through the house to the waiting carriage outside.

Isaac tears open the door and I scramble into the carriage as Eustace leaps onto the driver bench. Isaac slams the door as Eustace shouts to the horses. We're thrown against the back seat as the carriage surges forward and we thunder away from the mansion, into the dark night.

Isaac and I are thrown together and apart as the carriage rattles and jumps over the road. His skeletal hand flashes out to stabilize me, but I can't help shrinking from the touch of his flesh-dripping finger bones. We're slammed together and hurled apart. I don't think he notices my recoil.

Car horns blast outside and Eustace's gruff voice shouts commands to the startled horses. The carriage jerks and the warlock monocle slides out of my eye. I catch the chip in my palm, but another jolt sends the piece flying out of my hand and onto the carriage floor.

I blink at my handsome Isaac, the gory version of him now gone. He takes me in his arms, bouncing together on the bench. I lean into his flesh-covered chest, steeping in the comfort of my nose tucked against his neck, it's as if he's woke me from a nightmare.

The carriage takes a sharp turn and Isaac plants his heel to steady us. The warlock's monocle gives a sharp crack before it shatters beneath his boot. The horses settle into a cantor and I slump against Isaac.

I'm relieved.

Not because we're far enough from the Brethren for Eustace to slow the horses, but because the monocle is gone forever. I never want to see Isaac in that way again. It's not who he is. The longer his arms are wrapped around me, the more I consider telling him about his servant's betrayal, about the mysterious man who stole into the barn to deliver the spelled glass chip that ensured I saw Isaac as a monster.

It perplexes me that just the thought of that mysterious man turns off my desire to tell Isaac about him. Being so close to Isaac seems to pull at the truth, but I manage to keep it locked behind my lips. I have no idea why I feel so protective of the stranger.

"We have to get you a body soon," Isaac says, his voice a warm rumble against my ear. "It's the only way for the Brethren to accept my claiming of you."

"Yes." My voice is husky, like it belongs to someone else. That is the only logic explanation as to why any word of agreement drops out of my mouth.

I'm not sure the person I'm becoming with Isaac is the one I want to be, no matter how comfortable and easy it is to relax in his arms. It's tempting to accept what he's offering—a body in which I can feed him, in which Isaac believes we can finally be whole and complete together, an eternity of Isaac caring for me in exchange for my servitude. As I lie against him, the deal seems wildly stacked against me, but I can't make myself hate the idea of it.

"We'll have to go shopping," Isaac murmurs.

"For rings?" I ask, confused. Maybe *claiming* is the same as marriage in the vampire world.

"If you like, we can get that too," he chuckles, "but we'll need to find you a body to sport it first."

He mentioned some of this before, the whole poltergeist thing, but I didn't really believe it and didn't question the specifics much at all. I never considered *how* I would obtain a body, only that I would have one.

"How do you *shop* for a body?" I sit back, the vision of gruesome Brethren flashing through my head. I gulp. "We don't have to dig up bodies in a cemetery do we?"

This time, he laughs out loud. "You have such a morbid mind, Nova! Of course not! A revenant needs a living organism to slide into! How do you imagine a vampire could drink from a dried up well?"

"I…I have no idea," I stammer, scooting across the bench until my back is against the wall of the carriage. "If I don't jump into a dead body, are you saying I take over a live one? I *possess* someone?"

His expression turns serious, head tilted and eyes tightened, as if he takes some offense to my disbelief. "How did you think it would happen?"

"I don't know, but I can't steal someone else's life away from them!" I crank the carriage window open and stick my head out, gulping in the stream of city air. The smell of exhaust and restaurant food is clarifying, but it also makes me nauseous. Isaac is talking about murder. There's no other way to put it.

"Nova," he says, laying a hand on my arm.

I shake him off. "No! I am not killing anyone!"

He yanks me back into the carriage by one arm and hauls the window shut. "That's not something to scream out the window," he growls. "We don't need to attract anymore attention than we already are."

"Maybe we do!" I counter.

"Are you frightened?" he asks softly. His face is near mine, his breath on my cheek. His question turns to a suggestion in my head.

"No?" I turn my face toward the window, craving the fresh air, while knotting my fingers in my lap. Something is wrong, but I don't know what.

"Are you having second thoughts about being with me?" he asks.

The question gives me anxiety I can't escape. "No. I just don't want to—"

Isaac moves closer. "What don't you want?" he asks softly.

I don't know if it's the way he's staring at my lips, or the way I'm staring back at his, the excitement of escaping the party, or the threat of the Brethren that still hangs over our heads, but I can't remember. My brain is wiped clean. I look out the window, look back to Isaac.

"Addiction," I say, grasping for the film of a thought. "I don't want to be addicted."

He smirks. "You wouldn't be. You're not just any revenant. You'd be my *mate*. I wouldn't addict my mate."

"You can control it?"

"Yes," he says, pulling up his chin as he tears loose the knot in his tie.

"Don't you want this to change?" He opens the window a slit on his side of the carriage. A gentle breeze wafts through the carriage. The lovely scent of fresh air mixed with Isaac's cologne clears my head to what really matters.

"Change is all I want," I say.

"Then we need to begin by getting you a body," he says. "You can be whole again, Nova. Wouldn't you like that?"

Like it? It's all I have wanted since my memory began reforming and re-creating my life. Wholeness felt impossible on my own, but then Isaac came along and began filling in my gaps. I owe him everything. The blood I'll give him as a revenant is hardly payment, considering how much I will get out of having a body. I'll be able to hunt down that vial of my father's memories—it's got to be out there somewhere—and I'll finally know who I am. It's the only thing that matter to me.

Almost.

It's all that matters until I think of the egg we're going to have to crack to get there. I wish I could think of it in black and white—I'm acquiring a body. Simple. Like going to the store and buying a new dress. But it keeps getting messy when I think of the person who will lose their life, so I can have a second turn at living mine. It ruins the excitement and the joy.

"You deserve wholeness," Isaac whispers as if he's listening to my thoughts. His voice beckons agreement that I can't give him.

"At someone else's expense," I add, my eyes tearing up. I can't do this. My dreams are at my fingertips, I can feel them, but they're too far out of reach. Stealing someone else's body, hijacking it to live my life, is beyond my grasp. I'd forever be wearing an ill-fitting dress that was never meant for me. "I can't do it, Isaac. We can't. We're going to have to figure out some other way to make this work."

He drops back against the bench seat with a heavy sigh. "There is no other way, my love, but it is your choice and I will honor that, although it'd be nothing for me to take your blood, if that's all I wanted." A challenging flicker winks from the recesses of his stare. "But I want so much more from you than that."

"Like?"

"Isn't it obvious?" He inclines his head. "I want everything you are—your love, your body...I want your every thought to be of me. You are not and never would be *a meal* to me. You are a *feast,* Nova. I don't want a temporary arrangement of convenience with you...I desire a relationship that we will both savor, into eternity."

His short laugh is a spike of joy driven into the deepest, wanting parts of my body, but it doesn't even prick my compassion. It must not show on my face, because his enthusiasm builds in his tone as he continues. "I want everything you are capable of giving. I know how deeply you can love. I want all of it. And I want to give you the same."

My body tingles, even though I'm not comfortable with the thought. I don't have an answer for either reaction, but I know I have to shut this down now, before Isaac thinks that I'm in any kind of agreement with him. My lips are like concrete, but I manage to slip one word between them. "Never," I say, and let my answer hang there, dragging the joy out of his smile.

A frown settles slowly over his chin.

"It's true that I am the weak one, Nova," he says somberly, "but I promise you, you will desire my love, the way I desire yours. And now, just for being so callous when I have laid out my heart for you so honestly, now I'll have to insist that you beg. It won't bring me any pleasure, but it will convince you, when you finally recognize that our destiny is to be together, that trying to wound me is only hurting yourself. I am yours, and I promise that you will relish being mine."

I open my mouth to wound him, but it's a bad decision on my part. He is a fever in my non-existent veins, challenging my immunity with his charm and my resolve weakens with each passing second.

I should feel good that Isaac is being so easy about this, but I don't. As we cross the *vias* to the estate, the view disappears. Outside the window, an endless, bleak gray erases the ground, the sky, and everything in between. It's exactly how I feel.

Isaac and I have both lost.

We have a shot at being together forever, counting on one another, supporting each other, but I can't supply any of that without a body that can feed him. We can't create a bond between us, a circular connection of just him and me without me being in flesh form. Without a body, I'm never going to know the past I lived. Who I was, or the family and friends I had. Who might be looking for me still. It's haunting.

The deep night on the estate floods the carriage windows. The horses neigh as their hooves bite into the gravel drive.

"We're home," Isaac says, pinching a pant leg at the knee. "I have a few matters to tend to. Do you require me for anything?"

Whether it's there or not, I hear his lingering disappointment in my refusal to get a body. I want him to stay, to talk through this some more, but I'm not about to beg him to stick around just to make me feel better either.

"No, go do what you need to do," I tell him. Eustace opens the carriage door and Isaac steps down first, offering me his hand and leading me down the steps. The pearls' song is hoarse and quiet, as if I've worn them out.

Hoomstid stands off to the side like a faithful hound. "Welcome back, lady and gentlemen." He does a short bow.

Eustace burfs at the other servant and turns to Isaac. "Anything else tonight, Mr. Havrath?"

"No, that's all." Isaac says. No *thank you for saving our lives* or anything. Eustace climbs back up into the driver's seat and snaps the reins over the horse's backs. The carriage ambles away.

Isaac takes my hand and lowers his head toward it. His lips are dry on my knuckles, his eyes shrouded when he turns them up at me. "I will return shortly to you, my love."

With that, he lets loose of my hand and goes into the house without a glance back. I lock my knees so I don't follow him. My head spins. Isaac's exit has taken every thought I have with him. I don't know what to do next, but as my gaze runs into Hoomstid's, I push my shoulders back.

"Thank you for meeting us," I say.

Hoomstid's smile is starched. His eyebrows bunch in the center. "Certainly?" he says.

We stare at each other too long. My heels ache in my shoes, but I'll stand here until the world stops moving because my mind is utterly blank. A bead of sweat rolls down my spine. I'm suddenly afraid to say anything, afraid to wonder aloud if whatever happened before is happening again. If I'm in the process of forgetting everything that has happened up to this point.

"Miss?" Hoomstid says.

I don't know what he wants, or what the concern in his expression means. I put the back of my hand to my mouth.

Isaac is still on my skin. Comforting, calming, the scent of him reminds me that whatever I do, it's for him.

"I don't feel good and I'd like to wait for Isaac," I bumble to Hoomstid.

His brow pinches even more, but he nods. "I will take you upstairs to Mr. Havrath's suite. Esther can help you with your dress."

"Yes," I say, but I don't move until Hoomstid extends a hand toward the back door where Isaac disappeared. This time, I take the cue and walk up the back steps, through the kitchen where the servants stare, up the stairs, down the hall to Isaac's rooms.

Hoomstid lets me in.

"I'll have Esther come right up," Hoomstid whispers as he backs out and closes the door behind him.

I stand in the empty, silent suite with no idea what I'm doing here.

E sther stomps into Isaac's suite as if she is coming to kill a pig, rather than coming to help me out of my dress.

"Turn around," she commands through tight lips. When I don't turn fast enough, she grabs my shoulders and jerks me around, so my back faces her. The pearls shriek and Esther makes a sound of disgust deep in her throat. Her fingertips are icy as she unhooks the cascades of pearls and silences the strings as much as she can in the palm of her hand. The hanging ends continue to sing until Esther folds the strings in half and dump them on the love seat.

The sound halts, as if murdered. Esther begins on the buttons down the back then, yanking them free.

"Is something wrong?" I ask.

She makes the *ugh* sound again. "Everything," she mutters.

"Can I help?" I ask and her fingers pause from ripping free my buttons.

"Can you? No, I doubt it. It doesn't seem you're good for much."

That stings. I whirl free, knocking her hands away as I do. The dress glides down my legs and falls in a pool around me.

"Me?" I fire back. "How about you? One minute, you're

stuffing things into my bodice to *help me,* and next, you're knocking me around and ripping off my dress!"

Esther, holding out a shift to me, gapes. "All we've done is risk our necks to help you!"

I rip the shift from her fingers, yanking it down over my head. "Fat lot of good it's done!"

"You used the chip, then?" she dials down her volume, but her whisper still shrieks. "Don't you know that what you saw was true? Isaac's a monster!"

"I think you're a witch," I whisper back, my tone as icy as her fingers were. "You spelled that glass so I would leave Isaac alone and you could be with him!"

"He's managed to addict you with or without his venom, hasn't he?" she hisses. "I can tell by the way you defend him and by the way you think I had something to do with that glass! You're right —I would've protected Isaac with everything I have, but he's not worthy of it anymore. He's ruined my family and I let him, because I loved him."

I roll my eyes. "And you always will, right?"

"Yes," the maid says. Her expression pleads for a pity I won't give her. She turns her eyes away from mine. "Don't judge a weakness you don't have. Isaac is every bit the monster I say he is, as much as he is the monster you saw. He's also enchanting and despite how I hate him, I still love him more. You'll see."

"Maybe I already do."

She *tsks* as if I haven't got a brain in my head. "If you can't see him for who he is, you could be lost forever."

"Maybe I'm okay with that," I tell her. "But what about you? I don't see that having all this clarity about him has gotten you free."

"I was his for a decade, " she grinds her teeth, the skin in her cheek jumping. "On some level, I will always be lost when it comes to him, but that doesn't mean I can't administer some lessons."

"Tough love," I say.

"If it's with a vampire, it's the toughest," she says as she turns to the door. "Come with me if you'd like to see the beautiful monster I know."

I follow her out of the suite and down the hallway, in only my gauzy shift. The runner chews up any sound from our soft footsteps. Across from the stairway, Esther opens a door. A chill whisks down the raw panels of another staircase with ascending steps. At the top is another door.

A howl tears down the stairwell. Esther's eyes are clenched shut, her lips tight, pained. A tear rushes down her cheek. She opens her eyes, wiping the tears away with rough fingers, before lifting her skirts and urging me up the stairs with a flick of her chin.

I climb the stairs, slowed by the second noise that erupts from behind that high, closed door. It's not a howl, but the sound of a shredded breath, dragged inward through clenched teeth. Labored breathing, someone is trying to steal enough to keep themselves alive.

My legs turn to iron as I continue to climb. I am drawn by each tattered breath, each gurgle, each suffocated shriek.

At the top of the stairs, the maid stops. I reach past Ester for the knob, but she pushes my hand away.

"Go," she whispers, motioning for me to move through the door, rather than open it.

The horrible sounds rush out from beneath the wood floor like a cold whisper over my toes.

This way, not that. My body guides my movement.

That's it.

Don't think. Don't linger.

Just do.

I close my eyes and walk straight at the door. The core of the wood brushes me on all sides, coarse and thick, but I keep my eyes shut. I keep walking, *expecting* to reach the other side of the door, in order to keep the panic at bay.

The air pressure changes and I open my eyes.

It's impossible to miss Isaac, seated across the room in a dark wingback chair beneath a circular window. Hazy, blue moonlight spills over him and Lucy, Esther's daughter and Hoomstid's beloved, seated in Isaac's lap.

She is wedged between his legs, leaning back with her head cradled against his shoulder. He is wrapped around her like a serpent, every inch of her grasped, as he sucks from her neck.

He pauses. Her vein must be crimped like a chewed straw. He pulls back, a ridge rising in her neck. She cries out. Struggles. He tightens the knot of his body all around her and she moans.

He yanks out his fangs, the sound sickening as he rips the parchment of her skin. She cries out again and I recoil at the sight of her ruined neck.

Lucy's head lolls to the other side, limp as a soggy towel.

I think she's dead. I think it until she whispers, "More."

"Are you certain, my love?" Isaac whispers back.

I haven't moved any closer to them since I crossed through the wall, but hearing him call her the same thing he's called me—my heart freezes. My mind stops. Whatever life force I have rushes out of me as if I've been kicked in the chest.

Lucy's delicate fingers reach up, curling into Isaac's hair. She urges him down to her exposed skin and at the last moment, before his lips touch, he plunges his fangs into her neck.

She cries out.

I want to kick her.

I want to end him.

She fists his hair in her palm and presses him closer, lodging his fangs deeper into her skin. Isaac responds to the pressure of her grip with a long, powerful pull on the fresh vein, his head drawing back slightly as he suckles her jugular. His knees squeeze more tightly around her and she moans.

"What are you doing!" I shout.

Lucy jerks up, crying out in pain as Isaac's teeth snag in

her skin. He lifts his head and, seeing me, drags his fangs from her skin, sealing the open gashes with a quick flick of his tongue.

Lucy's gaze falls to her feet. Her porcelain skin forces a blush that doesn't quite cover her cheeks.

"I...I'm sorry, Miss," Lucy begins to cry, although no tears fall. Probably too dehydrated.

My emotions spin.

Part of me doesn't care what they were doing. Part of me wants her dead. As dead and incapable as I am of fulfilling him.

Isaac dumps her off his lap, prowling toward me.

"There's nothing to be ashamed of, Lucy," Isaac says over his shoulder, his eyes on me. "I needed to eat and I'm grateful you offered your services."

The maid's chest continues to heave, although the ducts of her eyes remain clear.

I hate him.

He moves in slowly, as if he's protecting me from myself. The audacity.

But something happens as he nears. My hate becomes a pliable thing. It slips through the slats of my thought and I'm left questioning if I saw what I saw.

I shake my head as if it can get me a clear answer.

The hatred turns itself on me. Isaac stands before me, his soulful eyes looking deep into mine, and I hate myself.

Deep inside me disgust pulls at me like a child tugging at a mother's arm, but I can't seem to dredge up enough of the emotion to stop myself from tipping my head to the side and baring my neck to him.

Isaac brushes close to me, a field of goose bumps rising up all over me. His breath stirs the hair behind my ear and my eyelids flutter in reflex.

"Is there something you want, Nova?" he whispers. The hair at the back of my neck stands up as if it is reaching for him.

I dredge up my eyelids and see Lucy across the room, shifting nervously from foot to foot. *Mine*, I think as I stare at her.

"I want her dead," I say.

Lucy lifts her head, eyebrows cresting in horror. She stamps around the back of the chair like a frightened colt, trying to hide. Isaac glimpses her long enough to flick his chin toward the door. The girl skitters past us, pressing her body flat to slip over the threshold without touching us.

He circles me and my gaze releases Lucy to track him instead. I laugh, uncomfortably drunk on him. "I don't want her dead. Holy cow, I don't mean that."

"You didn't mean you don't want her dead, or you do?" He exhales temptation, a warm gust over my ear. My thoughts tangle. "Or is there something else you'd like?"

"Something else," I say, but I didn't mean to say that either. I don't mean to say anything, but his proximity draws the words from my mouth like air gushing out of a balloon. The responsible, logical part of me scrambles in the back of my head, clinging to ideas that slide free. Isaac's gaze snares me at every turn.

"What else?" he purrs. "Just tell me what you want, Nova, and I'll get it for you."

Isaac smiles and his fangs weep.

"Skin," I say.

5 6

Isaac calls for the carriage immediately.

Eustace brings it around, although the carriage driver looks a little disheveled and equally put out, after having been told he'd have the night off hours ago. Isaac doesn't acknowledge it. He helps me into the carriage and tells Eustace to take us to the waterfront. Eustace answers with a gruff sound and the carriage rolls down the driveway.

"Are you sure we should be going out now?" I ask.

"You said you wanted skin," Isaac says with a slight frown. I can hardly stand to see disappointment on his face. "Have you changed your mind, my love?"

My love. It's a railroad spike in my spine. "I haven't. I was only thinking the Brethren may be looking for us."

"They're probably still busy fighting with one another," Isaac scoffs. "Don't worry about them. I can take care of them if they come looking."

He means Eustace. Eustace will take care of them. I wonder if the carriage driver thought to bring his gun along again.

The carriage swings right on Washington without even a ripple of resistance. Maybe I don't notice the drab, spreading gray of the

253

vias because Isaac's hair has all my attention. The blue-black color of his locks makes it easy to forget the Brethren, and Eustace, and that we're going out to shop for a body as if it is nothing more than a new gown.

What do I care. The metallic patchouli of Isaac's cologne is soothing and if I get my hands in his hair, I could play with the perfect, soft layers for hours. All too quickly, Eustace deposits us in a New Baltimore I barely know.

Isaac and I stroll down a bustling, dirt-road version of Washington. The sidewalks aren't concrete, but wood planks with a mud veneer. The historic buildings aren't aged either. In this New Baltimore, they are fresh builds without any of the familiar, elemental antiquing I knew. I have to look at them twice, as if they are the great, great grandchildren of the wizened grandparents I know.

The shops are different too. More practical than I expect. There is a hardware/mercantile, an undertaker, a barber shop, a hotel, and a butcher. If I could be excited about muslin bags of salt and sugar, fabric bought by the bolt, or a butcher shop with whole sides of meat hung from metal hooks in the window, then this shopping trip would be super exciting.

But we're not here shopping for any of that.

"Let's sit here," Isaac says, motioning to the empty bench outside the mercantile, overlooking the beach and bay. The air is damp and close in the dusk, but the women wear long sleeves and dresses with bustles, while the men wear suits. More like prom clothes than casual summer attire.

"Look there," Isaac says as a young woman strolls toward us on a man's arm.

He doesn't have to point her out—there's no way I wouldn't notice her. Even hidden beneath a bell-shaped cloche hat, she's exotic, with olive skin and gleaming, black, spiraled locks that escape the short, wavy brim.

They walk past us, engrossed in conversation. Her eyes flick to Isaac and me and she shivers.

"People are talking about us," she whispers to the man. With the breeze blowing in off the bay, their voices are amplified and their conversation gusts back to us, easy to overhear.

I wondered if she could tell that we're not human, but a ghost and a vampire who are low-key leering at her. I'm not even sure she can see me, or if she's even talking about us in particular.

The man's shoulders lift and drop, before planting his palm on her gloved hand, looped through his elbow. "Let them, Ruth," he tells her softly. "We're together and they can whisper all they like, so long as they leave us be. That's all that matters."

"Except that it's me they're talking about. They're never going to accept our marriage." She looks off to the left, away from him, and though I can't see her eyes, I imagine her eyes are glossy.

How lucky she is to have her troubles. Lack of acceptance seems like a tiny and luxurious problem, compared to my lack of a body and how I will have to go about acquiring one. Queasiness washes through me.

I shake my head at Isaac. "Not her. They're married," I murmur.

"What difference?" he whispers back. How different couples' secrets are. "We are in need of a body. Preferably one which is esthetically pleasing to us both. This body meets that requirement, does it not? It makes no difference what the body's past has been. Only that it is a healthy vessel, able to serve your needs as a vehicle through life at my side."

I level my gaze on his, struggling to stay free of his iris's cavernous depths.

"She's a *person*." A lump scales the back my throat. "We're taking someone's *life*."

"I thought you'd gotten past this. You can't think of a body that way. It will be much easier if you don't." His eyes are on the backs of the couple, or maybe it is just on her backside. "You need to focus on making the body your own."

I sit up straight and scoot a few inches away from him. Isaac closes the gap as soon as I make it, leaning over and capturing my chin in his fingertips. He tries to guide my lips to his, the scent of his cologne spilling over me, captivating me. It's a struggle, but I pull away as a tiny voice in the back of my mind whispers something I can't quite make out.

I squint into the darkness, as if it will make the tiny voice clearer, but I can't clear away the recurring desire to let Isaac kiss me. I press my feet into the soles of my shoes, fighting the urge to give into him.

His tender fingers press softly at my jaw again and I make the mistake of turning my head back to him.

"It's not a selfish desire, my love, it's a need." His gaze sucks at mine and I can't look away. "We will both benefit. I have a hunger, and you don't want to fade away. What makes our plight less important or less worthy of a life, when it will save two, instead of serve only one, who isn't even grateful for what they possess? That woman is complaining about gossip, when she should be appreciating the man who loves her." I know there's a message in his words, but it slips past my guard as I study the smooth planes of his cheeks, the delicate peaks of his lips. "That's all the justification we need."

"Is it?" I ask. I really don't know anymore. "How do we take her?"

Isaac offers me an arm and we get off the bench. "You return to the carriage and let me worry about the rest," he says. When he lets loose of me, I drift back to the carriage like the ghost I am.

"Are you ready?" Isaac's voice runs over me quick as a river current. The woman from the waterfront lies askew on the couch, one leg hanging off the edge.

I spin on one heel to face him, unable to fully close my mouth from the shock. "How did you get her here?"

"She's perfect, isn't she?" He turns back, admiring her. My jealousy stirs. Her breathing is shallow, her skin the wrong color of olive than when I last saw her.

"Her name is Ruth and I told you, *she's married.* I don't want her." Except that I do. I back away from the couch as if I can back away from the greed bubbling in me.

She's beautiful.

She has a life. A husband who loves her.

I could be her.

My voice sticks in my throat. "I'm not ready for this."

"No one is ever *ready.*" He flashes me a reassuring grin as he comes to me. He puts his head close, a warm breath down my neck, stirring the hair near my ear. "I can't wait until I can drink from you."

I breathe him in, my anxiety subsiding with every breath.

He leaves a kiss on my neck and moves away from me, drawing nearer to the unconscious woman. A possessive growl rumbles in my throat. It doesn't matter if she's unconscious, I can hardly stand the thought of his mouth on her. "She's nearly drained," he explains. "I will finish her and the moment she exits the body, you can take it."

"Whoa! Isaac!" I shriek, hands up as he moves to the edge of the bed. "I don't know if I can do this!"

If I can.

Not, *I don't want to take this woman's life.* I can't say that, because I do want it.

I want to slip into her body, slide it over my soul like a leather glove, and offer her neck to Isaac.

He's already at the woman's side, reaching for her. The jealousy climbs through me. I'm barely resisting the urge to join him at the bedside and huddle up, so I'm ready to go for the moment I can dive into her.

I knot my fingers, reminding myself of the price Ruth will pay. Isaac glimpses my fingers.

"Think of it like this: a stranger is moving out of a home I've bought for you," he says softly, dragging my fingers apart. "She's taking her thoughts with her, so you are free to move in."

"Ruth," I whisper. "She has a name."

"Had," he says with a gentle, encouraging smile. He kisses my forehead and the scent of him calms my nerves. I don't know what I'd do without him.

My arms hang loose at my sides as I stare down at her. The price I'm willing to pay swells within me. "Tell me how to do it again."

Isaac slides an arm beneath her shoulders. My spine prickles as he lifts her toward him, head lolling over his forearm, her midnight-hair spilling over the cushions.

"When she sighs," he says, "that is the moment to act. The soul exits the body and one of two things will happen. If her soul reenters, she will become a vampire and I will have to kill her immediately. However, if you claim the body, you will become a revenant."

"I have to fight her out of her own body," I groan

"You may see her, but if you do, ignore her. You need to locate the echoing pulse of her energy, which will remain for a few minutes after she's gone. Don't miss it, or this will be for nothing, and that would be a waste, as she is quite beautiful."

I grit my teeth at his compliment and then root myself, so I don't rush forward and seize Ruth's body. I snarl as I stare at her.

Isaac nods, silver streaking across his eyes. He places a fingertip over the low part of her forehead, between her eyes.

"Enter here," he says.

"How am I supposed to *enter* there? Break her skull?" I'm overwhelmed with how to do the impossible, but Isaac is calm. Like he does this every day.

"You put your finger there and follow the pulse of energy in, or place your forehead to the skin there and you'll be pulled in. However, don't waste any time, as you'll begin to fade from the moment she is out of the body, and she will, likewise, become more solid as a ghost. You don't want her to overpower you and retake the body." Isaac's fangs dribble on Ruth's neck and a surge of anxiety rushes over me. This is wrong. This is also my chance to feed Isaac. My chance to find out who I am.

"Okay," I say before I can circle back to my morals. "I'm ready."

Isaac cups the back of the woman's neck. Her breath is a flutter as he tips back his head to pierce her. There are already marks at her neck where he's drank from her.

I deserve her body and the blood she used to feed my vampire.

The sensation of breath stutters in my lungs. Probably for the last time.

This is really happening.

"Get ready to take the body," Isaac says.

"Her name is—"

"Her name is Nova!" he growls, plunging his fangs into her flesh.

The sigh comes too soon.

I'm not ready.

My panic explodes as I watch a milky fog erupt from the woman's skin. It starts like a breath of dry ice, and builds, rushing together and forming a foggy replica of the body on the bed. The woman that forms blinks hard, staring at me as if she can't quite get me into focus. She becomes more solid, more like me, with every second.

Isaac retracts his fangs, dropping Ruth's body on the couch. "Go now!" he tells me.

I hesitate, in awe of the spirit before me. "I'm sorry," I say.

"Ignore her!" Isaac prompts, but I can't.

Ruth's brow creases as she pieces together what's happening.

Then, it furrows.

She nails her furious gaze to me.

I should've listened to Isaac and ignored her. The thrum of energy vibrates from Ruth's body. I feel it in my chest, like bass blasting from a teenager's car.

I rush forward, thrusting my finger toward the spot between Ruth's eyes that Isaac showed me moments ago. A thin string of opal mist leads out of the skin, attached to the woman's spirit. I press my finger to the spot and the string snaps.

So does Ruth.

She lunges for me. A shadow, attacking me. She's got one foot in each world and not solid enough in either—her body isn't fully alive, even if there is a slight heartbeat, and she's not dead enough to be a full ghost.

"Get away!" she howls, frantically clawing to keep me away from her body. It's useless. She's a milky apparition and I can move right through her.

She spots the snapped end of the opal string dangling from the spot on the forehead and the matching, broken end trailing from her ghostly feet. Her translucent fingers slip right through the string at her feet. She reaches for the one drifting from her forehead, but her ghostly self is clumsy; she can't manipulate the objects, even as I see her ghostly skin show signs of thickening. The string doesn't respond to her grasp, but she tries again, as her thumb gels into something more solid.

"Nova, if she regains the body—" Isaac warns.

I have no choice now. My own form is beginning to thin from the inside out. My insides feel light and disconnected as I become ready to slip into the body. If Ruth jumps back into her body, I'll be left to fade into oblivion, without ever knowing who I was, who I truly am. And I'll lose Isaac forever.

Ruth's fingers are becoming more opaque by the second. She glimpses me, her mouth twisted as she presses her finger and thumb together. If she can pinch them together, it'll be a cinch for her to lift that string and reconnect her spirit to it.

There's no way I'm going to miss my opportunity.

I concentrate my energy as I lunge for the string myself.

My shoulder should hit her chest like a ram's horn, and my momentum should throw her backward, but there's still not enough to her yet, too newly a ghost. My arm goes right through her.

Ruth grabs a clump of my hair between the finger and thumb that have solidified. She yanks downward.

Hard.

I scream, twisting in her grasp. It's easy enough to shake loose even though she's got a few more fingers to work with.

I'm not interested in going easy on Ruth now.

It's not her body anymore.

It's mine.

All I've got to do is take it.

Ruth must see the change in my eyes; the craving. A hard crease ruins her ghostly brow.

I get hold of her fingers and fling her. The rest of her is weightless, so she's as easy to toss across the room as one of Meg's cigarettes.

But she's also dead, and ghostly enough to feel the impression of pain. She gets back on her feet with a howl and comes at me, fingers curled in front of her like she's going to dig out my eyes.

We both go for the string.

I plunge my elbow between her ghost ribs again, but I only manage to wrench my shoulder and lose my balance. I fall to my knees and Ruth slips past, running for her body and the string that is disintegrating into the air like an ignited fuse. I jump up and throw myself at her, swiping at anything tangible. I fall through her and land with my hands around something solid.

Her ankle. I jerk it back. She falls with an *oof*, but recovers quickly, kicking me in the face. My teeth crack but nothing falls out. The pain is gone as quickly as I release the thought of it.

More and more of Ruth is materializing—her palms are solid now, her arms and legs are milky instead of translucent. As her ghostly body emerges, the thinning inside me turns outward.

I'm beginning to fade.

With every second, Ruth is gaining strength, and I'm losing it. My shoulders turn translucent. My hands dangle at the end of my fading arms. If Ruth gets hold of my hair, soon there will be no way for me to fight back.

"Get in the body!" Isaac shouts. "Do it now!"

Ruth positions herself between me and the body and we come to blows like men. My fists are like blobs of iron at the end of my rubber band arms, but I fling them at her, pummeling her with everything I've got. There is no blood, but she's fully connecting with her pain from the sound of her groans and shrieks.

I keep at her until she sags and drops at my feet. I almost drop next to her.

I should feel victorious.

I don't.

Part of my own spirit is lying at my feet with her, watching her pant.

"You're going to lose the string!" Isaac shouts. The fuse of her energy is only a few centimeters from her forehead and there's nothing Isaac can do to help. It's all up to me.

I look down at Ruth. "I promise to take care of your body. I will find a way to do right by you, I swear it."

"Go to hell!" she puffs. "You have no right to my body or my life!"

"I don't want your life," I tell her, "I have my own."

"Nova," Isaac's softened tone captures me. "You have to claim the body *now*."

Ruth doesn't have enough energy to raise to her newly formed feet. She couldn't catch me now if she wanted to—my ghostly self has completely thinned to the same translucent shadow Ruth was when she left her body behind.

The eyes of the body are open and beautiful, a lovely brown.

I kneel before it and press my forehead to the one that used to belong to Ruth.

Used to.

59

I wasn't sure how I would slide into the body, but it's nothing like sliding.

It's like running into cement. My soul doesn't feel like fog, it's gel, squeezing through a hole the size of a pin prick. My imaginary bones still feel horribly real, as they crush to dust and filter into Ruth's body.

Once inside, my spirit unfurls fast. I crash into the confines of organs, muscles, fat, and bone. I merge with the body, joining the blood stream and shaking hands with the cells so they don't revolt and mutiny with disease. The skin clings to me, suctioning to my spirit like a rubber suit.

I open my mouth before my eyes, gasping for breath. This body is suffocating, like a housecoat made of bricks.

Isaac is beside me, I sense him more than see him, as if the sun is at his back and the rest of him is in a dark shadow. The light stings. Isaac's voice sounds deeper through these ears. Rich and dark as turned soil. I am eager to breathe him in, but his cologne is so strong it's stifling. I cough as if I just took a huff of car exhaust.

And then, there's the tongue.

It's a whole separate animal. A bloated, lazy worm lying

against the jaw. I'm not sure quite how to connect with it, to make it jump and twitch and curl with speech.

"Nova?" Isaac whispers.

At the same time, Ruth's voice—distant and weak—whispers, "Thief."

I scan the room. I can't see her with her own eyes.

"Are you in there?" Isaac asks.

My gaze settles on him. My tongue collapses as I exhale, "I'm…here."

60

I saac and I are lying in the estate's back field, watching the stars, because I asked him to. I couldn't stand another moment in his suite, that big bed taunting us from across the room, when he's told me a dozen times already that I need to be in this new skin and meet a bunch of criteria before he can safely drink from me.

"How much longer?" I ask. "Ruth's voice is long gone. I haven't heard her since yesterday night."

Without her whispers, it's been easier for me to accept that this body is mine now. The arms and legs felt a lot like trying to control a lead marionette with strings that were too long. All of my movements were heavy, awkward, and delayed at first, but it's only taken a day for me to get the hang of it.

"She's not the only thing we have to wait for." He lies on his side, staring at me instead of the moon and stars that peek from beneath thin clouds. His eyes are liquid shadows; his gaze obsessed. I don't think there's been a moment since I acquired this body that I haven't turned to find his eyes on me. I wonder if he's imagining me within these skin and bone layers of Ruth, or if it is just her beauty he is admiring. I can't think about it too long

267

without feeling disoriented and crazy. "We have to wait for the extra dermal layer to form too."

"When will we know—" I start and he pinches me. I shriek and slap his hand away. "Don't squeeze me like a grape!"

"But that's how we'll know," he says with a laugh. "Your skin has to be firm enough to handle my bite. Humans tear too easily— they're as delicate as tissue paper. A revenant forms their own soul barrier—a second skin—beneath the layer of the original body. Your organs and muscles and bones are all forming an extra strong layer. It's what makes a revenant durable. "

"And my blood?" I ask, "How is that changing?"

His eyelids drop at the mention. I know exactly what it's doing to him and I love teasing his reaction out of him. His breath fans over my neck, his gaze focusing on the pulse there.

"Your blood is fortifying," his voice is husky and the peaks of his fangs appear just under the sensual line of his lips. "Doubling in immunity…"

I move closer to him, watching his own breath hitch as I inhale him. "The mosquitos don't bite me."

"No, a revenant's blood is not right for their system," he says. "It's too rich. They know instinctually that they'll die from even a sip."

I turn my eyes back to the full length of the sky and all the stars sparkling across the canvas. "So, only vampires can drink from me?"

Isaac startles me with a hiss. "Not *vampires*." he growls, his fangs fully extended and eyes flashing with razor sharp streaks of metal that make me wince. "Me. Only me. Promise me."

I try to laugh it off and lighten the mood that's gotten darker than the night around us. "I forgot…you're competitive and stupid-jealous."

"I'm all those things," he agrees darkly, "but if you should betray me by allowing another to drink from you, something worse will happen than my wrath. Combining two vampire's venoms is explosive. Enough of it in the bloodstream and you'll combust."

He's got to be kidding.

I laugh.

He doesn't.

"Why do you think vampires guard their mates so closely?" he asks. "Forcing oneself on a mate that is not yours can cost a vampire their status and their life, but it doesn't mean it doesn't happen. Claiming protects you only from those vamps who respect the laws...but how respectful do you think any of them are? You've met them."

I think of the Brethren clambering to take me from Isaac. Their vicious battle we barely escaped.

"If any of them capture you and want to retain you, rather than kill you for the sake of spiting me—they will hold you until my scent has dissolved completely from your blood. Once my venom is gone, they can safely claim you for themselves without worry of you going up in flames."

Flames. I gulp.

"But I have a way for you to protect yourself." He slips his fingers in his trouser pocket and withdraws a chain with a vial the size of my pinky finger dangling from it. The glass bottle is wrapped in silver filigree, the fluid inside clear and a drop of blood floating within it like a tiny ruby. "You'll wear this vial of my distilled venom around your neck. If another vampire ever tries to feed from you, all you need to do is touch this vial to their skin."

"Your solution is a chemistry set?" I scoff. "Yeah, that sounds easy enough to do while they're trying to bite me."

"This isn't just any venom. My venom has been distilled by a seasoned warlock, and placed in this spelled container. The filigree heats when it comes in contact with skin that is neither mine nor yours. The glass will simultaneously crack, and when the venom touches an enemy's skin, it explodes. The venom is dynamite...in the wrong hands."

I don't reach for the necklace. Isaac drops it over my head before I can object. It falls against my skin and I blanch, but nothing happens. The silver is cool against my skin.

"Go ahead and touch it," Isaac says. "It won't break."

"What if it does?"

"You won't explode. It's just a mega dose of my venom. It would only make you hopelessly in love with me."

His smile sparkles like the stars. "That's not so bad," I say. "Do the Brethren have vials too?"

"The Brethren haven't made the friends I have," he chuckles. "But this little vial also took me around 100,000 venom collections to fill. It's taken nearly my entire existence as a vampire to create. I wanted the vial as a mating gift, to ensure your safety, in the rare moment when I may not be close by. There is enough in here to kill one vampire. Drop it in a vamp's mouth and BOOM."

"How do you know a vial will do it?"

"I know," he laughs.

"Then how big of a *boom* are you talking?"

Isaac holds up his hands, makes the noise of an explosion, and shakes his hands open, as if releasing a mushroom cloud that would melt a city.

"You would likely die with the attacker if you were too close." The planes of his face are flat, solemn, undecipherable. His meaning becomes clear when he says, "But would you want to live if another claimed you?"

The sick thing is, I wouldn't.

He's all I want.

So I could explode if another vamp drinks from me, or I have a shot at killing the vamp who tries and maybe going down with that ship in the process. It seems like a simple decision.

Why would I ever want to leave a male who harnesses his power purely to please me? It's thrilling to lay beside a lion who wouldn't hesitate to murder anyone who tried to come between us, yet manages me with the type of tenderness necessary to keep a dandelion puff intact. His power belongs to me; of course I won't hesitate to lay down my life for him.

"Let me see it," I say. He holds it up, although he doesn't hand it to me.

The venom catches the moonlight and sparkles as if it has the dust of stars floating in it.

The breeze shifts direction, blowing a lock of my hair toward Isaac.

"A storm must be coming," I laugh, tucking the loose spiral behind my ear.

My fingertips are still behind the cartilage, my eyes on the vial. The wind blows Isaac's wonderful cologne away and leaves behind something far less enjoyable: a streak of a memory that shoots through my head. A moment when I first stood in the moonlight on the grass of the Havrath Estate; a moment of panic when I couldn't find what I was looking for.

Something important.

I grasp for the thought as the breeze continues to rush over my face, forcing air through my nostrils. I breathe deep, the fog in my head barely clearing, but the hazy tail of the thought wiggles again and I catch it, repeating the thought over and over to strengthen the memory, if I can.

It is completely disconnected, a random thought that could almost be mistaken for a lie. Except that the emotions attached to it stick in my heart like thumb tacks.

My happiness dies as I recall the whole thought.

It wasn't *something* I was looking for.

It was someone.

I've forgotten Meg.

My beautiful cousin, Meg.

I haven't thought of her since the day I went searching for her in New Baltimore and couldn't find her. A second dart of panic chases the memory of her. She's got to be worried sick about me. My stomach rolls as I imagine her searching for me as I did for her. She'll be wondering what's happened, or she might be thinking I left without a thought of her.

Which is pretty much what I did.

Isaac notices the change in me as quickly as I feel it. "What's wrong?" he asks, swiftly dropping the coriander sprig and rolling back onto his hip to face me.

"My cousin, Meg. I forgot…to miss her." My throat swells. I twist the skin of my middle finger with my opposite hand. "I haven't even thought of her. She's probably scared to death that I haven't been home. I have to see her and let her know I'm okay."

He frowns. "I don't think it's a good idea."

I'm shocked. A solid wave of *push* wells up inside me, battering back the *pull* that holds me in Isaac's orbit. I scramble to my feet, staring down at him. Those feelings of enchantment dissolve. Isaac appears weak and needy, lying on the grass and staring up at me with his needy gaze. I have no idea why I thought he was a lion. He's about as virile as a pale, little corn snake.

"Why not?" I demand.

"You don't belong there anymore." He shrugs, rolling onto his feet. "Those people only saw you because of their altered minds."

"They still saw me for what I was," I snap. I move backward as he steps forward, maintaining a distance between us. Baseless disgust takes the place of the sadness that had blocked my throat when I thought of Meg. I don't know why it's all changed, but my feelings for Isaac have suddenly turned upside down and my emotions are strong enough, I can't deny them. Locks of my hair tumble loose in another gust and blow into my face. I shove them back harshly, locking my suspicious gaze on Isaac.

"They saw you *because of what they were*," he goes on. He raises his hands as if readying for the possibility of hand-to-hand combat. "It had nothing to do with you, and they won't recognize you now anyway."

Fury boils beneath my stolen skin. "I don't care what they are, or why they spoke to me, they still did. They treated me as if I existed."

"I would bet they barely noticed you, unless they had to," Isaac says.

It strikes a nerve. One that is truer than I'd like to admit. Uncle Leonard ignores me almost all of the time we're together. Murray too. But it's the hundreds of time that Meg has ignored me that really hurts, when she's chosen to get high over talking with me, or making out with Murray rather than talking to me. I've felt less valuable and it's changed me. I try not to talk much. I try to say things that they'll want to hear. I've never been able to make minimization feel okay.

Another gust of wind hits my back and Isaac sinks another arrow of truth through my heart.

"Why do you think your cousin is so worried about your whereabouts when she hasn't bothered to come looking for you?"

I want to rip him apart for that.

I lunge toward him and Isaac darts away. We move like boxers in the ring, sizing up one another for a take down. He stalks in a circle and I turn with him, keeping him in direct sight. The stars have disappeared overhead and dark clouds press in overhead. At least I'm facing the direction that allows the gusty fall air to brush my hair out of my eyes so I can see Isaac clearly.

"You can go and see her, if you like," he says softly.

The wind rushes over his shoulders and slams into me, filling my nose with the scent of him.

What am I doing? This is the man I love.

My emotions turn upside down again, my anger rushes out of me as quickly as the sand in a broken hourglass.

I straighten out of my fighter's crouch, prickling heat spilling over my cheeks. I fan my face, breaking eye contact and unwilling to meet Isaac's gaze again. I've betrayed the man I love.

Seconds ago, I hated him so intensely it was a dark fire beneath my skin.

I don't know what's wrong with me.

"Are you alright?" Isaac asks, inching closer. I won't look him in the face. He scoots closer and closer, until he wraps me in his arms. His touch is careful as he draws my head to his chest. "What was that? What happened?"

"I don't know," I say, gulping breaths so I don't break out in sobs. Holding in my tears, everything blurs around me. "I wanted to…fight you."

That's not true. Not one bit.

I wanted to *murder* him.

I can't tell him that. Between clogged breaths, I choke out, "I just miss Meg so much! I have to see her and make sure she's alright!"

His voice is gentle, calm. "Is there any reason she wouldn't be alright—besides wondering about you?"

"Her boyfriend, Murray." Sobs spill out of me as Isaac brushes his fingers through my hair. I close my eyes to savor the tenderness of his touch, the scent of his skin. I lean against him as if my legs aren't capable of holding me completely upright. "Murray's a mess and he's always dragging Meg into his chaos. I just miss her so much…I want to be sure she's alright…and she needs to know I'm okay."

He pulls me down with him and lays me back on the grass, one arm beneath my head. I wipe my eyes with my palms and when I'm done, Isaac plucks a stem of coriander from a nearby plant and twists it lazily in his fingers above our heads.

He squeezes the skin of my forearm and I don't yelp.

"Did you just pinch me?" I laugh. "It didn't even hurt."

"My girl with a tough skin," he says. He drops the coriander sprig and rolls over to kiss me, the tips of his fangs scratching my bottom lip. "It might be a good experiment for you to visit your cousin for an afternoon…to see if you can survive without me, after I've had my fill of you."

"Come here," he says, drawing me to lay beside him on the bed. He brushes my hair over my shoulder, his eyes loose on my neck. I see him swallow before he meets my gaze again. "It won't hurt very much," he promises softly.

I nod, numb. Of course it will hurt. Puncturing skin *hurts*.

He strokes my face and places his lips against my neck. He kisses me softly, brushing his lips against my skin.

My brain screams *jump up and run*—but I lean in, bathing my lungs in his scent.

I want him.

I press upward to meet his next kiss and he moves on top of me.

His weight settles over my body, pressing me into the quilt as he threads his arms beneath me. Holding himself on his forearms, he grips my shoulders gently, still dusting my skin with his lips. Nothing feels more right than this. He slides his legs along either side of mine, whispering *I love you* and *I am yours* between kisses. My excitement makes me squirm, but Isaac is wrapped around me, holding me tight.

His breathing grows faster, waves of heat fanning against my neck.

I try to crest upward; everything in me being drawn toward him —my heart, my soul, my body, my words.

"I am yours," I whisper and Isaac strikes.

I gasp.

His fangs are cold and sharp as they pierce my throat.

It hurts.

I scream and try to jerk away, but he winds round me even more tightly. His fingers snag my necklace and the chain breaks. The vial rolls into the sheets, but Isaac doesn't stop. He sinks his teeth deeper into me, slicing the vein wide open. I scream his name again, but he doesn't let me go. Instead, his thumb caresses my skin.

Tears sting the corners of my eyes, but don't fall. His fangs placed, Isaac grows still, but my nerves throb with the pain.

The first pull from my vein makes me shriek.

The sound of him drinking is wet and slippery. His lips move against my skin in a whispering kiss and I try not to cry, but I can't help twisting beneath him. My fight-or-flight response is trying to fly, but he's too heavy to push him off. I wiggle beneath him and manage to bring up my knee, wedging it between us.

Another pull on my vein like the first and I'm going to give him everything I've got with a knee to his groin.

He has to stop.

I don't want to hurt him, but he's hurting me.

Too much.

I let out a whimper, a final warning, and heat suddenly surges into my vein. It's like spilling warm milk. The sensation spreads through me. It saturates my nerves and I loosen without even meaning to.

I relax into the rhythm of his feeding, leaning my head back against the pillow. He takes a deep pull of my blood and the skin of my neck stretches. I feel my pulse moving into his mouth.

His throaty moan makes me tremble.

My thoughts liquefy, and I laugh. I run my fingers over Isaac's back, coaxing him closer, pushing the fangs deeper into my vein. This pain is full and beautiful. With each drink, first comes the sharp, painful pull of Isaac's fangs, which is swiftly followed by the soft, suckling sweep of his lips against my skin and the flood of warmth that flows through my veins, numbing the pain as he swallows from me.

It's ecstasy.

After a few times, I only gasp a little with the initial sting, but I have to bite my lip so I don't moan with the velvet brush of his lips.

My thoughts warp as the room spins. I am swirling in the center of Isaac's universe and I never want to leave it. I never want this to end.

When he's had his fill, Isaac seals my neck and pulls away, but my limbs are paralyzed.

Or I'm weakened to the brink of death.

I really can't tell and don't even care.

Isaac lays me back in the bed. The glow in my veins is so lovely, if my arms worked, I'd get ahold of Isaac's hair and pull him to the opposite side of my neck.

"Are you alright?" he asks. His eyes are black, full moons. I smile into them.

"Do it again," I whisper.

He grins. "Not yet," he says.

"Don't you like how I taste?" I frown, though the mellow sensation of his feeding still washes away any displeasure.

"That's not the problem," he says. "We've got to work up to full feedings. Your blood will adjust to my nutritional needs, so expect your own preferences to change."

"I don't have any," I say, but even as the words come out of my mouth, my stomach rumbles. I want eggs. But I still want him more. "That felt so good."

"It will feel better and better."

"You don't have to drink from the servants anymore."

"Only as absolutely necessary," he says, but squeezes my hand and quickly adds, "which will be rare, if ever."

"It will be never, ever necessary again," I say.

The residual venom in my blood sings with the promise, but my brain still wages a weak battle against just about everything I'm doing now.

Isaac walks me to the lot line, my arm looped through his.

I drag my feet, listening for how he is going to beg me to stay. I'll make him plead a little, but I'll give in.

My brain is obsessed with the thought of climbing the stairs to our suite, falling back on the sheets so they exhale the scent of him all around me as his fangs puncture the vein in my throat, my arm, my thigh. We've been trying different areas all over my body, sensual and necessary, so my veins don't collapse and my skin can heal.

The blue-black bruises Isaac leaves on my skin with each bite reminds me of the dark skin of grapes, ruined for wine. They also remind me of his kiss, and the way I feel when his venom spills through me. His passion is as blue-black as it is irresistible, a shooting star dying in my veins.

I wish he'd beg me to stay right now.

Not so long ago, I jumped the ditch to escape him and he dragged me back by the heels.

Isaac drops his arm, my own separating from his.

"Don't be long," he says.

My disappointment is lump the size of a full, cold moon lodges itself in my esophagus, but I try to stay brave and focused. As if leaving him is the same as going off to war. One word from him and I won't leave at all. Seeing Meg just doesn't feel like the priority I thought it was before.

"I'll tell my cousin all about you," I say.

"Good." He gives me a tight-lip grin and a short nod, as if he doesn't care what I say about him at all. His reaction tightens the muscle between my shoulder blades.

"I really should see her." The words are less for him and more to remind myself that I asked for this. I wanted to go, no matter how frantic and anxious leaving makes me feel now. Deep behind all of this drama swirling in my head is a bubble of reason that keeps burping four words: *stay focused, find Meg.*

It's sort of ridiculous. Like Isaac said before, she hasn't come looking for me. It'd be so lovely to walk back into the mansion instead. I could lie in the bathtub beneath the glass window—in a warm milk bath, to warm my blood like a fine glass of sherry, like Isaac had purred earlier. It would be bliss, compared to going, alone, back into my old world.

I can't believe he hasn't started asking me to stay yet. There are so many good excuses he could use and I'm prepared to agree with any one of them.

To encourage his pleading, I push back my shoulders and sigh, "Well, I should be going."

Isaac gives me a second, *who cares* kind of nod that crumples my pride and my posture. "Give your cousin my very best regards."

I dig my nails into my palms. Very best? Really? What about some concern for me, going unguarded into my old dimension?

"I hope I don't run into any of the Brethren," I say. If there's anything that might peak his eyebrows and get him thinking of what he could lose by letting me go, it's the threat of his Brethren.

He said vampires are competitive and territorial. This should do it.

But Isaac only says, "I don't think you have to worry. I've sent Eustace on ahead to keep an eye out."

"Oh. Great," is all I can manage. I guess Isaac cares enough to send his bodyguard. It still doesn't feel like it's enough. Isaac's indifference has got my goat and I'm not sure if I should feel guilty or infuriated.

I choose infuriated.

I spin away from him and step over the lot line, my foot falling onto the dusty, empty Washington Street that I used to know.

Isaac and the entire Havrath estate vanish in a blink.

The temperature shoots up. I'd like to think it's the moisture in the air that makes my lungs so heavy, but it's hard to breathe every time I think of being here without Isaac.

A full sun blazes overhead and I squint at the now-empty lot, so used to the perpetual dusk on the estate. Sweat beads up on my back and the fabric of my dress sticks to it like fly paper.

I want to cry.

I want to go home.

To Isaac.

I get how stupid it is that I want to go back, when Isaac didn't seem to care that I was leaving. The best I can do is let him miss me while I take my time visiting with Meg.

No matter how much I don't feel like visiting anymore. Leaving Isaac is like pulling a Band-Aid from an open, gaping wound.

Eustace is nowhere to be found, so I begin the long walk to Aunt Dena and Uncle Leonard's house on the opposite side of town.

The back door to the house is open, so I walk right in. Meg's not in her room. Not parked in front of the TV, not smoking out the bathroom window. She's not around, but Uncle Leonard is —hunched down over the kitchen table, gnawing on a chicken leg. The moment I step into the room, he drops the leg and sits up straight.

"Who the hell are you?"

He can still see me, but he can't *see* me hiding inside this new skin. "I'm looking for Meg."

"I don't care who you're looking for!" The grease on his chin coats his anger with a sheen of ridiculousness. "Who do you think you are, lady, walking into my house like you own the joint?"

I snort. Can't help it. "At least you're acknowledging you can see me now."

His head tips to the side like a confused dog. He squints at me as he stands up. "I can see you just fine! Now get the hell out of my house!"

"It's Nova," I say flatly.

That stops him dead. His eyes slide away. He wipes his brow. Plops onto his chair.

"I don't know nobody by that name," he mutters, fingers wiping independently over his bristly jaw.

"Sure you do." I take the chair beside his. "You ignored me for months. What did I ever do to you? I came here after my parents *died* and you ignored me. Do you know how awful that was?" His gaze remains focused somewhere beyond me. "Now, I just want to know where Meg's at."

Eyes large and distant, he raises the chicken leg to his mouth.

"Are you seriously going to try to ignore me again?" I grab his hand, yanking the food away from his mouth and he shrieks.

He drops the chicken leg as he shoots out of the chair.

"Stop acting like I don't exist!" I shout, jumping up too.

We're only a few feet apart, but he turns his head away, looking out the window beside the table.

"Tell me where Meg is!" I growl, stepping toward him.

He turns to bolt.

I jump in front of him.

He pivots the other way, but I block his escape again. He twists this way and that, trying to get away from me, but I counter his every move.

"I'm not crazy!" he shrieks.

"And I'm not invisible anymore," I snarl. We continue this horrible dance until I've got him pinned with his back in the corner. "Tell me where Meg is!"

Uncle Leonard throws his hands over his eyes and rolls toward the wall, smashing his face against the plaster. He begins to wail.

"You're not real!" he bawls. "You're not, *you're not*, YOU'RE NOT! You can't make me go back to the ward! I won't, because *you're not real*!"

Ward? What ward?

Hands still cupped over his sobbing face, he pushes off the wall and I fall back, watching him in shock. He staggers to the kitchen cupboard beside the stove. The place where Aunt Dena keeps cold medicine hidden in spice bottles, so Meg and Murray don't swallow them all.

At least, I thought it was cold medicine.

"I'll take my meds! I'll take them all, I swear!" Uncle Leonard swats around blindly for the cabinet, eyes still covered with the opposite hand so he doesn't have to look at me. He finally lands on the right cabinet and swings it open, fumbling through the bottles. A half dozen dark blue bottles spill out all over the counter, roll off, and drop on the floor. Between his fingers, he scans the bottles and dives for one. He gets the cap open and squints as he pours loose, blackberry tea into his hand. I can smell the waft of Aunt Dena's favorite tea from where I stand.

Meg must've found the treasure trove after all.

Uncle Leonard doesn't recognize that he's got a fist full of dried tea leaves instead of his medication.

Sliding down to the floor, with his ear against a cupboard, he stuffs the handful of leaves into his mouth. Still sobbing, he takes a breath and swallows hard, without water. Sweat trickles down his forehead, his eyes crushed shut beneath his splayed fingers.

"I don't see you. I don't see you. I don't see you!" he chants. "You're going to disappear. Go away. Go away!"

I go into the kitchen, keeping a few feet between us as I squat down beside him.

"You don't have to see me anymore," I whisper softly, "if you just tell me where I can find Meg."

A tear slips out from beneath his pinky finger.

"I don't know!" he howls. "Murray took her someplace, but then the weirdo came looking for her again too, and nobody's been back since!"

"Weirdo? What weirdo?" I ask. The hair rises on the back of my neck. Murray's the only weirdo, that I know of, who has ever come to the house. I scoot closer to Uncle Leonard. "Are you talking about one of Murray's friends?"

"I don't know!" he wails. "It's the guy with the tattoos up his face! I don't know anything else! I swear! Just go away and leave me alone!"

I stand up. I believe him, but I don't know of any weirdo with tattoos up his face either. Adrenaline pools in my stomach. Someone is looking for Meg and I have no idea if it is human, ghost, vampire, or something else I have yet to discover.

I stare at Uncle Leonard as he sobs for a few more moments and then let myself out, stumbling down the front steps. What Uncle Leonard did when I came to live with them, and what I actually deserved, isn't so clear anymore.

All I know is: I have to find Meg.

I spot Dorcas Boyle, the museum curator, the moment I turn the corner onto Washington Street. She's standing in front of the museum, fanning herself so enthusiastically with a pamphlet that she's blowing her crazy hair right out of her flower barrettes. They drop on the pavement and she picks them up, sliding them randomly back into her hair.

"Hello, hello," she greets me as I approach. "Are you here to see the famous Havrath Wedding Exhibit?"

"I've already seen it," I squirm for how to explain my new skin as I drop my words to a whisper. "This is kind of weird, but we've already met. You won't recognize me, but I talked to you a couple weeks ago, about the incorrect wedding dates."

The curator drops the pamphlet fan to her side, peering at me. She licks her lips. "I don't know what you mean. The dates are correct," she says, but there is a slight tremble in her voice.

"My name is Nova." She leans back as I tilt toward her. "You might not know this, but I was a ghost when you met me before."

Dorcas Boyle throws her head back in a laugh, before turning a more solemn face to me. "Oh! Ha! And?"

She peers at me as if this isn't unexpected news. I sputter and stutter; of all the reactions I anticipated, this isn't one of them.

"Well…I'm not anymore," I stammer. "A ghost, I mean. You knew what I was?"

"How would I have known? You never mentioned it." She snorts. "I'm not the kind to poke at other people's business, but if you're here," she reaches out and softly pinches my arm, "then it means you've taken a body."

I gape. "Yes…I have…you know about that too?"

"I'm a savant! I study *everything*. How would I not know about it?" She lifts the pamphlet and begins fanning her face again. "However, knowing something and actually seeing it in practice— well, this is an exciting day."

"You've only read about it? You've never seen anyone else like me before?"

She shrugs. "I don't know. Maybe. I'm not much of a meddler, or a gossip, but if you're no longer a ghost, then the only way you are capable of standing here with me, in a form I don't recognize, is as a revenant." Her eyes move up and down the street. "I assumed you'd gotten all the answers you needed from me, since you disappeared without a goodbye, but here you are again, so how can I help you?"

My head is spinning. "What else do you know that I don't?"

"Probably most subjects. Could you be more specific?"

"What do you know about revenants?"

"Revenancy occurs when a ghost who hasn't passed into the next realm takes the body of another who has passed—"

"Do you know anything about vampires?"

"Oh yes. Scads."

"Is there any way to hide from a bunch of them?"

Dorcas rests her elbow in her palm, her upraised fingers against her lips. "A nest? Hmmm, well, yes. In theory. It's said that you can use garlic to repel them, you can stake their sleeping bodies to kill them, or you can traverse the dimensions where they are not permitted, in order to avoid them."

I perk at the last suggestion. "Do you know about a thing called a *vias?* A barrier between dimensions?"

"I've heard of a barrier called the *in-between.*"

"Yes, that's it."

"Vias, hmmm? Interesting." She eyes me, as if she'll ask what I know about vampires, but she doesn't and I'm relieved. "The *in-between* makes traveling between dimensions tricky. One can be lost quickly and thoroughly if they dwell too long, but crossing the barrier is necessary to get into alternate dimensions. Are you trying to avoid a nest of vampires?"

"Yes." I swallow. "Do you believe in any of this?"

"Oh no." She laughs. "There isn't enough factual evidence to substantiate the hypothesis of mythical-based creatures and their realms."

Yet, she believes I was a ghost, and she acknowledges that I'm a revenant now. It seems that vampires aren't much of a stretch, but I'm not about to argue.

I might as well tell her the truth. "If I want to stay away from a bunch of vampires, do you know anything about how to identify their dimensions so I can stay out of them?"

Isaac called me into his dimension and I don't want that to happen with any of the other Brethren. And I certainly don't want to make a wrong turn somewhere and stumble into a dimension I didn't expect.

"Well, deep lore suggests you'd have to seek the help of a witch," Dorcas says, cupping her chin with one hand. "A good one, who can furnish you with an indicating charm."

"Do you know where I could find someone like that?"

The curator throws her head back with a cackle. "This is turning into a witch hunt, isn't it?" She's giggling so much, I doubt she's taking any of this seriously at all, which isn't really a bad thing. "I don't know many witches, but you're in luck. The Celtic Sisters is a shop just down the way. Three sisters run it and they've talked about the ghosts living in their shop. Try them. They might be able to help."

A round table near the door, tiered like a wedding cake, displays candles and soap in brown wrappers. The gentle combination of scents is the first thing to hit me as I enter the Celtic Sisters' shop and the smell is so appealing, I want to curl up in a corner and inhale it all day. I wonder if the stuff is enchanted, or if it just smells that good.

The rest of the shop is about the same: an eclectic mix of shelves and vintage cabinets divide up the space. One rack displays tee-shirts with slogans like, *It's a New Baltimore Thing* and *I'd rather be fishing on Anchor Bay.* Another is filled with jars of locally-gleaned honey, jam, and hard candy. At the back, there is a revolving display with key chains on hooks, and ceramic mugs on shelves. Framed oil paintings hang on the walls, each with a hand-written price tag tucked in a corner. The whole place is as welcoming and comfortable as a favorite sweater.

The wood floors creak beneath my feet. At the sound, a woman pops her head up from behind the counter at the opposite end of the shop. She's got the kind of lines in her face that make her look like she's smiling, even if she's not.

"Good afternoon to you." She stands with a grunt, her smile

aligning with her wrinkles. The shopkeeper, hands on her aproned hips, tips her head back to see me through the wedge of her bifocals. "Something I can help you find?"

"Dorcas Boyle sent me." I sound so ominous as I walk to the back of the shop, my heels clicking across the wood. I'm not sure how we'll get where I need to go in this conversation.

Beyond the counter is a hot dog roaster that squeaks as it turns, a slushee machine, an ice cream freezer with six buckets in it. At the very back, there is a bright, yellow wall with a staircase tucked behind it. The steps face the front of the shop, ascending to the second floor, and a little girl is seated half-way up.

The girl has sharp, black eyes and a huge black bow in her black hair, so it looks like she has pointy cat ears rather wearing a hair accessory. She's wearing a dress with a red bodice, black-with-white polka dots skirt, white stockings that end at her scuffed, black Mary Jane's. Her white legs and black shoes poke out through the banister rails. She sways her feet as she stares at me, scraping lines in the yellow paint with her heels.

I flash a smile at her and she smashes her face through the rails, smashing the bow on her head backward. The little girl looks just like her grandmother—their peaked upper lips don't quite hide their front teeth.

"Are you after some local history books?" the woman asks, wiping her hands on her apron front. "We carry *The History of New Baltimore* and *Ashleyville Isn't Anymore*. They're both pretty good reads."

"No, thank you, but I am looking for…a witch."

The little girl's legs still, but the woman doesn't skip a beat. "Oh! Dorcas must've told you about our ghost!"

"She mentioned that, but I'm actually looking for a witch."

"Our ghost is a witch!" the woman sputters as she comes out from behind the counter. "By the way, I'm Ellie, and that's my granddaughter up there on the stairs, in case you're wondering. I'm the middle sister. The china cabinet is right over here. It's where she lives."

I'm not sure how to respond, since this is a goose-chase. Ghosts don't live in cabinets. I should know.

Still, I follow behind her to the cabinet. I've got to see what she's talking about, if it's anything at all. As a revenant, I should be able to see any ghost that's in there. Ellie stops in front of a tall cabinet that someone painted over with a glossy, glowing, butter-yellow. Drawers on the bottom with white, ceramic pulls. Glass doors on top, enclosing three shelves. The top two are scattered with a dozen, small, clay tiles.

"She's a crier usually, I have to warn you," Ellie says. "But if she has a temper today, stay clear of the doors and I'll close her up again so she can settle down."

I don't know what she's got in the cabinet, but I don't think clay tiles bite.

Ellie opens the glass doors slowly, peeking inside as if she's worried about disturbing someone's slumber. I stare through the glass, but there's nothing. Just the tiles on the raw, wood shelves. No sign of a ghost.

"Miss Mack," Ellie calls. "Hello? It's Ellie of the three sisters. Are you interested in visiting today?"

This is ridiculous. I glance over at the little girl on the stairs. She's leaning as far as she can from between the stair rails, watching us. I give her a grimace-smile, but her face remains seriously bored. The most I can get out of her is a squint.

Ellie, however, continues to work the glass doors open a few centimeters at a time, while she croons through the opening at the shelves and the tiles.

Then, something in the cabinet begins to click.

I look through the glass. The tiles are trembling on the shelves, but there's no one in there doing it. I'd be able to see a ghost. This has got to be a hoax. A pressure plate beneath the cabinet that makes it rumble.

A tile drops onto the bottom shelf. Bracing the cabinet doors, Ellie reaches in and retrieves the tile.

I lean closer to her as she studies it. There is an arrow on the tile, pointed in my direction.

Ellie turns wide eyes on me. "Miss Mack would like to know your name."

The hair on my neck rises. I don't want to tell my name, in case this Miss Mack somehow knows Ruth. A distant relative or someone who would recognize Ruth's face and know that this woman went missing. My own name might raise suspicion if the skin is recognized. Either name I give Miss Mack may not make sense, and it could unravel the theft I committed in stealing Ruth's body away from her.

"I'd like to see her," I say instead, peering hard through the glass. "Who is she?"

The cabinet rumbles again and another tile falls onto the lower shelf. Ellie plucks it out. This tile has an elongated 'y' printed on it.

"She'd like to know why you want to see her."

"Why wouldn't I?" I laugh.

Two tiles fall this time.

"Wow. She's really talkative with you," Ellie says. She shows me two tiles, both with question marks. "I guess she's giving up on your name. Miss Mack would like to know what you want."

"I need three things. I need something to help me find a vial that is lost, something to help me find my cousin, and a charm that can help me avoid vampires."

Ellie's high-browed gaze is stuck on pause. She finally turns back to the cabinet. "Alrighty then," she drawls. "Hear that one, Miss Mack? Anything you can do?"

One tile drops. Ellie picks it up. The arrow on the tile points to a pegged shelf with polished stones on key chains. Ellie takes down a quartz in the shape of a heart, and a second stone that is an inch long, slim and jagged, like a fang, and a third that is just a stone. All are on key chains. Ellie brings it to the cabinet, holding it up in front of the paned doors as if they are eyes.

"Are these correct?" Ellie asks the cabinet. And she thinks I'm crazy for asking for a vampire charm.

A tile drops. Ellie holds it up.

"A '*Y*' for yes," she says. I hold out my hand for the charms, but Ellie shakes her head. "They're not infused with anything yet."

She slips them into the cabinet, on the bottom shelf, and closes the doors as if she's closing a microwave.

"Ok, Miss Mack," she says. "Do your thing!"

The cabinet rumbles and stills. Ellie opens up the door and retrieves the charms, along with another tile. She extends her hand to me and I put out mine, but her fingertips remain in my palm. She holds up the tile, pressed with a money symbol.

"Miss Mack says there is a price," Ellie says. The little girl on the stairs stands, the step creaks beneath her.

"What is it?"

A tile inside the cabinet drops on the lower shelf with a *tink*. Ellie pulls it out and holds it up. Another arrow, pointed in my direction.

"She wants your name. That's her price," Ellie says.

I close my fingers on Ellie's and she releases the charms. I suppose if I give her my own name, any similarity between Ruth and I could be explained away with a, *I must have a twin!* or *you don't say- I get that all the time.*

"My name is Nova," I say.

Ellie smiles in response, but the little girl on the stairs screams a scream that turns my borrowed blood to ice.

E llie slams the cabinet doors shut. "What's wrong with you, Annie?"

Her granddaughter barrels down the stairs and past the back counter machines.

"I told you, my name's not Annie!" the girl bellows as she sprints toward us.

I press my back against the side of the cabinet to avoid being run over, but the shopkeeper's granddaughter stops short, glaring up at me.

"What'd you say your name is?" the little girl growls. Anxiety floods me. Could this little kid somehow recognize Ruth? Her vicious expression snags on her tiny features, giving her the appearance of a rabid, wild animal. Her mouth opens wide as she snarls, "What's your name!"

"Nova," I stammer.

The girl lunges for me.

"Gracious!" Ellie grabs the little girl from the back, grasping her upper arms. "My word, what's gotten into you, Anna Marie?"

The girl bares her teeth at me as she squirms in the woman's grasp. "Let me go!"

I try to slide out of my trapped corner against the cabinet and almost make it, but Annie's shoe shoots out and strikes my shin, swift and hard.

I shriek and grasp my leg, jumping up and down.

"Goodness! I apologize for my granddaughter, ma'am!" Ellie shrills. She gives the little girl a shake. "Anna Marie, you apologize right now!"

"She's a thief!" the little girl insists.

I draw back. "I...I haven't touched a thing but these tiles," I say, holding out the tiles in my hand.

Ellie glimpses them and turns her attention back to her granddaughter. "What are you talking about?"

I've never seen this girl in my life and now I'm being framed.

"She stole my husband away from me!" the girl shrills.

Ellie relaxes with a laugh, although she doesn't let go of the girl's arms. I laugh too. This kid is maybe six years old—being accused of stealing her husband is comical.

"You don't have a husband yet, sweetheart," Ellie soothes, but the kid wiggles with a renewed burst of energy, freeing herself from her grandmother's clutches. Anna Marie spins to face me, eyes narrowed, and jabs her first little finger straight at my face.

"She is a dirty, rotten thief and she stole my Isaac away!"

I gape at the little girl, her bow slipped down on the side of her head. There's no way she could know about Isaac. She's six years old.

"Isaac who?" I ask.

The girl seethes. "Like you don't know!" Her voice lowers, along with her brow. Her hands wave, as if she's moving a fog I can't see. "I withdraw what I can, that which I gave of my own hand, as the circumstances have changed, and this beneficiary is to blame!"

The tiles tingle in my hand.

"What did you just do?" I ask.

Ellie shrugs as if I was talking to her. "I didn't even know she knew words like that," she says vacantly. "Where did you learn those words, Annie?"

"For the last time…my name's not Annie!" the girl screams. "It's Machara Milligen, and *she* is why Isaac sent me away!"

I stumble backward. That name couldn't have come out of nowhere, and this isn't a coincidence. Machara Milligen, the woman who was living in the cottage I burnt down, who was addicted to Isaac's blood, who was sent away…is in this little girl's body.

Miss Mack…it was Machara Milligen moving the tiles with her magic the whole time. No wonder Ellie said she's usually a crier—she's probably still mourning being separated from Isaac.

"You're the witch," I whisper to the little girl in front of me.

Ellie turns on me. "Don't call her that. She's just a little confused."

But Machara circles me and hisses, "Yes!" She yanks the bow off her head. The little girl flicks her fingers in Ellie's direction, as if she's dispelling something sticky from them, but the motion immobilizes the shopkeeper. Ellie is freakishly still, her breath so shallow I can't detect it. I'm not sure she's still alive.

"What did you do to her?" I snarl, but Machara flashes me a wry smile.

If Machara can do this to an innocent woman, I can't imagine what she's going to do to me. "You convinced Isaac to send me away and do this to me!"

I move backward as Machara advances, but back into a glass case with a display of honey and jam on top. Machara blocks the door, but anyone passing by and looking in the window would've been amazed to see this tiny girl backing up a full grown woman. But no one could guess how powerful a witch this little girl has within her either.

"I didn't even know you existed!" I tell her. "The night Isaac sent you away was the first time I ever saw you. I heard you screaming and I thought you were—"

"He sent for you, but he was mine!" Machara barks through the little girl's mouth. She raises her pinched fingers between us, as if she's drawing an invisible string up from the floor. At chest level, she flips her hand over and opens her palm. A dark red flame jumps in her palm. Machara flashes me a maniacal grin before her gaze flicks back to the tiny, burgundy blaze. "You shouldn't have come! I'm telling them you're here!" she shrieks. "They're going to take you away! They'll bed you and wed you and then Isaac will have me back in his arms again!"

A spear of jealousy pierces my patience. "He chose me," I growl.

"They *all* did," Machara spits out a scornful laugh. "I don't care which one has you, as long as it's not the one who belongs to me!"

She tips the flame out of her palm. It plops onto the floor like a teaspoon of jelly, but it soaks into the wood. A small dark circle appears, smoking in the center. A flame blazes up, my reflection in it. I grab one of the hand-quilted blankets from a rack and throw it on the fire, stomping on it to suffocate the fire.

"Too late! They know!" Machara says sweetly, kissing her shoulder with the tip of her chin.

The hair stands on my arms.

The little girl claps her hands and jumps straight up, as if she's taking a monumental leap into the sideways-eggbeater of a double-dutch jump rope. But instead of jumping in, her body rises up, turning from a body to a misty image clinging in the air above me. Machara's burning gaze anchors to me through the image of Ellie's granddaughter, which folds up like a napkin right in front of my eyes. The image creases and flops over onto another part of the image, until the final square of the little girl's body disappears into thin air.

I'm left with only one thought: she told *them*. She could only mean the Brethren.

My blood prickles. Isaac's not here to protect me, and I doubt I can take on one vampire by myself, let alone as many as might make up a *'them'*.

I'm in trouble.

Ellie's arm twitches. It doesn't feel right to leave her, but when she comes to, she's going to want to know what happened to her granddaughter and I have no way to explain it. Humans don't accept magic, I know that from living with Uncle Leonard and Aunt Dena. There's no way Ellie won't call the cops.

I can't be stuck here, trying to explain what humans won't believe. The ache of being away from Isaac so long spreads across my chest. I've got to get out of here.

Tiles in my palm, I bolt out the front door and run straight into the muscled chest of the man who was in the estate barn—Athen, with his mahogany eyes and whiskey-colored hair. He grabs hold of me and it knocks the air from my lungs. Not because of the impact of our bodies, but because his touch is electric.

"Nova?" he asks, but there's little doubt in his tone.

"You can see me?" I am stunned he knows who I am in Ruth's skin, but he certainly seems clear on it as he gives my arm a tug, sending me skittering down the sidewalk beside him.

"You've got to come with me right now." His entire face is tight as his gaze flashes up and down the street. His grip on my forearm firms. A quiver knocks its way down my borrowed spine. "Look, don't fight me on this. We've got to go—they know you're here!"

"Who?" I yelp as he drags me down the sidewalk close to his ribs.

With a downward slant of his chin he mutters in my ear, "The vamps!"

Like the waves rolling onto the beach from Anchor Bay, a strange and soothing wave of trust washes over me. Having met Athen only once before, I can't allow the feeling to saturate my logic. I don't know where Athen came from, or why he's here. Maybe Hoomstid and Esther had some reason to send him, but maybe they didn't. The strangely pleasant, electric sting of his touch could actually be some funky manipulative magic, for all I know.

I plant my feet, pulling Athen to a stop with me. "How did you know who I am?"

"I just know...look, I don't have time to explain..."

I yank my arm away from him. He stares at me a moment, I think it's disbelief raising his brow, but then he studies me and lets out a heavy sigh.

Evidently, I've effectively communicated that I'm not budging until I get an answer. I put my hands on my hips, resting back on them as I wait for a better answer.

He groans through a second sigh. "I can… *feel* you," he grumbles, as if he's just as confused about the admission as I am. "We don't have time for me explain it all to you right now, okay? We've got to get out of here!"

The intensity in his tone alarms me, but I'm not about to run off with him either. I side-eye up and down the street too and see no sign of Brethren in either direction. Waves lick the shore of the beach, and a teenage couple walking on the opposite side of the street giggle and kiss and the girl squeals, like Meg used to do with Murray.

Why do I keep forgetting about Meg? I came here to find her and I've done everything *but* hunt her down. Allowing Athen to jog me away from an invisible threat will only delay me further from finding my cousin.

"I can take care of myself," I tell Athen. "I can hide if I have to."

Come to think of it, I haven't seen a hair of Eustace since he dumped me off. I throw a glance over my shoulder to a fairly empty street. Nope, not a whiff of anyone—not the servant who's supposed to be protecting me, or the Brethren, or Meg.

Washington's wrought iron streetlights pop on in the dusk and I think of Isaac, waiting for me at the estate. I've been here too long, chasing the ghost of my lover, rather than finding Meg and now it's getting too late.

"It's not safe. You've got to come with me," Athen insists.

"I can't. I have to get home," I say.

Athen's hand snakes out and takes hold of my upper arm. The zinging electricity of his touch mellows and morphs to a powerful current, tingling through my skin. The sensation circulates inside me, settling my nerves, spreading over my thoughts, melding our wills together.

The tight space between my eyebrows relaxes.

My feet fall into sync with his stride.

Athen and I move together as if we are one body, as if being so near to one another is completely natural. Normal. Another wave of energy crashes through me, this one more intimate, warming my heart as well as other places.

As fast as the pleasure came, a searing throb replaces it. Nothing pleasant about it, the throb rips through me and I jerk away from Athen.

The thought of Isaac rakes across my mind like a storm cloud over a dark moon. His face floats in my vision. Switching my gaze in another direction doesn't help. All I see is Isaac, furious that I'm trying to look away from him. I'm blinded to anything else. This version of Isaac isn't the sweet one who laid beside me, admiring the stars from the tall grass on the estate. This Isaac bares his teeth with a snarl that exposes his fangs and furrows his brow. This Isaac pierces me with a stare that questions my love for him and it hurts.

Literally.

My muscles tense, everything squeezes. My toes knuckle up, my stomach grips the remnants of my last meal and forces them upward. My throat knots off the vomit, but it also strangles my breath.

Closing my eyes is no escape. Isaac's furious image lunges at me and I stumble backward in shock.

"Don't doubt me!" I gasp to the life-like image. Isaac's face retreats a sliver as I murmur, "I love you. Only you."

My muscles loosen. I inhale deeply.

Athen grabs my wrist. I don't see him do it—Isaac's face still blots out everything else—but Athen's warming touch is unmistakable. It sends a second, white-hot throb racing through me. I shriek and jerk back as Isaac lunges at me again.

Athen lets go at my cry of distress, but his desperation vibrates in my ear.

"What's happening, Nova?"

I grab my head. I still can't see Athen, but words explode out of me as if they have sole control of my tongue. "Leave me alone! I don't belong to you, I belong to Isaac Havrath!"

The moment I say it, Isaac's smiling, sweet face nods to me.

My vision clears and I wipe my eyes. "I've got to get home."

Athen grimaces.

"That's what I thought," he groans, glimpsing each end of the street again, before dragging me around the corner building, off Washington. "That bastard addicted you to his venom!"

"Who do you think you are?" I wrench my arm away, static snapping in the broken connection between us. The tension between us is so thick, it could light the darkness where we're standing, away from the streetlights. "I'm not addicted to anything!"

Not sure where Athen gets off accusing Isaac, especially when Isaac told me he could control the addictive properties in his venom and promised me he wouldn't addict me.

And he hasn't.

Addiction would feel terrible. It would feel scummy. Desperate. Sure, I really want to be home, but I wouldn't chew off an arm to get back to the estate. I would really just prefer to be with Isaac. It's not an addiction to want to stretch out beside him in his bed. My eyes nearly roll back in bliss when I think of the tantalizing brush of Isaac's lips against my neck.

That's not addiction.

It's love.

Clearly, Athen has the emotional capacity of a turnip to think otherwise.

A thick girl, with a spiky, blond pixie cut and a grungy,

cropped, denim jacket, rounds the storefront facing the beach, knocking right into Aiden and me.

"I've been looking for you!" The girl's eyes latch onto Athen and something jagged shifts in my belly. I make up my mind immediately—I don't like her. "This place is crawling with vamps and their revs! We've got to get low."

"*Their* revs?" I snarl. "What do you mean *their revenants*? We're not pets, you know!"

The girl scoffs, glancing over her shoulder. "The hell you aren't!"

"Amnesty," Athen growls at her. "Shut up. You're not helping."

"Did you even hear what I said?" she bites back in a whisper. "We've got to get low and quick! There's one in a carriage that will be circling back any minute and his *chihuahua's* going to give us away!"

"That's Eustace!" I say. "He's looking for me!"

"What'd I tell you," Amnesty scoffs at Athen.

I streak past her, dodging from the edge of the building, back onto Washington. The carriage is two blocks away and Eustace's head is turned. I open my mouth to shout, but the girl hooks my elbow. Her other hand clutches my throat, cutting off all sound, as she drags me backward. She shoves me and I stumble, my spine smacking against Athen's chest. Raw wires sizzle in my skin as he coils his arm around me, holding me to him. His palm against my lips, I gasp a breath between his fingers.

"Please…I can't let you go!" he whispers in my ear. Something in his tone keeps me from immediately stomping on his instep to escape.

I hear the carriage wheels grinding over the concrete and the horse hooves clomping closer. It reminds me of Isaac and a surge of heat, unpleasant as a rash, spreads over every inch of skin in contact with Athen.

"I can't stay," I tell him, lifting my foot to back-kick his knee. He'll drop like Goliath if I hit it right.

"Do it," Athen says.

I think he's taunting me, until the blond girl steps in front of me, palm up, and blows a handful of dust in my face.

Dust that sticks in my nostrils, weakening my thoughts, my muscles, and my consciousness, until I droop in Athen's arms like the broken stem of a sunflower.

I take a breath. The air is stifling in its humidity. It's musty in my nostrils and tastes stale on the back of my tongue. My brain plugs into my body and I feel the half-dozen rivers of sweat dribbling off my skin and onto the damp sheet beneath me.

"She's waking up, Amnesty!" a girl's soft voice chirps, not far from me. "What do I do? Tell me what to do!"

The answering voice is surly and familiar. "Let her wake up, Charity. What else are you going to do?"

Before I even open my eyes, I know who she is. The surly girl with Athen. Spiky pixie. The dust-blower. Amnesty.

Yes, that was her name.

"What if she's who they think she is—" Charity's voice is tiny, babyish and instantly annoying as I lay in my ever-growing pool of sweat.

Amnesty groans. "She's not."

"How do you know?"

"Look at her! She's nothing special! She's just like the rest of us."

Charity pauses a moment, then, "It's so hot down here."

"That's what happens when there's no money for air condition-ing. Quit talking about it—you're just making it worse."

A fingertip taps my forehead. I squint open my eyes to see a young girl's unfamiliar face, lined with stick-straight locks of blond hair that spill over her shoulders. She skitters backward the moment she realizes I'm looking at her. Her knees hit the edge of a chair ten feet away and she falls onto the seat.

Beyond her: cinder block walls painted white, a metal trash can, the raw beams of an unfinished ceiling. Laughter, the stomping of boots, drifts down from the wood planks. It seems wildly out of place in the dank basement.

About the same distance from me on the left, Amnesty sits atop a cluster of barrels. She's hunched over and frowning deeply, her focus laser-aimed at digging stuff out from beneath her nails.

"Hello." The blond girl gives me a wry smile, waving from her chair. "I'm Charity and this is—"

"I know who she is," I murmur. My usually-reliable voice sticks in my throat, creaking and crackling over each word. Amnesty doesn't look up. I don't care. "She's the one who called me a *pet*."

Amnesty scoffs. "Because you are."

Acidic saliva fills my mouth as I try to sit up, but there's only so far I can go. I pull and rope cuts into my wrists. I'm tied to the cot I'm lying on. The laughter overhead ebbs and then swells again. I swallow hard, my own saliva burning down my throat.

"Why am I tied down?" I growl. Amnesty's face is unsympa-thetic. Panic shivers in my veins as I turn my face to Charity. "Can you get these things off me?"

The girl looks back at Amnesty. I follow her gaze.

"It's for your safety," Amnesty says dully. Hard to believe, since there is such a bitter twist on her lips. "And ours."

"There's two of you and one of me," I say. "What could I do to you?"

"You're addicted to venom." The twist of her lips deepens, like it's the most disgusting thing she's ever had to say. "You'd do anything you could to get back to that *leach*."

The word rattles in my head. *Leach*. Adrenaline rockets through me, my mouth fills with searing saliva. I swallow hard. It burns down my throat. The upper floor party amplifies. The chatter and laughter, along with the sound of heeled shoes on the floor above us, would drown out any words I have, if I had anything I wanted to actually say to this stupid girl.

Words can wait; I just want to get her first. Kill her. Rip Amnesty to pieces for talking that way about Isaac. *My Isaac.*

Boiling hot saliva fills my mouth again and I choke it down, yanking upward on the ropes that bite into my skin. I don't care if my hands come clean off. I'll beat Amnesty with the bloody stumps of my forearms if I have to.

She scoffs again. The volume upstairs recedes. "If you were in your right mind, you'd agree with me."

"You're a smug little witch," I fire back.

"I wish!" Amnesty laughs. "My life would be so much easier if I could just *hufflepuff* whatever I needed. By the by, if you've got to spit, try to wait until we get the vials in here to bottle it."

Charity turns her baby-doll eyes and bowtie mouth in my direction. "I heard you've got one after you. A really nasty witch, I mean. She's got it worse than you do. Another victim of that *leach*."

"Don't work her up too much before we get the bottles," Amnesty says. "We don't want to waste any of the master's juice, do we, *Pet*?"

The volume of the party upstairs increases, like a gossip who won't let me get a murder in edgewise.

"Shut up!" I scream, pulling at my braided tether. It's drowned in the noise of boots clomping across the floor upstairs in a herd. Finally, the slam of a door.

The silence that follows feeds me. It clears my thoughts. I turn my predatory glare on Amnesty, keeping Charity solidly in my peripheral vision.

It's not just that I want to kill them, it's that I *have to.* They're insulting me and the man I love.

I thrust one arm out and the other is yanked to my side. I try to kick, but my ankles are cinched together too, even tighter than my hands. It doesn't matter what I do; they're out of range. I scream, raging against the ropes, eyes squeezed shut as I pour my concentration into tearing free.

"Nova!" A pair of heavy hands grips my shoulders. The sound of the deeply masculine voice launches my heart into my throat.

Isaac has come for me.

I'm sure of it.

I open my eyes, but Isaac isn't the one in front of me.

Athen hovers at the side of my bed. The crease between his brows softens the moment our gazes connect. The mellow haze I felt in his presence before, returns. He smells like fall. Fresh, like wind through the trees. His grasp loosens and I let my arms drift down to my sides.

"Why are you screaming?" His right eyebrow raises slightly with his question.

There is a kindness in his gaze that makes me want to cry. Or maybe I want to cry because I can't poke my thumbs through his eye sockets. Both thoughts swirl in my head and I can't make sense of either of them. I have an urge to wrap my arms around him as much as I have an urge to wrap him in a choke hold and slowly smother him to death. My eyes well up and saliva wells in my cheeks, burning my gums. I want to warn him that I'm fighting a bizarre compulsion to spit in his face. I want to spit in his face and laugh.

A bit of what's in my cheek slides down my throat. It burns like hot sauce all the way down and sloshes around in my unsteady stomach, making me sick.

I can't tell if it is the burning, the overabundance of saliva in my cheeks, or the fact that every time I think of how pleasing Athen is, another searing wave of spit gushes into my mouth and gives me the unnerving urge to spew it in his face.

Whatever it is, I jerk my head to the edge of the cot and lean as much as I can over the side, the rope only allowing so much range. I open my mouth and let the saliva surge out in a hot stream, burning my tongue before it splatters on the cement floor. Athen jumps backward to avoid being hit.

A line of stinging drool sticks to my lip. I try to spit it off, my head still hanging over the edge of the cot, but it won't let go. My eyes water.

"This will help," Athen says softly. His hand appears with a square of clean, white terry cloth. He swipes the cool washcloth across my mouth, washing away the burning saliva and tossing the cloth into the metal trashcan against the wall.

I fall back against the cot, finding Athen's tranquil gaze again.

"I hate you," I whisper. As fast as I say it, I shake my head with a snap. Those are not the words I meant to say. I try again. "I hate you, *I hate you*, I HATE YOU!"

The more I try to thank him for helping, the louder I shout how much I hate him. My tone gets deeper and my stomach roils with the spit I keep choking down. Frustration and fury builds inside me, until I'm shrieking and yanking at the ropes again, the thought of digging out Athen's beautiful eyeballs with nothing but my fingernails broadcasting through my brain.

Athen smiles with confusing compassion. It's so kind.

A scream blasts from my lungs, as hard and unforgiving as a musket ball.

"This is normal," Athen says, squatting beside the cot so we don't break our eye contact. "You're going to say and do a lot of things you don't mean, until the venom works its way out of your system. It's a vampire's way of protecting his property—his venom will make you repel anyone who might be interested in you at all."

"I HATE YOU!" I scream so hard my voice finishes in shreds.

"I'm going to stay right here and look after you," he says.

It makes my heart ache. The saliva wells up so quickly, I can't clamp my lips shut fast enough. I spit, hard and fast, in that targeted-bullet way that Murray does.

Athen jumps backward and the bullet of spit just misses him, landing on the floor, sizzling and crackling on the cement.

"You know better than to get that close," Amnesty snipes from atop the crate, but then she goes back to carving crap out from beneath her fingernails. "You're going to get a hole burnt in your face."

"Be careful, Athen!" Charity's baby eyes are agape. "You'll need a whole new body if she gets you, and the one you have is so...*nice*. Stay away from her. It'd be a terrible waste."

Athen looks away. Charity's gaze drops to the floor.

So. Charity is into Athen, and I can spit flesh-eating acid.

I glance at my restraints. I'm not sure I can spit so precisely that I can burn off the rope, without setting the entire bed on fire, or burning off my hands.

Amnesty clicks her tongue and rolls her eyes. "The waste is that we still don't have those bottles down here to get our collections. Why don't you go up and see what's keeping Raze and Juan Pablo, Charity."

Charity frowns, but follows the order.

Athen clears his throat once she's gone, drawing my attention.

"I hate you." The words pluck my strangled vocal cords. I knit my brow, hoping it will signal to Athen that I don't mean them. I really, really don't.

His gentle smile makes me ache, as if he's reading my mind without even having to.

My chin jerks upward. I spit at him again. Hard.

The saliva lands on the tip of his boot. Athen jumps backward and kicks off the boot. The acid dissolves the leather and chews straight through the metal toe, leaving only shreds and slivers behind.

mnesty kicks over the barrels of water she was sitting on. The water surges across the floor, flooding the pock-marked cement, sloshing up against the cinder block walls. When she's finished emptying the barrels, the entire floor is covered in about an inch of water and the dank, musty smell of the basement doubles.

It takes Charity three trips down the stairs, tucked within a doorframe at the opposite end of the basement, to bring back weird glass jugs with short necks and broad, edged plates on top; tongs; and heavy gray gloves that reach to the elbows. Crossing the room to Amnesty and Athen, each step looks as though she's jumping in a puddle. The water splashes and tides roll over the gray floor.

It's more obvious now—how Charity can't keep her eyes off Athen. Every time I notice her mooning over him, the red-hot venom wells up in my mouth. But instead of dousing Charity, I am only able to spit it at Athen. However, the sputum never reaches him, but drops into the water on the floor with a sizzle or a hiss.

"Wait, wait!" Amnesty says, pulling on a pair of the gloves Charity hands her. Once on, she grabs the tongs from Charity too. Amnesty clasps the tongs around the jug's tapered neck and makes a tiny grunt when she lifts it. The tongs extend her reach by an arm length, but they seem flimsy compared to the weight of the bottle swaying awkwardly at the end. "Ready," Amnesty says.

For what, I'm not sure.

Charity scrambles to keep her footing once she's gloved up and tries to lift the jug with her pair of tongs. "Whoa!" she lurches across the floor, splashing as she tries to steady the awkward tong-grasp on the bottom-heavy jug.

She's so busy giggling, she runs right into Athen. He loses his grip. His jug crashes to the floor, the bottle shattering in the water.

"Oh no! I'm so sorry!" Charity shrills, still wobbling with her jug still clenched between her tongs.

Amnesty rolls her eyes—hard. There is a hair of bonding between us in that eye-roll.

"It's okay," Athen says tightly. "Just keep a good grip on yours."

"I'm so clumsy," Chastity says, but now she's giggling again.

"Concentrate so you don't break another." Athen says. Charity frowns, but focuses on her jug.

Amnesty jerks her chin in my direction. "Say something sweet to her."

I spit at her—surprisingly not because any compulsion drives me, but because she's such a snot.

She laughs, lunging forward with the bottle, soaking her knees with a spray of water. My spit lands on the plate with a sizzle. Amnesty tilts the bottle so the fluid drizzles through the neck and into the jug more quickly.

"Do it again," she goads with a wide smile. "We need as much as we can get."

I turn my head away. Why would I care what she wants and more so, why would I give it to her?

"Come on," Charity pleads, pouting with her delicate lip.

Like that will change my mind.

"Why would I do anything you want?" I snap back. I pull up

my tied hands so the rope scrapes the side of the bed as a reminder of why they don't deserve anything from me.

"The venom in your saliva will help us—" Athen begins, but catches himself, and his words drift away.

"Help you with what?" I ask.

He sighs, looking to Amnesty as he shakes his head. Whatever it 'helps' with, he doesn't want to say it.

The bottle held out in front of her, Amnesty lifts her left shoulder, wiping the sweat from her face on it. "It'll help you get see that blood sucker a whole lot quicker. That's what you want, right?"

Athen's grimace tells me it's not the whole truth—if it's even the truth at all.

"How would it do that?" I ask.

Athen's still not looking at me.

"The Blood Suckers know we got you," Amnesty says. "So they made a deal with us."

Athen scoffs, turning his head away.

"What's the deal?" I ask.

"They say they've got the Sunshine Vial. They claim they've had it all along—waiting for the moment to make a valuable trade."

"I'm telling you…it's food coloring in a bottle," Athen growls.

"I'm not saying you're wrong," Amnesty says with a shrug. Her gaze roots on Athen. "I don't believe for a sec that she's the one they think she is, but that's all the better for us. We'll finally see if you're who we think you are."

"I'm not," Athen says. "It's a waste."

"You're not a waste," Charity chimes in, her big moon eyes on Athen.

I push up on my elbows, a surge of relief breaking like a champagne bottle in my veins. Sharp and distressing at first, the feeling overwhelms me and I am suddenly drunk on the idea of seeing

Isaac again. "The vampires are going to trade me for the Sunshine Vial?"

"Yup," Amnesty says. "Unlike most of us, the leaches think you're a big freakin' deal."

Charity nods, but Athen plants his hands on his hips, aiming a glare so hostile at Amnesty, I wait a moment for it to cut her in half.

"You are a big deal," Athen says to me, but his glare dares Amnesty to say different. She remains silent.

"To Isaac, I am," I whisper.

My eyes sting at the thought of Isaac convincing Sarkazian to trade me for something so valuable. It's proof that the mating bond is every bit as sacred to the Brethren as Isaac said it was. They may want to kill each other, but down deep, they must love each other. I'm shocked at the thought of it, having seen their vicious brawl during the meeting I attended, but there must be love, or honor, or even just a regard for one another, in order to consider trading their most valuable asset in exchange for one of their Brethren's mates.

Athen makes a low, sharp, violent sound—a sound that makes voicing his disapproval unnecessary.

It tugs at me, but when I look at him, all I do is spit. Spit, build up a mouthful more and spit again. Amnesty gets the first projection, but Athen dodges as Charity reaches out with her tongs and captures the second amount on her plate.

"Gotcha!" She winks at me and I spit a precise, bullet-shot of venom that razors through the hair over her shoulder, shearing off a chunk that falls to the floor like an ignited curtain.

"Set down the jug!" Amnesty shouts.

Charity plops it down with a thunk, but the impact doesn't break the glass. The room fills with the stink of burnt hair as Charity slaps at her remaining, smoldering locks with gloved hands to keep her whole head from going up in flames.

I have to work on my aim. I was aiming for the dead-center of her face, even though I would've settled for a good hole in her cheek. That might shut her up.

Once she's extinguished herself, she grabs the tongs and tilts the bottle side to side, drizzling my acidic-spit into the jug. Her glare is nearly as acidic as my venom, though her laugh is more of a taunt. "I think we have enough to wipe them all out now, don't we, Am?"

"Shut up." Athen growls so deeply, it snuffs Charity's laughter and clamps her mouth shut.

I rise up on the bed, as far as the ropes will allow. "Wipe them out? What do you mean...wipe them out? What are you doing?" I yank on the restraints around my wrists, the rope biting into me, blood bubbling through my raw skin.

"We might as well tell her," Charity bubbles up again, looking to Athen as if he will suddenly approve. His scowl cuts deep lines in his cheeks, but Charity keeps blabbing. "It doesn't make any difference now—we've got the venom!" She throws her head back with a wild laugh, despite a second snarl from Amnesty. "We're making a venom *bomb* and it's going to kill all those blood sucking leaches once and for all!"

A bomb. I don't know why I didn't expect they'd know that one vampire's venom is highly combustible when mixed with another. With enough of it, the revenants could wipe out most of the Brethren. Including my Isaac. The rope fibers sizzle as blood seeps from my skin.

"Shut up, Charity!" Amnesty barks, but her eyes are wide, dialed in on my wrists as a trickle of blood smolders through the rope.

The smell of the burning cord replaces the smell of Charity's fried hair.

I yank upward as hard as I can, shrieking as the rope chews through my skin. My effort is rewarded. Blood douses the rope and a flame leaps up, blue and orange. I scream as the fire swells, singeing my skin, but I'll take it...the flame burns through my bindings. With one tug, the burnt rope breaks free from my wrist and falls to the floor. I pull at the other side, rubbing my raw and bleeding skin on the rope that still binds me.

"Get out of here!" Athen yells at the girls.

"Leave his bottle!" Amnesty shouts to Charity. Then to Athen, "Get whatever you can!"

The two of them splash through the doorframe to the stairs. Charity turns back to drag the heavy, oak door closed behind her, fighting the tide of water. A frown cuts deep grooves in her face and her eyes are glossy, but she manages to close the door, despite whatever regret she feels over leaving Athen in here with me.

I like her a tiny bit more for that.

The echo of each bolt shakes my spine. Each scrape locks us in, locks us up, and locks Athen into the knowledge that he will die in this room, at my hand.

A then glimpses the bottle Amnesty left behind, the tong handles resting on the cement in the inch of water. The jug is closer to me than him, and his face reminds me of the news on TV, when a major story is being broadcast, but the words of equally compelling stories crawl across the bottom of the screen. His general expression is calm, but the wary glimpse at the jug tells me he's weighing his ability to get that bottle without getting burned.

He only wants my venom.

Something about that sends prickling tears to my eyes. It leaves the back of my throat feeling both raw and swollen. Athen's been pretending to be concerned about me, so he can harvest my venom.

My jaw juts and rubs my freed, bleeding wrists on the ankle ropes, my blood burning through the last bit of the restraint. The ropes drop into the water beneath the cot.

Athen inches closer to the stairway door, although his head is inclined, his squint curious.

"Why are you crying?" The question is butter-soft and heart breaking. He sounds so genuinely interested in my emotions, I struggle to believe anyone could be such a convincing liar.

I spit at him again and he jumps out of the way. Still, I lock my knees and battle the muscles in my legs that ache to jump off the cot and splash across the floor. My brain doesn't want to hurt Athen, but my tongue is marinating in acidic venom. I shoot another bullet of spit at him and this time, I catch his arm. The venom grazes his flesh and he curses. An angry, red welt immediately bubbles up on the skin.

My heart squeezes at the sight of his clenched jaw. Athen drops down, scooping water onto his arm to douse the burn. The worse I feel, the more venom wells in my mouth, until I can't hold it back any longer.

"Move!" I gurgle through another projection of spit. Athen ducks out of the way, relying on my warning alone. I spit three more times, digging my fingers into the cot to stay put. Athen's far enough that the saliva doesn't reach him.

The venom lets out a hissing sputter as it dies in the water.

Athen stands, drawing his hand away from his arm. The welt on his skin is upraised and open, a thin river of blood dribbling into his palm.

"I'm sorry," I say, the saliva overflowing my lips. I look away, hoping to shut off my emotions. "I can't...help it."

"I know you can't," he says softly. "The scar will remind us that we're still friends, even when it's difficult."

Friends. Nothing about that feels right and my salivary glands agree. I fire another gob at Athen, but he dodges aside and the sizzle of the venom is lost in the splash of the water. Once Athen stands still, rings skim outward across the surface of the water. My eyes are as flooded as the room.

"It's okay," he says.

I spit at him, choking when I try to stop it.

"Don't try to stop it." His brows steeple in the center of his forehead.

"I don't want to hurt you," I say, but I spit again.

"Yeah, sure you don't," Charity says from the stairway door. To think, I initially thought she was adorable.

I slide one leg off the cot, dangling it toward the watery floor. Charity's gaze follows it, eyes widening as reality hits her: I'm no longer restrained. She slides her foot up, blindly locating the step behind her.

"Wanna go home to your blood sucker?" she sneers.

Athen shakes his head. "Knock it off. She's not going anywhere."

My palms are raw from hanging onto the cot. Charity's smug face makes me itch to let go, but I keep my grip, interested in what she has to say.

"The leaches just sent word," Amnesty says, walking down the stairs. She kicks Charity's locator foot out of the way. "The vamps have the Sunshine Vial."

Athen glimpses the two females on the staircase. His left cheek lifts in disbelief. "They've been saying that forever."

"It's true this time," Charity says. "Raze verified it."

"Why would they—"Athen begins.

"Because they want her," Amnesty flicks her chin in my direction. "They're trading the vial for her."

"Good riddance," Charity scoffs.

Athen doesn't respond to it. Instead, he roots his gaze on me.

Isaac has actually done it.

He's convinced Sarkazian to trade the vampire's most valuable asset…for me.

My mouth goes dry.

7 3

"Catch," Amnesty says. She produces a thick, glass cylinder on a rope from her back pocket and tosses it to Athen. He catches it with his welted, bloody hand.

Charity's eyes widen, leaning forward, momentarily forgetting her fear. "What did she do to you?"

"It's nothing." Athen dismisses it with a slight shake of his head.

"Listen," Amnesty says, "this *bit* is supposed to be *spelled,* but I'm not sure the witch that did it knew what she was doing. Hopefully, it will get us enough time to get her to the meeting place, but it's not guaranteed."

"You're not sticking that in my mouth," I snarl.

Athen shakes his head, swinging the ball from the rope in his fist. "There's already a meeting place?"

"They want her back *now.*"

My heart jumps. Isaac is coming for me.

"Who's going to put it in her mouth?" Charity's little mouth forms a dramatic *o* as she looks from Amnesty to Athen and back.

"Juan Pablo, Xander, and Honor all volunteered—" Amnesty says.

"No," I say, tightening my grip on the cot. "You and me, Athen. We'll do this together."

Athen's lips twitch a grin.

I spit at him.

"She's going to kill you the first chance she gets!" Charity squeaks.

"No, she won't. If she was going to kill me, she would've already done it." He says it with such conviction, I can almost let it go.

But not quite.

I spit hard at Athen. My eyes burn with the force.

Isaac is my only loyalty. My bones vibrate with it, and it doesn't matter if the notion doesn't resonate through me, the way every thought of Athen does. My loyalty is like a brace...or a fetter...clamped around my heart. I belong to Isaac and he belongs to me. Always.

Amnesty leans past Charity, grabbing the door and slamming it shut. Athen and I are alone again. He holds out the glass cylinder. "Are we going to do this?"

I nod. I'm going back to Isaac. Nothing can be better than that. But, as Athen circles around the back of me and I grip the edges of the cot to keep myself in place, the hollow feeling spills into me again and inflates. It presses against my enthusiasm, squeezes thoughts of Isaac to the edges of my mind.

I want something, but the emptiness doesn't give any clues.

Athen laces the cylinder around my neck. The cold glass sits heavily on my collar bone.

"Do it," I say before he says anything that makes me singe off his hands.

He pulls backward and I lift the cylinder into my mouth myself. I feel his knuckles brush against my hair as he ties the knot behind my head. Venomous spit drips out of my mouth, running down my hands and dripping onto the cot. The sheets, the mattress, the bed, smokes where the saliva soaks through, but I can hardly see it through the tears that sting much worse.

Then, he slips a blindfold over my eyes and shackles my wrists.

74

It all goes very fast. I suppose it has to, since the cylinder begins breaking down almost immediately, like a cheap jaw-breaker.

Luckily, I can see through the bottom of the blindfold.

Athen leads me upstairs, the tips of our fingers latched. His skin is warm and dry, his grip reassuring. The more I consider that, the more drool drips down my chin and burns holes in the ratty carpet on the stairs. I focus on what was once a diamond print and wonder what color it was when it was tacked to the steps. Now, it's gray.

Like my memories.

Aside from the increase of saliva, something tickles my skull when I think of Athen.

All I'd have to do is lean forward and pull his arm back, and I could sear off his hand at the wrist. I glimpse his hand, wide and square, and the saliva bubbles up in my mouth. When I pull Athen to a halt, he doesn't try to drag me forward. He waits as I let the spit drizzle out, the cylinder crackling on my tongue as it is basted in venom, the spittle burning through the steps. I'm not sure they'll ever be structurally sound again.

On the landing at the top of the stairs, the carpet switches to waxy looking vinyl and then, Athen leads me out the back door.

Male and female voices speak at a distance, but all around me, urging one another to move faster, get in, scoot over. The voices are mixed with the sounds of vehicle doors opening, engines roaring hoarsely to life, squeaking springs, thunks and thuds on hard surfaces.

Athen lifts me into the back of a truck. The frame creaks and I'm thrown off balance by the grooves of the metal bed as Athen jumps up behind me. I stumble and fall against his body, his arms on my elbows, keeping me upright.

The saliva runs off my chin and the smell of smoking metal coats my nostrils. It reminds me of Isaac and the drool shuts off like a faucet.

The truck bed dips at the same time the sound of boots thud behind me. A gruff, male voice adds, "Quit touching her. She's wrecking the truck."

Athen's fingertips leave my elbows. Relief ribbons into the hollowness inside me, like throwing ribbons into a pit.

The glass cylinder snaps on my tongue. It's already shrunken a quarter from what it was. My jaw aches less, but it still aches.

"Lean forward," Athen whispers in my ear. The sound of him tingles and the saliva wells up in response. I bend in half as the cylinder crackles again. I don't need liquefied glass running down my throat. From the bottom edge of the blindfold, I drool into the same glass jug Amnesty and Charity used to catch my venomous spit.

The voices all around me hush, but there's no mistaking the cocking of a rifle.

"Don't try nothing or we'll blow your head off," a female snarls.

There's no one else she'd be talking to, but me.

"Shut up, Honor," Athen says. "She could've killed all of us, but she didn't—"

"There's still time," the female scoffs.

"Let's go!" a male shouts.

A fist pounds the side of the truck. I lurch against Athen as the truck takes off. He shoves me gently away, back over the jug, as my mouth overflows, but it stops as we bump along in the back of the truck.

I am going home to Isaac.

75

The truck stops.

The tailgate opens with a bang.

The bed bounces as at least a half dozen bodies pile out.

Athen lifts me down, stifling a pained curse. Some of my spit must've got him. Despite his discomfort, he still sets me down as if I'm as fragile as a light bulb.

"Here," Amnesty's familiar voice says. I hear the slosh of water. It splashes on the dirt I glimpse beneath my feet.

"They're coming," a male says. From all around me, I hear the Revenants cursing and slandering the Brethren, as engines roar closer. My mouth goes bone dry as I hear the clop of horse hooves and the grind of Isaac's carriage wheels once the sound of the motors and slamming vehicle doors die away.

Silence cloaks everything.

Isaac is waiting for me. I step forward and someone jerks me back by my elbow. Athen hisses, so I know it wasn't him. The revenants are keeping me from Isaac. The cylinder between my teeth shrinks as my mouth waters.

"We've got to do this fast, before that bit disintegrates," an unfamiliar female strains a whisper from my right.

"Put the vest on her," a male says.

"Now listen to me," Athen whispers close to my face. The glass splinters and I have to lean forward to let the shard flow out of my mouth. Once I'm upright again, the vest, scratchy and heavy, is pulled down over my head. I tip my head back and gaze down at a sliver of Camouflage green canvas vest with large, full pockets. The thing weighs a ton.

"Hurry up, Athen." The anxiety in Amnesty's voice surprises me.

Athen continues, his tone calm, yet stretched tight, as if he is peering through thin ice at a raging current, waiting to carry him away. "This vest is loaded with the venom we collected in the front pockets and the back of it is loaded with another vamp's venom."

A quiver rattles my bones and the vibration of it rattles bottles in the vest. They made me into *the bomb*. The cylinder slips between my teeth and I slide my tongue over the glass, hoping to dissolve it, to spit it out, to kill some of them before they detonate me.

"Listen to me!" Athen says, gripping my arm tightly. The cylinder in my mouth crackles, but Athen leans in dangerously close—I could burn a hole through his eye…if the glass bit wasn't in my mouth. And if I wanted to.

Which I don't.

"Here's the deal," he says, his breath stirring the hair by my ear. It's warm against my skin. "The vest is radio-controlled. As long as you do what I'm telling you, you are *not* going to explode. It's heavy because it is lined with a protective armor that should shield you if one of the vials breaks, but the bottles are spelled to keep the venom intact. They're sealed in the front and back pockets. Totally separate. Just walk to that tree, half way between us and the blood—*the vamps*. They're going to bring you the Sunshine Vial. One of us will retrieve it, remove the vest, and then you are free to return to your vampire." He swallows hard. I can't tell if it is sadness or disgust.

The cylinder is small enough now that I could spit it out, but I hold it behind my teeth and listen for the rest of the instructions.

"If you don't do it exactly like he said," Amnesty snipes from beside me, "we'll have to assume you *want* to be with them and Raze will hit 'detonate'. The bottles will explode, blowing you and all your corpses to pieces. And just so you know, the bloodsuckers won't have time to save you if you try anything, got it?"

I open my mouth and what is left of the cylinder falls out. The thin shard of glass hits my chin and I spit in the direction of Amnesty's voice. I hear her curse and scramble away from me, along with the shuffle of several other feet, although there is no sizzle of venom.

"Got it," I say with a wide smile.

Someone yanks off my blindfold and I squint into the orange blaze of the sun.

The Revenants part to either side of me. We're standing on a long, dirt road, flanked by short grass. A half mile away, a huge and rickety garage stands like an abandoned appendage in the middle of this unrecognizable nowhere. The wide garage door is swung open, creating a protective overhang. To the side, a corridor draped with black damask, likely attached to each vehicle so the Brethren could enter without being scorched in the sun.

I grasp a breath and hold it tight in my chest the moment I see Isaac's carriage. I squint so hard my eyelids ache, but within the dark depths of the structure, I see the shadows move.

The Revenants are wise to meet with the Brethren during the day. However, I'm not sure the Revenants stand a chance of survival anyway.

My heart catches, pounding beneath the weight of the vest over my empty rib cage. I try not to track Athen in my peripheral as Isaac's words drift through my mind like a salve that doesn't quite bring relief: *vampires are territorial. They'll kill for what they believe is theirs.*

"Start walkin' and stop half way…at that tree," a dark-haired male at my right points toward the garage. There's only one tree, a dead sapling that looks like it never had a chance out in the middle of this nowhere place. "When you get the Sunshine Vial, give us a thumbs up and you can start walking back."

I take a step forward and Raze lifts up a thick, black box with red and black buttons. He shakes it with the warning, "Honor and Xander will be watching with binoculars, so be sure you remain in clear sight. Remember: only half way and no farther, got it?"

I glance Athen. Lips tight, hands clamped together in front of him, shoulders rigid.

I start the slow walk back to the love of my life, who is shrouded in shadows.

I spit the rope right off my wrists and keep walking. The sun beats down, making me sweat. It doesn't help that the weight of the vest feels like I'm carrying a man on my back. The bottles, insulated in each pocket, don't slosh or clink, but they bump against my skin with each step and don't let me forget, I'm carrying *bombs*.

"Only half way!" the Revenant with the remote controller hollers the reminder. His voice sounds smaller with distance.

The tree isn't much farther. I stop once I'm beside the leafless, brittle branches.

I squint at the garage, but the shadows within don't even move. No sign of life. The memory of what I saw when I slipped the spelled chip into my eye rushes back to me. The vision of the Brethren, fighting each other, in all their gory deadness.

I shiver beneath the canvas vest, the bottles of volatile venom chafing against my skin.

Maybe it's the idea that I could explode, or maybe it's because I keep thinking of Athen's breath in my ear, but I'm suddenly unsure of why I'm standing here, in the blazing sun, waiting for Isaac, when being with him feels like emptiness.

And when it's the exact opposite of what I feel when Athen's near me.

I'm not even being realistic. It's crazy to think I feel anything for Athen. I've seen him all of twice—once in the barn and again on Washington Street, where he snatched me and took me to the Revenant's house.

At the same time, whenever Athen is around, I'm enchanted with him. Not the way I am consumed by the thought of Isaac's lips on my neck and the excruciating bliss of his bite. With Athen, the desire is just to be near him. To listen to him. To touch him. I want to consume *him*, rather than wishing he'd consume *me*.

Isaac's carriage pulls around the back of the garage. Eustace, from the driver's bench, guides the two horses toward me. I stand in the road, not moving a foot past the dead tree, in case the Revenants think I'm trying to run off. The horses trot straight to me, veering to the right and slowing..

"Ho!" Eustace says and the horses come to a full stop, the carriage three steps from me.

The thick black curtains are drawn inside the carriage, but the door opens slightly.

"Come, Nova," Isaac calls to me.

His voice weakens the muscles in my legs. It weakens my entire resolve.

"I can't," I call back. "I'm wearing a vest full of venom."

"I know. Come into the carriage. It won't move, I promise you. I will give you the vial to return to them and then you will be free to come back to me."

I take a look over my shoulder at the Revenants, standing around the trucks. The guy with the remote gestures for me to go to the carriage.

Athen, standing off to the side, watches without expression.

I go to the carriage, open the door, and climb in, keeping the door open enough to remain in full view for Xavier, Honor, and their binoculars.

At least, I hope it is.

An odor washes over me. I put my hand over my face. Eustace must've been transporting something awful. The interior is thick with the sharp and bitter smell of metal and a lilting, sour undertone that reminds me of rotting fish.

Another thick, black curtain partitions the right bench from any direct sunlight. Once I close the carriage door, Isaac draws back the curtain. He smiles and I begin to cry.

"You're okay now, my darling," Isaac says, taking my hand in his. "You are with me and you know I will protect you with my life."

My stomach rolls. He cannot protect me with something he no longer possesses.

This is not the reunion I expected.

I quiver beneath the heavy vest as Isaac kisses my knuckles. He has no idea that the tears are because all the light seems to have gone out of my heart the moment I closed the carriage door and I doubt he would believe that the shivers pulsing through my body are triggered by repulsion, instead of desire. The smell hasn't gone away either.

"I have to take the Sunshine Vial back to the Revenants," I say, drawing my hand away.

"Yes," he says slowly, ticking his head slightly to the side. He smiles, but raw silver sparks in his eyes remind me of the glint of a sharp blade. "Are you happy to return to me, Nova?"

The stench is overwhelming and the intensity of his gaze feels like he's slicing through my chest and drawing out my heart for inspection. This is supposed to be the love of my life, but the only emotions racing through me are those of terror. Terror at the surge of love that feels a lot like eating sugared cereal that ends up cutting up the roof of my mouth.

I swallow hard and force a smile across my lips. "You're all I live for, Isaac. You know that. I just want to get this over with. I want to come home to you."

He reaches into his pocket and retrieves a glowing vial, the size of my ring finger. The fluid inside is sparkling and clear, laced with pale lemon and gold. It looks like someone bottled actual sunshine. Despite my apprehension, I'm mesmerized.

"They can have the Sunshine Vial," Isaac says with a scoff. "But I'd like you to give it to them with a little extra." He reaches into his pocket again and withdraws another vial. This one I recognize. It's the vial of distilled venom he gave to me the first time he drank my blood. He broke the chain and it was lost in the sheets, but he has a new chain on it now. He holds it out, dangling from his fingertip. I don't take it.

"You want to blow up the Revenants?" I can barely keep the shiver out of my voice.

"That little group has turned against us," he says, ticking his chin toward the opposite end of the road. "They want us dead, do you know that? They would blow you up with us—without blinking—if they thought they could get their hands on the Sunshine Vial without you. Honestly, I'm surprised that you seem to be taking up for them."

"I'm not," I answer. Maybe it is too quick. The silver flashes across Isaac's eyes.

Isaac holds out the vial of distilled venom again. "If you're not with them, you're with us, and if you are indeed with *me,* you'll help send a message to any of these *cups* who consider rising up against us."

"Is losing the Sunshine Vial worth all of this?" My throat is dry as I take it. "There's not a lot of them out there."

"Protecting ourselves is worth this," he says firmly. "Carry the Sunshine Vial in one hand and the vial of my venom in the other. It's no longer in the spelled vial, so it's quite volatile. Be sure it doesn't touch the vest at all. Once you deliver the Sunshine Vial to the Revenants, they are supposed to remove that vest and release you back to me. When you get a reasonable distance, I want you to turn and throw the vial of my venom back at them. Throw it as hard as you can and aim for the vest. The vial will shatter and if even a drop lands on that vest you left behind…we could be rid of the lot of them at once. "

"What if I miss?"

"You'll spatter enough of them, and chances are, most of them have been other vampires' cups before. They'll explode on contact."

That makes his vision crystal clear. Even a drop of the distilled venom, in contact with a contrasting venom, creates a huge explosion. It will create a chain reaction, and then it doesn't matter if any of the Revenants were never cups themselves. The proximity of the blasts will still kill them.

"You know who you are when you are with me. You are not alone anymore." His tone is pleading and soft. "Don't you want to protect what we have, Nova?"

"That's all I want," I say weakly. My body warms with it, which, in turn, curdles everything in my stomach.

Isaac leans forward, pressing the Sunshine Vial into my opposite hand.

"Good girl," he says. "Now go and do what needs to be done to preserve us."

I step down from the carriage and onto the road. The moment the door closes, Eustace whistles to the horses, and with a stroke of the whip, moves the carriage back in the direction of the garage. I cough on the dust cloud left behind.

It's just me and the dead tree in the middle of the road again, the vest heavier than ever.

I watch the carriage retreat and finally pull around the back of the garage. Eustace probably wants to be sure the horses are safely out of the way of any blast. That they won't be spooked.

For not being alone anymore, I feel very, very alone. Isaac tried to impress me with our love for each other, but all I could think about in the carriage was the awful smell, the weight of the vest, the way that I don't feel *at all* the way I did before. I loved Isaac before Athen snatched me, but now, thinking about Isaac leaves a sour coating on my thoughts.

I turn away from the garage and back toward the direction of the Revenants. I give the thumbs up. The glass vials in both hands are glazed with my sweat.

I stand in the center of the road, trying to get my head straight.

Athen snatched me. He tied me to a cot and harvested what he could from me. Despite the charge of emotions I feel when he's near me, the facts are still the facts. All he wants is Isaac's venom.

Looking off to the left, the garage stands off in the distance, open and dark, the phantoms waiting in the shadows for me to bring them proof of my love for Isaac. Waiting for me to bring them the Revenant's demise.

I turn my head to the right. The Revenants stand at their vehicles in the blazing sun, waving for me to return to them, desperate to get the Sunshine Vial and certain that the vamps have fulfilled their end of the deal.

Somewhere in the small crowd of Revenants, Athen is waiting, but with what expectations, I have no idea. Neither of us has ever mentioned the strange spark between us—and why would we when we are strangers who have only met twice? I can't explain why Athen appeals to me, but even my addiction to Isaac's venom haven't been able to fully wipe it out. That says something. Doesn't it?

The Revenants shout louder, urging me to return to them, but I stay rooted to the spot.

Maybe because weighing my options makes me feel like I'm coming up short.

The vampires want me to kill the Revenants for them. The Revenants want the Sunshine Vial and who knows? Maybe they'll kill me once they get it.

Isaac is waiting for me to show him my loyalty.

Athen is waiting for the same thing.

I take a deep breath. Where do I figure into all of this? I have two men waiting for me to choose between them, but what if I don't want to choose anyone? I still don't have any answers and being pulled in both directions isn't helping me make up my mind.

I look down at my hands. Venom in one palm. Sunshine Vial in the other.

Suddenly, it's clear exactly who I will choose.

The one who wants the answers most.

The one who is most loyal to me.

I lift the Sunshine Vial to my chest as I slam the vial of Isaac's venom against the vest.

I am the nucleus of the explosion. Ruth's body disintegrates, the dust of our shared anatomy blasting both upward and out, a hot cloud spreading over the road.

I am cast out—a ghost again.

Wind laces up from the ground, the gusts tying around me. My feet leave the ground.

This is new. Uncomfortably new.

I flail, caught off balance, but the wind continues to lift me. My muscles are tight and I keep twitching as if I'm falling, but I'm rising.

I can't get my balance.

I drift toward the Vampires, but then, the breeze reverses direction and I'm blown toward the Revenants. I can't control my movement. It makes me dizzy.

What have I done.

What have I done.

A gust hits my chest and I soar upward.

The faces of the Revenants are upturned, but I rise so quickly, I can't make out their expressions. The wizened tree in the road becomes smaller and smaller, until it looks like pen marks on the brown parchment of the road. I continue to grab at the air, trying to gain balance, as if the air will become solid in my hands.

It doesn't.

I continue upward, through the clouds, the humidity clinging to my skin. My head spins, thoughts thrown to the edges like an out-of-control centrifuge. The clouds are thick. There is no above or below—just clouds—until my head slams against a darker gray puff of cirrus.

Whatever this is, it's definitely solid. I put my hands against the cold wisps and they skitter from my fingertips. Beneath the vapors lies a sheet of solid, cold ice.

The problem isn't only the bizarre wind or weird ice, it's the gusts that keep slamming me against the frosty glass like a ghostly door knocker. Each time I hit the icy cirrus, wisps of precipitation scatter. Despite my ghostliness, every whack knocks the wind out of me and the back of my head feels bruised. I smack against it again and this time, there is a vibration at my back.

I turn my head and see feet…the bottom of petite, perfect, bare *feet*…skittering toward me, on the opposite side of the frozen barrier. After the next smack, I flip myself over.

Terrible idea.

My face slams into the ice hard enough that, were I still in Ruth's body, I would've broken our nose. As it is, I just feel as if I have.

Another gust bashes me against the cirrus as the owner of the feet bends down, wiping her side of the ice as she peers down at me. My cheek pounds the barrier as the woman on the other side shouts at me. Her voice is distorted but as the side of my head hits the ice beneath her feet again, I make out her words.

"I can't…open the door!" she shouts.

There's a door? And she's still standing there just gaping at me?

"What!" I shout. It's a knee-jerk answer and as I slam into the underside of her floor, I rethink my question more carefully. "By *life*...if there's a door...open it!"

"I..." she begins, but startles back with a gasp at the next jarring smack of my body against the ice. I groan for emphasis. If there's a door, maybe it will save the last of my non-existent bones from shattering inside my face.

"Open it!" I shout.

The woman jumps up and after a panicked look around, she hauls open a trap door that is seamless with the ice. I would've never known it was there. I shoot up through the opening and land on my feet, wavering to get my balance, beside the woman.

"You can't be here!" she whispers hotly, peering over my shoulder, and then, behind her own.

"Where's here?" I ask.

"You don't remember yet," she groan-whispers, scanning all around us.

What's around us is unexpected. The upper side of the ice is not cold. It's strangely and perfectly comfortable. We're in a cloud pond, standing on what seems like it should be foggy water. All around the edge of the pond is tall grass, greener than I've ever seen and beyond that, trees.

"Who are you and what is this place?" I say.

"I'm Nissa, and in a moment you'll know," she whispers.

The air is clean. I breathe deep and my thoughts suddenly run clear and swift. It only takes moments before the number of them accumulates and pile up, gushing through my mind so quickly, I stagger backward, holding my head.

This isn't *thinking*.

It's more like *downloading*.

Memory after memory explodes in my brain, linking together, populating my mind. After craving memories for so long, I should be happy to have them now, but I'm completely overwhelmed. I'm hardly able to review one memory before three more pop up. It's like gobbling a bowl full of never-ending strands of spaghetti. My brain is choking on all the memories flooding my mind.

Crazy things come…

Meg…

Wait, that was a flash of Meg…

but an elderly man's voice comes out of my mouth and calls my cousin *Meganira*.

It's a strange and unfamiliar name, but it *is* her name. Meg's real name. It hums inside my throat, in my lungs, and my heart.

Meganira.

The thought of her bursts in my heart. She meant as much more to me then, even more than she does now, which is hard to believe. Our bond was as far reaching as the sight of an ocean from a beach, and just as mysterious and consuming in its depth.

Memory after memory of my cousin pop up, of her as a little girl playing beside a dark-haired little girl, except Meg isn't playing. Meg is watching the dark-haired girl play, Meg's eyes sharp and scrutinizing as she watches everything happening around the two of them. Meg's eyes constantly scan across the terrain, flick over the faces of whoever is nearby, while also monitoring the dark-haired girl as she plays a game, spinning coins on the ground.

More sparks of memories show Meg taking a sharp stick away from the dark-haired girl; Meg stepping between the dark-haired girl and a third girl who wears an unsettling sneer; Meg knocking over a boy who kept jumping forward, trying to touch the dark haired girl on the shoulder.

The memories come faster and faster, Meg and the little girl growing, but always with Meg hovering around the dark-haired girl, defending, protecting, safeguarding, shielding, supporting.

After so many memories, the thought imprints itself on my brain: the little girl is Meg's sister.

Except that Meg doesn't have a sister.

There's no Aunt Dena or Uncle Leonard.

No double decker, falling-down house with stumps of snuffed Mary Janes dumped in the upstairs window tracks.

This is a Meg I don't know, even though I recognize her on sight.

I focus on the little girl who Meg treasures so much. I sift through the memories, grasping the ones with the little girl and letting the other memories filter through the sieve.

The little girl grows and grows, morphing into someone more familiar. As the memories reveal her more and more, recognition chimes in my head. I am shocked by what I see.

I try to dig in my mental heels to halt the memories, and can't.

But what I'm seeing in my head can't be.

I am looking into my own startled face, at a version of me, standing beside Meg, although Meg looks straight at *me* who is looking back at her now.

Shaking my head doesn't arrange the thoughts into any order that makes sense.

"Daddy," Meg pleads to me.

Wait another minute…these memories are from Meg's *father*? I'm looking through her father's eyes? Not Uncle Leonard's, but her birth father's eyes.

Who the heck was Meg's real father?

I look down at my hands and they are definitely not Uncle Leonard's beefy, bloated mitts. These hands belong to a powerful man. These strong hands are strangely familiar.

"Silvia is her best friend," Meg argues. "Nova has to be there! It's the only wedding gift Silvia wants!"

The man's hands drop, exasperated, before me.

The Silvia? Is she talking about Isaac's Silvia? What other Silvia could she mean? I was Silvia's best friend? My heart lifts as my stomach does a sickening flop. I don't know what to feel about any of this.

"You know it means everything to her, Daddy, and Nova's never asked for anything before. Not once."

"I haven't," the me-standing-before-me peeps.

The two words echo in the shell of this man with the same whomping vibration as a rubber ball hitting a fun house mirror. If I had a stomach, I'd barf.

"Besides," Meg carries on, "I will be there to look after her and so will Athen."

Athen? This other me and this other Meg knew Athen?

A man's voice responds through my mouth, the sound husky and thick, "It is not done, *Meganira*. It would be reckless to allow all three of you to go."

"It would be *safest*." Meg crosses her thin arms over her waist. She is unfamiliarly clear. Her eyes are bright and lucid, her voice definite and sharp, her shoulders pressed back with a pride the Meg I know never quite wears.

"It is forbidden," my male voice answers sternly this time. My face vibrates with the power of his voice.

Meg doesn't shrink away even a millimeter. She studies her nails.

"Despite what Nova desires," the man's voice in my throat growls, "the idea of transforming to human form for such a meaningless event as a *human wedding* is foolhardy enough, but the three of you? It is out of the question. It would leave the entire Realm vulnerable. If you were detected by another *caste,* it could be the end of the Realm altogether. To continue on with this foolish request brings shame upon us all."

The me-standing-before-me breaks into tears, but my masculine voice continues to reason in a deeper, even more booming octave, "The Gods would banish all of you and you wouldn't ever be welcomed back into the Realm!" The voice catches in my throat and the man swallows it down hard before Meganira can detect it. The lump sticks half way, but the man's voice works around it. "Do not defy me, Meg," he says. "Do. Not."

I gather from the knot behind my esophagus that this man

already realizes she will, but Meg does a sideways nod without looking into my eyes.

"I won't. I *won't*." Meg assures him with a shrug that is anything but assuring.

Meg disobeyed her father.

"You cannot compromise your position," the man warns. He's looking straight at the version of me standing before him. "You are Goddess of Night, Nova, and your wedding to Athen is coming soon. I want nothing to jeopardize it."

Goddess of Night?

Wedding to Athen?

"I am aware," the me-standing-before-me says. She stands tall, shoulders back, chin lifted. I'm proud of her, although I am still inwardly choking on both the *Goddess of Night* and the *wedding Athen* parts.

"Is this human worth risking banishment and being denied your bonding?" the man asks.

"It is worth every risk, father," the other me says, and I lose my footing. I stumble backward, out of the memory, out of the eyes of the man whose memory I've somehow hijacked. The woman who opened the icy door grabs me before I fall.

"You have received your father's gift," Nissa says. "It is the only way you could ascend to the God Realm, but for now, you must leave."

I hear her words, but they don't make sense. They scramble as all my attention turns to: *my father.*

I am looking through my father's eyes, reviewing the memories he sacrificed for me.

My father is the God of the Sun.

Meg is my sister.

I was going to marry Athen.

Meg, Athen, and I risked everything to attend Isaac and Silvia's wedding.

Suddenly, everything comes together in horrifying clarity.

Nissa squeezes my hand as her gaze nervously darts all around us. "I'm sorry, Nova, but you are not welcome in the God's Realm any longer. Not after how you've put us all in harm's way. When the three of you died down there, you were scattered as ghosts, because the majority of the gods decided you had all lost your rights to ascend and rejoin us. I could be severely punished for allowing you in this far. You must return to the Earth dimension."

"No," I murmur stubbornly. I'm unsure if it is me speaking, or my father's will somehow emerging. Either way, I know in my being what is right now. I plant my feet amidst the clouds. "This is my home."

"You are not welcome here," another male's voice breaks in from behind us. Nissa gasps and we both turn to face the newcomer.

"Oh, Phane, it's just you." Nissa exhales. She seems relieved, but judging by the murderous glare slicing through his dark eyes— the sharpness of his gaze is a thousand times more cutting than Isaac's teeth—I'm not relieved at all. "Nova ascended!"

"Not without proving her worthiness!" Phane snarls at Nissa. He turns to me, barking in a whisper, "You do not belong here! Get out!"

I do everything I can to call up my father's memories, rather than wilt before this man, but Phane leans in close and his gaze slices right through my determination.

"If the other gods find you here, you'll be slaughtered before you have a chance to speak in your own defense!" Is that fear adhered to the edge of his furious gaze? "Go back to where you came and if you wish to return, then do what must be done to prove yourself to the others!"

"What am I supposed to do?" I fix my glare on Phane's long face.

"Right now? Get out of here, before we're banished along with you." Phane grabs my shoulders, pushing me toward the trapdoor in the ice. My feet slide uselessly as I try to stand my ground.

"Then what?" I ask, struggling to hold my ground as he shoves me

"Kill the vampires. All of them," Phane snaps as he shoves me toward the opening in the floor.

"Yes, *all of them*," Nissa adds. "Phane and I will try to help, but—"

Isaac flashes through my mind, but the thought of him comes alone and without emotion. The intense passion I felt for him before is completely gone. The only emotion I feel for him now is a strange hollowness, slowly populated with thoughts of Isaac insisting I should want to die for him; thoughts of him locking me in the cottage; thoughts of him and his Brethren, and how they all looked with the glass chip in my eye that revealed their truly gory forms.

However, the monumental task they're talking about—to kill all the vampires—whether I want to or not—isn't something I can do on my own. I'm only a ghost. They're too powerful.

"How do you think I'm going to do that?" I ask. "What kind of help are you talking about? Isaac's clutch has fourteen vampires!"

"As the Goddess of New Life, I'll help by granting you your father's memories," Nissa says, "and we'll drop you back into the dimension where you came from. Then, we're going to continue to be the sanity in the Realm, so the gods don't find you and kill you before you manage to figure out a plan of attack."

"By myself?" I ask.

"Phane may be God of Death," Nissa muses, as if I know what she's talking about already, "but he can't do this for you. You must do fulfill this request from the Realm yourself."

"You got into this trouble on your own," Phane says, moving toward me. "You'll need to get out of it that way too."

I step backward and one of my feet drops through the trapdoor hole where I entered. Losing my balance, I twist and claw for Nissa, who takes a step backward.

So much for helping.

Then, Phane shoves me through the opening.

I plummet through the clouds, through the breathtaking blast of air, through Earth's atmosphere and toward the road I just left.

The dying tree beside the road comes into view, closer by the second. I close my eyes, overwhelmed.

I must find Meg.

I don't know how to explain everything to Athen, or if I should.

I have to destroy the vampire race.

When I hit the ground, I am relieved I am not a revenant in a fragile body.

No, I am unbreakable now.

I am a ghost again.

THE END

If you enjoyed the story, posting a review is greatly appreciated.

If you would like updates on the next story in the series, join the newsletter at mistyprovencherauthor.com and you'll also receive a free book!

ACKNOWLEDGEMENTS

Thank you, God,

for my every blessing of family, friends, and this beautiful life. It is always about you.

Hugs & sloppy kisses to Casey L. Bond, brainstorming buddy, beta reader, and all-around amazing friend. *I myself am strange and unusual...*

Props and shouts to Cristie Alleman, who pulled quotes for all my teasers. You have an incredible eye and can't thank you enough for putting them all over my pages.

Deep thanks and love to my Jes Ekker, beta reader, beautiful baby mama, the friend I've never met face to face. I adore you.

Thanks to my Book Babes, who share and who care. Thank you for being all kinds of fun!

Congrats to North Oldham Middle School's Juan Pablo and Xander, both for their outstanding essays that earned them their names in this book. Hope you enjoy the characters that share your names!

ALSO BY MISTY PROVENCHER

ADULT BOOKS BY MISTY PAQUETTE

Literary Fiction

WEEDS of DETROIT (based on true events)

STRONGER

Science-Fantasy

THE FLY HOUSE

Contemporary Romance

THE CROSSED & BARED SERIES

HALE MAREE (Book One)

FULL OF GRACE (Book Two)

CARELESS WHISPER (An 80s Love Story)

Erotica

THE BROWN BAG SERIES

THE RELEASE CLUB

*Misty Provencher writing as Misty Paquette

ABOUT THE AUTHOR

Misty Provencher is a prolific writer who creates fantasy stories for young adult readers and up. She also writes contemporary romance for adults under the name Misty Paquette.

While Provencher can ride a motorcycle, knows how to karate chop, and has learned enough French, Spanish, and sign language to get herself slapped, Misty's life is dedicated to connecting with, and understanding, the people who cross her path. She is totally enchanted with spending her time translating her everyday muses into words.

Misty Provencher lives in the mitten. Knock on her internet door at the following addresses, or find her wherever great coffee is sold:

For more information:
mistyprovencherauthor.com
misty@mistyprovencherauthor.com
You are also invited to join her Facebook Reader Group: CLICK HERE.

www.ingramcontent.com/pod-product-compliance
Lightning Source LLC
Chambersburg PA
CBHW030632020726
47493CB00006B/1681